"METICULOUSLY CONSTRUCTED . . .
Perry's images of the carnage and confusion of battle are relentless in their intensity, unflinching in their truth-telling detail."
—*The New York Times Book Review*

"[Perry's] concern for pressing social issues and her ability to set a scene are always strong—never more so than when depicting the terrifying battle of Manassas."
—*The Seattle Times*

"Pure, hearty escapism enhanced by a rich tapestry of period details . . . Perry keeps up the suspense right to the end."
—*The Baltimore Sun*

"A welcome and entertaining read . . . Perry writes with a deft sense of history and place. Her dialogue, suitable for the drawing room, sheds much light on the manners and codified pursuit of Victorian life."
—*The Cincinnati Post*

"*Slaves of Obsession* combines all the action of a modern thriller with an enjoyable look at a time when people took all day to travel a few miles and there were no phones, fingerprints, or databases to help catch killers."
—*The Orlando Sentinel*

By Anne Perry
Published by The Ballantine Publishing Group:

Featuring William Monk

THE FACE OF A STRANGER
A DANGEROUS MOURNING
DEFEND AND BETRAY
A SUDDEN, FEARFUL DEATH
THE SINS OF THE WOLF
CAIN HIS BROTHER
WEIGHED IN THE BALANCE
THE SILENT CRY
A BREACH OF PROMISE
THE TWISTED ROOT
SLAVES OF OBSESSION

Featuring Thomas and Charlotte Pitt

THE CATER STREET HANGMAN
CALLANDER SQUARE
PARAGON WALK
RESURRECTION ROW
BLUEGATE FIELDS
RUTLAND PLACE
DEATH IN THE DEVIL'S ACRE
CARDINGTON CRESCENT
SILENCE IN HANOVER CLOSE
BETHLEHEM ROAD
HIGHGATE RISE
BELGRAVE SQUARE
FARRIERS' LANE
THE HYDE PARK HEADSMAN
TRAITORS GATE
PENTECOST ALLEY
ASHWORTH HALL
BRUNSWICK GARDEN
BEDFORD SQUARE
HALF MOON STREET

SLAVES OF OBSESSION

Anne Perry

BALLANTINE BOOKS • NEW YORK

A Ballantine Book
Published by The Ballantine Publishing Group

www.ballantinebooks.com

Library of Congress Catalogue in Publication Data is available upon request.

ISBN 0-449-00592-5

Manufactured in the United States of America

First Hardcover Edition: October 2000
First Mass Market Edition: October 2001

10 9 8 7 6 5 4 3 2 1

To
Moreen, James and Nesta, née MacDonald,
for their friendship

SLAVES OF OBSESSION

1

"WE ARE INVITED to dine with Mr. and Mrs. Alberton," Hester said in reply to Monk's questioning gaze across the breakfast table. "They are friends of Callandra's. She was to go as well, but has been called to Scotland unexpectedly."

"I suppose you would like to accept anyway," he deduced, watching her face.

He usually read her emotions quickly, sometimes with startling accuracy, at others misunderstanding entirely. On this occasion he was correct.

"Yes, I would. Callandra said they are charming and interesting and have a very beautiful home. Mrs. Alberton is half Italian, and apparently Mr. Alberton has traveled quite a lot as well."

"Then I suppose we had better go. Short notice, isn't it?" he said less than graciously.

It was short notice indeed, but Hester was not disposed to find unnecessary fault with something which promised to be interesting, and possibly even the beginning of a new friendship. She did not have many friends. The nature of her work as a nurse had meant that her friendships were frequently of a fleeting nature. She had not been involved with any gripping cause for quite some little time. Even Monk's cases, while financially rewarding, had over the last four months of spring and early summer been most uninteresting, and he had not sought her assistance, or in most of them her opinion. She did not mind that; robberies were tedious, largely motivated by greed, and she did not know the people concerned.

"Good," she said with a smile, folding up the letter. "I shall write back immediately saying that we shall be delighted."

His answering look was wry, only very slightly sarcastic.

They arrived at the Alberton house in Tavistock Square just before half-past seven. It was, as Callandra had said, handsome, although Hester would not have thought it worth remarking on. However, she changed her mind as soon as they were in the hallway, which was dominated by a curving staircase at the half turn of which was an enormous stained-glass window with the evening sun behind it. It was truly beautiful, and Hester found herself staring at it when she should have been paying attention to the butler who had admitted them, and watching where she was going.

The withdrawing room also was unusual. There was less furniture in it than was customary, and the colors were paler and warmer, giving an illusion of light even though in fact the long windows which overlooked the garden faced the eastern sky. The shadows were already lengthening, although it would not be dark until after ten o'clock at this time so shortly after midsummer.

Hester's first impression of Judith Alberton was that she was an extraordinarily beautiful woman. She was taller than average, but with a slender neck and shoulders which made more apparent the lush curves of her figure, and lent it a delicacy it might otherwise not have possessed. Her face, when looked at more closely, was totally wrong for conventional fashion. Her nose was straight and quite prominent, her cheekbones very high, her mouth too large and her chin definitely short. Her eyes were slanted and of a golden autumn shade. The whole impression was both generous and passionate. The longer one looked at her the lovelier she seemed. Hester liked her immediately.

"How do you do," Judith said warmly. "I am so pleased you have come. It was kind of you on so hasty an invitation. But Lady Callandra spoke of you with such affection I did not wish to wait." She smiled at Monk. Her eyes lit with a flare of interest as she regarded his dark face with its lean bones and broad-bridged nose, but it was Hester to whom she addressed her attention. "May I introduce my husband?"

The man who came forward was pleasing rather than handsome, far more ordinary than she was, but his features were regular and there was both strength and charm in them.

"How do you do, Mrs. Monk," he said with a smile, but when courtesy was met he turned immediately to Monk, behind her, searching his countenance steadily for a moment before holding out his hand in welcome and then turning aside so the rest of the company could be introduced.

There were three other people in the room. One was a man in his mid-forties, his dark hair thinning a little. Hester noticed first his wide smile and spontaneous handshake. He had a natural confidence, as if he were sure enough of himself and his beliefs that he had no need to thrust them upon anyone else. He was happy to listen to others. It was a quality she could not help but like. His name was Robert Casbolt, and he was introduced not only as Alberton's business partner and friend since youth, but also Judith's cousin.

The other man present was American. As one could hardly help being aware, that country had in the last few months slipped tragically into a state of civil war. There had not as yet been anything more serious than a few ugly skirmishes, but open violence seemed increasingly probable with every fresh bulletin that arrived across the Atlantic. War seemed more and more likely.

"Mr. Breeland is from the Union," Alberton said courteously, but there was no warmth in his voice.

Hester looked at Breeland as she acknowledged the introduction. He appeared to be in his early thirties, tall and very straight, with square shoulders and the upright stance of a soldier. His features were regular, his expression polite but severely controlled, as if he felt he must be constantly on guard against any slip or relaxation of awareness.

The last person was the Albertons' daughter, Merrit. She was about sixteen, with all the charm, the passion and the

3

vulnerability of her years. She was fairer than her mother, and had not the beauty, but she had a similar strength of will in her face, and less ability to hide her emotions. She allowed herself to be introduced politely enough, but she did not make any attempt to pretend more than courtesy.

The preliminary conversation was on matters as simple as the weather, the increase in traffic on the streets and the crowds drawn by a nearby exhibition.

Hester wondered why Callandra had thought she and Monk might find these people congenial, but perhaps she was merely fond of them and had discovered in them a kindness.

Breeland and Merrit moved a little apart, talking earnestly. Monk, Casbolt and Judith Alberton discussed the latest play, and Hester fell into conversation with Daniel Alberton.

"Lady Callandra told me you spent nearly two years out in the Crimea," he said with great interest. He smiled apologetically. "I am not going to ask you the usual questions about Miss Nightingale. You must find that tedious by now."

"She was a very remarkable person," Hester said. "I could not criticize anyone for seeking to know more about her."

His smile widened. "You must have said that so many times. You were prepared for it!"

She found herself relaxing. He was unexpectedly pleasant to converse with; frankness was always so much easier than continued courtesy. "Yes, I admit I was. It is . . ."

"Unoriginal," he finished for her.

"Yes."

"Perhaps what I wanted to say was unoriginal also, but I shall say it anyway, because I do want to know." He frowned very slightly, drawing his brows together. His eyes were clear blue. "You must have exercised a great deal of courage out there, both physical and moral, especially when you were actually close to the battlefield. You must have made decisions which altered other people's lives, perhaps saved them, or lost them."

That was true. She remembered with a jolt just how des-

4

perate it had been, how remote it was from this quiet summer evening in an elegant London withdrawing room, where the shade of a gown mattered, the cut of a sleeve. War, disease, shattered bodies, the heat and flies or the terrible cold, all could have been on another planet with no connection to this world at all except a common language, and yet no words could ever explain one to the other.

She nodded.

"Do you not find it extraordinarily difficult to adjust from that life to this?" he asked. His voice was soft, but edged with a surprising intensity.

How much had Callandra told Judith Alberton, or her husband? Would Hester embarrass her with the Albertons in future if she were to be honest? Probably not. Callandra had never been a woman to run from the truth.

"Well, I came back burning with determination to reform all our hospitals here at home," she said ruefully. "As you can see, I did not succeed, for several reasons. The chief among them was that no one would believe I had the faintest idea what I was talking about. Women don't understand medicine at all, and nurses in particular are for rolling bandages, sweeping and mopping floors, carrying coal and slops, and generally doing as they are told." She allowed her bitterness to show. "It did not take me long to be dismissed, having to earn my way by caring for private patients."

There was admiration as well as laughter in his eyes. "Was that not very hard for you?" he asked.

"Very," she agreed. "But I met my husband shortly after I came home. We were . . . I was going to say friends, but that is not true. Adversaries in a common cause, would describe it far better. Did Lady Callandra tell you that he is a private agent of enquiry?"

There was no surprise in his face, certainly nothing like alarm. In high society, gentlemen owned land or were in the army or politics. They did not work, in the sense of being employed. Trade was equally unacceptable. But whatever family background Judith Alberton came from, her husband showed no dismay that his guest should be little better than

5

a policeman, an occupation fit only for the least desirable element.

"Yes," he admitted readily. "She told me she found some of his adventures quite fascinating, but she did not give me any details. I presumed they might be confidential."

"They are," she agreed. "I would not discuss them either, only to say that they have prevented me from missing any sense of excitement or decision that I felt in the Crimea. And for the most part my share in them has not required the physical privation or the personal danger of nursing in wartime."

"And the horror, or the pity?" he asked quietly.

"It has not sheltered me from those," she admitted. "Except for a matter of numbers. And I am not sure one feels any less for one person, if he or she is in desperate trouble, than one does for many."

"Quite." It was Robert Casbolt who spoke. He came up just behind Alberton, putting a companionable hand on his friend's shoulder and regarding Hester with interest. "There is just so much the emotions can take, and one gives all one has, I imagine? From what I have just overheard, you are a remarkable woman, Mrs. Monk. I am delighted Daniel thought to invite you and your husband to dine. You will enliven our usual conversation greatly, and I for one am looking forward to it." He lowered his voice conspiratorially. "No doubt we shall hear more of it over dinner—it is totally inescapable these days—but I have had more than sufficient of the war in America and its issues."

Alberton's face lightened. "So have I, but I would wager you a good carriage and pair that Breeland will regale us again with the virtues of the Union before the third course has been served."

"Second!" Casbolt amended. He grinned at Hester, a broad, shining expression. "He is a very earnest young man, Mrs. Monk, and fanatically convinced of the moral rightness of his cause. To him the Union of the United States is a divine entity, and the Confederate desire to secede the work of the devil."

Any further comment was cut short by the necessity of re-moving to the dining room, where dinner was ready to be served.

Monk found the house pleasing although he was not certain why. It was something to do with warmth of color and simplicity of proportion. He had spent the earlier part of the evening talking with Casbolt and Judith Alberton, with the occasional comment from Lyman Breeland, who seemed to find light conversation tedious. Breeland was too well mannered to show it overtly, but Monk at least knew that he was bored. He wondered why Breeland had come at all. It excited Monk's curiosity. Looking around the room, including himself and Hester, it seemed an oddly disparate group of people. Breeland appeared to be in his early thirties, a year or two younger than Hester. The rest of them must have been in their middle to later forties, apart from Merrit Alberton. Why had she chosen to attend this dinner when she could surely have been in the company of other young girls, if not at a party?

Yet he saw in her no sign of tedium or impatience. Was she remarkably well mannered, or was there something which drew her here by choice?

The answer came at the end of the soup course and as the fish was served.

"Where do you live in America, Mr. Breeland?" Hester asked innocently.

"Our home is in Connecticut, ma'am," he replied, ignoring his food and gazing at her steadily. "But at present we are in Washington, of course. People are coming in from all over the northern part of the Union to gather to the cause, as no doubt you know." He raised his level eyebrows very slightly.

Casbolt and Alberton glanced at each other, and away again.

"We are fighting for the survival of an ideal of freedom and liberty for all men," Breeland continued emphatically. "Volunteers are pouring in from every town and city and from the farms even far inland and to the west."

7

Merrit's face was suddenly alight. She looked for a moment at Breeland, her eyes shining, then back to Hester. "When they win, there will be no more slavery," she proclaimed. "All men will be free to come and go as they choose, to call no man master. It will be one of the greatest and noblest steps mankind has taken, and they will do it even at the cost of their lives, their homes, whatever it takes."

"War is usually at that cost, Miss Alberton," Hester answered quietly. "Whatever the cause of it."

"But this is different!" Merrit's voice rose urgently. She leaned forward a little over the exquisite china and silver, the light from the chandeliers gleaming on her pale shoulders. "This is true nobility and sacrifice for a great ideal. It is a struggle to preserve those liberties for which America was founded. If you really understood it all, Mrs. Monk, you would be as passionate in its defense as the Union supporters are . . . unless, of course, you believe in slavery?" There was no anger in her, just bewilderment that anyone should do such a thing.

"No, I don't believe in slavery!" Hester said fiercely. She looked neither to right nor left to see what other people's feelings might be. "I find the whole idea abhorrent."

Merrit relaxed and her face flooded with a beautiful smile. An instant warmth radiated from her. "Then you will understand completely. Don't you agree we should do all we can to help such a cause, when other men are willing to give their lives?" Again her eyes flickered momentarily to Breeland, and he smiled back at her, a faint flush of pleasure in his cheeks, and he looked away again, perhaps self-consciously, as if guarding his emotion.

Hester was more guarded. "I certainly agree we should fight against slavery, but I am not sure that this is the way to do it. I confess, I don't know sufficient about the issue to make a judgment."

"It is simple enough," Merrit replied, "when you cut away the political quarrels and the matters of land and money, and are left with nothing but the morality." She waved her hand

8

and, without realizing it, blocked the way of the footman trying to serve the entree. "It is a matter of being honest." Again the lovely smile transformed her face. "If you were to ask Mr. Breeland, he would explain the matter to you so you would be able to see it with such clarity you would burn to fight the cause with all your heart."

Monk looked across to see how Daniel Alberton felt about this intense loyalty in his daughter to a war five thousand miles away. There was a weariness in his host's face which told of many such discussions, and no resolution.

Newspapers in London carried many stories about Mr. Lincoln, the new president, and of Jefferson Davis, who had been elected president of the provisional government of the Confederate States of America, those states that had broken away from the Union one by one over the last several months. For a long time many had hoped to avoid outright war, while others actively encouraged it. But with the bombardment of Fort Sumter by the Confederates, and its subsequent surrender on April 14, President Lincoln had asked for seventy-five thousand volunteers to serve for a period of three months, and proposed a blockade of all Confederate ports.

Newspapers suggested that the South had called for a hundred and fifty thousand volunteers. America was now at war.

What was far less obvious was the nature of the issues at stake. To some, like Merrit, it was simply about slavery. In reality it appeared to Monk to have at least as much to do with land, economics and the right of the South to secede from a Union it no longer wished to be part of.

Indeed, much sympathy in Britain lay with the South, although the motives for that were also mixed, and perhaps suspect.

Alberton's patient tones came with an effort which for an instant was naked in his face.

"There are many causes, my dear, and some of them conflict with each other. There are no ends I know of which justify dishonorable means. One must consider—"

"There is nothing which justifies slavery!" she said hotly,

cutting across him with no thought for the respect she owed him, especially in company. "Too many people use sophistries to defend not risking themselves or what they own in a fight."

Judith's hand tightened on her silver fork, and she glanced at her husband. Breeland smiled. A flush of irritation crossed Casbolt's face.

"And too many people rush in to espouse one cause," Alberton replied, "without taking a moment to weigh what their partisanship might cost another cause, equally just and equally in need of their help, and perhaps as deserving of their loyalty."

It was apparent it was no philosophical argument. Something of immediate and highly personal importance was at stake. One had only to glance at Lyman Breeland's stiff shoulders and unsmiling face, at the high color in Merrit's cheeks, at Daniel Alberton's very evident impatience, to know that.

This time Merrit did not reply, but her temper flared very visibly. She was in many ways still not much more than a child, but her emotion ran so deep that Monk found the situation on the verge of embarrassment.

The entree plates were removed and cherry pie and cream were served. They ate in silence.

Judith Alberton made some pleasant remark about a musical recital she had been to. Hester expressed an interest Monk knew she did not feel. She did not care for sentimental ballads, and he wondered, looking at Judith's remarkable face, if his hostess really did either. It seemed a taste at odds with the strength of her features.

Casbolt caught Monk's eye and smiled as if secretly amused.

Gradually the conversation began again, gentle and well mannered, with an occasional shaft of wit. The pie was succeeded by fresh grapes, apricots and pears, then by cheese. Light gleamed on silver, crystal and white linen. Now and then there was laughter.

Monk found himself wondering why Breeland had been

10

invited. Discreetly he studied the man, his expression, the tensions in his body, the way he listened to the conversation as if intent upon interpreting from it some deeper meaning, and waiting his chance to intercede with something of his own. Yet it never came. Half a dozen times Monk saw him draw breath and then fail to speak. He looked at Merrit, when she was speaking, and there was a momentary softness in his eyes, but he scrupulously avoided leaning close to her or making any other gesture which might appear intimate, whether to guard her feelings or his own.

He was polite with Judith Alberton, but there was no warmth in him, as if he were not at ease with her. Considering her remarkable beauty, Monk did not find that difficult to understand. Men could be intimidated by such a woman, become self-conscious and prefer to remain silent rather than to speak, and risk sounding less than as clever or as amusing as they would have desired. He was probably ten years younger than she, and Monk had begun to suspect he was in love with her daughter, without her approval.

Casbolt showed no such lack of ease. His affection for Judith was apparent, but then as cousins they had probably known each other all their lives. Indeed he made several references, often in jest, to events in the past they had shared, some of which had seemed disasters at the time but had now receded into memory and no longer hurt. The pain or laughter shared made a unique bond between them.

They spoke of summer visits to Italy when the three of them—she, Casbolt, and her brother Cesare—had walked the golden hills of Tuscany, found gentle and idiosyncratic pieces of statuary that predated the rise of Rome, and speculated on the people who might have made them. Judith laughed with pleasure, and Monk thought he saw a shadow of pain as well. He glanced at Hester, and knew she had seen it also.

Casbolt's voice held it too: the knowledge of something too deep ever to be forgotten, and yet which could be shared because they had endured it together; he, she and Daniel Alberton.

11

Nothing overt was said during the entire course of the meal, and certainly nothing remotely offensive. But Monk formed the opinion that Casbolt did not much like Breeland. Perhaps it was no more than a dissimilarity in temperament. Casbolt was a sophisticated man of wide experience and charm. He was at ease with people, and conversation came naturally to him.

Breeland was an idealist who could not forget his beliefs, or allow himself to laugh while he knew others were suffering, even for the space of a dinner. Perhaps it was a certain strangeness, being far away from his home at a time of such trial, and among strangers. And obviously he could not help responding to Merrit's youth and her charm.

Monk had some sympathy with him. He had once been as passionate about great causes, brimming with zeal over injustices that affected thousands, perhaps millions. Now he felt such heat only over individuals. He had tried too often to affect the course of law or nature, and tasted failure, learning the strength of the opposition. He still tried hard and grieved bitterly. The anger seized up inside him. But he could also lay it aside for a space, and fill his heart and mind with the sweet and the beautiful as well. He had learned how to pace his battles—at least sometimes—and to savor the moments of respite.

The last course was almost completed when the butler came to speak to Daniel Alberton.

"Excuse me, sir," he said in little above a whisper. "Mr. Philo Trace has called. Shall I tell him you are engaged, or do you wish to see him?"

Breeland swiveled around, his body stiff, his expression so tightly controlled as to be almost frozen.

Merrit was far less careful to hide her feelings. The color rose hot in her cheeks and she glared at her father as if she believed he were about to do something monstrous.

Casbolt glanced at the others in apology, but his face was alive with interest. Monk had the fleeting impression that Casbolt actually cared what he thought, then he dismissed it as ridiculous. Why should he?

12

Alberton's expression made it plain that he had not expected the caller. For a moment he was taken aback. He looked at Judith questioningly.

"By all means," she said with a faint smile.

"I suppose you had better ask him to come in," Alberton instructed the butler. "Explain to him that we are at dinner, and if he cares to join us for fruit, then he is very welcome."

There was an uncomfortable silence while the butler retreated, and then returned, ushering in a slender, dark-haired man with a sensitive, mercurial face, the type whose expression conveyed emotion and yet perhaps hid his true feelings. He was handsome, as if charm came easily, and yet there was something elusive about him, and private. Monk judged him to be perhaps ten years older than Breeland, and the moment he spoke it was apparent he came from one of those Southern states which had recently seceded from the Union and with whom the Union was now at war.

"How do you do," Monk replied when they were introduced, after the butler had brought another chair and discreetly set an additional place at the table.

"I'm truly sorry," Trace said with some embarrassment. "I seem to have the wrong evening. I certainly did not intend to intrude." He looked for a moment at Breeland, and it was clear they already knew each other. The animosity between them crackled in the air.

"That's quite all right, Mr. Trace," Judith said with a smile. "Would you care for a little fruit? Or a pastry?"

His eyes lingered on her with pleasure and a certain earnestness.

"Thank you, ma'am. That is most generous of you."

"Mr. and Mrs. Monk are friends of Lady Callandra Daviot. I cannot remember whether you met her or not," Judith continued.

"No, I didn't, but you told me something of her. A most interesting lady." He sat down on the chair, which had been drawn up for him. He regarded Hester with pleasant curiosity. "Are you connected with the army also, ma'am?"

"Indeed she is," Casbolt said enthusiastically. "She has

13

had a remarkable career . . . with Florence Nightingale. I am sure you must have heard of her."

"Naturally." Trace smiled at Hester. "I'm afraid in America these days we are obliged to concern ourselves with all aspects of war, as I daresay you know. But I am sure it is not what you wish to discuss over dinner."

"Isn't that what you have come about, Mr. Trace?" Merrit asked, her voice cold. "You did not call socially. You admitted as much when you had mistaken the evening."

Trace blushed. "I don't know how I came to do that. I have already apologized, Miss Alberton."

"I'm sure I don't know either!" Merrit said. "I can only think you were worried in case Mr. Breeland might at last persuade my father of the justice of his cause, and you should find yourself without the purchase you expected." It was a challenge, and she made no concession to courtesy. Her passionate conviction rang in her voice so sincerely it almost robbed it of rudeness.

Casbolt shook his head. He looked at Merrit patiently. "You know better than that, my dear. However profound your convictions, you understand your father better than to think he would go back on his word for anyone. I hope Mr. Trace knows that also. If he doesn't, he soon will." He looked across at Monk. "We must apologize to you, sir, and to you," he said, including Hester for an instant. "This must all seem inexplicably heated to you. I daresay no one explained to you, Daniel and I are dealers and shippers, among other things. Guns of good quality are in great demand, with the United States at war, as it regrettably is. Men from both the Union and the Confederacy are scouring Europe and buying up everything they can. Most of the available weapons are quite possibly inferior, as likely to blow up in the faces of the men who use them as to do any damage to the enemy. Some of them have aims so bad you would be lucky to hit the broad side of a barn at twenty paces. Do you know anything about guns, sir?"

"Nothing at all," Monk said truthfully. If he ever had such knowledge, it had gone with the coach accident five years

14

ago which had robbed him of all memory before that time. He could not recall ever having fired a gun. However, Casbolt's explanation made clear the turbulence of emotions Monk had felt in the room, the presence of both Breeland and Trace, and the bitter emotion between them. It had nothing to do with Merrit Alberton, or any of the family.

Casbolt's face lit with enthusiasm. "The best modern gun—say, for example, the P1853, last year's model—is built of a total of sixty-one parts, including screws and so on. It weighs only eight pounds and fourteen and a half ounces, without bayonet, and the barrel is rifled, of course, and thirty-nine inches long. It is accurate over at least nine hundred yards—well over half a mile."

Judith looked at him with a slightly reproving smile.

"Of course!" He apologized, glancing at Hester, then at Monk again. "I'm sorry. Please tell us something of your business, if it is not all confidential?" His expression held an interest so sharp it was difficult to imagine it was affected purely for the sake of mere politeness.

Monk had never been asked such a question in the society of a dinner party. Normally it was the last thing people wished to speak of, because he was present to investigate something which had caused them recent pain and in all likelihood was still doing so. Crime not only brought fear, bereavement, and inevitably suspicion, it ripped from quiet lives the decent masks of secrecy everyone put over all manner of smaller sins and weaknesses.

"Robert!" Judith said urgently. "I think you are asking Mr. Monk to tell us about people's tragedies."

Casbolt looked wide-eyed and not in the least put out. "Am I? What a shame. How can I circumvent that? I really would like to hear something of Mr. Monk's fascinating occupation." He was still smiling, but there was a determination in his voice. He sat back from the table a little, picking up a small bunch of a dozen or so green grapes in his fingers. "Tell me, do you spend a lot of time on robberies, missing jewels, and so on?"

It was a far safer subject than guns or slavery. Monk saw

15

the interest flicker in Judith's face, in spite of her awareness that the subject was possibly not one a polite society would pursue.

Daniel Alberton also seemed relieved. His fingers stopped twisting the fruit knife he held.

"Mrs. Monk says that her involvement in your cases has replaced the exhilaration, the horror, and the responsibility she felt on the battlefield," Casbolt prompted. "They can hardly be affairs of finding the lost silver saltcellar or the missing great-niece of Lady So-and-so."

They were all waiting for Monk to tell them something dramatic and entertaining which had nothing whatever to do with their own lives or the tensions which lay between them. Even Hester was looking at him, smiling.

"No," he agreed, taking a peach off the dish. "There are a few of that order, but every so often there is a murder which falls to me, rather than to the police—"

"Good heavens!" Judith said involuntarily. "Why?"

"Usually because the police suspect the wrong person," Monk replied.

"In your opinion?" Casbolt said quickly.

Monk met his eyes. There was banter in Casbolt's voice, but his look was level, unflickering and highly intelligent. Monk was certain this remark at least was not made idly, to relieve the previous embarrassment between Breeland and Trace.

"Yes, in my belief," he answered with the weight he thought it deserved. "I have been seriously wrong at times, but only for a while. I was once convinced a famous man was innocent, and worked very hard to prove him so, only to find in the end that he was horribly and cold-bloodedly guilty."

Merrit did not wish to be interested, but in spite of herself she was. "Did you manage to put right your mistake? What happened to him?" she asked, ignoring the grapes on her plate.

"He was hanged," Monk said without pleasure.

She stared at him, a shadow flickering in her eyes. There

16

was something in his manner she did not understand, not the words but the emotion. "Weren't you pleased?"

How could he explain to her the anger he had felt at the loss of the woman who had been killed, and that revenge, which was all that a hanging was, brought nothing back? Justice, as the law contained it, was necessary, but there was no joy in it. He looked at the soft lines of her face; she had barely outgrown the roundness of childhood, and she was so certain she was right about the American war, so burning with indignation, love and consuming idealism.

"No," he said, needing to be honest to himself whether she understood or not. "I am pleased the truth was known. I am pleased he had to answer for his crime, but I regretted his destruction. He was a clever man, greatly gifted, but his arrogance was monstrous. In the end he thought everyone else should serve his talents. It consumed his compassion and his judgment, even his honor."

"How tragic," Judith said softly. "I'm glad Robert asked you; your answer is better than I had expected." She glanced at her husband, whose expression confirmed her own.

"Thank you, my dear." Casbolt flashed her a sudden smile, then turned back to Monk. "Tell us, how did you catch him? If he was clever, then you must have been even cleverer!"

Monk answered a trifle smugly. "He made mistakes—old cases, old enemies. I uncovered them. It is a matter of understanding loyalties and betrayals, of watching everything, and never giving up."

"Hounding him?" Breeland asked with distaste.

"No!" Monk replied sharply. "Seeking the truth, whether it is what you want it to be or not. Even if it is what you dread most and cuts deepest at what you want to believe, never lie, never twist it, never run away, and never give up." He was surprised at the vehemence with which he meant what he said. He heard it in his voice and it startled him.

He saw the agreement in Hester's face, and felt himself color. He had not realized her respect mattered so much to him. He had never intended to be so vulnerable.

17

Merrit was staring at him with a sudden interest, as if in a space of moments he had metamorphosed into a man she could like and she did not know how to deal with the change.

"There you are," Casbolt said with evident pleasure. "I knew you had invited a most interesting man, my dear," he said to Judith. "Are you ever defeated, Mr. Monk? Do you ever retire from the fray and concede to the villain?"

Monk smiled back, a trifle wolfishly. Now the passion was gone; they were fencing to entertain.

"Not yet. I've come close a few times. I've feared my own client was guilty, or that the person I was employed to protect might be, and I have wanted to let go, just walk away and pretend I did not know the truth."

"And did you?" Alberton asked. He was leaning forward a little across the table, his plate ignored, his eyes intent upon Monk's face.

"No. But sometimes I liked the villain better than the victim," Monk answered honestly.

Judith was surprised. "Really? When you understood the crime you had more sympathy with the murderer than the person he killed?"

"Once or twice. There was a woman whose child was systematically molested. I liked her far better than the man she killed for it."

"Oh!" She sucked in her breath sharply, her face blanched with pain. "Poor creature!"

Trace looked at her, his eyes wide, then at Merrit. "Was he guilty?"

"Oh, yes. And a victim himself."

"A . . ." Judith started, then understanding, her eyes filled with pity. "Oh . . . I see."

Breeland pushed his chair back from the table and rose slowly to his feet.

"I am sure Mr. Monk's adventures are fascinating, and I regret having to excuse myself so early, but since Mr. Trace has called on what is apparently business, I feel I should either stay and argue my cause over his, or withdraw and retain your goodwill by not allowing this most agreeable evening to descend into acrimony." He lifted his chin a little higher. He was angry and self-conscious, but would yield his convictions to no one. "And since you already know every reason why the Union is fighting to preserve the nation we have founded in freedom, against a Confederacy which would encircle us in slavery, and I have argued it with every reason and every emotion in my power, I shall thank you for your hospitality and wish you good night." He inclined his head stiffly in something less than a bow. "Mrs. Alberton, Miss Alberton." He looked at Daniel coldly. "Sir. Ladies and gentlemen," he said, including everyone else. Then he turned on his heel and left.

"I'm so sorry," Trace repeated. "That was the last thing I meant to have happen." He turned from Judith to Daniel Alberton. "Please believe me, sir, I never doubted your word. I did not know Breeland was here."

"Of course you didn't," Alberton agreed, rising to his feet also. "Perhaps if the rest of you will excuse us, we shall be able to conclude our business quite quickly. It seems unfortunate, and unnecessary, now that Mr. Trace is here, for me to require him to come again tomorrow." He looked apologetically to Hester and Monk.

"I daresay it is my fault." Casbolt looked at Trace and shrugged very slightly. "It was I who last spoke to you about it. I may have given the wrong date. If I did, I am sorry. It was most careless of me." He turned to Judith, then to Monk and Hester.

"It is quite all right," Monk said quickly, and he meant it. The friction between Trace and Breeland was more interesting than a blander party might have been, but of course he could not say so.

"Thank you," Casbolt said warmly. "Shall you and I remain here while the ladies retire to the withdrawing room and Daniel and Mr. Trace conduct their business?"

"By all means," Monk accepted.

Casbolt looked at the port bottle nestling in its basket, and the sparkling glasses waiting for it, and grinned broadly.

Judith led Hester and Merrit through to the withdrawing room again. The curtains were still open and the last of the evening light still bathed the tops of the trees in a warm apricot glow. An aspen shimmered as the sunset breeze turned its leaves, glittering one moment, smooth the next.

"I am so sorry for the intrusion of this miserable war in America," Judith said ruefully. "It seems we can't escape from it at the moment."

Merrit stood very straight, her shoulders squared, staring out of the long windows at the roses across the lawn.

"I don't think it is morally right that we should try to. I'm sorry if you feel that it is bad manners to say so, but I honestly don't believe Mrs. Monk is someone who would use manners as an excuse to run away from the truth." She turned her head to stare at Hester. "She went to the Crimea to care for our soldiers who were sick and injured when she could have stayed here at home and been comfortable and said it was none of her business. If you had been alive at the time, wouldn't you have campaigned with Wilberforce to end the slave trade through Britain and on the high seas?" There was a challenge directed at Hester, but in spite of the ring in her voice, her eyes were bright, as if she knew the answer.

"Please heaven, I hope so!" Hester said vehemently. "That we even entered into it was one of the blackest pages in all our history. To buy and sell human beings is inexcusable."

Merrit gave her a beautiful smile, then turned to her mother. "I knew it! Why can't Papa see that? How can he be there in his study actually proposing to sell guns to the Confederacy? The slave states!"

"Because he gave his word to Mr. Trace before Mr. Breeland came here," Judith replied. "Now please sit down and don't place Mrs. Monk in the middle of our difficulties. It is quite unfair." Taking Merrit's obedience for granted, she turned to Hester. "Sometimes I wish my husband were in a different business. I am not sure if there is anything entirely without contention. Even if you were to sell tin baths or turnips, I daresay there would be someone on your doorstep declaring your demands were unrighteous or prejudicial to somebody else's livelihood. But armaments arouse more emotions than most other things, and seem to depend upon so many reverses of fortune that cannot be foreseen."

"Do they?" Hester was surprised. "I would have thought governments at least could see the probability of war long before it became inevitable."

"Oh, usually, but there are times when it comes right out of nowhere at all," Judith replied. "Naturally my husband, and Mr. Casbolt as well, study the affairs of the world very closely. But there are events that take everyone by surprise. The Third Chinese War just last year was a perfect example."

Hester had no knowledge of it, and it must have been clear in her face.

Judith laughed. "It was all part of the Opium Wars we have with the Chinese every so often, but this one took everybody by surprise. Although how the Second Chinese War began was the most absurd. Apparently there was a schooner called *Arrow*, built and owned by the Chinese, although it had once been registered in British Hong Kong. Anyway, the Chinese authorities boarded the *Arrow* and arrested some of the crew, who were also Chinese. We decided that we had been insulted—"

"What?" Hester said in amazement. "I mean . . . I beg your pardon?"

"Precisely," Judith agreed wryly. "We took offense, and used it as a pretext to start a minor war. The French discovered that a French missionary had been executed by the Chinese a few months before that, so they joined in as well. When the war finished various treaties were signed and we felt it safe to resume business with the Chinese as usual." She grimaced. "Then quite unexpectedly the Third Chinese War broke out."

"Does it affect armament sales?" Hester asked. "Surely only to the advantage, at least for the British?"

Judith shook her head very slightly. "Depends upon whom you were selling to! In this instance, not if you were selling

21

to the Chinese, with whom we were going through a period of good relations."

"Oh . . . I see."

"Then perhaps we should be more careful to whom we sell guns?" Merrit said fiercely. "Instead of just to the highest bidder!"

Judith looked for a moment as if she were about to argue, then changed her mind. Hester formed the opinion that her hostess had had some variation of this conversation several times before, and on each of them failed to make any difference. It was eminently none of Hester's business, and better left alone, yet the impulse in her, which so often Monk told her was arbitrary and opinionated, formed the words on her lips.

"To whom should we sell guns?" she asked with outward candor. "Apart from the Unionists in America, of course."

Merrit was impervious to sarcasm. She was too idealistic to see any moderation to a cause.

"Where there is no oppression involved," she said without hesitation. "Where people are fighting for their freedom."

"Who would you have sold them to in the Indian Mutiny?"

Merrit stared at her.

"The Indians," Hester answered for her. "But perhaps if you had seen what they had done with them, the massacres of women and children, you might have felt . . . confused, at the least. I know I am."

Merrit looked suddenly very young. The gaslight on her cheeks emphasized their soft curve, almost childlike, and the fair hair where it curled on her neck.

Hester felt a surge of tenderness towards her, remembering how ardent she had been at that age, how full of fire to better the world, and sure that she knew how, without the faintest idea of the multitudinous layers of passion and pain intertwined with each other, and the conflicting beliefs, all so reasonable if taken alone. If innocence were not reborn with each generation, what hope was there that wrongs would ever be fought against?

"I am not happy about the morality of it either," she said contritely. "I would rather have something relatively uncomplicated, like medicine. People's lives are still in your hands, you can still make mistakes, terrible ones, but you have no doubt as to what you are trying to do, even if you don't know how to do it."

Merrit smiled tentatively. She recognized an olive branch and took it. "Aren't you afraid sometimes?" she asked softly.

"Often. And of all sorts of things."

Merrit stood still in the fading light. Only the very top of the aspen beyond her still caught the sun. She was fingering a rather heavy watch which had been tucked down her bosom, and now she had taken it out. She caught Hester's eyes on it and the color deepened in her cheeks.

"Lyman gave it to me . . . Mr. Breeland," she explained, avoiding her mother's gaze. "I know it doesn't really complement this dress, but I intend to keep it with me always, to the devil with fashion!" She lifted her chin a little, ready to defy any criticism.

Judith opened her mouth, then changed her mind.

"Perhaps you could wear it on your skirt?" Hester suggested. "It looks like a watch for use as much as ornament."

Merrit's face lightened. "That's a good idea. I should have thought of that."

"I tend to wear a useful watch rather than a pretty one," Hester said. "One I cannot really see defeats the purpose."

Merrit walked over to the chair opposite Hester and sat down. "I have the most tremendous admiration for people who dedicate themselves to the care of others," she said earnestly. "Would it be intrusive or troublesome of me to ask you to tell us a little more about your experiences?"

Actually it was something Hester was very willing to leave behind her when there was nothing she could accomplish and no one to persuade. However, it would have been ungracious to refuse, so she spent the next hour answering Merrit's eager questions and waiting for Judith to lead the conversation in another path, but Judith seemed to be just as interested, and her silence was one of deep attention.

When Trace had completed his business with Alberton he took his leave, and Alberton returned to the dining room, glanced at Casbolt, then seeing a slight nod, invited him and Monk to find more comfortable seats, not in the withdrawing room with the ladies but in the library.

"I owe you an apology, Mr. Monk," Alberton said almost before they had made themselves comfortable. "I have certainly enjoyed your company this evening, and that of your wife, who is a most remarkable woman. But I invited you here because we need your help. Well, principally I do, but Casbolt is involved as well. I am sorry for misleading you in such a way, but the matter is very delicate, and in spite of Lady Callandra's high opinion of you—which, by the way, was given as a friend, not professionally—I preferred to form my own judgment."

Monk felt a moment's resentment, mostly on Hester's behalf, then realized that he might well have done the same thing himself, were he in Alberton's position. He hoped it was nothing to do with guns, or a choice between Philo Trace and Lyman Breeland. He found Trace the more agreeable man, but he believed in Breeland's cause far more. He did not feel as passionately as Hester, but the idea of slavery repelled him.

"I accept your apology," he said with a slightly sardonic smile. "Now, if you can tell me the matter that troubles you, I will make my judgment as to whether I can help you with it—or wish to."

"Well taken, Mr. Monk," Alberton said ruefully. He made light of it, but Monk could see the tension underlying his words. His body was rigid; a tiny muscle ticked in his jaw. His voice was not quite even.

Monk felt a stab of guilt for his levity. The man was neither arrogant nor indifferent. His self-control all evening had been an act of courage.

24

"Are you facing some kind of threat?" he asked quietly. "Tell me what it is, and if I can help you, I will."

The flicker of a smile crossed Alberton's face.

"The problem is very simple to explain, Mr. Monk. As you know, Casbolt and I are partners in the business of shipping, sometimes timber, but mostly machinery and armaments. I imagine after the conversation of our other dinner guest, that much is obvious." He did not look at Casbolt while he spoke but fixed his gaze unwaveringly on Monk. "What you cannot know is that some ten years ago I was introduced to a young man named Alexander Gilmer. He was charming, very beautiful to look at, and a trifle eccentric in his style of living. He was also ill and had been earning his way as an artists' model. As I said, he was of striking appearance. His employer had abandoned him, Gilmer said, because he had refused him sexual favors. At that time he was desperate. I paid his debts as a matter of compassion." He took a deep breath but his eyes did not waver.

Casbolt did not attempt to interrupt. He seemed content that Alberton should tell the story.

"Nevertheless," Alberton went on, his voice even lower, "the poor man died . . . in very tragic circumstances. . . ." He drew in his breath and let it out in a sigh. "He had tried to get more work as a model, but each time with less respectable people. He was . . . somewhat naive, I think. He expected a standard of morality that did not exist in the circles in which he moved. He was misunderstood. Men thought he was offering sexual favors, and when he refused they became angry and put him out on the street. I suppose rejection very often produces such emotions." He stopped, his face filled with pity.

This time it was Casbolt who took up the thread, his voice earnest.

"You see, Mr. Monk, poor Gilmer, whom I also helped financially on one occasion, was found dead several months ago in a house known for male prostitution. Whether they merely sheltered him out of compassion, or if he worked

25

there, is not known. But it made any money passed to him, whether a gift or a payment, fall under suspicion."

"Yes, I see that." Monk could visualize the picture very clearly. He was not sure precisely how much he believed, but it was probably irrelevant. "Someone has discovered proof of this gift of yours and wishes you to continue it . . . only to them?"

A flicker crossed Alberton's face. "It is not quite as simple as that, but that is the substance of it. It is not money they wish. If it were, I could be tempted, to protect my family, although I realize that once you have paid there is no end to it."

"It also appears to be an admission that there is something to hide," Monk added, hearing the edge of contempt in his own voice. Blackmail was a crime he loathed above any other kind of theft. It was not just the extortion of money; it was a form of torture, long-drawn-out and deliberate. He had known it to drive people to their deaths. "I'll do all I can to help," he added quickly.

Alberton looked at him. "The payment they want is one I cannot give."

Casbolt nodded very slightly, but there was anger and pain in his face. He watched Monk intently.

Monk waited.

"They want me to pay them in gun sales," Alberton explained. "To Baskin and Company, a firm which I know is merely a front for another which sells directly to pirates operating in the Mediterranean." His hands were clenched into fists till his knuckles shone white. "What you may not know, Mr. Monk, is that my wife is half Italian." He glanced momentarily at Casbolt. "I think you heard mention of it at dinner. Her brother and his wife and children were murdered while at sea off the coast of Sicily . . . by pirates. You will understand why it would be impossible for me to sell them guns in those circumstances."

"Yes . . . yes, of course I do," Monk said with feeling. "It is never good to pay blackmail, but this is doubly impossible. If you give me all the information you have, I will do everything I can to find out who is threatening you, and deal with it. I may be able to find proof that your gift was no more than compassion, then they will have no weapon left. Alternatively, there may be the same weapon to use against them. I assume you would be willing for me to do that?"

Alberton drew in his breath.

"Yes," Casbolt said without hesitation. "Certainly. Forgive me, but it was to form some judgment of your willingness to pursue a difficult and even dangerous case to the conclusion, to fight for justice when all seemed stacked against you, that I asked you so much about yourself earlier in the evening, before you knew the reason why. I also wished to see if you had the vision to see a cause greater than satisfying the letter of the law."

Monk smiled a trifle twistedly. He also took few men at their word.

"Now, if you would tell me how they got in touch with you, and everything you know about Alexander Gilmer, both his life and his death," he replied, "I will begin tomorrow morning. If they get in touch with you again, delay them. Tell them you need to make arrangements and are in the process of doing so."

"Thank you." For the first time since he had mentioned the subject, Alberton relaxed a little. "I am deeply obliged. Now we must discuss the financial arrangements."

Casbolt reached out his hand. "Thank you, Monk. I think we now have room to hope."

2

MONK HAD DESCRIBED the case to Hester on their way home from the Albertons' house. She was entirely at one with him about his acceptance. She found blackmail as abhorrent as he did, and apart from that, she had liked Judith Alberton and was distressed to think of the amount of embarrassment and pain that might be caused to the family were scandal to be created over the circumstances of Alberton's help to Alexander Gilmer.

Monk set out early to go to Little Sutton Street in Clerkenwell, where Alberton had told him Gilmer had died. It was only eight o'clock as he walked rapidly towards Tottenham Court Road to find a hansom, but the streets were full of all kinds of traffic: cabs, carts, wagons, drays, costermongers' barrows, peddlers selling everything from matches and bootlaces to ham sandwiches and lemonade. A running patterer stood on the corner with a small crowd around him while he chanted a rough doggerel verse about the latest political scandal and caused roars of laughter. Someone threw him a coin and it flashed for a moment in the sun before he caught it.

The musical call of a rag and bone man sounded above the noise of hooves and the rumble of wheels over the rough road. Harness clinked as a brewer's dray went by laden with giant barrels. The air was heavy with the smells of dust, horse sweat and manure.

Monk glanced at a newsboy's headlines, but there was

nothing about America. The last he had heard was the rumor that the real invasion of the Confederate states was not to take place until the autumn of this year. Back in mid-April President Lincoln had proclaimed a naval blockade of the Confederate coast right from South Carolina to Texas, then later extended it to include Virginia and North Carolina. Fortifications had been begun to protect Washington.

Today was Tuesday the twenty-fifth of June. If anything had happened since then more than the occasional skirmish, news of it had not yet reached England. That took roughly from twelve days to three weeks, depending upon the weather and how far it had to travel overland first.

He saw an empty hansom and waved his arm, shouting above the general noise. When the driver pulled the horse up Monk gave him the address of the Clerkenwell police station. He had already considered how he intended to begin. He did not suppose either Alberton or Casbolt was lying to him, although clients certainly had in the past and no doubt would again. But even the best-intentioned people frequently make mistakes, omit important facts, or simply see an incomplete picture and interpret it through their own hopes and fears.

The cab arrived at the police station; Monk alighted, paid the fare and went in. Even five years after the accident, and with so much of a new life built, he still felt a surge of anxiety, the unknown returning to remind him of those things he had discovered about himself. Right from the beginning he had had flashes of familiarity, moments of recollection which vanished before he could place them. Most of what he knew was from evidence and deduction. He had left his native Northumberland for London, and begun his career as a merchant banker, working for a man who had been his friend and mentor, until his ruin for a crime of which he was innocent, although Monk had been unable to help him prove it. That had been the force which had driven Monk into the police and away from the world of finance.

Too many discoveries had made it evident that he had

30

been a brilliant policeman, but with a ruthless streak, even cruel at times. Juniors had been afraid of his tongue, which had been too quick to criticize, to mock the weaker and the less confident. It was something he disliked, and of which he could at last admit, even if only to himself, he was ashamed. A quick temper was one thing, to demand high standards of courage and honesty was good, but to ask of a man more than his ability to give was not only pointless, it was cruel, and in the end destructive.

Every time he went into an unfamiliar police station, he was aware of the possibility that he would meet another reflection of himself he would not like. He dreaded recognition. But he refused to let it shackle him. He went in through the door and up to the desk.

The sergeant was a tall man, middle-aged, with thin hair. There was no expression in his face but polite interest.

Monk breathed a sigh of relief.

"Mornin', sir," the sergeant said pleasantly. "What can I do to help you?"

"Good morning," Monk replied. "I need some information about an incident that happened in your area some months ago. A friend of mine is threatened with involvement in a scandal. Before I undertake to protect him, if I can, I should like to be certain of the facts. All I am looking for is what is recorded." He smiled. "But from an unimpeachable source."

The sergeant's polite skepticism was replaced by a certain understanding.

"I see, sir. And which particular incident would that be?" A look crossed his eyes as if he might already have a good idea, at least of its nature, if not specifically which occasion.

Monk smiled apologetically. "The death of Alexander Gilmer in Little Sutton Street. I am sure you will have records of it and someone who knows the truth." It was at times like these he missed the authority he used to have when he could simply have demanded the papers.

"Well, sir, the records are here, sure enough, but they

31

won't be open to the public, like. I'm sure you'll understand that, Mr. . . . ?"

"I'm sorry. Monk, William Monk."

"Monk?" Interest flared in the sergeant's eyes. "Would you be the Mr. Monk as worked on the Carlyon case?"

Monk was startled. "Yes. That was a few years ago now."

"Terrible thing," the sergeant said gravely. "Well, I s'pect since you used to be one of us, like, we could tell you all we know. I'll find Sergeant Walters as was on the case." And he disappeared for several minutes, leaving Monk to look around at the various wanted posters on the walls, relieved that the sergeant knew of him only since the accident.

Sergeant Walters was a thin, dark man with an enthusiastic manner. He took Monk to a small, chaotic room with books and papers piled everywhere, and cleared a chair by lifting everything off it and putting it all on the floor. He invited Monk to sit down, then perched on the windowsill, the only other space available.

"Right!" he said with a smile. "What do you wanter know about Gilmer, poor devil?"

"Everything you know," Monk said. "Or as much as you have time and inclination to tell me."

"Ah! Well." Walters settled himself more comfortably. It seemed he often sat on the sill. This was apparently the normal state of the room. How he found anything was a miracle.

Monk leaned back hopefully.

Walters stared at the ceiling. "About twenty-nine when he died. Tubercular. Thin. Haunted sort of look to his face, but good features. Not surprised artists wanted to paint him. That's what he did, you know? Yes, I suppose you do know." He seemed to be waiting for confirmation.

Monk nodded. "I was told that."

"Only saw him when he was dead," Walters went on. He spoke quite casually, but his eyes never left Monk's face, and Monk formed the very clear impression that he was being measured and nothing about him taken for granted. He could imagine Walters writing notes on him the moment he was gone, and adding them to the file on Gilmer, and that Walters would know exactly where in this chaos the file was.

Monk already knew the name of the artist from Casbolt, but he did not say so.

"Fellow called FitzAlan," Walters went on when Monk did not speak. "Quite famous. Found Gilmer in Edinburgh, or somewhere up that way. Brought him down here and took him in. Paid him a lot. Then grew tired of him, for whatever reason, and threw him out." He waited to see Monk's reaction to this piece of information.

Monk said nothing, keeping his expression bland.

Walters understood, and smiled. It was a measuring of wits, of professionalism, and now they both acknowledged it.

"He drifted from one artist to another," Walters said with a little shake of his head. "Downhill all the time. Be all right for a while, then he seemed to quarrel and get thrown out again. Could've left of his own choice, of course, but since he had nowhere to go, and his health was getting worse, seems unlikely."

Monk tried to imagine the young man, alone, far from home and increasingly ill. Why would he keep provoking such disagreements? He could not afford it, and he must have known that. Was he a man of ungoverned temper? Had he become an unusable model, the ravages of his disease spoiling his looks? Or were the relationships those of lovers, or by then simply user and used, and when the user grew bored the used was discarded for someone else? It was a sad and ugly picture, whichever of these answers was true.

"How did he die?" he asked.

Walters watched him very steadily, his eyes almost un-blinking. "Doctor said it was consumption," he replied. "But he'd been knocked around pretty badly as well. Not exactly murder, not technically, but morally I reckon it was. I'd find a way to beat the daylights out of any man who treated a dog like that man'd been used. I don't care what he did to get by or what his nature was." Under the calm of his manner there was an anger so hot he dared not let it go, but Monk saw it behind his eyes, and in the rigid set of his shoulders and in his arms where the fingers were stiff on the windowsill, knuckles white.

He had found Walters instantly agreeable. Now he liked him the more.

"Did you ever get anybody for it?" he asked, although he knew the answer.

"No. But I haven't stopped looking," Walters replied. "If you find anybody in your . . . help for your friend . . . I'd be obliged." He looked at Monk curiously now, trying to assess where his loyalties lay and exactly what sort of "friend" he had.

Monk himself was not sure. The blackmail letter Alberton had shown him was comparatively innocuous. It was awkwardly worded, made up from pieces cut from newspapers and pasted onto a sheet of very ordinary paper one might buy at any stationer's. It had stated that the payments could be interpreted as purchase of several forms, and in light of the way in which Gilmer had died, public knowledge of it would ruin Alberton's standing in society. No suggestion had been made that either Alberton or Casbolt was responsible for Gilmer's death. Possibly the blackmailer was afraid they could prove themselves elsewhere at the time. More likely such a threat was unnecessary. He thought he could obtain what he wanted without going so far.

"If I find out," Monk promised, "I shall be happy to assist you to dispense justice. I gather it was a male brothel where he was found?"

"That's right," Walters agreed. "And before you ask me what he was doing there, I'll tell you that I don't know. The owner said he took pity on him and fetched him in off the streets, an act of charity." There was no irony in his eyes, and his look dared Monk to differ. "Could be true. Gilmer, poor devil, was in little state to be any use as a worker, and he had neither strength nor money to be a client, assuming he was that way inclined, which no one seems to know.

34

We've just got it down officially as death by natural causes. But we all know damned well that someone beat him pretty badly too. Could have had them for assault if the poor sod hadn't died anyway."

"Any idea who it was that beat him?" Monk asked, hearing the edge in his own voice. "Privately, even if you couldn't prove it?"

"Ideas," Walters said darkly. "Not much more. Clients in places like that don't leave their names on a list. Some of them have some pretty sordid tastes that they can't exercise at home and aren't keen to have known."

"Think it was a client?"

"Sure of it. Why? Your friend one of them?" The sneer in Walters's voice was too bitter to hide.

"He says not. If you tell me when Gilmer died, exactly, I may be able to ascertain where my friend was."

Walters took out his notebook and rifled through it.

"Between eight and midnight on September twenty-eighth last year. Is your friend being blackmailed over Gilmer's death?"

"No, over having given him some money, which is open to misinterpretation."

"Nobody gave him much, poor devil." Walters shrugged. "Got himself into debt pretty badly. Thought it might have been one of his creditors beat him to teach him to pay up more promptly. We went and interviewed the man we suspected." He smiled, showing his teeth. It was more of a snarl, although there was definitely pleasure in it. "Somewhat vigorously," he added. "But he said Gilmer had paid everything he owed. Didn't believe that for a moment, but the bastard could unarguably prove where he was all that night. He spent it in jail! Only time I was sorry to see him there."

"Do you know how much it was?" Monk enquired. He knew exactly how much Alberton had said he gave Gilmer.

"No. Why?" Walters said quickly. "Do you know something about it?"

Monk smiled at him. "I might. How much was it?"

"Told you, I don't know. But it was over fifty pounds."

Alberton had paid sixty-five. Monk was unreasonably pleased. He realized only now how profoundly he had wanted to find Alberton honest.

"That answer you?" Walters was staring at him.

"No," Monk said quickly. "It confirms what I thought. My friend claimed to have paid it. It looks as if he did."

"Why?"

"Compassion," Monk said immediately. "Are you thinking it was for services rendered? I'd like to meet the boy that commands that much!"

Walters grinned. His eyes opened wide. "Looks like a good man caught in an unpleasant situation."

"It does, doesn't it," Monk agreed. "Thank you for your help."

Walters straightened up. "Hope it turns out to be true," he said pleasantly. "I'd like to think someone helped him . . . whatever he was."

"Did you know of him when he was alive?" Monk rose slowly also.

"No. Learned the rest when we were looking into his death. Got too much to do to investigate prostitution, if they aren't causing a public nuisance." He shrugged. "Anyway, most of the time the 'powers that be' would rather we didn't draw attention to it, and they'd certainly rather we didn't take names and addresses." He did not need to explain what he meant. "But let me know if you find out who did that to him, will you?"

"I will," Monk promised, picking his way through the piles of papers to the door. "Because I'd like you to meet up with him . . . and because I owe it to you."

It was early afternoon, and far too hot to be comfortable, when Monk reached the large house in Kensington which was Lawrence FitzAlan's studio. The midsummer sun beat on the pavements, shimmering back in waves that made the

36

vision dance. The gutters were dry and the unswept manure was pungent in the air.

The maid who answered the door was remarkably pretty, and Monk wondered if FitzAlan painted her as well. He had already decided how he would approach the artist, and had no compunction whatever in lying. Perhaps based quite unfairly on Walters's anger, he had formed a dislike of FitzAlan.

"Good afternoon," he said as charmingly as he could, and he knew that was very effective indeed; he had used it often enough. "I should very much like to have a portrait painted of my wife, and so I have naturally come to the finest artist I know of. May I make an appointment to see Mr. FitzAlan at his earliest convenience? Unfortunately, I am in London only a short while before returning to Rome for a month or two."

She looked at him with interest. With his dark hair and lean face he filled her idea of a mysterious Italian very well. She invited him into an ornate hall in which were several expensive pieces of statuary, and went to tell her master of the visitor.

FitzAlan was a flamboyant man with a high sense of his own talent, which Monk could see, having glanced at the canvases in his studio, was very real. Five were turned face out in various places, hung or stacked so they were well displayed, although to the casual eye they appeared to be placed with no regard. The draftsmanship was excellent, the play of light and shade dramatic, the faces arresting. In spite of himself Monk found his eye going to them instead of to FitzAlan.

"You are an art lover!" FitzAlan said with satisfaction.

Monk could imagine him playing this scene with every visitor, always the slight surprise in his voice, as though the world were peopled with Philistines.

Monk forced himself to meet FitzAlan's gaze. The artist was not tall, but he was a big man, broad-shouldered, in his fifties and now running to paunch. His gingerish hair had faded but there was still plenty of it, and he wore it affectedly long. It was a proud face, strong-featured, self-indulgent.

It galled Monk to flatter him, but it was necessary if he were to remain long enough to learn what he wanted to.

"Yes. I apologize for my discourtesy, but your paintings took my eye, regardless of my intention to be civil. Forgive me."

FitzAlan was pleased. "You are forgiven, my dear sir," he said expansively. "You wish for a portrait of your wife?"

"Rather more than that, actually. A friend of mine saw a very remarkable painting of a young man, done by you," Monk replied, making himself smile disarmingly. "But he was unable to purchase it because the owner, very naturally, would not sell. I wondered if you had any others of the same subject I might tell him of. He is very anxious to possess one. In fact, it is something of an obsession with him."

FitzAlan appeared suitably flattered. He tried to hide it, but Monk had assumed that his hunger for praise was far from filled even by the fame he already enjoyed.

"Ah!" he said, standing still as if thinking hard, only the brilliance of his eyes and the slight smile giving him away. "Let me see. Not certain which young man that might be. I paint anyone whose face intrigues me, regardless of who they are." He was watching Monk's reaction. "Can't be bothered to paint pretty pictures to make famous men look better than they do." He said it with pride. "Art, that is the master . . . not fame or money, or being liked. Posterity won't give a damn who the subject was, only how they were on canvas, how they spoke to the soul of the man who looked at them decades later—centuries, maybe."

Monk agreed with him. It was an acute and honest perception—but it galled him to say so.

"Of course. That is what divides the artist from the journeyman."

"Can you describe the subject?" FitzAlan asked, basking in the praise.

"Fair-haired, thin-faced, with a spiritual air, almost haunted," Monk replied, trying to visualize how Gilmer must have looked in the earliest days of his modeling, before his health deteriorated.

"Ah!" FitzAlan said quickly. "Think I know who you mean. I've got a couple upstairs. Been keeping those against the day when they'd be appreciated for what they are."

Monk controlled his anger with difficulty. He coughed, raising his hand to his face to conceal the revulsion he felt for a man who could speak so casually about a youth he had known and used, and whom he must have heard was dead.

"Excuse me," he apologized, then continued. "I should like very much to see them."

FitzAlan was already going to the door, leading the way back into the hall, past a naked marble Adonis and up the stairs to a larger room obviously used for storage. He went without hesitation to two canvases, concealed by other, later ones, and turned them so Monk could see and admire.

And much as it cut him, he did admire them. They were brilliant. The face that stared out from the colored oils was passionate, sensitive, already shadowed by some vision beyond the pedestrian needs of life. Perhaps even at this time he had known he was consumptive and would not have long to savor the joys or the grief he then knew. Had they been the sweeter for that, the more poignant? FitzAlan had caught all that was precious and swift to pass in the eyes, the lips, the almost translucent pallor of the skin. It was a disturbing painting. It flashed through Monk's mind to ask Alberton for the price of it as his reward. It hurt him to think he would never see it again after these few moments. It was a reminder of the sweetness of life, never to waste or disregard a moment of its gift.

"You like it," FitzAlan said unnecessarily. Monk could not have denied it. Whatever sins lay in the soul of the painter, the picture was superb. He recalled his purpose. "Who is he?" It was not difficult to ask. It seemed the only natural thing to do.

"Just a vagrant," FitzAlan replied. "A young man I saw in the street and took in, for a while. Wonderful face, isn't it?"

Monk turned away from FitzAlan in order to hide his own emotion. He could not afford to have his loathing show.

"Yes. What happened to him?"

"No idea," FitzAlan said with slight surprise. "Nobody else will paint him like that, I assure you. He was consumptive. That look won't be there anymore. That's what is so valuable, the moment! The knowledge of mortality. It's universal, the perception of life and death. It's a hundred and fifty guineas. Tell your friend."

That was half the price of a good house! FitzAlan certainly did not underestimate his own worth. Even so, Monk found ideas racing through his mind as to how he might acquire the picture. He would never have that sort of money to spend in such a way. He would probably never have it at all. He might be able to bargain down a good deal, but still not into his financial possibilities. Was there some trade? He would profoundly have liked to force FitzAlan into it, twist him until something hurt enough for him to be glad to give up the picture in exchange for relief.

"I'll tell him," he said between his teeth. "Thank you."

Monk spent the rest of that day, and the next two as well, tracing Gilmer's fairly rapid decline from one artist to another, each of lesser skill than the last, until finally he was destitute and on the street. In each case he had seemingly quarreled and left in some anger. No one had wished him well or given him any assistance. In the end, roughly the middle of the previous summer, he had been taken in by the master of a male brothel.

"Yeah, poor devil," he said to Monk. "On 'is last legs, 'e were. Thin as a rake an' pale as death. I could see as 'e were dyin'." His scarred face was pinched with pity as he sat in the overstuffed chair in his crowded parlor. He was an extraordinarily ugly man with a humpbacked, misshapen body, but with beautiful hands. Who or what he might have been in other circumstances Monk would never know, but it crossed his mind to wonder. Had he been drawn to this, or taken it up out of greed? He chose to think it was the former.

"Did he tell you anything about himself?" Monk enquired.

The man looked at him narrowly. Monk had not asked his name. "A bit," he answered. "What's it to you?"

40

"Did he work for you?"

"When 'e was well enough . . . which weren't often."

Monk could understand it, but he was still disappointed.

" 'E did the laundry," the man said wryly. "Wot was you thinking?"

To his amazement Monk was blushing.

The man laughed. " 'E weren't o' that nature," he said firmly. "Yer can turn boys, but 'is age it's 'arder, an' beside that, the way 'e looked like death, an' coughed blood, no one'd fancy 'im anyway. Whether you believe it or not, I took 'im in because I was sorry for 'im. I could see it wouldn't be for long. 'E'd bin 'ard enough used as it was."

"Any idea who knocked him around?" Monk tried to keep the anger out of his voice, and failed.

The man looked at him with a slight squint. "Why? Wot yer goin' ter do about it?"

There was no point in being less than honest. The man had already seen his feelings. "Depends upon who it is," he replied. "There are several people who would be happy to make life very difficult for whoever it was."

"Startin' wi' you, eh?"

"No, I'm not the first. I'm several steps along the line. He quarreled with many of the artists he worked for. Was it one of them?"

"I reckon so." The man nodded slowly. "But 'e didn't rightly quarrel with them. The first one just got bored and threw him out. Found it more profitable ter paint women for a while. The second couldn't afford to keep him. The third and fourth both asked favors of him like wot I sell—at an 'igh price. 'E weren't willing—that's why they threw 'im out. An' by then 'e were losing 'is looks an 'e got iller an' iller."

"Was it one of them?"

The man sized up Monk carefully, the dark face, the lean bones, broad-bridged nose, unblinking eyes.

"Why? Yer gonna kill 'im?"

"Nothing so quick," Monk replied. "There's a police

41

sergeant who would like to exact a slow vengeance . . . through the law."

"An' you'd tell 'im so 'e could?"

"I would. If I were sure it was the right one."

"Customer o' mine took a fancy to 'im an' weren't minded ter take no fer an answer. I'd 'ave 'ad 'im beat ter within an inch of 'is life, meself, but I can't afford ter. Get a name fer that, an' I'll be out o' business, an' all me boys wi' me."

"Name?"

"Garson Dalgetty. A gent, but a right sod underneath it. Told me 'e'd ruin me if I laid an 'and on 'im. And 'e could!"

"Thank you. I'll not say where I got this information. But I want a favor in return."

"Yeah? Why don't that surprise me none?"

"Because you're not a fool."

"Wot's yer favor?"

Monk grinned. "Not your trade! I want to know if Gilmer told you of anyone giving him money to pay his debts, and I mean giving, not paying."

The man was surprised. "So you know about that, do yer?"

"The man who gave it told me. I wondered if it was the truth."

"Oh, yeah. Very generous, 'e were." He rocked a little in his red chair. "I never asked why. But 'e kept it up till Gilmer come 'ere, an' after. Stopped when 'e died."

Monk realized with a jolt what the man had said.

"He went on incurring debts?"

"Medicine, poor sod. I couldn't afford that."

"Who was it?"

"Yer said yer knew."

"I do. But do you?"

The man's ugly face lit with bitter amusement. "Black-mail, is it? No, I don't. Gilmer would never tell me, an' I never asked."

"Who did know?"

"God . . . and the devil! How do I know? Don't suppose it

would be that 'ard ter find out, if yer put yer mind ter it. I never wanted ter."

Monk stayed a little longer, then thanked the man and took his leave, choosing not to look to either the right or the left as he went out. He had found compassion in the man, and he wanted to know nothing of his trade.

The man had been perfectly correct in saying that it would not be difficult to trace the payments, now that Monk knew they were made regularly. It took him the rest of that day, and required no skills beyond ordinary knowledge of banking and common sense. Any number of other people could have done the same.

He also wrote a note to Sergeant Walters, telling him the name of the man he was seeking was Garson Dalgetty.

Leaving Clerkenwell, he wondered why Alberton had not mentioned that he had made Gilmer an allowance of five guineas a month. It was not an enormous amount. It would get him a little extra food, enough sherry and laudanum to ease his worst distress, no more. It was an act of charity, nothing to be ashamed of, very much the opposite. But was it all it seemed?

He did not bother to trace any gift made by Casbolt. Alberton's gift was enough for his purposes. If he found no blackmailer in that, he could go back to Casbolt again.

The next thing he would do was trace the gun dealers through whom Alberton was requested to make the payment. But before that he would report to Alberton, as he had promised.

The evening went far from the way Monk had planned. He arrived at the house in Tavistock Square and was received immediately. Alberton looked anxious and tired, as if some negotiations of his own had not been easy.

"Thank you for coming, Monk," he said with a brief smile, welcoming him into the library. "Do sit down. Would you like a glass of whisky, or something else?" He gestured to the crystal-and-silver tantalus on a side table.

43

Monk was seldom treated as if he were a social equal, even in the most delicate cases. He had found that the more embarrassed people were by their need, the less did they wish to unbend to those whose help they asked. Alberton was a pleasant exception. Nevertheless he declined, wishing not only to keep a totally clear head, but also to be seen to.

Alberton did not take anything either. It seemed the invitation was purely hospitable, not a desire to excuse indulging himself.

Monk began to tell him briefly what he had learned of Gilmer and his life and death. He was giving an account of his visit to FitzAlan when the butler knocked on the door.

"I'm sorry to disturb you, sir," he apologized. "But Mr. Breeland is here again, and very insistent. Shall I ask him to wait, sir, or . . . or have one of the footmen show him out? I am afraid it could prove most unpleasant, and bearing in mind that he has been a guest . . ."

Alberton looked at Monk. "I'm sorry," he said bleakly. "This is a very awkward situation. You met young Breeland the other evening. As you must have observed, he is fanatical in his cause and cannot see any other point of view. I am afraid he will wait until I do speak to him, and to tell you the truth, I would rather my daughter did not meet with him again, as she may do if I do not see him straightaway." There was tenderness and exasperation in his face. "She is very young and full of ideals. She is rather like he is. She can see the justice of only one cause, and nothing at all of any other."

"By all means see him," Monk agreed, rising to his feet. "I can very easily wait. I really have little to say anyway. I came because you asked me to report regardless."

Alberton smiled briefly. "Actually, I think that was rather more Robert than I, but I can see his purpose. One can feel helpless, out of control, if one has no idea what is happening. All the same, I should be obliged if you would remain while I see Breeland, if you would? Another presence here may calm his excess a trifle. I really thought I had

44

made myself plain before." He turned to the butler, who was still waiting patiently. "Yes, Hallows, ask Mr. Breeland to come in."

"Yes, sir." Hallows withdrew obediently, but for an ir. stant, before he masked it, his opinion of Breeland's impor tunity was clear in his face. Monk imagined Hallows would wait well within call.

Lyman Breeland appeared a moment later, as if he had been on the butler's heels. He was dressed very formally in a dark, high-buttoned suit and well-cut boots with a fine polish.

He was quite clearly disconcerted to see Monk present.

Alberton observed it. "Mr. Monk is my guest," he said coolly. "He has no interest in armaments and is not a rival for anything you would wish. But I have told you before, Mr. Breeland, the guns that interest you are already sold—"

"No, they are not!" Breeland interrupted him. "You are in negotiation. You have not been paid, and believe me, sir, I know that. The Union has its ways of gaining information. You have been given a deposit, but the Rebels are short of funds, and you may be fortunate to see the second half of your price."

"Possibly," Alberton said with a distinct chill. "But I have no reason to suppose those I deal with are not men of honor, and whether they are or not, it is not your concern."

"I have the money in full," Breeland said. "Tell Philo Trace to produce the same! See if he can."

"I have given my word, sir, and I do not withdraw it," Alberton replied, his face set in hard lines, his anger unmistakable.

"You are conniving at slavery!" Breeland's voice rose. His body was stiff, his shoulders high. "How can any civilized man do that? Or have you passed beyond civilization into decadence? Do you no longer care where your comforts come from or who pays for them?"

Alberton was white to the lips. "I don't set myself up as a judge of men or of nations," he said quietly. "Perhaps I should? Maybe I should require every prospective purchaser to justify himself before me and account for every shot he

45

will take with any gun I sell him. And since that is manifestly preposterous, then perhaps I should not sell guns at all?"

"You are reducing the argument to absurdity!" Breeland countered, splashes of pink in his cheeks. "The moral difference between the attacker and the defender is clear enough to any man. So is the difference between the slave owner and the man who would free everyone. Only a sophist of the utmost hypocrisy would argue differently."

"I could argue that the Confederate who wishes to set up his own government according to his belief in what is right has more justification to his cause than the Unionist who would oblige him to remain in a union he no longer wishes," Alberton replied. "But that is not the issue, as you well know. Trace came to me before you did, and I agreed to sell him armaments. I do not break my word. That is the point, Mr. Breeland, and the only point. Trace has not misled me or deceived me in any way that would cause me to renege on my commitment to him. I have no guns to sell you; that is the sum of the situation."

"Give Trace back his deposit," Breeland challenged him. "Tell him you are no slaver! Or are you?"

"Insults offend me," Alberton said grimly, his face dark. "They do not change my mind. I agreed to see you because I was afraid you would not leave my house until I had. There is nothing more for us to discuss. Good evening, sir."

Breeland did not move. His face was pale, his hands clenched at his sides. But before he could find the words to retaliate, the door opened behind him, and Merrit Alberton came in.

Her gown was deep pink, her fair hair elaborately coiled but now in some disarray. Her cheeks were flushed and her eyes brilliant. She ignored Monk, glanced only briefly at Breeland, but deliberately stood close beside him. She addressed her father.

"What you are doing is immoral! You have made a mistake in offering the guns to the Confederates. You would never have thought of doing it were they rebels against England!" Her voice was rising higher and sharper all the time in her indignation. "If we still had slavery here, would you sell guns to slave traders so they could shoot at our army, and navy, even our men and women in their own homes, because we wanted all people to be free? Would you?"

"That is hardly a comparison, Merrit—"

"Yes, it is! The Rebels keep slaves!" She was shaking with emotion. "They buy men and women, and children, and use them like animals! How could you sell guns to people like that? Have you no morality at all? Is it just money? Is that it?" Almost unconsciously she was moving even closer to Breeland, who was watching with an almost impassive face.

"Merrit—" Alberton began.

But she cut him off. "There's no argument can justify what you are doing! I am so ashamed of you I can hardly bear it!"

He made a gesture of helplessness. "Merrit, it is not so simple as—"

Again she refused to listen. She still seemed unaware of Monk's presence. Her voice rose even more shrilly as her outrage drove her on. "Yes, it is! You are selling guns to people who keep slaves, and they are at war with their countrymen who want to prevent that and set the slaves free." She flung her arm out furiously. "Money! It's all about money, and it's pure evil! I don't know how you, my own father, can even try to justify it, let alone be part of it. You are selling death to people who will use it in the worst possible cause!"

Breeland moved as if to put his hand on her arm.

At last Alberton's temper gave way. "Merrit, be quiet! You don't know what you are talking about! Leave us alone. . . ."

"I won't! I can't," she protested. "I do know what I am talking about. Lyman has told me. And so do you, that's the worst of it! You know, and still you are prepared to do it!" She took a step towards him, ignoring Monk and Breeland, her face crumpled, brows drawn down. "Please, Papa! Please, for the sake of all the enslaved, for the sake of justice and freedom, above all for your own sake, sell the guns to

47

the Union, not to the Rebels! Just say you can't support slavery. You won't even lose any money . . . Lyman can pay you the whole amount."

"It's not about money." Alberton's voice was also louder now, and sharp with hurt. "For God's sake, Merrit, you know me better than that!" He ignored Breeland as if he had not been present. "I gave my word to Trace and I won't break it. I don't agree with slavery any more than you do, but I don't agree with the Union's forcing the South to remain part of it under their government either, if they don't want to! There are lots of different kinds of freedom. There's freedom from hunger and the bondage of poverty as well as the sort of slavery you're talking about. There's—"

"Sophistry!" she said, her face flooding with color. "You're happy enough to live here and make your own way. You aren't standing for Parliament to try to change our lives to stop hunger and oppression. You're a hypocrite!" It was the worst word she could think of, and the bitterness of it was in her eyes and her voice.

Breeland stared coldly at Alberton. It seemed at last he understood that he would not change his mind. If all that Merrit had said did not affect him, there was nothing else for him to add.

"I am sorry that you have seen fit to act against us, sir," he said stiffly. "But we shall prevail, nevertheless. We shall obtain what we need in order to win, whatever sacrifice it requires of us and whatever the cost." And with only a glance at Merrit, as if knowing she would understand, he turned on his heel and strode out. They heard his footsteps move sharply across the wooden floor of the hall.

Merrit stared at her father, her eyes hot and wretched. "I hate everything you stand for!" she said furiously. "I despise it so much I am ashamed that I live under your roof or that you paid for the food in my mouth and the clothes on my back!" And she too ran out, her feet light and rapid, heels clattering across the floor and up the stairs.

Alberton looked at Monk.

"I am profoundly sorry, Monk," he said miserably. "I had no idea you would be subjected to such unpleasantness. I can only apologize."

Before he could add anything further, Judith Alberton appeared at the door. She looked a little pale, and quite obviously she had overheard at least the last part of the argument. She glanced at Monk, embarrassed, then at her husband.

"I am afraid she is in love with Mr. Breeland," she said awkwardly. "Or she thinks she is." She watched Alberton with anxiety. "It may take a little while, Daniel, but she will think better of this. She'll be sorry she spoke so . . ." She faltered, uncertain what word she could use.

Monk took the opportunity to excuse himself. He had said all he had meant to about his enquiry. The Albertons should be permitted privacy in which to resolve their difficulties.

"I shall keep you informed of everything else I hear," he promised.

"Thank you," Alberton said warmly, holding out his hand. "I . . . I am very sorry for this unpleasantness. I am afraid emotions run very high in this American affair. I think we have barely seen the beginning of it."

Monk feared he was correct, but he said no more, wishing them good night and allowing the butler to show him out.

He woke confused, wondering for a moment where he was, struggling to separate the persistent noise from the last shreds of his dream. He sat up quickly. It was daylight, but shadowy and thin. The noise continued.

Hester was awake. "Who can it be?" she asked anxiously, sitting upright, her hair falling around her shoulders. "It's quarter to four!"

Monk climbed out of bed and grasped his dressing gown. He put it on hastily and went through to the front of the house, where the knocking was now louder and more persistent. He had not bothered with boots or trousers. Whoever it was seemed so desperate they were determined to wake someone even if it meant disturbing the entire neighborhood.

49

Monk fumbled for a moment with the lock and then opened the door.

Robert Casbolt stood on the step in the thin dawn light, his face unshaven, his hair rumpled.

"Come in." Monk stepped back, holding the door wide.

Casbolt obeyed without hesitation, and began speaking even before he was over the threshold.

"I'm sorry to disturb you in such a frantic manner, but I'm terribly afraid something irreparable may have happened." His words stumbled as if he could barely control his tongue. "Judith—Mrs. Alberton sent me a note. She is beside herself with worry. Daniel left shortly after you did and he has not returned. She said Breeland was there yesterday evening and was very angry indeed . . . even threatening. She is terrified that . . . I'm sorry." He brushed his hand across his face as if to clear his vision and steady himself. "What is worse is that Merrit has disappeared too." He stared at Monk with horror in his eyes. "She seems to have gone straight up to her room after the quarrel with her father. Judith assumed she would stay there, in temper, and probably not come down until morning."

Monk did not interrupt.

"But when she was unable to sleep with anxiety over Daniel," Casbolt went on, "she went to Merrit's room—and found her gone. She was nowhere in the house, and her maid looked and said a bag and some of her clothes were gone . . . a costume and at least two blouses. And her hairbrush and combs. For God's sake, Monk, help me look for them, please."

Monk tried to collect his thoughts and form some clear plan as to what to do first. Casbolt seemed close to the edge of hysteria. His voice was erratic and his body so tense his hands clenched and unclenched as if stillness were unbearable.

"Has Mrs. Alberton called the police?" Monk asked.

Casbolt shook his head very slightly.

"No. That was the first thing I suggested, but she was afraid if Merrit has gone to Breeland that she would be involved in scandal and it would ruin her. She . . ." He took a

50

deep breath. "Honestly, Monk, I think she is afraid Breeland has done Daniel some harm. Apparently when he left the house he was in a terrible rage, and said that he would win one way or another."

"That is true," Monk agreed. "I was there when he said it." He remembered with a chill the passion in Breeland's voice. It was the fire of the artist who creates from nothing a great vision for the world, the explorer who ventures into the unknown and opens the way for lesser men, the inventor, the thinker, the martyr who dies rather than deny the light he has seen . . . and the fanatic who sees any act justified by the cause he serves.

Casbolt was right to be afraid of Breeland; so was Judith Alberton.

"Yes, of course I'll come with you," he answered. "I'll go and dress, and tell my wife. I'll be five minutes, or less."

"Thank you! Thank you very much."

Monk nodded, then went hastily back to the bedroom.

Hester was sitting up with a shawl around her.

"Who is it?" she asked before he had closed the door.

"Casbolt," he answered, taking off his dressing gown and putting on his shirt. "Alberton went out shortly after I left and hasn't come home, and Merrit is missing. It looks as if she might have gone after Breeland. Stupid child!"

"Can I help?"

"No! Thank you." He fastened his shirt with clumsy fingers, moving too hastily, then reached for his trousers.

"Be careful what you say to her," Hester warned.

He would have been delighted to put Merrit Alberton over his knee and spank her until she was obliged to eat off the mantelpiece for a week. It must have shown in his face, because Hester stood up quickly and came to him.

"William, she is young and full of ideals. The harder you argue with her, the more stubborn she will be. Fight with her, and she'll do the last thing she really wants to rather than be seen to give in. Plead for her help, her understanding, earn her mercy, and she'll be reasonable."

51

"How do you know?"

"Because I was sixteen once," she said a trifle tartly.

He grinned. "And in love?"

"It is a natural state of affairs."

"Was he a gun buyer for a foreign army?" He put his jacket on. There was no time to shave.

"No, actually he was a vicar," she replied.

"A vicar? You . . . in love with a vicar?"

"I was sixteen!" There was warm color in her cheeks.

He smiled and kissed her quickly, feeling her respond after only an instant's hesitation.

"Be careful," she whispered. "Breeland may be . . ."

"I know." And before she could add anything further he went out and back to where Casbolt was standing near the door impatiently.

Casbolt's carriage was waiting outside in the street, and he climbed in ahead of Monk, shouting at the driver sitting huddled on the box. The summer dawn was hardly cold, but too chilly to wait in, and the man had been woken barely halfway through his sleep.

The carriage lurched forward and reached a good speed within moments. It was altogether fourteen minutes since Casbolt had interrupted Monk's dream.

"Where are we going?" Monk asked as they rolled over the cobbles and were flung together by the swerve around a corner.

"Breeland's rooms," Casbolt answered breathlessly. "I nearly went straight there without you, but for the cost of a street or so out of my way, I could have you with me. I don't know what we should find there. It may need more than one of us, and I formed the opinion you are a good man to have beside me in a scrap—if it should come to that. God knows what is in Merrit's mind. She must have lost all sense of . . . everything. She hardly knows the man! He . . ." He gasped as they were bumped again and the carriage swerved the other way, this time throwing him half on top of Monk.

"He could be anything!" he went on. "The man's a fanatic, prepared to sacrifice everything and everybody to his damned cause! He's madder than any of our own military men, and God help us, they are insane enough." His voice was rising with a wild note in it. "Look at some of their antics in the Crimea. Any price to be a hero—glory of victory, blood and bodies all over the place, and for what? Fame, an idea . . . medals and a footnote in history."

They were clattering through a leafy square, the trees making a temporary darkness.

"Damn Breeland and his idiotic ideals!" he said in an explosion of fury. "He has no business preaching to a sixteen-year-old girl who thinks everyone else is as noble and as uncomplicated as she is." There was a startling venom in his voice, a passion so deep it broke through his control and was raw in the air in the broadening light as they careered through the dawn streets.

Monk wished there were some help he could offer, but he knew that what Casbolt said was true. He deplored fatuous words, so he remained silent.

Suddenly the carriage drew up, Casbolt glanced out to make sure it was not a crossroads, apparently recognized where he was, and all but threw himself out.

Monk followed after him as he strode across the pavement to a doorway, opened it abruptly, and went inside. It was merely the outer entrance to a set of apartments, and the night doorman was sitting comfortably half asleep in a chair in the hallway.

"Breeland's rooms!" Casbolt said loudly as the man started awake.

"Yes, sir." He scrambled to his feet, fishing for his cap and setting it crookedly on his head. "But Mr. Breeland in't 'ere. 'E's gorn, sir."

"Gone?" Casbolt looked staggered. "He was here last night. What do you mean 'gone'? Where to? When will he be back?"

" 'E won't be back, sir." The doorman shook his head. " 'E's gorn for good. Paid up an' took 'is bags. Not that 'e 'ad but the one."

"When?" Casbolt demanded. "What time did he go? Was he alone?"

The doorman squinted. "I dunno, sir. 'Bout 'alf-past eleven, or summink like that. Were before midnight, anyway."

"Was he alone?" Casbolt persisted. His body was shaking and his face was white, a fine sweat on his brow.

"No, sir." The doorman was definitely frightened now. "There were a young lady wif 'im. Very pretty. Fair 'air, much as I could see of it. She 'ad a bag wif 'er as well." He swallowed. "Was they elopin'?" His breath caught in his throat and he coughed convulsively.

"Probably," Casbolt replied, the pain naked in his voice.

The doorman controlled his coughing. "Are you 'er father? I din't know, I swear ter Gawd!"

"Godfather," Casbolt replied. "Her father may have come looking for her as well. Was there anyone else here?"

The doorman screwed up his face. "There were a message for Mr. Breeland, but it just come wi' a reg'lar lad. Took it up ter Mr. Breeland, personal, an' went orff again. An' there were someone after that too, but I only just saw the back of 'im as 'e went up."

"What time was the message?" Casbolt said, desperation rising in his voice.

"Jus' afore 'e went orff." The doorman was now thoroughly alarmed. "I gave Mr. Breeland a knock an' 'e answered the door. The lad give 'im the message. Wouldn't trust me ter do it. Sounds as 'e'd bin paid ter give it personal, like I said, an' wouldn't take no for an answer."

"About half-past eleven?" Monk interrupted.

"Yeah, or a bit later. Anyway, Mr. Breeland came out jus' minutes arter that, wi' 'is things in 'is bag and the young lady arter 'im, and paid me wot 'e owes, for me ter give the landlord, an' orff 'e goes. An' 'er wif 'im."

"May we see his rooms?" Casbolt asked. "It may tell us something, although I have little hope."

"Course, if yer want." The doorman was more than amenable and started leading the way.

"Have you any idea what was in the note?" Monk asked, keeping pace with him. "Any idea at all? How did he look when he read it? Pleased, surprised, angry, distressed?"

"Pleased!" the doorman said immediately. "Oh 'e were right pleased. 'Is face lit up an' 'e thanked the lad, give 'im sixpence!" He was clear the extravagance spoke volumes about his pleasure. "An' in a terrible 'urry ter be gorn, 'e were."

"But did he give you any idea where to?" Casbolt urged, so agitated he moved his weight from one foot to the other, unable to keep still.

"No. Jus' said as 'e 'ad ter 'urry, be very quick, an' 'e were. Out in ten minutes, 'e were." He came to the door of Breeland's room and opened it, stepping back to allow them in.

Casbolt went straight past him and turned around slowly, staring.

Monk followed. The room seemed stripped of all personal belongings. He saw only a little crockery, a bowl for water, a ewer and a pile of towels. There was a Bible and a few scraps of waste paper on the dressing table. There was nothing left to indicate who had occupied the room only a few hours before.

Casbolt went straight to the dressing table, rifling through, then around pulling out the drawers. He yanked the bedclothes back right to the mattress, his actions growing wilder as he found not a thing beyond the landlord's few furnishings.

"There's nothing here," Monk said quietly.

Casbolt swore, fury and desperation sharp-pitched in his voice.

"There's no point in staying," Monk cut across him. "Where else can we look? If Breeland's gone, and Merrit is with him, perhaps Alberton went after them both? Where would they be most likely to head?"

Casbolt put his hands up to cover his face. Then his body stiffened and he stared at Monk wide-eyed. "The note! Merrit was with him, so it couldn't have been from her. He was pleased by it—very pleased. The only thing he cares about is the damned guns! It must be to do with them." He was moving towards the door already.

"Where?" Monk went after him out into the hallway.

"If he's held Merrit to ransom, then the warehouse. That's where the guns are," Casbolt called, racing to the front door and out into the street. "It's on Tooley Street!" he shouted to the driver, and pulled the door open, scrambling in a stride ahead of Monk. The carriage lurched forward and picked up speed, throwing Monk hard on the seat. It was moments before he was upright and had regained his balance.

They rode in silence, each consumed by fear of what they would find. It was clear daylight now and a few laborers were on their way to work. They passed wagons going to the vegetable market at Covent Garden, or others like it. It was all a familiar blur.

They crossed the river at London Bridge, the water already busy with barges, the smell of damp and salt coming in with the tide. The light was hard, a brittle reflection off the shifting surface.

They turned right, then pulled up sharply outside high, double wooden gates. Casbolt leapt out and ran across to them. He threw his weight against them and they swung wide, no lock or bar holding them.

Monk followed and burst into the warehouse yard. For an instant in the cold morning light he thought it was empty. The warehouse doors were closed, the windows blind. The cobbles were splattered with mud, clear tracks leading in several directions, as if something heavy had turned.

There were fresh horse droppings.

Then he saw them, dark, awkward mounds.

Casbolt stood paralyzed.

Monk walked across, his stomach cold, his legs shaking. There were two bodies lying close to each other, a third a little distance away, perhaps nine or ten feet. They were all in strangely contorted positions, as if they had been on the ground when someone had passed a broom handle under

56

their knees and over their arms. Their hands and ankles were tied, preventing them from moving, and they were gagged. The first two were strangers.

Monk walked over to the third, his stomach sick. It was Daniel Alberton. He, like the others, had been shot through the head.

3

M**ONK STARED DOWN** in horror at Alberton until the sound of Casbolt choking brought him abruptly to the realization that they must act. He turned around to see Casbolt was haggard, apparently incapable of moving. He looked as if he might faint.

Monk went over to him. He took him by the shoulders, forcing him to turn away. His body under Monk's hands was rigid and yet curiously without balance, as if the slightest blow would knock him over.

"We . . . we should do something. . . ." Casbolt said hoarsely, stumbling and leaning heavily on Monk. "Get . . . someone . . . Oh God! This is . . ." He could not complete the sentence.

"Sit down," Monk ordered, half easing him to the ground. "I'll look around and see what I can. When you're fit to, you go for the police."

"M-Merrit?" Casbolt stammered.

"I don't think there's anyone else here," Monk answered. "I'm going to look. Stay where you are!"

Casbolt did not reply. He seemed too stunned to move unaided.

Monk turned back and walked across the cobbled yard to the bodies of the two men lying close to each other. The nearest one was strongly built, thickset, and although it was hard to tell in his doubled-up position, Monk guessed he was of less-than-average height. His head and what was left of his face were covered with blood. The hair still visible was light brown with no gray in it. He could have been in his thirties.

Monk swallowed hard and moved to the next body. This second man seemed older; his hair was sprinkled with gray, his body leaner, his hands gnarled. His clothes had been pulled away from his shoulders at the back, and there was an almost bloodless cut on his skin below and to the side of his neck. It was T-shaped. It must have been made after death.

Monk walked back to the first man and looked more carefully. He found the same thing on his shoulder, half obscured by the way he had fallen, although there was so little bleeding this cut also must have been made after his heart had stopped. It was a curious, savage thing to do to a dead man. Was there great hatred behind it? Or some other bitter purpose? It had to matter, or why would anyone waste time remaining here to do it? Surely after such a murder one would escape as quickly as possible?

At first Monk had been too appalled to touch the flesh to see if it was still warm. He must do it now.

He glanced across at Casbolt, who was sitting on the ground, staring at him.

He bent and touched the dead man's hand. It was growing cold. He touched the shoulder under the jacket and shirt. There was still a trace of warmth in the flesh. They must have been killed two or three hours ago, at perhaps about two in the morning. Alberton must have arrived not long after midnight. The other two must be the watchmen normally employed.

The relief would be coming soon. He could hear the sound of carts in the street beyond the gates, and now and then voices. The world was awakening and beginning its day. He stood up and walked over to where Daniel Alberton lay, curled over in the same grotesque position. The shooting here had been neater. More of his face was recognizable. The same T-shaped mark was cut into his shoulder.

Monk was startled at how angry he felt, and how grieved.

60

He realized only now how much he had liked the man. He had not expected such a sense of loss. He understood why Casbolt was so shattered he could barely move or speak. They had been lifelong friends.

Nevertheless he must make Casbolt get mastery of himself and go to find the nearest constable on duty, and have him fetch a senior officer and the mortuary wagon for the bodies. He turned and began to walk back. He was almost up to Casbolt when his foot kicked something solid in the mud over the cobbles. At first he thought it was a stone and he barely glanced at it. But a gleam of light caught his eye and he bent to look. It was metal, yellow and shining. He picked it up and brushed off the caked mud. It was a man's watch, round and simple, with engraving on the back.

"What is it?" Casbolt asked, looking up at him.

Monk hesitated. The name on the watch was "Lyman Breeland" and the date was "June 1, 1848." He put it back exactly where it had been.

"What is it?" Casbolt repeated, his voice rising. "What have you got?"

"Breeland's gold watch," Monk said quietly. He wished he could offer more compassion, but nothing he said would alter the horror of it, and they needed to act. "You had better gather your strength and go and fetch the police." He looked closely at Casbolt's white face to judge if he was up to it. "There's bound to be a constable on the beat somewhere near here. Ask. There are people about. Someone'll know."

"The guns!" Casbolt cried, staggering to his feet, swaying for a moment, then going at a shambling run towards the great double wooden doors of the warehouse.

Monk followed after him and had almost caught up with him when Casbolt yanked at the handle and it swung open. Within the visible part of the warehouse there was nothing at all, no boxes, crates, or anything else.

"They're gone," Casbolt said. "He's taken them . . . every last one. And all the ammunition. Six thousand rifled muskets and above half a million cartridges to go with them. Everything Breeland wanted and five hundred more besides!"

61

"Go and find the police," Monk told him steadily. "We can't do anything here. It's not just robbery, it's triple murder."

Casbolt's jaw fell. "Good God! Do you think I give a damn about the guns? I just wanted to know if it was he who did this. They'll hang him!" He turned and walked away, stiff-legged, a little awkwardly.

When he was out of the yard and the main gate closed, Monk began again to examine the whole place, this time more closely. He did not go back to the bodies. The sight of them, beyond all human help, sickened him, and he did not feel there was anything he could learn from them. Instead he looked closely at the ground. He began at the entrance, it being the one place any vehicle must have come. The yard was cobbled, but there was a definite film of mud, dust, smudges of soot from nearby factory chimneys, and the dried remnants of old manure. With care it was possible to trace the most recent wheel tracks of at least two heavy carts coming in, probably backing around and turning so their horses faced the exit and the wagons were tail to the warehouse doors.

He paced out roughly where the horses would have stood, possibly for as long as two hours, to load six thousand guns, twenty to a box, and all the ammunition. Even using the warehouse crane it would have been an immense task. That would explain what the men were doing for the two hours between midnight and their deaths—they had been forced to load the guns and ammunition first.

He found fresh manure squashed flat by at least two sets of wheels.

Would they have left any carts outside waiting?

No. They would draw attention. They might be remembered. They would have brought them all in at the same time and had them wait idle in the yard. It was large enough.

Obviously, Breeland had had accomplices, ready and only waiting for the word. Who had the message come from? What had it said? That they were ready, wagons obtained, even a ship standing by to take them out on the morning tide? The police would look into that. Monk had no idea when the river tides were. They changed slightly every day.

He walked all around the yard, and then the inside of the warehouse, but he found nothing more that told him anything beyond what was already obvious. Someone had brought at least two wagons, more probably four, sometime last night after dark, probably about midnight, and killed the guards and Alberton, and taken the guns. One of them had been Lyman Breeland, who had dropped his watch during the physical exertion of loading the cases of guns. It was conceivable it had been in some other exertion, a fight between his own men, or with the guards, or even with Alberton. The varieties of possibility did not alter the facts that mattered. Daniel Alberton was dead, the guns were gone, so was Breeland, and it appeared as if Merrit had gone with him, whether or not she had had any idea what he planned. If she was now with him willingly or as a hostage there was also no way to tell.

Monk heard wheels stop outside and the yard gate opened. A very tall, thin policeman came in, his limbs gangling, his expression at once curious and sad. His face was long and narrow, and looked as if by nature it was more suited to comedy than this present stark death. He was followed by an older, more stolid constable, and behind him an ashen-faced Casbolt, shivering as if with cold, although it was now broad daylight and the air mild.

"Lanyon," the policeman introduced himself. He looked Monk up and down with interest. "You found the bodies, sir? Along with Mr. Casbolt here . . ."

"Yes. We had cause to believe something was wrong," Monk explained. "Mrs. Alberton called Mr. Casbolt because her husband and daughter had not returned home." He knew the procedure, what they would need to know, and why. He had been in similar positions himself often enough, trying to get the facts that mattered from shocked and bereaved people, trying to weed out the truth from emotion, preconceptions, threads of half observations, confusion and fear. And he knew the difficulties of witnesses who say too much, the shock that makes one need to talk, to try to convey

63

everything one has seen or heard, to make sense of it long before there is any, to use words as a bridge simply not to feel drowned by the horror.

"I see." Lanyon still regarded Monk closely. "Mr. Casbolt says you used to be in the police yourself, sir. Is that right?"

So Lanyon had never heard of him. He was not sure whether he was pleased or not. It meant they started without preconceptions now. But what about later, if he heard Monk's reputation?

"Yes. Not for five years," he said aloud.

For the first time Lanyon gazed around, his eyes ending inevitably on the crumpled bodies twenty yards away.

"Best look at them," he said quietly. "Surgeon's on his way. Do you know when Mr. Alberton was last seen alive?"

"Late yesterday evening. His wife says he left home then. It will be easy enough to confirm with the servants."

They were walking towards the bodies of the two guards. They stopped in front of them and Lanyon bent down. Monk could not avoid looking again. There was a peculiar obscenity in the grotesqueness of their positions. The sun was high enough to shed warmth into the yard. There were one or two small flies buzzing. One settled in the blood.

Monk found himself almost sick with rage.

Lanyon made a little growling sound in his throat. He did not touch anything.

"Very odd," he said softly. "Looks more like a sort of execution than an ordinary murder, doesn't it? No man sits like that because he wants to." He reached out his hand and touched the skin at the side of the nearest man's neck, half under the collar. Monk knew he was testing the temperature, and that he would come to the same conclusion he had earlier. He also knew he would find the T-shaped incision.

"Well . . ." Lanyon said with an indrawn breath as he uncovered the cut. "Definitely an execution, of sorts." He looked up at Monk. "And the guns were all taken, Mr. Casbolt said?"

"That's right. The warehouse is empty."

Lanyon stood up, brushing his hands down the sides of

64

his trousers and stamping his feet a little, as if he were cold or cramped. "And they were the best-quality guns—Enfield P1853 rifled muskets—and a good supply of ammunition to go with them. That right?"

"That's what I was told," Monk agreed. "I didn't see them."

"We'll check. There'll be records. And daytime staff. The constable will keep them outside for the moment, and the new watch, if there is one." He glanced at the bodies again. "The night shift can't tell us, poor devils." He led the way over to where Alberton lay. Again he bent down and looked closely.

Monk remained silent. He was aware of the constable and Casbolt in the distance, examining the warehouse itself, the doors, the tracks in the thin film of mud, crisscrossing where the wagons had backed and turned, where they must have loaded the cases of guns.

Lanyon interrupted his thoughts.

"What does T stand for?" he said, biting his lip. "T for thief? T for traitor, perhaps?" He stood up frowning, his long face full of anger and sadness. He was a plain man, but there was something likable in him that dominated one's impression. "This Mr. Breeland who wanted to buy the guns is American, that right?"

"Yes. From the Union."

Lanyon scratched his chin. "We heard the Union army executes its soldiers something like this, when it has to. Very nasty. Can't see the need for it, myself. Ordinary firing squad seems good enough to me. I suppose they have their reasons. Why didn't Mr. Alberton sell him the guns? Was he a Southern sympathizer, do you know?"

"I don't think so," Monk answered. "He'd just committed himself to sell them to the Southern buyer and he wouldn't go back on his word. I don't believe for him there is any question of ideological difference between the sides, just his own honor in keeping a promise." He found that oddly difficult to say. He saw Alberton alive in his mind, and then the crumpled figure on the ground, its face almost unrecognizable.

"Well, it cost him dear," Lanyon said quietly.

"Sir!" the constable called out. "I got summink 'ere!"

Lanyon turned.

The constable was holding up the watch.

Lanyon walked over, Monk close behind him. He took the watch from the constable and looked at it carefully. The name in script was very clear to read.

"Looks like someone found this already," he said, glancing at Monk.

"I did. I cleared the name, then put it back."

"And I presume you would have told us?" Lanyon observed with a sharp glance. He had very clear, pale blue eyes. His hair was straight and tended to stick out.

"Yes. If you hadn't retrieved it yourselves. I assumed you would."

Lanyon said nothing. He took a piece of chalk out of his pocket and marked the cobbles, then gave the watch to the constable, telling him to look after it.

"Not that it matters much where it was," he remarked.

"Except that it can't have been there long," Monk pointed out. "If it had been in a corner, it might have lain there for days."

Lanyon eyed him curiously. "You doubt it was Breeland?"

"No," Monk was honest. "We went to his rooms. He's cleared everything out, almost an hour or less before they must have come here, judging by how long it would take to load the crates and how long since the men were killed."

"Yes. Mr. Casbolt told me. That's what brought you here. And it seems Miss Alberton has disappeared from home as well." He did not add any conclusion.

"Yes."

Casbolt moved forward.

"Sergeant, Mrs. Alberton doesn't yet know anything except that her daughter is missing. She doesn't know about . . ." He gestured towards the bodies, but did not look at them. "May we . . . may Monk and I go and tell her, rather than . . . I mean . . ." He swallowed convulsively. "Can you leave her at

66

least until tomorrow? She will find this . . . she will be devastated. They were devoted . . . both her husband and her daughter . . . and by a man who had been a guest in her home."

Lanyon hesitated only a moment. "Yes, sir. I know of no reason why not. Poor lady. It looks pretty plain this was a robbery carried out in a particularly vicious manner." He shook his head. "Though why they did this to them I don't know. Seems as if Breeland felt he'd been betrayed, but from what you say the Confederate got there first. Maybe there was something in the deal we don't know about. We'll look into it, but it doesn't make any difference to the murders. People get cheated in business every day. Yes, Mr. Casbolt, you and Mr. Monk go and tell Mrs. Alberton the news, and stay there and look after her. But I shall need to speak to you again, later in the day."

"Thank you," Casbolt said with profound emotion.

Outside in the street Monk turned to him. "I don't know why you said I should go with you, but you should tell Mrs. Alberton alone. You're her cousin. I am almost a stranger. And anyway I would be more use here than anywhere else." He had already stopped as he spoke. Casbolt's carriage was still waiting, the driver peering anxiously up and down. The street was busy with laborers, dockers and other workmen arriving for their duties. A cart laden with bricks passed one way, a heavy wagon of coal the other.

Casbolt shook his head impatiently. "We can't help Daniel now." His voice was hoarse. His eyes looked as if he had seen hell and the image of it was stamped on him forever. "We must think of Judith, and of Merrit. The police may believe she went willingly with Breeland, or they may think she is a hostage." He shook his head minutely. "But if they have already left England, there is nothing they can do. America is consumed in its own civil war. There will be little or no point in anyone here making representations to Washington to have Breeland deported to face a charge of triple murder. He will be the hero of the hour. He has just taken the Union enough guns to arm nearly five regiments. They will simply refuse to believe he obtained them by murder."

67

He licked dry lips. "And there is still the matter of the black-mail. Please . . . come with me. See what Judith would like. Isn't that the least we can do?"

"Yes," Monk said softly, more moved than he wished to be. He dreaded going to tell Judith Alberton that her husband was dead. He had been filled with relief that this time it was not his task. He understood only too well why Lanyon was willing to allow Casbolt to do it. And now it was inescapable. He could alter nothing about what had happened, but Casbolt was right, he might be able to help with Merrit in a way the police could not, and it was impossible to refuse. It did not even seriously occur to him to try.

They rode in silence from the warehouse through the morning streets away from the heavy industrial area with its traffic and smoke, the grime-stained shirts and cravats of men in grays and browns moving towards other yards, factories and offices. Still without speaking, they entered the smarter city streets with men in dark suits, traders, clerks, and paperboys calling the morning news.

Too soon they arrived at Tavistock Square. Monk was not ready yet to face Judith, but he knew delaying would not help. He got out of the carriage behind Casbolt and followed him up the steps.

The front door opened before Casbolt could touch the bell. The butler, pale-faced, ushered them in.

"Mrs. Alberton is in the withdrawing room, sir," he said to Casbolt, barely acknowledging Monk's presence. He must have seen from Casbolt's face the nature of the news he brought. "Shall I fetch her maid, sir?"

"Yes, please." Casbolt's voice was little above a whisper. "I am afraid the news is . . . terrible. You might also send word for Dr. Gray."

"Yes, sir. Is there anything else I can do?"

"I could use a brandy, and I daresay Mr. Monk could also. It has been the worst morning of my life."

"Did you find Mr. Alberton, sir?"

"Yes, I am afraid he is dead."

The butler drew in his breath and swayed for a moment,

then regained his self-control. "Was it the American gentleman, sir, over the guns?"

"It looks like it, but say nothing to anyone yet. Now I must go and—"

He got no further. Judith opened the withdrawing room door and stood staring at them. She read in Casbolt's agonized face what she must already have dreaded.

He stepped forward as if to catch her should she fall, but with an effort so intense it was plain to see, she steadied herself and remained upright.

"Is he . . . dead?"

Casbolt seemed to be beyond words. He merely nodded.

She breathed out very slowly, her face ashen. "And Merrit?" Her voice cracked.

"No sign of her." He took her by the arm, gently, but almost supporting her weight. "There is no reason to suppose any harm has come to her," he said clearly. "That is why I brought Monk. He may be able to help us. Come in and sit down. Hallows will send for Dr. Gray and bring us some brandy. Please . . . come in. . . ." He turned her as he spoke, half leading her into the room, and Monk followed after, closing the door. He felt like an intruder in an intensely private grief. Casbolt was family, perhaps all she had left now. They had known each other since childhood. Monk was an outsider.

Judith stood in the middle of the floor, and it was not until Casbolt guided her to a chair that she finally sank into it. She looked devastated, hollow-eyed, her skin bloodless, but she did not weep.

"What happened?" she asked, looking at Casbolt as if to lose sight of him would somehow be to abandon all help or hope.

"We don't know," he answered. "Daniel and the two guards at the warehouse were shot. It was probably very quick. There will have been no pain." He did not say anything about the extraordinary positions they had been in, or the T-shaped cuts in their flesh. Monk was glad. He would not have told her either. If she did not ever have to know, so

69

much the better. If it became public, it would be later, when she was stronger.

"And the guns and ammunition were all gone," Casbolt added.

"Breeland?" she whispered, searching his face. He was sitting close to her and she reached toward him instinctively.

"It looks like it," he replied. "We went to his rooms first, looking for him," he went on. "For Merrit, really, and he was gone, all his belongings, everything. He received a message and packed and left within a matter of minutes, according to the doorman."

"And Merrit?" There was terror in her voice, in her eyes, the slender hands clenched in her lap.

He reached out and rested his fingers over hers. "We don't know. She was at his rooms and left with him."

Judith started to rock sideways, shaking her head in denial. "She wouldn't! She can't have known! She would never . . ."

"Of course not," he said softly, tightening his hand on hers. "She won't have had the faintest idea of what he intended to do, and it may be he will never tell her. Don't think the worst; there is no occasion to. Merrit is young, full of hotheaded ideals, and she was certainly swept off her feet by Breeland, but she is still at heart the girl you know, and she loved her father, in spite of the stupid quarrel."

"What will he do to her?" There was agony in her eyes. "She'll ask him how he got the guns. She knows her father refused to sell them to him."

"He'll lie," Casbolt said simply. "He'll say Daniel changed his mind after all, or that he stole them . . . she wouldn't mind that because she believes the cause is above ordinary morality. But she wouldn't ever countenance violence." His voice rang with conviction, and for a moment there was a flicker of hope in Judith's face. For the first time she turned to Monk.

"He obviously had allies," Monk said to her. "Someone came to his rooms with a message. He could not have moved the guns by himself. There must have been at least two of them, more likely three." He did not mention the forced help at gunpoint he believed had been the case. "Merrit may have been looked after by someone else during that time."

"Could . . ." She swallowed and took a moment to regain her composure. "Could she just have eloped with Breeland, and neither of them had anything to do with the . . . the guns?" She could not bring herself to say "murder." "Could that have been the blackmailer?"

Casbolt was startled. He glanced questioningly at Monk and then back at Judith.

"He didn't tell me," she said quickly. "Daniel did. I knew there was something wrong, and I asked him. I don't believe he ever kept secrets from me." The tears welled in her eyes and spilled over.

Casbolt looked wretched and helpless. He was gaunt with shock and exhaustion himself. Suddenly, Monk felt an overwhelming sympathy for him. He had lost his closest friend, and with the theft of the guns, also a great deal of money. He had seen the bodies themselves in all their grotesque horror, and now he had to try to support the widow who had lost not only her husband but also her child. It would be days before she even thought of her share of the financial loss, if she ever did.

"I'm sorry you had to know." Casbolt found his voice. "It was all very silly. Daniel befriended the young man because the poor creature was ill and alone. He paid his bills, nothing more."

"I know . . ." she said quickly.

"It is just a matter of reputation," he went on. "He wanted to protect you from the distress, but he would never have sold guns to the blackmailers because of where they would be used." His eyes were gentle, full of understood pain. After all, her brother had been his cousin and friend also. "And I don't believe he would have paid anything," he added bitterly. "Once you pay a blackmailer you have tacitly admitted that you have something to hide. It never stops. That's why

I brought Mr. Monk now. Perhaps we could still use his help. . . ." He left it hanging, for her to answer.

"Yes," she said, shaking. "Yes, I suppose we still need to find them. I'm afraid I . . . I hardly thought of it." She turned to Monk.

"I'll do whatever you want, Mrs. Alberton," he promised. "But now I'd like to go with the police and see what's happening in their investigation. That is the first thing to know."

"Yes . . ." Again the hope flashed in her eyes. "Maybe . . . Merrit . . ." She did not dare to put it into words.

It was plain in Casbolt's face that he held no such illusion, but he could not bring himself to tell her so.

"Yes," he added, nodding to Monk. "I'll stay here. You should see what Lanyon has found. Go with him. Please consider yourself still on retainer to do that. Help us in any way you can. Make your own judgments . . . anything at all. Just keep us informed . . . please?"

"Of course." Monk rose to his feet and excused himself. He was immensely relieved to escape the house of tragedy. Judith's grief was painful to be so close to, even though he would carry the knowledge of it with him wherever he went. Even so, to involve himself in some physical action was a kind of relief, and he strode towards Gower Street, where he could find a hansom and go back to the warehouse. From there he would start to look for Lanyon.

He began in Tooley Street with the constable who had been posted outside the warehouse gates and was perfectly willing to tell him that Lanyon had questioned people closely. Then he set off in the direction of Hayes Dock, which was the closest point on the river with a crane at hand from which they could transfer the guns to barges.

Of course it was possible they could have gone instead to the railway terminus, or across London Bridge back to the north side of the river. But movement by water seemed the obvious choice, and Monk followed the policeman's directions to the dock, although he did not expect to find Lanyon still there.

The place bustled with life now, teeming with carts and wagons laden with all kinds of goods. The shops were open for business and men and women carried bundles in and out. They seemed to be of every possible nature, groceries, ships' supplies, ropes, candles, clothes for all weather, both on land and at sea.

He walked quickly along the waterfront, traveling south, downriver. Gulls wheeled and circled, their harsh cries clear above the sound of the incoming tide against the stones, the wash of passing barges, lighters and the occasional heavier ship, and the shouts of men to each other as they worked at loading and hauling. The smells of salt, fish and tar were thick in his nostrils and with them came sudden memory of the distant past, of being a boy on the quayside in Northumberland. There he was by the sea, not a river, looking out at an endless horizon, a small stone pier, and hearing the lilt of country voices.

Then it was gone again, and he was at Hayes Dock, and the tall, thin figure of Lanyon was unmistakable, his straight, fairish hair standing up like a brush in the wind. He was talking to a heavyset man with a dark, grimy face and hands almost black. Monk knew without asking that he was a coal backer, carrying sacks up the twenty-foot ladders from the holds of ships, across as many as half a dozen barges to the shore, and up or down more ladders, depending on the tide and the loading of the ship. It was a backbreaking job. Usually a man was past doing it anymore by the time he was forty. Often injury had taken its toll long before that. Monk could not remember how he knew. It was another of the many things lost in the past.

But that was irrelevant now.

Lanyon saw him and beckoned him over, then resumed his questioning of the coal backer.

"You finished at nine yesterday evening, and you slept on the deck of that barge there, under the awning?" He smiled as if he were repeating the words to clarify them.

"S'right," the coal backer agreed. "Drunk, I was, an' me ol' woman gave me an 'ard time of it. Always goin' on, she

73

is. Never gives it a rest. An' the kids screamin' an' wailin'. I jus' kipped down 'ere. But I weren't so tired I din' 'ear them comin' in an' loadin' them boxes, an' the like. Dozens of 'em, there were. Went on fer an hour or more. Crate arter crate, there was. An' nobody said a bleedin' word. Not like normal folks, wot talks ter each other. Jus' back an' for'ard, back an' for'ard with them damn great crates. Must 'a bin lead in 'em, by the way they staggered around." He shook his head gloomily.

"Any idea what time that was?" Lanyon pressed.

"Nah . . . 'ceptin' it were black dark, so this time o' the year, reckon it were between midnight an' about four."

Lanyon glanced at Monk to make sure he was listening.

"W'y?" the coal backer asked, running a filthy hand across his cheek and sniffing. "Was they stolen?"

"Probably," Lanyon conceded.

"Well, they're long gorn nah," the man said flatly. "Be t'other side o' the river past the Isle o' Dogs, be now. Yer've no chance o' getting 'em back. Wot was they? Damn 'eavy, wotever they was."

"Did the barge go up the river or down?" Lanyon asked.

The man looked at him as if he were half-witted. "Down, o' course! Ter the Pool, mos' like, or could 'a bin farver. Ter Souf'end fer all I knows."

Barges were passing them all the time on the water. Men called to each other. The cry of gulls mixed with the rattle of chains and creak of winches.

"How many men did you see?" Lanyon persisted.

"Dunno. Two, I reckon. Look, I were tryin' ter get a spot o' kip . . . a little peace. I din't look at 'em. If folks wanna shift stuff around 'alf the night in't none o' my business—"

"Did you hear them say anything at all?" Monk interrupted.

"Like wot?" The coal backer looked at him with surprise. "I said they didn't talk. Said nuffin'."

"Nothing at all?" Monk insisted.

The man's face tightened and Monk knew he would now stick to his story, true or not.

74

"Did you notice what height they were?" he asked instead.

The man thought for a moment or two, making Monk and Lanyon wait.

"Yeah . . . one of 'em were shortish, the other were taller, an' thin. Very straight 'e stood, like 'e 'ad a crick in 'is back, but worked real 'ard . . . the bit I saw," he amended. "Made enough noise, clankin' around."

Lanyon thanked him and turned to walk back towards the road along the river edge. Monk kept level with him.

"Are you sure it was the wagon from the warehouse?" he asked.

"Yes," Lanyon said without hesitation. "Not many people about in the middle of the night, but a few. And I sent men in other directions as well. Searched around in other yards, just in case they moved them only a short way. Not likely, but don't want to overlook anything." He stepped off the curb to avoid a pile of ropes. They passed Horsleydown New Stairs, and ahead of them, close together, were four more wharfs before they had to bear almost a quarter of a mile inland to go around St. Saviour's Dock, then back to the river's edge and Bermondsey Wall, and more wharfs.

The Tower of London was sharp gray-white on the far bank, a little behind them. The sun was bright in patches on the water, thin films of mist and smoke clouding here and there. Ahead of them lay the Pool of London, thick with forests of masts. Strings of barges moved slowly with the tide, so heavy laden the water seemed to lap at their gunwales.

Behind them were the dark, disease-infested, crumbling buildings of Jacob's Island, a misnamed slum which had suffered two major outbreaks of cholera in the last decade, in which thousands had died. The smell of sewage and rotting wood filled the air.

"What do you know about Breeland?" Lanyon asked, increasing his stride a little as if he could escape the oppression of the place, even though they were following the curve of the river into Rotherhithe and what lay ahead was no better.

"Very little," Monk answered. "I saw him twice, both times at Alberton's house. He seemed to be obsessed with

75

the Union cause, but I hadn't thought of him as a man to re-sort to this kind of violence."

"Did he mention anyone else, any friends or allies?"

"No, no one at all." Monk had been trying to remem-ber that himself. "I thought he was here alone, simply to arrange purchase—as was the man from the Confederacy, Philo Trace."

"But Alberton had already promised the guns to Trace?"

"Yes. And Trace had paid a half deposit. That was why Alberton said he couldn't go back on the deal."

"But Breeland kept trying?"

"Yes. He didn't seem to be able to accept the idea that for Alberton it was also a matter of honor. He was something of a fanatic." Should he have been able to foresee that Breeland was so closely poised to violence that a final refusal would break his frail links with decency, even perhaps sanity? Had preventing this been his moral task, even though it was not the one for which he had been hired?

Lanyon seemed to be deep in thought, his narrow face tight with concentration. They walked quickly. It was half a mile around the dock, and they had to avoid bales and crates, piles of rope, chains, rusty tin, men heaving loads from the towering wharf buildings across to where barges lay, riding the slurping water, bumping and scraping sides as the wash of a passing boat caught them.

The dockers were men of all ages and types. It was labor anyone could do if his strength permitted it. It surprised Monk that he knew that. Somewhere in the past he had been to places like this. He knew the different sorts of men as he saw them: the bankrupt master butchers or bakers, grocers or publicans; lawyers or government clerks who had been suspended or discharged; servants without references, pen-sioners, almsmen, old soldiers or sailors, gentlemen on hard times, refugees from Poland and other mid-European coun-tries; and the usual fair share of thieves.

"It must have been very well planned," Lanyon interrupted his thoughts. "Everything worked to time. The question is, did he stage the quarrel just to keep himself informed about

76

Alberton's movements and whether or not the guns had already gone? Did he know perfectly well that Alberton wouldn't change his mind?"

That had not even occurred to Monk. He had assumed the quarrels were as spontaneous as they had seemed. Breeland's indignation had sounded entirely genuine. Could any man act so superbly? Breeland had not struck him as a man with sufficient imagination to simulate anything.

Lanyon was waiting for an answer, looking sideways at Monk curiously.

"It was certainly planned," Monk admitted reluctantly. "He must have had men ready to help, with a wagon. They must have known the river and where to hire a barge. Perhaps that was the message he received which made him leave his lodgings and go that night. I had wondered where Merrit Alberton fitted in, if it was her leaving home that precipitated it."

Lanyon grunted. "I'd like to know her part in it too. How much idea had she as to the kind of man Breeland really is? What is she now—lover or hostage?"

"She's sixteen," Monk replied, not knowing really what he meant.

Lanyon did not answer. They were back at the water's edge. On both sides of the river tall chimneys spewed out black smoke which drifted upwards, staining the air. Massive sheds had wheels vaulting up through their roofs like the paddles of unimaginably huge steamers. Monk remembered from somewhere in the past that the London docks could take about five hundred ships. The tobacco warehouses alone covered five acres. He could smell the tobacco now, along with tar, sulfur, the saltiness of the tide, the stench of hides, the fragrance of coffee.

All around were the noises of labor and trade, shouts, clanging of metal on metal, scrape of wood on stone, the slap of water and whine of wind.

A man passed them, his face dyed blue with the indigo he unloaded. Behind him was a black man with a fancy waistcoat, such as a ship's mate might wear. A fat man with long gray hair curling on his collar carried a brass-tipped rule, dripping spirit. There was a stack of casks a dozen yards away. He had been probing them to test their content. He was a gauger—that was his work.

A whiff of spice was sharp and sweet for a moment, then Monk and Lanyon were negotiating their way around a stack of cork, then yellow bins of sulfur, and lead-colored copper ore.

Somewhere twenty yards away, sailors were singing as they worked, keeping time.

Lanyon stopped a brass-buttoned customs officer and explained who he was, without reference to Monk.

"Yes, sir," the customs man said helpfully. "Wot was it about, then?"

"A triple murder and robbery from a warehouse in Tooley Street last night," Lanyon said succinctly. "We think the goods were loaded onto a barge and sent downriver. Probably got this far about one or two in the morning."

The customs man bit his lip dubiously. "Dunno, meself, but yer best chance'd be to ask the watermen, or mebbe even river finders. They often work by night as well, lookin' fer bodies an' the like. Never tell what the river'll fetch up. Not lookin' fer bodies too, are yer?"

"No," Lanyon said grimly. "We have all the bodies we need. I was going to try the watermen and river finders. I thought you would know of any ships bound for America from the Pool, especially any that might have gone this morning." There was a wry expression on his lugubrious face, as if he were aware of the irony of it.

The customs man shrugged. "Well, if there was, I reckon your murderer and thief is long gone with it!"

"I know," Lanyon agreed. "It'll do me no good. I just have to be sure. He may have accomplices here. It took more than one man to do what was done last night. If any Englishman helped him, I want to catch the swine and see him hang for it. The American might be able to find some justification, although not in my book, but not our men. They'll have done it for money."

78

"Well, come with me into my office, an' I'll see," the customs man offered. "I think the *Princess Maude* might have gone on the early tide, and she was bound that way, but I'd 'ave ter check."

Lanyon and Monk followed obediently, and found that two ships had left, bound for New York, that morning. It took them until early afternoon to question the dockers, sackmakers, and ballast heavers before being satisfied that Alberton's guns had not gone on either vessel.

With a feeling of heavy disappointment they went to the Ship Aground for a late lunch.

"What in hell's name did he do with them, then?" Lanyon said angrily. "He must intend to ship them home. There's no other use he would have for them!"

"He must have taken them further down," Monk said, biting into a thick slice of beef and onion pie. "Not a freighter, something fast and light, especially for this."

"Where? There's no decent mooring along Limehouse or the Isle of Dogs, not for something to sail the Atlantic with a load of guns! Greenwich maybe? Blackwall, Gravesend, anywhere down the estuary, for that matter?"

Monk frowned. "Would he take a barge that far? I know it's late June, but we can still get rough weather. I think he'd get it into a decent ship and up anchor as soon as possible. Wouldn't you?"

"Yes," Lanyon agreed, taking a long draft from his ale. The room around them was packed with dockers and river men of one sort or another, all eating, drinking and talking. The heat was oppressive and the smells thick in the throat. "I suppose that leaves us nothing to do but try the watermen and the finders. Watermen first. Anyone working last night might have seen something. There'll have been someone around; there always is. It's just a matter of finding him. Like looking for a needle in a haystack. Customs man had a good point. Why bother?"

"Because Breeland didn't do it alone," Monk replied, finishing the last of his pie. "And he certainly didn't bring a barge over from Washington!"

79

Lanyon shot him a wry glance, humor in his thin face. He finished his meal as well, and they stood up to leave.

It took them the rest of that afternoon and into the evening to work their way as far as Deptford, to the south of the river, and the Isle of Dogs, to the north, going back and forth in the small ferryboats used by the watermen, questioning all the time.

The following morning they started again, and finally crossed from the West India Port Basin in Blackhurst, just beyond the Isle of Dogs, over the Blackwall Reach to Bugsby's Marshes, on the bend of the river beyond Greenwich.

"Ain't nuffin' 'ere, gents," the waterman said dolefully, shaking his head as he pulled on the oars. "Yer must 'a bin mistook. Jus' marsh, bog, an' the like." He fixed Monk with a critical, sorrowful eye, having already examined his well-cut jacket, clean hands and boots that fit him perfectly. "Yer in't from 'round 'ere. 'Oo tol' yer there was anyfink worth yer goin' ter the Bugsby fer?"

"I'm from right around here," Lanyon said sharply. "Born and raised in Lewisham."

"Then yer oughter 'ave more sense!" the waterman said unequivocally. "I'll wait for yer an' take yer back. Less yer wanter change yer mind right now? 'Alf fare?"

Lanyon smiled. "Were you out on the river the night before last?"

"Wot of it? Do some nights, some days. Why?" He leaned on the oars for a minute, waiting till a barge went past, leaving them rocking gently in its wake.

Lanyon kept his smile half friendly, half rueful, as if he were an amateur experimenting at his job and hoping for a little help. "Three men were murdered up on Tooley Street, beyond Rotherhithe. A shipload of guns was stolen and brought in a barge downriver. Don't know how far down. Beyond this, anyway. We think they may have been loaded on board a fast, light ship somewhere about here, bound for America. If they were, you would have seen them."

The waterman's eyes widened as he started to pull again. "A ship for America! I never saw no ship anchored 'ere.

80

Mind, it could 'a bin around the point, opposite the Victoria Docks. Still, I'd 'a thought I'd see the masts, like."

Monk felt disappointment unreasonably bitter. How far down the river could they go? There were no watermen in the estuary. Unlikely to be anyone at all around before dawn. Although if Breeland had gone that far, negotiating a heavily laden barge through the Pool of London at night, along Limehouse Reach, around the Isle of Dogs and past Greenwich, it would have been well into the early morning by then, and full daylight by the time he reached anything like open water.

"Did you see anything?" he pressed, aware of how the urgency in him was making his voice harsh.

"Saw a barge come down 'ere, big black thing it were, low in the water," the man replied. "Too low, if yer ask me. Lookin' fer trouble. I dunno why fellas take risks like that. Better ter 'ire another barge than risk losin' the lot. Greed, that's wot it is. Seen some o' the wrecks ter prove it. Ask some o' them finders! More men drowned through greed than anyfink else."

Lanyon stiffened. "A heavy-laden barge?"

"That's right. Went on down the river, but I never saw no ship."

"How close were you to it?" Lanyon pressed, leaning forward now, his face eager. Gulls wheeled and circled overhead. The heavy mud smell of the water was thick in the air. The low marshes lay ahead of them.

"Twenty yards," the waterman replied. "Reckon they 'ad yer guns?"

"What did you notice? Tell me everything! It's the men I'm after. They murdered three Englishmen to get what they took. One of them anyway was a good man with a wife and daughter; the other two were decent enough, worked hard and honestly. Now, describe that barge!"

"Do you wanter go ter the Marshes or not?"

"Not. Tell me about the barge!"

The waterman sighed and leaned on his oars, letting the

81

boat drift gently. The tide was on the turn and he could afford to allow the slack current to carry him. He was concentrating, trying to picture the barge in his mind again.

"Well, it were very low in the water, piled 'igh wi' cargo," he began. "Couldn't see what it were 'cos it were covered over. It weren't proper light, but there was streaks in the sky like, so I could make out the shape of it plain. An' o' course it 'ad riding lights on it." He was watching Lanyon. "Two men, I saw. Could 'a bin more, but I jus' saw two at any time . . . I think. One were tall an' thin. I 'eard 'im yell at the other one, an' 'e weren't from 'round 'ere. Mind, I got proper cloth ears w'en it comes ter speech. I dunno a Geordie from a Cornishman."

Neither Lanyon nor Monk interrupted him, but they glanced at each other for an instant, then back at the waterman sitting slumped over his oars, his eyes half closed. The boat continued to drift very gently in the slack water.

"I don' remember the other one sayin' much. Tall one seemed ter be in charge, like, givin' the orders."

Lanyon could not contain himself. "Did you see his face?"

The waterman looked surprised; his eyes suddenly opened very wide and he stared past Lanyon at the river beyond. "No—I never saw 'is face clear. It were still afore dawn. They must 'a come down the river pretty good if they was from north o' Rother'ithe. But 'e 'ad a pistol in 'is belt, I can see that clear as if 'e were in front o' me now. An' 'e 'ad blood on 'is hands, smeared like. . . ."

"Blood?" Lanyon said sharply. "Are you sure?"

"Course I'm sure," the waterman replied, his eyes steady, his face set grimly. "I saw it red w'en 'e passed under the riding light, an' summink dark on 'is shirt an' trousers, splattered. I never took no thought ter it then." He rubbed his hand across his face. "Yer reckon it were 'im as killed your three men in Tooley Street, then?"

"Yes," Lanyon said quietly. "I do. Thank you, you have been extremely helpful. Now I need to find out where the barge went back to, whose it is, and what happened to the other man. Someone took it back up the river again."

82

"Never seen it come back. But then I were gorn 'ome by then, mebbe."

Lanyon smiled. "We'll go back too, if you please. I've no desire to get out at Bugsby's Marshes. It looks disgusting."

The waterman grinned, although his face was still pale and his hands were clenched tight on the oars. "Told yer."

"Just one more thing," Monk said quietly as the man leaned his weight on the oars to turn the boat. The tide was beginning to run the other way, and suddenly he needed to put his back into it. Monk could almost feel the pull on his own muscles as he watched.

"What's that?"

"Did you see any sign of a woman . . . a young girl? Or she could even have been dressed as a boy, perhaps?"

The waterman was startled. "A woman! No, I never seen a woman on one o' them barges. What would a woman be doing out 'ere?"

"A hostage, perhaps. Or maybe willingly, going to board the seagoing ship farther down the river."

"I never saw 'er. But then them barges 'as cabins, sort o'. She could 'a bin below. . . . Gawd 'elp 'er. Wish I'd 'a known. I'd 'a done summink!" He shook his head. "There's river police!" His expression betrayed that that would have been a last resort, but in times of extremity he would have abandoned his own principles and turned to them.

Lanyon shrugged ruefully.

Monk said nothing, but settled in his seat for the journey back to Blackwall, and then eventually to the city, to tell Mrs. Alberton that Breeland had got away and there was nothing he and Lanyon, or anyone else, could do about it.

Monk arrived at Tavistock Square early in the evening. He was not surprised to find Casbolt there. And in truth he was relieved to see him. It was easier to tell him such bare facts as he had, simply because his emotion could not possibly be as deep or his bereavement as dreadful as Judith's.

He was shown into the withdrawing room immediately. Casbolt was standing by the empty hearth, the fireplace now

83

covered with a delicate tapestry screen. He looked pale, as if his composure cost him great effort. Judith Alberton stood by the window as if she had been gazing out at the roses just the other side of the glass, but she turned as Monk came in. The hope in her face twisted inside him with pity, and with guilt because he could do nothing to help. He brought no news that was of any comfort.

The atmosphere was electric, as if the air even inside the room were waiting for thunder.

She stared at him, as if to guess from his face what he would say, trying to guard herself from pain, and yet she could not let go of all hope.

He cleared his throat. "They put the guns on a barge and took them downriver as far as Greenwich. They must have had a ship waiting, and loaded them there." He looked at Judith, not at Casbolt, but he was acutely conscious of him watching, hanging on every word. "There was no sign of Merrit," he added, dropping his voice still further. "The last witness we spoke to, a waterman near Greenwich, saw two men, one tall and upright with an accent he couldn't place, and a shorter, heavier man, but no woman. Sergeant Lanyon, who is in charge, won't give up, but the best we can hope for is that he finds the barge owner and proves his complicity. He could prosecute him as an accomplice."

He thought of adding something about there being no evidence that Merrit had come to any harm, then knew it would be stupid. Nothing would have been easier than to take Merrit along and dump her body as soon as they were clear of the estuary. Judith must surely have thought of that too, if not now, then she would soon, in the long days ahead.

"I see . . ." she whispered. "Thank you for coming to tell me that. It cannot have been easy."

Casbolt moved toward her. "Judith . . ." His face was gray, twisted with pity.

She held up her hand quite gently, but as if to keep him from coming any closer. Monk wondered whether if he touched her she would not be able to keep her control. Sympathy might be more than she could bear. Perhaps any emotion would be too much.

She walked forward very slowly to Monk. Even in this state of distress she was remarkably beautiful, and quite unlike any other woman he had ever seen. With that large mouth she should have been plain, but it was sensuous, quick to smile in the past, now tightly controlled on the edge of tears, speaking all her vulnerability. Her high, slanted cheekbones caught the light.

"Mr. Monk, where do you believe Lyman Breeland has gone?"

"To America with the guns," he said instantly. He had no doubt of it at all.

"And my daughter?"

"With him." He was not so certain, but it was the only possible answer to give her.

She kept her composure. "Willingly, do you believe?"

He had no idea. There were all sorts of possibilities, most of them ugly. "I don't know, but none of the people we spoke to saw anything of a struggle."

She swallowed with an effort. "She may also have been taken with him as a hostage, may she not? I cannot believe she would have had any willing part in her father's death, even if she did not disapprove of stealing the guns. She is hotheaded and very young." Her voice cracked and nearly broke. "She does not think things through to the end, but there is no malice in her. She would never condone . . . murder." She forced herself to use the word, and the pain of it was sharp in her voice. "Of anyone."

"Judith!" Casbolt protested again, his agony for her naked in his face. "Please! Don't torture yourself! There is no way we can know what happened. Of course Merrit would not willingly have any part in it . . . in violence. She almost certainly knows nothing of it. And she is obviously in love with Breeland."

He was standing very close to her now, but he refrained from making any attempt to touch her, no matter how slightly. "People do many extraordinary things when they are in love. Men and women will sacrifice anything at all for the person they care for." His voice was husky, as if he spoke through continual fear so intense it had become physical. "If Breeland loves her, he will never harm her, no matter what else he may do. You must believe that. The most evil man can still be capable of love. Breeland is obsessed with winning his war. He has lost all sight of the morality you and I would hold a necessity of civilized life, but he may still treat the woman he loves with tenderness and consideration, and even give his life to protect her." At last he did touch her, gently, with trembling hands. "Please, do not fear he will harm her. She has chosen to go with him. She almost certainly has no idea what he has done. He will keep it from her, for her sake. She will never know. Perhaps when she reaches America she may even write and tell you she is well and safe. Please . . . don't despair!"

She turned to him at last, the very faintest smile on her lips.

"My dear Robert, you have been a strength to me as you always have, and I love you for it. I trust you as I do no one else at all. But I must do what I believe to be right. Please do not try to dissuade me. I am quite determined. I shall value you even more, if that were possible, if you could support me, but regardless, I must do this. You have already done a great deal for us, and were the situation not so desperate I would ask no more, but my child is in a danger from which I can do nothing to protect her. At the very best, she has eloped with the man who murdered her father, and he may or may not wish her harm. But he is an evil man, and even if he believes he loves her, he cannot be the man she would wish."

"Judith . . ." Casbolt began to protest.

She ignored him. Perhaps she did not even hear. "At worst he has no care for her, and simply took advantage of her love for him to take her with him as hostage, and if he fears the British police will pursue him, he will use her to effect his escape. When she is no longer of use to him, he . . . he may kill her also."

Casbolt drew in his breath in a gasp.

Monk did not argue. It was true, and it would be cruelty to allow her to doubt it and then have to gather her courage to face it again.

"Mr. Monk, will you go to America and do everything you can to bring Merrit back home . . . by force if persuasion will not move her?"

"Judith, that is most . . ." Casbolt tried again.

"Difficult," she said for him, but without moving her eyes from Monk's face. "I know. But I must ask you to do everything that can be done. I will pay all I have, which is considerable, to see her free of Breeland and back home."

Casbolt tightened his fingers on her arm. "Judith, even if Mr. Monk were to succeed, and bring her back, willingly or unwillingly, he is a man, and traveling with him would compromise her so she would be effectively ruined in England. If you—"

"I have thought of that." She put her hand over his, curling her fingers to tighten the pressure very slightly. "Mr. Monk has a brave and most unusual wife. We have already met her and heard something of her experience on the battlefields of the Crimea. She could not lack the courage, the spirit or the practical ability to go to America with him and help him persuade Merrit to return. Once Merrit knows what Breeland is, she will need all the help we can give her."

Casbolt closed his eyes, the muscles clenched in his jaw, a nerve jumping on his temple. When he spoke his voice was only just audible.

"And what if she already knows, Judith? Have you thought of that? What if she loves Breeland enough to forgive him? It is possible to love enough to forgive anything."

She stared at him, her eyes wide.

"Do you want her brought home even then?" he asked. "Believe me, if I could find any way not to have to say this to you, and still care for you, be honest to your happiness, I would. But Merrit may not be as free to return to England as you think."

Her lips trembled for a moment, but she did not look away from him. "If she had any willing part in her father's death, however indirectly, then she must come back here and answer for it. Loving Breeland, or believing in the Union cause, is no excuse." She turned again to Monk but she did not move from Casbolt's side or release herself from his arm. "I will pay passage for you and your wife to America, and all expenses while you are there, and whatever your charge is for your time and your skill, if you will do all within your power to bring my daughter back. If you are able to arrest Lyman Breeland as well, and bring him to stand trial for the murder of my husband and the two men who died with him, then so much the better. Justice requires that, but I am not seeking vengeance. I want my daughter safe, and free of Breeland."

"And if she does not wish to come?" he asked.

Her voice was low and soft. "Bring her anyway. I do not believe that when she realizes the full truth she will wish to remain with him. I know her better sometimes than she knows herself. I carried her in my own body and gave birth to her. I have watched her and loved her since she first drew breath. She is full of passions and dreams, undisciplined, too quick to judge, and sometimes very foolish. But she is not dishonorable. She is looking for a dream to follow, to give herself to . . . but this is not it. Please, Mr. Monk, bring her back."

"And if she answers to the law, Mrs. Alberton?" he asked. He had to know.

"I do not believe she is guilty of any evil, only perhaps of stupidity and momentary selfishness," she answered. "But if she is guilty of those, then she must answer. There is no happiness in running away."

"Judith, you don't know what you are saying!" Casbolt protested. "Let Monk go after Breeland, by all means. The man should swing on the end of a rope! But not Merrit! Once she is here, you cannot protect her from whatever the law may do. Please . . . reconsider what it may mean for her."

"You speak as if you think her guilty," she returned, hurt now and angry with him.

88

"No!" He shook his head, denying it. "No, of course not. But the law is not always fair, or right. Think of what she might suffer, before you do anything so hasty."

She looked at Monk, her eyes wide, pleading.

"I shall ask my wife," he replied. "If she is willing, we will go and see if we can find Merrit. And if we can, we shall learn the truth from her of what happened and how much she knew. Will you trust me to make my own decision as to whether she would be best served by coming home or remaining in America, with Breeland or alone?"

"She cannot do either!" she said desperately, her voice at last beginning to crack. "She is sixteen! What can she do alone? Finish up in the streets! She went with Breeland, unmarried to him." Her hand tightened on Casbolt's, still holding her. "What decent man would care for her? Breeland is at best a murderer, at worst . . . a kidnapper as well. Bring her back, Mr. Monk. Or . . . or, if she is guilty . . . take her to Ireland . . . somewhere where she is not known, and I will go and join her there. I will come for her. . . ."

Casbolt's fingers clenched so tightly on hers she winced, but he did not speak. He stared at Monk, beseeching him for a better answer.

But there was none.

"I will speak to my wife," Monk promised again. "I shall return tomorrow with her answer. I . . . I wish I could have brought you something better." It was an idle thing to say, and he knew it, but he meant it so fiercely the words were spoken before he weighed their emptiness.

She nodded, the tears at last spilling down her cheeks.

He said nothing more, but turned and took his leave, going out into the summer night with his head already full of plans.

4

Hᴇꜱᴛᴇʀ ʜᴀᴅ scarcely seen Monk over the last two days. He had come home late and exhausted, too worn out even to eat, and had washed and gone to bed almost straightaway. He had risen early, eaten a solitary breakfast of tea and toast, and been gone again before eight. He had told her nothing, except that he had no hope of catching up with Breeland, who must be far out into the Atlantic by now.

She could do little to help, except not ask questions he could not answer and keep the kettle singing softly on the hob.

When he came home from Judith Alberton's a little after nine o'clock on the second evening she knew immediately that something vital had changed. He was still white-faced with distress, and so weary he moved slowly, as if his body ached. His mouth was dry, and his first glance, after greeting her, was at the kettle. He sat down and loosed his bootlaces and was obviously waiting to talk. Impatiently his eyes followed her as she made him tea, urging her to hurry. And yet he did not begin until she brought the pot, cup and milk on a tray. Whatever he had to say was not simple, nor unmixed good or bad. She found herself hurrying for her own sake as much as his.

He began by telling her about following the trail of evidence down the river as far as Greenwich, and the inevitable conclusion that the guilty had escaped. The purpose of stealing the guns was to get them to America. Why would Breeland waste even an hour?

But she knew from his face, the urgency in his voice in spite of his words, that there was something else, something further to say.

She waited impatiently.

He was looking at her as if trying to weigh in his mind her reactions.

"What is it?" she demanded. "What else?"

"Mrs. Alberton wants us to go to America and do everything we can to bring Merrit home—regardless of the circumstances—or her own wishes."

"Us? Who is us?" she said instantly.

His smile was tired, wry. "You and me."

"You . . . and me?" She was incredulous. "Go to America?" Even as she said it she could see a glimmer of sense, tiny, a spark of light in the darkness.

"If I find her," he explained, "if I can persuade her to come back, or must bring her by force, I shall need help from someone else. And I shall need someone to chaperon her. I can't arrive in England alone with her." He was watching her as if he could read not just her words but her thoughts, and the emotions which lay deeper than that, perhaps what she refused to think.

The idea was overwhelming, even with the reasoning that sounded so eminently sensible. To America! Across the Atlantic to a country already in armed conflict with itself. No word of pitched battles had reached England, but without a miracle, it would be only a matter of time before it became war.

Yet she also saw in his eyes that he had made his own decision already, not in his mind, perhaps, but deeper than that. He had thought of plans, ways to persuade her. Was it for the adventure of it, the challenge, for a sense of justice, of anger for Daniel Alberton, for the arrogance of Breeland? Or out of a misplaced guilt, because it was Daniel Alberton who had asked him to help, and he had failed? It hardly mattered that it had been Breeland and not the blackmailer who had ruined him.

Or was it pity for Judith Alberton, who, in one dreadful night, had lost everything she loved most?

It was for Judith that Hester answered.

"All right. But are you sure Merrit didn't have anything to do with it, even unwittingly? I think she was very deeply in love with Breeland. She thought of him as some kind of warrior saint." She frowned. "I suppose you are sure it was Breeland? It couldn't possibly have been the blackmailer . . . could it? After all, the price of his silence was guns."

"No." He lowered his eyes, as if protecting some inner hurt. "I found Breeland's watch in the warehouse yard. It couldn't have been there long; there was just a little mud on it, near where the cart tracks were. It would have been seen by anyone in daylight, and picked up. And since Alberton refused to sell him the guns, he would have no legitimate reason to be in the yard."

She felt a dizzy sort of coldness sweep through her.

"Breeland's watch?" she repeated his words. "What does it look like?"

"Look like?" He was puzzled. "A watch! A round, gold watch that you wear on a chain."

"How do you know it was his?" she persisted, knowing argument was futile but still compelled to try.

"Because it had his name on it, and the date."

"What date?"

A flicker of impatience crossed his face. He was too tired and too hurt for quibbles. "What does it matter?"

"What date?" she insisted.

He was staring at her; his shoulders sagged with exhaustion and disappointment. "June 1, 1848. Why? Why are you making an issue over it, Hester?"

She had to tell him. It was not something she could conceal, allow him to go to America unknowing.

"It wasn't Breeland who dropped it," she said very quietly. "He gave it to Merrit for a keepsake. She showed it to me the evening we had dinner there. She said she would never let it out of her sight."

93

He looked at her as if he barely comprehended what she was saying.

"I'm sorry," she added. "But she must have been there, whether it was willingly or not." Another thought occurred to her. "Unless he took the watch from her and dropped it himself, on purpose. . . ."

"Why on earth would he do that?"

But she saw in his eyes that he had thought of the answer before she said it.

"To incriminate her . . . so we wouldn't go after him . . . a sort of warning that he had her with him . . . a hostage."

He sat silently, turning it over in his mind.

She waited. There was no point in detailing the possibilities. He could think of them all as well as she could, perhaps better. She poured more tea for both of them, well steeped, and now not quite so hot.

"Mrs. Alberton knows he might hold her hostage," he said at last. "She wants us to try anyway."

"And if she went willingly?" she asked. It had to be faced.

"She knows Merrit is hotheaded and idealistic and acts before she thinks, but she doesn't believe that in any circumstances whatever she would condone murder." Now he was looking at her, searching her eyes to read in them if she agreed.

"I hope she's right," she answered.

"You don't think so?" he said quickly.

"I don't know. But what else could any woman say of her own child?"

"Do you want me to refuse?"

"No." The answer slipped out before she had time to weigh it, surprising her more than it did him. "No," she repeated. "If it were me, I think I would rather have the truth than live with hope of the best, and fear of the worst, all my life. If I loved someone, I would like to think I would have the faith to put it to the test. Anyway, it doesn't matter what I think, or you. It's what Mrs. Alberton wants."

"She wants us to go to America and bring Merrit back, willingly or unwillingly, and Breeland too, if we can."

She was startled. "Breeland too!"

"Yes. He's guilty of triple murder. He should stand trial and answer for it."

"That's all?" In spite of herself there was a lift of desperate sarcasm in her voice. "Just that?"

He smiled, his eyes wide and steady. "Just that. Shall we?"

She took a deep breath. "Yes . . . we shall."

The following day, Sunday, June 29, Hester packed the few things it would be necessary for them to take, almost entirely clothes and toiletries. Monk returned to Tavistock Square to give Judith Alberton their answer. It was a sort of relief to know that at least it was the one she wished.

He found her alone in the study, not concealing the fact that she had been waiting for him. She was wearing black unrelieved by any ornament and it accentuated the pallor of her skin, but her hair still had the same warmth of color, and the sun streaming through the window caught the brightness of it.

She wished him good morning with the usual formal phrases, but her eyes never left his and the question was in them, betraying her emotion.

"I spoke to my wife," he said as soon as she had resumed her seat and he had sat opposite the desk. "She is willing to go and to do all we can to bring Merrit back here." He saw her relax, almost smile. "But she was concerned that Merrit may be implicated in the crime," he went on, "even by association, and that it may, after all, not be what you wish to happen. That would be beyond our control."

"I know that, Mr. Monk," she said levelly. "I believe in her innocence. I am prepared to take that risk. And I am perfectly aware that I am taking it for her, as well as for myself." She bit her lip. Her hands on the desktop were slender, white-knuckled. She wore no jewelry but her wedding ring. "If she were older, perhaps I would not, but she is still a child, in spite of her opinion to the contrary. And I am prepared to live with the fact that she may hate me for it. I have thought about it all night, and I believe absolutely that in spite of the risks of coming back to England, the dangers if she remains in America with Breeland are greater, and there will be no one else to fight for her there."

She lowered her eyes from his. "Apart from that, she must face what Breeland has done, and if she had a part in it, however small or unintended, she must face that also. One cannot build happiness upon lies . . . as terrible as this."

There was nothing for him to say. He could not argue, and even to agree seemed somehow impertinent, as if he were qualified to share in her pain. That would belittle it.

"Then we shall go as soon as arrangements can be made," he replied. "My wife is already packing cases."

"I am very grateful, Mr. Monk." She smiled at him faintly. "I have the money here, and the name of the steamship company. I am afraid it is in Liverpool. That is where they sail most frequently for New York . . . every Wednesday, to be precise. It will require haste to catch the next ship, since this is Sunday. But it can be done, and I beg you not to delay. In the hope that you would accept, I telegraphed the steamship company yesterday reserving a cabin for you." She bit her lip. "I can have it canceled."

"We shall go tomorrow morning," he promised.

"Thank you. I also have money for your use while in America. I do not know how long it will take you to accomplish your task, but there should be sufficient for a month. It is all I can supply at such short notice. My husband's affairs are naturally not disposed of yet. I have sold some jewelry of my own."

"A month should be more than enough," he said quickly. "I hope we shall find her long before that. And either she will be eager to come home, if she was not aware of Breeland's acts or if he is holding her against her will, or, if she is not, then we shall have to take her as soon as possible, in case Breeland finds a way to make it more difficult for us. Whatever the circumstances, these will be adequate funds."

"Good." She passed a large bundle of money across the desk. There was no hesitation in her, as if it had not crossed her mind that he would be anything but honest.

"I should sign a receipt for this, Mrs. Alberton," he prompted.

"Oh! Oh, yes, of course." She reached for a piece of notepaper and picked up a pen. She dipped it in the inkwell and wrote, then passed the paper to him to sign.

He did so, then gave it back.

She blotted it and put it away in the top drawer of the desk without glancing at it. He could have written anything.

There was a knock on the door, and a moment later it opened.

"Yes?" she said with a frown.

"Mr. Trace is here, ma'am," the butler said anxiously. "He is eager to speak to Mr. Monk."

Her brow smoothed out. The mention of Trace's name seemed not to displease her. "Ask him to come in," she requested, then turned to Monk. "I trust you are agreeable?"

"Of course." He was curious that Trace should still be in touch with the Alberton household, since the guns were now gone and he must be aware of it.

Trace came in a moment later, noticing Monk, but only just. His attention was entirely upon Judith. The distress in his face was too palpable to be feigned. He did not ask her how she was, or express sympathy, but it was naked to read in his face with its dark eyes and curious, sensitive asymmetry. Monk was startled by it. When Trace spoke, his words were ordinary, no more than the formalities anyone might have offered.

"Good morning, Mrs. Alberton. I am very sorry to intrude on you, especially now. But I am most concerned not to miss Mr. Monk. Mr. Casbolt told me of your intention to employ him to go after Breeland, and I intend to go also." This time he looked at Monk for a moment, as if to ascertain that he had accepted the task. He was apparently satisfied.

Judith was startled. "Do you? It was not so much after Breeland, but to bring back my daughter that I wish Mr. Monk to go. But of course if he could bring him back also that would be most desirable."

"I will help any way I can," Trace said intently, his voice

97

charged with emotion. "Breeland deserves to hang, but of course that is far less important than saving Miss Alberton from him, or from further grief." He stood, slender and very straight, a little self-conscious of his hands, as if he were not quite sure what to do with them. He sought her company, and yet he was not comfortable in it.

It was at that moment, watching the tension in him, the earnestness in his face, hearing the edge to his voice, that Monk realized Philo Trace was in love with Judith. Possibly his offer had very little to do with the guns.

Monk was not sure if he wanted him along or not. He would rather have had complete autonomy. He was used to working alone, or with someone who was junior to him and whom he knew.

On the other hand, Trace was American and might still have friends in Washington. Certainly he would know the land, and would be familiar with transport by both train and ship. More important still, he would know the manners and customs of the people and be able to facilitate events where Monk might find it impossible.

He studied the man as he stood in the sunlit room, his face turned to Judith, waiting for her decision, not Monk's. He looked more of a poet than a soldier, but there was a self-discipline in him under the charm, and the grace of his slender body suggested a very considerable strength.

"Thank you," Judith accepted. "For my part I should be very grateful, but you must counsel with Mr. Monk whether you join with him or not. I have given him the freedom to do as he thinks best, and I think that is the only circumstance in which he could undertake such a task."

Trace looked at Monk, the question in his eyes. "I fully intend to go, sir," he said gravely. "Whether I go with you or just behind you is a matter for your choice. But you will need me, that I swear. You think we speak the same language and so you will be able to make yourself understood. That is only partly true." A shadow of humor crossed his face, sad and self-mocking. "I have discovered that to my cost over here. We use the same words, but we don't always mean the same things by them. You don't know America, the state we are in at the present. You can't understand the issues. . . ."

A sudden uncontrollable pain pulled at his lips. "No one does, least of all ourselves. We see our way of life dying. We don't understand. Change frightens us, and because we are frightened we are angry, and we make bad judgments. A civil war is a terrible thing."

Sitting here in this quiet, sunlit withdrawing room, bright and furnished with the proceeds of munitions, Monk was acutely aware that he had never seen war at all. At least, not as far as he remembered. He knew poverty, violence, a little of disease, a great deal about crime, but war as a madness that consumed nations, leaving nothing untouched, was unknown to him.

He made the decision instantly. "Thank you, Mr. Trace. With the provision that it is agreed I make my own judgments, and that I am free to take your advice or to leave it, I should welcome your company and such assistance as you are willing to give."

Trace relaxed, a little of the weariness easing from his face. "Good," he said succinctly. "Then we shall leave tomorrow morning. In case I do not see you at the station or on the train, we shall meet at the steamship company offices in Water Street in Liverpool. The next sailing is on the first tide Wednesday morning. I promise I shall not let you down, sir."

Monk and Hester set out for the Euston Square station in the morning. It was a strange feeling, and for Hester it brought back memories of leaving seven years before to go to the Crimea, also not knowing what she was facing, what the land would be like, the climate, the taste and smell of the air. Then it had also been with a mission filling her mind. She had been so much younger in a dozen ways, not just her face and her body, but immeasurably so in experience and understanding of people and of how events and circumstances can change one. She had been certain of far more, convinced she understood herself.

Now she knew enough to have some grasp of the magnitude of what she did not know and of how easy it was to make mistakes, particularly when you were convinced you had it right.

She had no idea what waited for them in Washington. She did not know if they had any chance of succeeding in bringing Merrit Alberton back to England. The only things she was certain of were that they could not refuse to try and, most important of all, this time she was going with Monk, not alone. She was no longer young enough to be sure about much. She had learned by experience her own fallibility. But sitting in the train as it belched steam and lurched forward out of the vast arching canopy of the station, she knew she had a sense of companionship that was different from every other journey. She and Monk might quarrel over all sorts of things, great and trifling, and frequently did. Their tastes and views differed, but she knew as deeply as she knew anything at all that he would never willfully hurt her and that his loyalty was absolute. As the steam from the engine drifted past the window and they emerged into daylight, she found she was smiling.

"What is it?" he asked, looking across at her. They were passing gray rooftops, narrow streets with back alleys facing each other, grimy and cramped.

She did not want to sound sentimental. It would certainly not be good for him to tell him the truth. She must say something sensible and convincing. He could read her far too well to believe any hasty evasion.

"I think it is a good thing Mr. Trace is coming also. I am sure he will be here, even though we haven't seen him. Do you think we should tell him about the watch?"

"No," he said immediately. "I would rather wait until we hear from Merrit what her account is of that night."

She frowned. "Do you believe Breeland could have taken it from her and dropped it deliberately? That would be a very cold and terrible thing to do."

"It would be effective," he answered, his face registering

100

his contempt. "It would be an excellent warning that he will stop at nothing, if we pursue him."

"Except that he did not know we were aware he had given it to her," she argued. "The police would see only his name on it. Judith would not tell them, especially if she knew it had been found."

"No, but she would know," he answered, his lips thinning bitterly. "That is all he needs. He didn't count on her courage to send someone privately, or on her resolve to face the truth, whatever it is."

They were coming to the outskirts of the city now, great open stretches of field spread out in the morning light. Trees rested like billowing clouds of green over the grass. It was going to be a long day, and two nights in a strange bed before they embarked on the Atlantic crossing and landed again on an unknown shore. She wondered fleetingly how she had had the courage, or the lunacy, to do it before, and alone.

They arrived late in Liverpool and it was as they were following the porter along the platform towards the way out that they saw Philo Trace. He came striding over to them, his face lighting up with relief. He greeted them warmly, and they went together to find a hansom, directing it to a modest hotel not very far from the waterfront where they could spend the time before sailing.

Judith Alberton had telegraphed the shipping office as she had said, and their berths were reserved for them. It was a ship largely crowded with emigrants hoping to make a new life for themselves in America. Many were looking to travel west beyond the war into the open plains, or even to the great Rocky Mountains. There they could find refuge for their religious beliefs, or wide lands where they could hack from the wilderness farms and homesteads they could not aspire to in England.

The ship was scheduled to pick up more passengers from Queenstown in Ireland, half-starved men and women fleeing the poverty that followed the potato famine, willing to go anywhere, to work at anything to make a life for their families.

It was a strange sensation to be at sea again. The smell of the closed air of a cabin brought back to Hester the troopships to the Crimea more sharply than the pitch and roll of the deck, the sounds of the sea, of erratic waves, and the wind. She heard the cries of seamen one to another, the creaking of timber. The squawking of chickens and the squeal of pigs troubled her because she knew they were kept to be eaten as they drew farther and farther away from land and provisions became stale and short. The wind was against them off the coast of Ireland. It would be a long crossing.

They were in a first-class cabin with tiny bunks, a single small basin, a chamber pot to be emptied out of the porthole, a small desk and a chair. Clothes were to be hung on a hook behind the door. Monk said nothing, but watching his face, hearing the tension in his voice, she knew he found it almost unbearably oppressive. She was not surprised when he went up on the deck as often as he could, even when the weather was rough and the seas drove hard in their faces, and cold, in spite of it being early July.

Thank heaven they had not had to travel steerage, where men, women and children had no more than a few square feet each and could not take a pace without bumping into someone else. If a person were sick or distressed there was no privacy. Fellowship, good temper and compassion were necessities of survival.

The crossing took just a day under two weeks, and they landed in New York on Monday, July 15.

Hester was fascinated. New York was unlike any city she had previously seen: raw, teeming with life, a multitude of tongues spoken, laughter, shouting, and already the hand of war shadowing it, a brittleness in the air. There were recruitment posters on the walls and soldiers in a wild array of uniforms in the streets.

There seemed to be copies of every kind of military dress from Europe and the Near East, even French Zouaves looking like Turks with enormous baggy trousers, bright sashes around their waists and turbans or scarlet fezes with huge tassels hanging to the shoulder.

The star-spangled banner flew from every hotel and church they passed, and was echoed in miniature on the trappings of the omnibus horses and in rosettes on private carriages.

Business seemed poor, and the snatches of talk she overheard were of prizefights, food prices, local gossip and scandal, politics and secession. She was startled to hear suggestions that even New York itself might secede from the Union, or New Jersey.

She, Monk and Philo Trace took the first available train south to Washington. It was crowded with soldiers in both blue and gray, the same chaos of uniform prevailing here. How they were meant to know one another on the battlefield Hester could not imagine, and the thought troubled her, but she did not speak it aloud.

Memory crowded in on her as she saw the young faces of the men, tense, frightened and trying desperately to hide it, each in his own way. Some talked too much, voices loud and jerky, laughing at nothing, a paper-thin veneer of bravado. Others sat silently, eyes filled with thoughts of home, of an unknown battle ahead, and perhaps death. She was horrified to see how many of them had no canteens of water and carried weapons that were so old, or in such a state of disrepair, that they posed more danger to the men who fired them than to any enemy. They were of such variety that no quartermaster could be expected to obtain ammunition for all of them. They were all muzzle-loaders, but smoothbore, not rifled. Some were old flintlock muskets which misfired much more often and were far less accurate than the new precision weapons that Breeland had stolen.

Hester found herself sick with anticipation of the blind slaughter which would follow if the war came to a pitched battle. From the snatches of desperate, youthful boasting she heard, or the passion to preserve the Union, it could not be far away.

She overheard snatches of conversation during the times she stood up and stretched her back and legs.

A thin, young redheaded man wearing a Highland kilt

was leaning up against the partition, speaking with a fresh-faced youth in gray breeches and jacket.

"We'll drive those Rebels right out of it," the kilted youth said ardently. "There's no way on earth we're gonna let America break up, I'm tellin' ye. One nation under God, that's us."

"Home by harvest, I reckon," the other youth said with a slow, shy smile. He saw Hester and straightened up. "Pardon me, ma'am." He made room for her to pass and she thanked him, her heart lurching to think what he was going into so innocently. From his lean body, work-hardened hands and threadbare clothes, he clearly knew poverty and labor well, but he had no conception of the carnage of battle. It was something no sane person could create in the imagination.

She smiled back at him, looking into his blue eyes for a moment, then moved on.

"You all right, ma'am?" he called after her. Perhaps he had seen the shadow of what she knew, and recognized its hurt.

She forced herself to sound cheerful. "Yes, thank you. Just stiff."

On the way back she passed an older man chewing on the stem of an unlit clay pipe.

"Got to go," he said gravely to the bearded man opposite him. "Way I see it, there's no choice. If you believe in America, you've got to believe in it for everyone, not just white men. In't right to buy an' sell human beings. That's the long an' the short of it."

The other man shook his head doubtfully. "Got cousins in the South. They in't bad people. If all the Negroes suddenly got free, where are they gonna go? Who's gonna look after 'em? Anybody thought o' that?"

"Then what are you doin' here?" The first man took the pipe out of his mouth.

"It's war," the other said simply. "If they're gonna fight us, we gotta fight them. Besides, I believe in the Union. That's what America is, isn't it . . . a Union?"

Hester continued back to her seat, oppressed by the sense of confusion and conflict in the air.

They stopped in Baltimore and more people got on board. As they pulled out she was sitting by the window, having changed places with Monk for a while. They both looked out at the passing countryside. Opposite them, Philo Trace sat growing more and more tense, the lines in his face etched more deeply and his hands clenched together, one moment moving as if to do something, then knitting around each other again.

Looking through the window, Hester saw for the first time pickets guarding the railroad tracks. Occasionally to begin with, then more and more frequently. She saw beyond them the pale spread of army camps. They increased in both size and density as the train moved south.

It had been hot in New York. As they approached Washington the heat became suffocating. Clothes stuck to the skin. The air seemed thick and damp, heavy to breathe.

As they pulled into Washington itself the wasteland around the outskirts was covered with tents, groups of men marching and drilling, white-covered wagons and all manner of guns and carts drawn up. The fever of war was only too bitterly apparent.

They drew into the depot and at last it was time to alight, unload cases and begin to look for accommodation for such time as they would be in the city.

"Breeland will be here all right," Trace said with assurance. "The Confederate armies are only about two days' march away to the south. We should stay at the Willard if we can, or at least go there to dine. It's the best place to pick up the news and hear all the gossip." He smiled with painful amusement. "I think you'll hate the noise. Most English people do. But we haven't time to indulge in dislikes. Senators, diplomats, traders, adventurers all meet there—and their wives. The place is usually full of women and even children too. An evening there, and I'll know where Breeland is, I promise you."

Hester was fascinated with the city. Even more than New York had been it was unlike any she had seen before. It was apparently designed with a grand vision, one day to cover the whole of the land from the Bladensburg River to the Potomac, but at present there were huge tracts of bare grass and scrub between outlying shanty villages before they reached the wide unpaved main thoroughfares.

"This is Pennsylvania Avenue," Trace said, sitting in the trap beside Hester, watching her face. Monk rode with his back towards them, his expression a curious mixture of thought and suspense, as if he were trying to plan for their mission here but his attention was constantly being taken by what he saw around him. And indeed it was highly distracting. On one side, the buildings were truly magnificent, great marble structures that would have graced any capital in the world. On the other were huddled lodging houses, cheap markets and workshops, and now and then bare spaces, unoccupied altogether. Geese and hogs wandered around with total disregard for the traffic, and every so often one of the hogs would get down and roll in the deep ruts left by carriage wheels after rain had turned the street into mire. There was no rain or mud now, and their movement caused clouds of thick dust that choked the lungs and settled on everything.

Far ahead of them, the Capitol looked at first glance like some splendid ruin from Greece or Rome surrounded by the wreckage of the past. Closer, it was clear that the opposite was true. It was still in the process of being built. The dome had yet to be constructed, and pillars, blocks and statues stood amid the rubble, the timber and the workers' huts and the incomplete flights of steps.

Hester wanted to say something appropriate, but all words escaped her. There seemed to be flies everywhere. It had not occurred to her in England, or even on the ship, that America would feel like somewhere tropical, the clammy air like a hot, wet flannel wrapping.

They reached the Willard, and after a great deal of persuasion from Trace were shown to two rooms. Hester was exhausted and overwhelmingly relieved to be, for a few moments at least, in private away from the noise, the dust and the unfamiliar voices. The heat was inescapable even here, but at least she was out of the glare of the sun.

Then she looked across at Monk and saw the doubt in his face. He stood very still in the center of the small room, his jacket crumpled, his hair sticking to his forehead.

She was suddenly aware of the ridiculousness of their situation. It was a moment either to laugh or to cry. She smiled at him.

He hesitated, searching her eyes, then slowly he smiled back, and then sat down on the other side of the bed. At last he began to laugh, and reached over and took her in his arms, falling back with her, kissing her over and over again. They were tired and dirty, totally confused and far from home, and they must not allow it to matter. If they even once looked at it seriously, they would be crippled from trying.

They met Philo Trace again at breakfast the following morning. It was an enormous meal. It put even the English country house breakfast to shame. Here as well as the usual ham, eggs, sausages and potatoes, were fried oysters, steak and onions and blancmange. This was apparently the first of five meals to be served through the day, all of equal enormity. Hester accepted two eggs lightly poached, some excellent strawberries, toast with preserves which she found far too sweet, and coffee which was the best she had ever tasted.

Philo Trace looked tired; his face was marked with lines of fatigue and distress. There were shadows around his dark eyes and his nostrils were pinched. But he was immaculately shaved and dressed, and obviously he intended to make no parade of the emotions which must torment him as he saw too closely his country lurch from the oratory of war to the reality of it.

The hotel dining room was full, mainly of men, several army officers among them, but there were a considerable number of women, more than there would have been in a similar establishment in England. Hester noticed with surprise that several of the men had long, flowing hair, which they wore loose, resting over their collars. Very few were clean-shaven.

Trace leaned forward a little, speaking softly.

107

"I've already made a few enquiries. The army left two days ago, on the sixteenth, going south towards Manassas." His voice cracked a little; he could not keep the pain from it. "General Beauregard is camped near there with the Confederate forces, and MacDowell has gone to meet him." A shadow covered his eyes. "I expect they have Breeland's guns with them. Or I suppose I should say Mr. Alberton's guns." His food sat on his plate ignored. He did not say whether he had held any hope of stopping the arms from reaching the Union forces. Hester thought him blind to reality if he had, but sometimes one cannot bear to look, and blindness is a necessity, for a while.

All around them the dining room hummed with the babble of talk, now and then rising in excitement or anger. The air was clouded with tobacco smoke and, even at half-past eight in the morning, clammily hot.

"We can't stop that." Monk spoke with calm practicality. "We are here to find Merrit Alberton and take her home." There was surprising compassion in his voice. "But if you wish to leave us and join your own people, no one will ask you to remain here. It may even be dangerous for you."

Trace shrugged very slightly. "There are still plenty of Southerners about. Probably every man you see here with long hair comes from the South, the 'slave states' as they refer to them." There was bitterness in him now. "It's a fashion the North doesn't follow."

Hester liked him, but she had wondered many times during the journey how he could espouse something she considered an abomination, by any standards an offense against natural justice. She did not wish to know his answer, in case she despised him for it, so she had not asked. She heard the suppressed anger in him now as he gave it regardless.

"Most of them have never even seen a plantation, let alone thought about how it worked. I haven't seen many myself." He gave a harsh little laugh, jerky, as if he had caught his breath. "Most of us in the South are small farmers, working our own land. You can go for dozens of miles and that's all you'll see. But it's the cotton and the tobacco that we live on. That's what we sell to the North and it's what they work in their factories and ship abroad."

He stopped suddenly, lowering his head and pushing his hand across his brow, forcing his hair back so hard it must have hurt. "I don't really know what this war is all about, why we have to be at each other's throats. Why can't they just leave us alone? Of course there are bad slave owners, men who beat their field slaves, and their house slaves, and nothing happens to them even if they kill them. But there's poverty in the North as well, and nobody fights about that! Some of the industrial cities are full of starving, shivering men and women—and children—with nobody to take them in or feed them. No one gives a damn! At least a plantation owner cares for his slaves, for economic reasons if not common decency."

Neither Monk nor Hester interrupted him. They glanced at each other, but it was understood Trace was speaking as much to himself as to them. He was a man overwhelmed by circumstances he could neither understand nor control. He was no longer even sure what he believed in, only that he was losing what he loved and it was rapidly growing too late to have any effect on the horror that was increasing in pace from hour to hour.

Hester was passionately sorry for him. In the two weeks she had known him, on the ship and the train to Washington, she had observed him in moments of solitude when there seemed a loneliness which wrapped around him like a blanket, and at other times when he had had a quick empathy with other passengers, also facing the unknown and trying to find the courage to do it with grace, and not frighten or burden their families even further by adding to their fears.

Aboard ship, there had been one gaunt-faced Irishwoman with four children who struggled to comfort them and behave as if she knew exactly what she would do when they landed in a strange country without friends or a place to live. And alone, staring over the endless expanse of water, her face had shown her terror naked. It was Trace who had

109

gone and stood silently with his arm around her thin shoulders, not offering platitudes, simply sharing the moment and its understanding.

Now Hester could think of nothing to say to him as he faced the ruin of his country and tried to put it into words for two English people who had come on a single, and possibly futile, mission but who could return to peace and safety afterwards, even if they had to explain failure to Judith Alberton.

"We can't know what we're doing," Trace said slowly, now looking up at Monk. "There has to be a better way! Legislation might take years, but the legacy of war will never go away."

"You can't change it," Monk replied simply, but his face showed the complexity of his feelings, and Trace saw it and smiled very slightly.

"I know. I would be better employed addressing what we came for," he acknowledged. "I'll say it before you do. We must find Breeland's family. They'll still be here, and Merrit Alberton will be with them." He did not add "if she is still alive," but the thought was in the quick pulling down of his lips, and it was easy to read because it was in Hester's mind as well, and she knew it was in Monk's.

"Where do we begin?" Monk asked. He glanced around the huge dining room, where all the tables were full. Crowds of people had been coming and going all the time they had been there. "We must be discreet. If they hear that English people are asking for them, they may leave, or at worst, get rid of Merrit."

Trace's expression tightened. "I know," he said quietly. "That's why I propose to do the asking myself. It's what I came for. At least it's part of it. You'll also need help leaving here with her. We may be able to go north, but maybe not. I can guide you south through Richmond and Charleston. It will depend upon what happens in the next few days."

Monk hated being dependent on someone else, and Hester read it in his face. But there was no alternative, and to refuse would be childish, and risk even less chance of success.

Perhaps Trace was aware of that too. Again the ghost of a

110

smile lit his expression. "Learn what you can about the army," he suggested. "Movements, equipment, numbers, morale. The more we know, the better we can judge which way to go when we have Merrit . . . and Breeland, if possible. There will be plenty of war correspondents from British newspapers. No one will think it odd." He shrugged minutely and a shred of humor filled his eyes. "In this war you are neutral, at least in theory."

"In fact," Monk added, "I may wish to see Breeland hang from the nearest tree, but I don't tar the entire Union with the same brush."

"Or the slave owners of the South?" Trace's eyes were wide.

"Or them either." Monk smiled back and rose to his feet, the last of his breakfast unfinished. "Come on," he said to Hester. "We are going to research a brilliant and perceptive article for the *Illustrated London News*."

They spent the rest of the day moving from one place in the city to another, listening to people, observing those in the streets and in the foyer of the hotel, seeing their anxiety, sensing the frenzy in the air. A few were openly afraid, as if they expected the Confederate armies to invade Washington itself, but the vast majority seemed certain of victory and had hardly any perception of what the cost would be, even if they won every battle.

Monk listened to complaints about the overwhelming presence of the army everywhere, the upheaval to the city, and especially the offensive odor of the drains, which could not cope with the sudden influx of people. And overriding everything there were the political arguments about how the issue of slavery had changed into the issue of preserving the Union itself.

Hester saw the men and women in the street, especially the women, who had sent their sons and husbands and brothers to the battlefront imagining glory, and with only the faintest notion of what their injuries could be, what horror they would be part of which would change who they were forever. The amputated limbs, the scarred faces and

111

bodies would be only the outward wounds. The inner ones they would not have the words to share, and would be too confused and ashamed to try. She had seen it before in the Crimea. It was one of the universals of war that it bound friend and foe together, and set them apart from all those who had not experienced it, however deep the loyalties that tied them.

Twice she spoke to women in the hotel and tried to tell them how much linen they would need for bandages, which simple things for keeping injured men clean, like lye and vinegar and rough wine. But they did not understand the scale of it, the sheer number of men who would be wounded, or how quickly someone can bleed to death from a shattered limb.

Once she tried to say something about disease, the way typhoid, cholera and dysentery can spread through the closely packed men in an army camp like fire through a dry forest. But she met only incomprehension, and in one case deep offense. They were good people, honest, compassionate and utterly blind. It had been the same in England. The agonizing frustration was not new to her, or the rage of helplessness. She did not know why it should hurt more the second time, thousands of miles from home among a people who were in many ways so different from her own and whose pain she would not stay to see. Perhaps it was because the first time she had been ignorant herself, not seeing ahead, not even imagining what was to come. This time she knew; the reality had already bruised her once, and she was still tender from it, still raw in places she could not reach to heal.

By evening Trace had already managed to find Breeland's parents and contrived that he and Hester and Monk should dine in the same place. It was forced, but by ten o'clock they were in a small group talking and by five minutes past they were introduced.

"How do you do," Hester replied, first to Hedley Breeland, an imposing man with stiff white hair and a gaze so direct it was almost discomfiting, then to his wife, a woman of

112

warmer demeanor, but who stood close to him and regarded him with obvious pride.

"Happy to meet you, ma'am," Hedley Breeland said courteously. "You've come at an unfortunate time. They say the weather is always oppressive in Washington in midsummer, and right now we have problems which I daresay you've heard of even over in England."

She was not sure if some of that was intended as a criticism of their choice of time; there was nothing in his face to mitigate the brusqueness of it.

Mrs. Breeland stepped in. "We just wish we could make you more welcome, but all our attentions are taken up with the fighting. Lord knows, we've done everything we could to avoid it, but there's no accommodating slavery. It's just plain wrong." She smiled at Hester apologetically.

"It's not just about slavery," her husband corrected. "It's about the Union. You can't expect foreigners to understand that, but we must be truthful."

A flicker of annoyance crossed Mrs. Breeland's face and vanished immediately. Hester could not help wondering what her true feelings were, what emotions filled her life, of which perhaps her husband had no idea.

"Our son has just become engaged to marry an English girl," Mrs. Breeland went on. "And very charming she is. All the courage in the world to just pack up and come out here with him, all alone, because her father was against it."

Hester felt a surge of relief that Merrit was here and apparently had come willingly. The girl could not possibly know the truth.

Hester felt Monk stiffen beside her, and tightened her hand on his arm warningly.

"She knew a fine man when she saw him," Hedley Breeland said with a lift of his chin. "She couldn't do better for herself in any country on God's green earth, and she had the sense to know it! Fine girl."

"Is your son here?" Hester asked disingenuously. "I should be delighted to meet this girl. I do admire courage so much. We can lose all we value in life without it."

113

Breeland stared at her as if he had become aware of her existence for the first time but was now uncertain whether it pleased him or not.

She realized she had said something he considered vaguely unseemly. Perhaps Breeland did not think women should express opinions on such a subject. She had to force herself to think of Judith Alberton and bite her tongue not to tell him what she felt about the quiet courage of women the world over who bore pain, oppression and unhappiness without complaint. She could not contain herself entirely.

"Not all courage is obvious, Mr. Breeland," she said in a small, tight voice. "Very often it consists of hiding a wound rather than showing it."

"I can't say I understand you, ma'am," he said dismissively. "I'm afraid my son is at the battlefront, where all good soldiers belong at a time like this."

"How brave," Monk said in an unreadable voice, but Hester knew it was his coldest irony, and that he was thinking of the grotesque bodies shot to death in the Tooley Street warehouse yard.

There was music, laughter and the clink of glasses around them. Women with bare shoulders drifted by, magnolia blossoms caught up in their gowns and wafting a sweet perfume. It seemed to be the fashion to wear real flowers.

"Surely his fiancée is here with you?" Hester said quickly, she hoped before Breeland would wonder about Monk's remark.

"Of course," Breeland replied, turning to her. "But she is very keen to do her duty also. You should be proud of her, ma'am. She has a clear vision of right and wrong and a hunger to fight for freedom for all men. I admire that greatly. All men are brothers and should treat each other so." He made it a statement, and looked to Monk as if he expected to be challenged on it.

A wave of panic passed through Hester, burning her cheeks as she thought of all the answers Monk might make to that—most of them with razor-cruel sarcasm.

But instead Monk smiled, perhaps a trifle wolfishly. "Of

114

course they should," he said softly. "And I can see that you are doing everything within your power to make sure that they do."

"That's right, sir!" Breeland agreed. "Ah! There's Merrit! Miss Alberton, my son's fiancée." He turned, and they could see Merrit coming towards them. She was dressed in wide skirts pinched into a tiny waist, and a softly draped bodice decorated with gardenias. She looked flushed with excitement and quite lovely.

"Brothers?" Hester said very softly to Monk. "Hypocrites!"

"Cain and Abel," he replied under his breath.

Hester swallowed her snort of abrupt laughter and turned it into a cough just as Merrit saw them and stopped. For an instant her face registered only shock. There was a brief moment while she struggled to remember from where she recognized them. Then it came, and she walked forward, her smile uncertain but her head high.

Hester had thought she knew how she would feel when she saw Merrit again; now it all vanished and she struggled to read in the girl's face whether it was brazen defiance which lit her expression or if she had no idea what had happened in the warehouse yard. Certainly there was no fear in her at all, and no apology.

Breeland introduced them, and there was a brief instant when they were all uncertain whether to acknowledge past acquaintance or not.

Merrit drew in her breath and then did not speak.

Hester glanced at Monk.

"Good evening, Miss Alberton," he said with a slight smile, just enough to be courteous. "Mr. Breeland speaks very highly of you." It was ambiguous, committing him to nothing.

She blushed. It obviously pleased her. She looked very young. For all the womanly curves of her body and the romantic gown, Hester could see the child in her. It did not take much imagination to put her back in the schoolroom with her hair down her back, a pinafore on and ink on her fingers.

In a wild moment Hester longed for any escape from the truth, any answer but the dead bodies in the warehouse yard and Lyman Breeland on his way to Manassas with the Union army—and Daniel Alberton's guns.

They were talking and she had not heard.

Monk answered for her.

Somehow she stumbled through the rest of the conversation until they excused themselves and moved on to speak to someone else.

Later that night Trace came to Monk and Hester's room, his face grave, his dark eyes hollow and deep lines from nose to mouth accentuating his weariness.

"Have you made your decision?" he asked, looking at each of them in turn.

Hester knew what he meant. She turned to Monk, who was standing near the window which opened over the rooftops. It was close to midnight and still stiflingly hot. The sounds of the city drifted up in the air along with the smell of flowers, dust and tobacco smoke, and the overtaxed drains that everyone complained about.

Monk answered softly, aware of other open windows.

"We don't think she knows of her father's death," he answered. "We plan to tell her, and what we do after that depends upon her reaction."

"She may not believe you," Trace warned, glancing at Hester and back to Monk again. "She certainly won't believe it was Breeland."

Hester thought of the watch. She remembered Merrit's pride in it and how her fingers had caressed its shining surface.

"I think we can persuade her," she said grimly. "But I don't know what she will do when she realizes."

"At all costs, we must keep them apart." Monk was watching Trace. "If he can, Breeland may hold her as hostage. He won't go back to England without a fight." His voice made it half a question. Hester knew he was trying to judge what stomach Trace had for a confrontation and the violence that might go with it.

He could not have been disappointed in the reaction. Trace smiled, and for the first time Hester did not see in him the gentle man who had such pity for the Irishwoman on the ship, or who behaved with such charm at Judith Alberton's dinner table, nor the person who grieved for the conflict that engulfed his people. She saw instead the naval officer who went to England to buy guns for war and who had beaten Lyman Breeland to the purchase.

"I'd dearly love to take him back to face a court and answer for Daniel Alberton's death." He spoke in little above a whisper, but his words were sharp and clear as steel. "Daniel was a good man, an honorable man, and Breeland could have taken the guns without killing him. That was a barbarity that war doesn't excuse. He killed out of hate, because Alberton refused to go back on his word to me. I say we go after him, unless it costs us Merrit to do that."

"We'll tell her tomorrow," Monk promised.

"How?" Trace asked.

"We've thought of that." Monk relaxed a little and came farther into the room, away from the window. "The battle is going to come soon, perhaps as soon as tomorrow. The women are preparing some sort of ambulances for the wounded. Hester has more experience of field surgery than anyone else here is likely to. She will offer to help." He saw Trace's look of skepticism. He smiled tightly. "I couldn't stop her even if I didn't think it a good idea. Believe me, neither could you!"

Trace looked uncertain.

"But it is a good idea," Monk continued. "She can easily scrape a reacquaintance with Merrit, who will want to help as well. They are two Englishwomen caught up in the same circumstances, far from home, and with the same beliefs on slavery and nursing the wounded."

Trace was still dubious. "Are you sure?" he said to Hester.

"Positive," she answered succinctly. "Have you ever seen a battle?"

"No." He looked suddenly vulnerable, as if she had unwittingly obliged him to face the reality of the coming war at last.

117

"I'll start in the morning," she said simply.

Trace stood up. "God be with you. Good night, ma'am."

It was as uncomplicated as Monk had said for Hester to join the efforts of the many women trying to assemble some help for the one assistant army surgeon to each regiment and to convey supplies nearer the battlefield, which was going to be almost thirty miles away. A little questioning, frequently interrupted by her own overwhelming sense of urgency to help what she knew was coming far better than these optimistic, good-hearted and innocent women, and at last she found herself in a yard with Merrit Alberton. They were handing up rolls of linen into a cart which would serve to carry the wounded back to the nearest place where they could set up a field hospital. It was dirty and exhaustingly hot. The air seemed too thick to breathe, clogging the lungs as if it were warm water.

It was a moment before Merrit recognized her. At first she was just another pair of arms, another woman with hair tied back, sleeves rolled up and skirts scuffed and stained with dirt from the unpaved streets.

"Mrs. Monk! You're staying to help us!" Her expression softened. "I'm so glad." She pushed her hair out of her eyes with a dusty hand. "I hear you have experience that will be invaluable to us. We are grateful." She took a bundle of supplies—bandages, splints, a few small bottles of spirits—from Hester.

"We'll need far more than this," Hester said, avoiding the truth for a moment, although perhaps she spoke about a reality that mattered more. They were hopelessly unprepared. They had never seen war, only dreamed it, thought of great issues, causes to be fought for without the faintest idea of what the cost would be. "We'll need far more vinegar and wine, lint, brandy, more linen to make pads to stop bleeding."

"Wine?" Merrit asked dubiously.

"As a restorative."

"We have enough for that."

118

"For a hundred men. You may have a thousand badly wounded . . . or more."

Merrit drew in her breath to argue, then perhaps she remembered something of the conversation at the dinner table in London. Her face pinched with recognition that Hester knew the enormity of what they were facing. There was no point in saying this was different from the Crimea. Certain things were always the same.

Hester could not put off her mission any longer. For a few moments they were alone as the other women moved away to begin a different task.

"There was another reason I wanted to speak to you," she said, hating what she was about to do, the pain she would cause and the judgments she must make.

There was no shadow of premonition in Merrit's face, which was beaded with perspiration, a smear of dust on her cheek.

Time was short. War overshadowed murder and would soon sweep it away, but for every person bereaved, their own loss was unique.

"Your father was killed the night you left home," Hester said quietly. There was no way to make it kinder or blunt the edge of it, nor could she afford to. She, Monk and Trace would decide their actions upon what Hester judged to be Merrit's complicity in the crime.

Merrit stood still, as if she had not understood the words, her face blank.

"I'm sorry," Hester said slowly. "He was murdered in the yard of his warehouse in Tooley Street."

"Murdered?" Merrit struggled for sense in what seemed incomprehensible. "What do you mean?"

Hester stared at her, watching every shadow of emotion in her face, every trace of pain, confusion and grief. It was grossly intrusive, but if they were to keep their promises to Judith Alberton, she had no choice.

"He was tied up and shot," she said clearly. "So were the two guards. Then the whole shipment of guns and ammunition was taken—stolen."

119

Merrit looked stupefied, as if a friend had struck her so hard she was breathless, gasping to fill her lungs. Her knees wobbled and she sank back and sat awkwardly on the wheel of the cart behind her, still staring at Hester, wide-eyed with horror.

Hester could not afford to show pity, not yet.

"Who . . . who did it?" Merrit said hoarsely. "Philo Trace? Because Papa sold the guns to Lyman after all!" She let out a long groan of misery and rage, her hands clenched tight.

Only with difficulty did Hester restrain herself from bending to her. She would have sworn to anyone, to Monk or to Judith, that Merrit believed what she was saying. But she must test it further. This chance would never come again.

"Lyman Breeland's watch was found in the yard," she went on. "The one he gave you and you swore you would never let out of your sight."

Merrit's hand unclenched and flew to her breast pocket, but it was instinctive, not thought, because the moment after, she remembered. "I changed my dress," she said in a whisper. "I put it down. . . ."

"The watch was found in the mud in the yard," Hester said again. "And there was no money paid for the guns. They were stolen."

"No! That's impossible!" Merrit stood up quickly, staggering a little. "Philo Trace must have done it . . . and I don't know what happened to the money. But Lyman bought the guns! I was there! He would never . . . never steal! And . . . and to think he would . . . murder . . . is monstrous . . . it couldn't be true, and it isn't!" Her belief was not a matter of will; it was absolute, shining in her face. There was anger in her, and grief, but nothing that looked like guilt.

Hester could not disbelieve her. There was no judgment to make, no weighing of evidence one way or another. Breeland must have taken the watch himself and left it in the yard, either by mistake or intentionally. But why?

There was a clatter of hooves and a moment later voices raised.

"Hurry! Get those wagons! The battle will be tomorrow for certain, at Manassas! We must get there by dawn!"

Hester responded without hesitating even an instant for thought. There was only one thing to do now. Breeland, Merrit, the questions of hostage or murderer must all wait. There were men who the next day would be wounded, and the tide of war drowned everything else. Horror filled her, familiar as an old nightmare, and she answered as she always had. "We're coming."

5

HESTER AND MERRIT left Washington and set out on the journey towards Bull Run. The immediacy of war overtook even personal tragedy, and perhaps Merrit at least found it easier for a few hours to think of the small, practical difference she could make to the scores of men who would be wounded, rather than fill her mind with what had happened in the warehouse yard in London.

They traveled at the best speed they could make out through the streets and then the strange, open patches where one day the city might stretch, across the Long Bridge over the river to the now almost deserted camps in Alexandria. The men here were those wounded in earlier skirmishes to the south and west, and the numerous sick with fevers, typhoid and the dysentery that plagued all such groups of people where there were no sanitary arrangements. Here it was even worse than it might have been in a cooler climate, or among men with military training. These were raw recruits with no knowledge of how to take the smallest precautions against disease, lice, or poisoning from spoiled or contaminated food and water. Each man was responsible for cooking his own provisions, which were given him in bulk. Most of them had no idea how to ration them so they lasted, and very little notion of how to cook.

Hester passed through trying not to stop and recognize everything. There was so much needless suffering, and the stench of it assailed her as they joggled over the rough track in the stifling heat, choked by the dust of those ahead of them. She heard the groans of distress, and fury mounted inside her at the agony she could picture in her mind as vividly as if Scutari and the dying there were only yesterday. She was clenched up inside, all her muscles locked tight, her body aching from the tension of it, her mind trying not to picture it, and failing.

Merrit sat beside her in silence. Whatever her thoughts were, she did not voice them. She was white-faced, her eyes on the road even though it was Hester who drove the cart. She might have been thinking of the battlefield ahead, wondering and fearful of what they would find, whether they had supplies remotely fit for the task, whether her own courage would be good enough, her nerve steady, her knowledge adequate. Or she might have been remembering her furious parting with her father and the things she had said to him which could not now be taken back. It was too late to say she was sorry, that she had not really meant it, or even that for all their differences she loved him, and that her love was far greater; it was lifelong, part of who she was. Or perhaps she was thinking of her mother and the grief that must now be consuming her.

Or maybe she wondered what had happened in the warehouse yard, and what had been Lyman Breeland's part in it. That was assuming she did not know. And Hester could not believe she did.

The noonday heat was almost unbearable. It was over ninety even in the shade. What it was in the glare of the dust-choked road could not even be guessed.

They drove all day, stopping only as was necessary to rest the horse and allow the animal to cool itself in the shade of roadside trees, and to take a little water. They had to watch carefully that neither it nor they drank too much. They did not speak, except of the other traffic bent on the same errand as themselves, or how much longer the journey would be and where they would finally settle.

Once Merrit looked as if she were going to broach the subject of Breeland's honor again. She stood on a patch of withered grass, swatting away the tiny, black thunder flies that irritated all the time. But at the last minute she changed her mind, and spoke of the outcome of the battle instead.

"I suppose the Union will win. . . ." It was not quite a question. "What happens to the wounded of the side that loses?"

There was no point in indulging in euphemisms. The truth would be apparent within hours. To be prepared for it at least reduced the paralysis of shock, if not the horror.

"It depends how fast the battle travels," Hester replied. "With cavalry it moves on and leaves them. They help each other as they can. With infantry it goes only as fast as a man can run. Everyone does his best to stagger away, to carry others, to find wagons or carts or anything else to move those who can't walk."

Merrit swallowed. Other wagons were passing along the road, dust swirling up behind them. "And the dead?" she asked.

Memory washed over Hester with such power for a moment that her vision blurred and a wave of grief and nausea engulfed her. She was back in the Crimea, stumbling across the floor of the valley strewn with bodies of the dead and dying after the massacre of the Light Brigade, the earth trampled and soaked with blood, the smell of blood in the air, clogging her nose and throat, the sounds of agony all around her. She was helpless with the enormity of it. She could feel the tears running down her face again, and the hysteria and despair.

"Mrs. Monk!" Merrit's voice brought her back to the dust and sweat of the moment, to Virginia, and to the battle yet to happen.

"Yes . . . I'm sorry."

"What happens to the dead?" Merrit's voice shook now, as if she knew the answer in her heart.

"Sometimes they're buried," Hester said huskily. "You do if you can. But the living are always more important."

Merrit turned away and went to fetch the horse. There were no more questions to which she wanted to know the answers, except the simple, practical ones of how to harness a horse, of which she had no idea.

They reached the small town of Centreville at dusk. It was no more than a stone church, a hotel and a few houses lying between five and six miles from Bull Run Creek and Henry Hill beyond it.

Hester was exhausted and certainly aware of how dirty she was, and she knew Merrit must feel the same, only she would be far less accustomed to it. But the girl had a fever of enthusiasm for the Union cause to spur her on, and if she wondered about Lyman Breeland even for a moment, it did not show in the deliberation with which she greeted the other women who had come to share in the work and offer their help also, or the few men from the army who were detailed off for medical duties.

They had already turned the church into a hospital, and other buildings also, and seen their first casualties from earlier, brief engagements. The last of those who could be moved were being put into ambulances to be taken to Fair-Fax Station, seven miles away, and from there to Alexandria.

A tall, slender woman with dark hair seemed to be in charge. There was a moment when she and Hester came face-to-face, having given conflicting orders on the storage of supplies.

"And who are you, may I ask?" the woman said abruptly.

"Hester Monk. I nursed in the Crimea, with Florence Nightingale. I thought I could be of help. . . ."

The anger in the woman's face melted away. "Thank you," she said simply. "General MacDowell's men have been scouting the battlefield all day. I think they will probably attack about dawn. They cannot all be here yet, but they will be by then, or soon after."

"That's if they are to attack at first light," Hester said quietly. "We had better get our rest so we have our strength to do what is necessary then."

"Do you think . . ." The woman stopped. There was a moment's blank fear in her face as she realized the reality was only hours away. Then her courage reasserted itself and the

126

determination was back. There was only the slightest tremor in her voice when she continued. "We cannot rest until we are certain we have done all we can. Our men will be marching through the night. How can they have confidence in us if they find us asleep?"

"Post a watch," Hester said simply. "Idealism has its place, and morale, but common sense is what will keep us going. We will need all our strength tomorrow, believe me. We will have to be working long after the battle itself is won or lost. For us that is only the beginning. Even the longest battle is very short, compared with the aftermath."

The woman hesitated.

Merrit came into the room, her face white, her hair straggling out of its pins; she had tied it back with a torn kerchief. She looked dizzy with exhaustion.

"We need rest," Hester said. "Tired people make mistakes, and our errors could cost soldiers their lives. What's your name?"

"Emma."

"There's nothing more we can do now. We have lint, adhesive plasters, bandages, brandy, canteens of water, and instruments to hand. Now we need the strength to use them, and a steady hand."

Emma conceded, and in weary gratitude they ate a little, drank from the water canteens, and settled in for what was left of the short night. Hester lay next to Merrit, and knew that she was not asleep. After a little while she heard her crying quietly. She did not touch her. Merrit needed to weep, and privacy was best. Hester hoped if anyone else were awake and heard her they would take it for fear and leave her to conquer it without the embarrassment of being noticed.

Monk and Trace also heard word that battle was bound to commence on Sunday, the twenty-first of July, and that the last of the volunteers and supplies had gone out to Centreville and the other tiny settlements near Manassas Junction, ready to do all they could to help.

127

They were in the street just outside the Willard Hotel. People were shouting. A man ran out of the foyer, waving his hat in the air. Two women clung to each other, sobbing.

"Damnation!" Trace said vehemently. "Now there's no chance of getting Breeland before the fighting. It'll be the devil's own job to find him. He could be wounded and taken back to one of the field hospitals, or even evacuated back here."

"There was never any chance of getting him before the battle," Monk said realistically. "Chaos is our friend, not our enemy. And if he's injured we'll just have to leave him behind. If he's killed, it hardly matters. Except it will be harder to blacken the name of a man who died fighting for his beliefs, whatever they were."

Trace stared at him. "You're a pragmatic devil, aren't you. Our nation is about to tear itself apart, and you can be as cold as one of your English summers."

Monk smiled at him, a wry baring of the teeth.

"Better than this suffocation!" he retorted. "I'll recover from a cold in the head faster than from malaria."

Trace sighed and smiled back, but his expression was shaky, too close to weeping.

A man careered by on horseback, shouting something unintelligible, sending up a cloud of dust.

Monk stiffened. "Our best chance of getting Breeland is if we can find him in the battlefield and take him by force, as if we were Confederates capturing a Union officer. No one will think anything odd of it, and from the fancy dress party of uniforms you've got, no one will know who anybody else is anyway! You could probably be joined by ancient Greeks and Romans without causing a stir, from what I've seen. You've already got Scots with kilts, French Zouaves in every color of the rainbow, not to mention sashes around the waist and everything on their heads from a turban to a fez!"

"They were supposed to be in gray," Trace said with a shake of his head. "And the Union in blue. God! What a mess! We'll be shooting friends and foes alike."

Monk wished desperately that he could offer any comfort.

128

If it had been England fighting its own he would not know how to bear it. There was nothing good or hopeful to say, nothing to ease the terrible truth. To try would be to show that he did not understand—or worse, that he did not care.

They took horses—there were no more carts or carriages to be hired—and rode through the night towards Manassas, stopping only for a short while to rest. The knowledge of what lay ahead prevented anything but the most fitful sleep.

By early Sunday morning just before dawn they passed columns of troops marching at double speed, others at a full run. Monk was horrified to see their sweating bodies stumbling along, some with haggard faces, gasping for breath in air already hot and clinging in the throat, thick with tiny flies.

Some men even threw away their blankets and haversacks, and the roadside was strewn with dropped equipment. Later, as the sky paled in the east and they got closer to the little river known as Bull Run, there were exhausted men tripped or fallen and simply lying, trying to regather some strength before they should be called upon to load their weapons and charge the enemy. Many of them had taken off their boots and socks, and their feet were rubbed raw and bleeding. Monk had heard at least one officer trying to get the men to slow down, but they were constantly pressed forward by those behind and had no choice but to keep moving. He could see disaster closing in on them as inevitably as the heat of the coming day.

Monk started as he heard the sharp report of a thirty-pounder gun firing three rounds, and he judged it to be on the side of the river he was on and aimed across to the other, close to a beautiful double-arched stone bridge which took the main turnpike over the Bull Run. It was the signal for the battle to begin.

He looked at Trace beside him, sitting half slumped in the saddle, his legs covered with dust, his horse's flanks sweating. This would be the first pitched battle between the Union and the Confederacy; the die was cast forever, no more skirmishes—this was war irrevocable.

Monk searched Trace's features and saw no anger, no hatred, no excitement, only an inner exhaustion of the emotions and a sense that somehow he had failed to grasp the vital thing which could have prevented this, and now it was too late.

Again Monk tried to imagine how he would feel if this were England, if these rolling hills and valleys dotted with copses of trees and small settlements were the older, greener hillsides he was familiar with. It was Northumberland he saw in his mind, the sweep of the high, bare moors, heather-covered in late summer, the wind-driven clouds, the farms huddled in the lea, stone walls dividing the fields, stone bridges like the one crossing the creek below them, the long line of the coast and the bright water beyond.

If it were his own land at war with itself it would wound him so the pain would never heal.

Behind them more men were drawing up and being mustered into formation, ready to attack. There were carts and wagons rigged up as ambulances. They had passed pointed-roofed tents that would serve as field hospitals, and seen men and women, white-faced, trying to think of anything more they could do to be ready for the wounded. To Monk it had an air of farce about it. Could these tens of thousands of men really be waiting to slaughter each other, men who were of the same blood and the same language, who had created a country out of the wilderness, founded on the same ideals?

The tension was gathering. Men were on the move, as they had been since reveille had been sounded at two in the morning, but in the dark few had been able to gather themselves, their weapons and equipment, and form into any sort of order.

Hester waited in an agony of suspense as she heard the gunfire in the distance. Merrit kept glancing towards the door of the church where they were waiting for the first wounded. Nine o'clock passed. A few men were brought in, half carried, half supported. The military surgeon took out a ball from one man's shoulder, another's leg. Now and then word came of the fighting.

"Can't take the Stone Bridge!" one wounded man gasped, his hand clutching his other arm, blood streaming through his fingers. "Rebels have got a hell of a force there." Hester judged him to be about twenty, his face gray with exhaustion, eyes wide and fixed. The surgeon was busy with someone else.

"Come and we'll bind that up for you," she said gently, taking him by the other arm and guiding him to a chair where she could reach him easily. "Get me water," she said over her shoulder to Merrit. "And some for him to drink too."

"There's thousands of them!" the man went on, staring at Hester. "Our boys are dying . . . all over the ground, they are. You can smell blood in the air. I stood on . . . someone's . . ." He could not finish.

Hester knew what he meant. She had walked on battlefields where dismembered bodies lay frozen in a last horror, human beings torn or blown apart. She had wanted never to see it again, never to allow it back into her mind. She turned away from his face, and found her hands shaking as she cut his sleeve off and exposed the flesh of the wound. It was mangled and bleeding heavily, but as far as she could judge the bone was untouched, and it was certainly not arterial bleeding, or he would not still be alive, let alone able to have staggered to the church. The main thing was to keep the wound clean and remove the shot. She had seen gangrene too often. The smell was one she could never forget. It was worse than death, a living necrosis.

"It'll be all right." She meant to say it strongly, reassuringly, soothe away his fear, but her voice was wobbly, as if she herself were terrified. Her hands worked automatically. They had done it so many times before, probing delicately with tweezers, trying not to hurt and knowing that it was agony, searching to find the little piece of metal that had caused such damage to living tissue, trying to be certain she

131

had it all. Some of them fragmented, leaving behind poison-ous shards. She had to work quickly, for pain, or shock which could kill, and before too much blood was lost. But equally she had to be sure.

And while she was working her mind was caught in a web of nightmare memory until she could hear the rats' feet as if they were around her again, scuttering on the floor, their fat bodies plopping off the walls, their squeaking to each other. She could smell the human waste, feel its texture under her feet on the boards overrun with it, from men too weak to move, bodies emaciated from starvation and dysentery or cholera. She could see their faces, hollow-eyed, knowing they were dying, hear their voices as they spoke of what they loved, tried to tell each other it was worth it, joked about the tomorrows they knew would never come, denied the rage they had so much cause, so much right, to feel at their betrayal by ignorance and stupidity.

She could remember some of them individually: a fair-haired lieutenant who had lost a leg and died of gangrene, a Welsh boy who had loved his home and his dog, and talked of them until others told him to be quiet and teased him about it. He had died of cholera.

There were others, countless men who had perished one way or another. Most of them had been brave, hiding their horror and their fear. Some had been shamed into silence; to others it came naturally. She had felt for all of them.

She had thought that the present, her love for Monk, all the causes and the issues there were to fight now, the puzzles, the people who filled her life, had healed the past over in forgetting.

But the dust, the blood, the smell of canvas and wine and vinegar, the knowledge of pain, had brought it back again with a vividness that left her shaking, bewildered, more drenched with horror than those new to it, like Merrit, who had barely guessed at what was to come. The sweat was run-ning down Hester's body inside her clothes and turning cold, even in the suffocating, airless heat.

She was terrified. She could not cope, not again. She had done her share of this, seen too much already!

She found the shot and drew it out; it came followed by a gush of blood. For an instant she froze. She could not bear to watch one more person die! This was not her war. It was all monumentally stupid, a terrible madness risen from the darkness of hell. It must be stopped. She should rush outside, now, and scream at them until they put away the guns and saw the humanity in all their faces, every one, the sameness, not the difference, saw their own reflections in the enemy's eyes and knew themselves in it all!

But as her mind was racing, her fingers were stitching the wound, reaching for bandages, pads, binding it up, testing that the dressing was not too tight, calling for a little wine to mix with the water. She heard herself comforting the man, telling him what to do now, how to look after the wound, and to get it dressed again when he reached Alexandria, or wherever he would be shipped.

She heard his voice replying, steadier than before, stronger. She watched him climb to his feet and stagger away, supported by an orderly, turning to smile before he left the tent.

More wounded were brought in. She helped fetch, roll bandages, hold instruments and bottles, carry things, lift people, speak to them, ease their fear or their pain.

News came in of the battle. Much of it meant little to Hester or to Merrit, neither of whom knew the area, but whether it was good or ill was easily read on the faces of those who did.

Some time after eleven the surgeon came in, white-faced, his uniform blouse covered with blood. He stopped abruptly when he saw Hester.

"What the hell are you doing?" he demanded, his voice sliding up close to hysteria.

She stood up from the man whose wound she had just finished binding. She turned towards the surgeon and saw the fear in his eyes. He was not more than thirty and she knew that nothing in his life had prepared him for this.

"I'm a nurse," she said steadily. "I've seen war before."

"Gunshot . . . wounds?" he asked.

"Yes."

"More Rebel troops have arrived on Matthews Hill," he said, watching her. "There are a lot more wounded coming in. We've got to get them out of here."

She nodded.

He did not know what to say. He was foundering in circumstances beyond his skill or imagination. He was grateful for any help at all, even from a woman. He did not question it.

An hour later a man with a badly shattered arm told them with a smile through his agony that Sherman had crossed the Bull Run River and the Rebels were pulling back to Henry Hill. There was a cheer, mostly through gritted teeth, from the other wounded men.

Hester glanced across at Merrit, the front of her dress wrinkled and smeared with blood, and saw her smile. The girl's eyes brightened for a moment, and then she turned back to pass more bandages to the surgeon, who had barely taken time to look up at the news.

During the next hour the wounded grew fewer. The surgeon relaxed a trifle and sat down for a few moments, taking time for a drink of water and wiping his hand across his brow. He smiled ruefully at Merrit, who had been working most closely with him.

"Looks like we're doing well," he said with a lift in his voice. "We'll drive them back. They'll know they've had a battle. Maybe they'll think better of it, eh?"

Merrit pushed her hair off her brow and repositioned a few of her pins.

"It's a hard price to pay though, isn't it!"

Hester could still hear the gunfire, cannon and rifles in the distance. She felt a sickness creeping through her. She wanted to escape, to find some way of refusing to believe, to feel anymore, to be involved in it at all. She understood very clearly why people go mad. Sometimes it is the only way to survive the unbearable when all other flight has been cut off.

When the body cannot remove itself, and emotions cannot be deadened, then the mind simply refuses to accept reality.

She walked away a moment before speaking. If she waited too long she might not do it at all.

"What?" The surgeon turned to her, his voice incredulous.

She heard her answer hollowly, as if it were someone else speaking, disembodied. "They are still fighting. Can't you hear the gunfire?"

"Yes . . . it seems farther away . . . I think," he replied. "Our boys are doing well . . . hardly any wounded, and those are slight."

"It means the wounded haven't been brought," she corrected him. "Or there are too many dead. The fighting is too heavy for anyone to leave and care for them." She saw the denial in his face. "We must go and do what we can."

It was definitely fear she saw in his eyes, perhaps not of injury or death to himself, more probably of other people's pain and of his own inability to help. She knew exactly what it was like; it churned in her own stomach and made her feel sick and weak. The only thing that would be worse was the hell of living with failure afterwards. She had seen it in men who believed themselves cowards, truly or falsely.

She turned towards the door. "We need to take water, bandages, instruments, all we can carry." She did not try to persuade him. It was not a time for many words. She was going. He could follow or not.

Outside she met a soldier who was climbing into a blood-spattered ambulance.

"Where are you going?" she asked.

"Sudley Church," he replied. "It's about eight miles away . . . nearer where the fighting is now."

"Wait!" Hester ordered. "We're coming!" And she ran back inside to get Merrit. The surgeon was still busy trying to evacuate the last of the wounded.

Merrit came with her, carrying as many canteens as she could manage. They scrambled up into the ambulance and set out the eight miles to Sudley.

135

The heat was like a furnace; the glare of the sun hurt the eyes. Clouds of dust and gunpowder marked easily where the fighting was densest, on a rise beyond the river, whose course was well marked by the trees along the banks.

It took them over an hour, and Hester got off at least a mile before the hospital, carrying half a dozen canteens and setting out to reach the men still lying where they had fallen.

She passed broken carts and wagons, a few wounded horses, but there was very little cavalry. There were shattered weapons lying in the grass. She saw one which had obviously exploded; its owner was dead a couple of yards away, his face blackened, the ground dark with blood. Beside him others lay wounded.

She swore blindly at the ignorance and incompetence which had sent young men into battle with guns that were so old and ill-made they slaughtered the users. The irony brought tears of helplessness to her eyes. Was she really sure it would be better if they fired properly, and killed whoever was in their sights instead? Guns were created to kill, to maim, cripple, disfigure, cause pain and fear. It was their purpose.

The firing ahead was very heavy. The sound of grape and canister being shot from cannon screamed through the air. She could clearly see the lines of men, blue-gray against the parched grass, half obscured by dust and gun smoke. Battle standards were high above them, hanging limply in the hot air. It must be after three o'clock. Sudley Church was a few hundred yards away.

She passed more shattered carts, guns, bodies of the dead. The ground was red with blood. One man was lying half propped against a caisson, his abdomen ripped open and his intestines bulging out over his torn and bloody thighs. Incredibly, his eyes were open; he was alive.

This was what she hated most, worse than the dead, those still in agony and horror, watching their own blood pour away, knowing they were dying and helpless to do anything about it. She wanted to walk on, pretend she had not seen, wipe it out of her memory. But of course she could not. It

136

would have been easier to put a bullet through his head and stop the pain.

She bent down in front of him.

"There ain't nothin' you can do for me, ma'am," he said through dry lips. "There's plenty o' fellows further on. . . ."

"You first," she answered softly. Then she lowered her eyes to his dreadful wound and the hands clenched over it, as if they could actually do something.

Perhaps she could? It seemed to be the outer flesh which was torn; his actual organs looked undamaged. She could barely see for the dirt and blood.

She put down the canteens of water and took out the first roll of bandages. She poured water onto a pad, and a little wine, and began to unclench his hands and wash the dirt off the pale flesh of his intestine. She tried in her mind to separate it from the live man watching her, to think only of tiny detail, of the little grains of earth, sand, the oozes of blood, to keep it all clean and try to place it where it should be in the cavity of his body.

For a few moments she was even unaware of the heat burning her skin, the sweat dripping on her face, under her arms and down the hollow between her breasts. She moved as quickly as she could; time was short. He needed to be carried from here to Sudley Church, and then Fairfax or Alexandria. She refused to think of failure, that he might die here in the heat and sound of gunfire before she was even finished. She refused to think of the other men within a stone's throw of her who were in as much pain, perhaps dying as she knelt here, simply because there was no one to help them. She could do only one thing at a time, if she were to do it well enough for it to matter.

She was nearly finished. Another moment.

The gunfire in the distance was growing heavier. She was aware of people passing her, of voices and cries and the bump of a cart over the dry ruts of the ground.

She looked up at the man's face, sick with dread that he might already be dead and that she had been laboring blindly, refusing to see the truth. The sweat was cold on her

137

skin for an instant, then hot. He was staring back at her. His eyes were sunken in his head with shock and the sweat was dry on his cheeks, but he was definitely alive.

She smiled at him, placing a clean cloth over the awful wound. She had nothing with her with which to stitch it. She picked up the canteen she had been using and moistened a new cloth and held it to his lips. After a moment she gently washed his face. It served no real purpose, except to comfort, and perhaps to give some kind of dignity, a shred of hope, an acknowledgment that he was still there, and his feelings mattered, urgent and individual.

"Now we need someone to move you," she told him. "You'll be all right. A surgeon will sew and bandage it. It'll take a while to heal, but it will. Just keep it clean . . . all the time."

"Yes, ma'am . . ." His voice was faint, his mouth dry. "Thank you . . ." He trailed off, but his meaning was in his eyes, not that she needed it. The reward was in the doing, and in the hope. There was a little less horror and, if he was lucky, another life not destroyed.

She stood up awkwardly, her muscles locked for a moment, a trifle dizzy in the heat. Then she looked around for someone to help them. There was a soldier with a broken arm, another with blood splattered down his chest but apparently still able to walk. After a moment she saw Merrit on her way back from Sudley Church, dirty, bloodstained, staggering along under a weight of water canteens. She stooped every now and then to help the wounded or to look at someone and see whether he was already dead and beyond her power to aid.

Hester told the man not to move, under any circumstance, and picking up her skirts she ran and stumbled across the rough turf to Merrit, calling out as she went.

Merrit turned, her face twisted with fear and exhaustion, then she recognized Hester and came to her at a run, jumping over the rough tussocks of grass.

Briefly Hester told her about the man with the abdominal injury, and the necessity of finding some kind of transport to

138

take him and any other wounded they could carry to the church.

"Yes," Merrit said with a gulp. "Yes . . . I'll . . ." She stopped. There was panic barely concealed in her eyes. All the brave words were absurd now, irrelevances from another life. Nothing could have prepared her for the reality. Hester could see that she wanted to say so, to deny the things she had said before. She needed Hester to know what she felt, to acknowledge the difference of everything.

Hester smiled at her, a tiny rueful gesture. There was no time to waste in explanations of how they felt. The wounded came first, and there was going to be no second or third.

"Go and get help," Hester repeated.

Merrit dropped most of the canteens, squared her shoulders and turned to obey, tripping on the rough ground, straightening up again, then moving a little faster.

Hester picked up the canteens and walked towards the battle, tending others who were wounded, seeing more and more of the dead. Beyond the Bull Run the firing never stopped and the air was thick with dust and gun smoke. The heat was searing, parching the mouth, burning the skin.

Finally she headed back towards the church. It was a small building surrounded by farmhouses about half a mile from Bull Run and had become the principal depot for the Union wounded.

The seats from the body of the church had been removed and placed outside. Many men were propped up awkwardly, lying under trees and makeshift shelters. Others were in the open in the full glare of the sun. Some had no wounds but were suffering from the heat and dehydration.

All around men were groaning and crying out for help. Some less hurt tried to assist the two or three orderlies struggling to make order out of the chaos.

As Hester approached the door, the surgeon, scarlet-fronted, came out and dropped an arm on the pile of amputated and mangled flesh against the wall, and without even seeing her, turned and went back in again.

An ambulance came jolting over the rough ground with more wounded.

Hester pushed open the wooden door. Inside the church floor had been covered over with the blankets that could be spared. Hay from a nearby field had been scattered in loose heaps for men to rest on. There were several buckets of water, some fresh, others red with blood.

In the center of the room was the operating table, instruments laid out on a board between two chairs next to it. There were pools of blood, making the floor slippery, and dried blood darkening. The smell caught in her throat. In the heat it was almost choking.

She swallowed her nausea and began to work.

All the sweltering afternoon the battle went on over Henry Hill. At first it looked to Monk and Breeland as if the Union troops would take it. It would be a crushing blow to the Confederacy. Perhaps it would even be enough to end the open conflict. Then they could return to diplomacy, maybe even agree that such bloodshed was too high a price to force union on a people who were prepared to die rather than accept it.

But by late afternoon the Confederate troops were reinforced and Henry Hill stood against everything MacDowell could throw at it. Henry House itself seemed unreachable. Crouching in a patch of scrub on the side of Matthews Hill and looking across the stream that he had been told was called Young's Branch, Monk could see Confederate troops holding the crown of the hill. Union men had been charging it again and again, flags held high in the swirls of dust and gun smoke amid the trees, and had been repulsed each time.

There were soldiers as close as twenty yards away. The roar of cannon was deafening. There was a constant crackle of muskets and every now and then the whine of a bullet and the spurt of dust as it hit the ground. One had grazed Monk's arm, tearing his shirt and drawing scarlet blood. The sting of it shocked him, slight as it was compared with the agony of others.

140

"I'm going to find that bastard!" Trace shouted over the din. "I don't give a damn what the outcome of this battle is, he's not getting away with it. . . ." He gave a bitter shrug. "Unless he's dead! Then the devil will have beaten me to him. But if God's on my side, I'll get to him first." He shaded his eyes and stared from where he knelt across Young's Branch and over to Henry Hill. Union lines stretched as far as Chinn Ridge to the right, and all the way to Henry Hill to the left.

The wind changed a little, sending the smoke across the fighting. A cannonball screamed past them and scythed through the trees, shearing away some branches and leaving them hanging.

Monk wondered briefly why Trace did not join the battle himself. Why was he so determined, above all else, to pursue Breeland? He seemed obsessive about it, out of balance. Monk did not fight. It was not his war. He had no feeling for either side over the other. The issue of slavery did not give him a moment's thought. He was irrevocably against it, but he could appreciate the Confederacy view that the economic oppression of the North was in actuality no better for the poor. One changed deeply rooted institutions slowly, but violence was not the answer.

Neither did he understand the passion for union above all else. These things were intellectual arguments to him. What he felt was the reality of men maimed, crippled, bleeding to death here on these dusty hillsides. He saw no difference between Union and Confederate; they were all equally flesh and blood, passion, dreams and fears. For the first time he understood something of what Hester must feel as she worked with friend and foe without difference, seeing only the person.

He hardly dared think of Hester. He looked at the wounded and the dying all around him, and had no idea how to help them. Horror made him feel sick. His hands shook; his legs almost failed to support him. He was dizzy with revulsion as his mind drowned in the abomination of it. How did she keep

141

her head, bear all the pain, the dreadful mutilation of bodies? She had a strength beyond his power to imagine.

Philo Trace was scanning the hill ahead, perhaps trying to recognize a uniform, or battle colors, to know where Breeland might be.

"Would you go into that to look for him?" Monk shouted.

"Yes," Trace answered without turning, his eyes wrinkled up against the sun. "Any Southerner can fight for the Confederacy and our right to decide our own fate. I'm the only one who can take Breeland back to England and show everyone what he is . . . what a Union gun buyer will do to get arms."

Monk said nothing. He could understand, and it frightened him. He had seen crime and poverty before, individual hatred and injustice. This was on a scale of enormity, a national madness from which there was no escape, no rational core where one could find healing, or even respite.

Over on Henry Hill men were killing and dying, and neither side appeared to gain.

Trace set off down the slope towards Chinn Ridge. Monk turned back.

There were wounded men on the ground, covered in blood and dust, limbs crooked, lying side by side with the dead. Carts were overturned, wood splintered, gun barrels cracked and pointing to the sky. Wheels were tilted at crazy angles.

Monk did what he could to help, but he had no knowledge, no skills to call on. He did not know how to set a bone, how to stop bleeding, who could be moved and who would be harmed if he were moved. The heat burned the skin and clogged the throat, sweat stinging the eyes, and wet fabric rubbed the skin raw over his bullet-grazed arm. The glare of the sun was merciless. Flies were everywhere.

Time and again he scrambled down the bank to the stream and filled canteens, carrying them back amid a rain of gunfire, to hold them up for the wounded.

He carried men where he knew they should be taken, to

142

the field hospitals, doing what they could to stanch bleeding, pad wounds, splint bones, there on the grass of the hillside.

He saw Merrit at about half-past four, also carrying water, stopping where the wounded were capable of drinking.

Her skirts were torn and she looked exhausted, almost sleepwalking. Her face was ashen, her eyes filled with horror. He was not certain if she even recognized him.

Together they helped into a cart a man with a badly broken leg, and another man with a crushed hand, two more with heavily bleeding chest wounds, and Monk pulled the cart over the rough ground, straining his shoulders, feeling his muscles ache. The bullet graze on his arm seemed to have stopped bleeding.

There were no horses around loose and unhurt themselves. There was something in him that hated seeing an animal hurt even more than a man. They had not chosen to fight. They were creatures with no part in war. But he knew better than to say so. Perhaps half the men in the battle had no will in it either, no decision not driven by fear or someone else's idealism.

He got the cart to within twenty yards of the field hospital at Sudley Church. He could go no farther. He and Merrit helped the men out, and leaning on each other, they staggered the last little distance.

The shooting sounded closer behind them, as if the Rebels had held Henry Hill and were coming down towards them.

Inside the church he saw Hester. He recognized the set of her shoulders instantly, square, a little thin, the cotton of her dress pulling tight as she moved quickly, deftly. Her hair was scraped back, poking out of its pins, and a tiny strand fell down her back. Her skirts were filthy, and several smears and splatters of blood showed even from the back.

His heart lurched. His eyes stung with tears of pride, and so powerful an admiration welled up in him that for seconds he saw only her; the rest of the room was a dark cloud over the periphery of his vision. There need not have been other people, wounded men, a man standing still, uniform blue or gray, another woman on her knees.

143

Hester had a saw in her hand and was cutting through the bone of a man's forearm, moving quickly, with no hesitation, no time for weighing or judging. She must have done all that before she set the blade to the flesh. There was light, wet blood everywhere, on pads and bandages on the floor, in pools and spatters, staining her hands scarlet, and forming a dark stain on the thighs of the man's uniform. His face was gray, as if he were already dead.

She went on working. The useless arm, what was left of it, fell to the floor and she began stanching the wound, binding a loose flap of skin over it, holding a pad hard, so hard it compressed the vessels. All the time she did not speak. Monk watched her tense face, lips pressed together, sweat running down her brow and standing out on her lip. Once she brushed a hair out of her eyes, using the back of her wrist.

When she was finished and the bleeding had stopped, she took a piece of cloth and dipped it into wine and held it to the man's mouth, very gently.

His eyelids fluttered.

She gave him a few drops more.

He opened his eyes, turned to focus on her face, and drifted into unconsciousness again.

Monk had no idea whether the man would live or not. He did not know whether Hester knew. He looked at her face and could not read it in her. She was beyond exhaustion not only of body but of spirit. She was hardly even aware that anyone else was there, let alone that it was he, yet he was overwhelmed with the knowledge that he had never seen another woman so beautiful. Physically she was totally familiar. He knew every part of her, had held her, touched her, but the soul of her was something apart, amazing and unexplored, a thing that filled him with awe. And it frightened him, because he knew the dark regions within himself, and felt he would never be worthy of what he saw in her. He also knew that he would never measure or touch the end of his hunger that she would love him equally, that he would be worthy of it, unclouded and whole.

144

Hester turned and saw him, and the moment broke. Her eyes met his long enough for understanding and a flood of relief. She spoke his name, smiling, then began to work again.

He did what he could to help, increasingly aware with every moment that he had no skill, he did not even know the names of the instruments she needed or the types of bandages, and the blood and pain horrified him. How did anyone deal with this day after day, for weeks . . . years . . . and cling to sanity?

He went out again, back to the battlefield, and found to his quickening fear that it had moved closer. It was after five in the afternoon and the Union forces had not taken Henry Hill—far from it; the Rebels were streaming down the slope and hard fighting was now backing towards where he stood. Clouds of dust obscured the details.

He went back into the church.

"The battle's coming this way!" he said sharply. "We must get these men out."

The surgeon was there now, ashen-faced, moving as in a dream.

"Don't panic," he said crossly. "It just looks closer than it is."

"Come and see it yourself, man!" Monk retorted, hearing his own voice rise, almost out of control. "The Rebels are coming this way! The Union troops are in retreat!"

"Don't be ridiculous!" the surgeon shouted at him. "If you can't keep from hysterics, get out of here! That's an order, mister! Get out of our way!"

Monk went outside again, shaking with anger and shame. Was he panicking in front of Hester, who was so calm in this inferno of horror?

He must steady himself. His legs were shaking. The sweat poured off his body. That was heat! It was like an oven.

No, it was not panic! Not in him. But the Union forces were in complete disarray, running towards him, throwing weapons and cartridge belts aside, hurling away anything that cumbered their flight. Blind terror galvanized their legs.

145

Monk turned on his heel and charged back into the church.

"They're in retreat!" he yelled. "They're all making for the road to Washington. Get the wounded and get out of here! Everyone that can walk, do it!"

Hester turned to stare at him, her eyes steady, questioning. It was only an instant before she believed him.

"Out!" she ordered. "Merrit, you stay with me!" Her eyes were still on Monk's. She had not forgotten why they had come.

There was a volley of shots close outside.

As if it were the spur he was needing, the surgeon moved at last. He pushed past her and ran to the door, the others following on his heels.

Outside, they stopped abruptly. A small detachment of Rebel cavalry was twenty yards away and approaching fast. A bullet whined past Hester and slammed into the church wall, sending splinters flying. One grazed her hand, and she gasped involuntarily, putting it to her lips to stop the blood.

The Rebels stopped and the surgeon stepped forward to speak to the officer.

"This is a field hospital," he said, his voice shaking. "Will you give us safe conduct to evacuate our wounded?"

The officer shook his head. "Get them out the best you can, but I can't give you any promise." He looked him up and down. "And you're coming with us . . . back to Manassas Junction."

The surgeon pleaded, but the Rebels would brook no argument, and ten minutes later they were gone, and the surgeon with them, leaving Monk, Hester, Merrit and the two orderlies to help the wounded.

They were carrying men into the carts and about to begin the journey back towards Centreville and Washington when a Union cavalry officer rode up, his arm in a sling across his chest, his tunic dark with blood.

"You'll have to go west!" he shouted. "You can't go by the turnpike. The bridge over Cub Run River is blocked. There's a cart turned over on it and there are civilians all over the

146

place, sightseers out from Washington to watch the battle, picnic hampers an' all. Now they're overrun and nothing can get through ... not even ambulances." He waved his good arm. "You'll have to go that way." He swung his horse around and headed off, picking up speed and disappearing into the dust and smoke.

"Has the Union really lost?" Hester said miserably.

Monk was standing close to her. He could give his reply quietly enough in the momentary lull that even Merrit could barely hear him.

"This battle, by the look of it. I don't know what's going to happen along the road." He could hardly believe what the cavalryman had said. Who on God's earth would look at this voluntarily?

But the shock he had expected to see in Hester's face was not there. He stared, puzzled. Why did it not horrify her?

She read his thoughts.

"It happened in the Crimea as well," she said with a sad, lopsided grimace. "I don't know what it is ... a failure of the imagination. Some people cannot think themselves into anyone else's pain. If they don't feel it themselves, then it isn't real." Then she started to move again, picking up what few belongings were most important and passing around the canteens of water to anyone who could carry them.

The firing was growing closer all the time, but it was very sporadic now.

Merrit was standing frozen with dismay. In the distance they could hear the strange, high Rebel yell on the wind.

"Where's Trace?" Hester said urgently.

Monk made the decision in the instant, even as he spoke. "He's gone into the battle. He's hell-bent on finding Breeland, whatever happens. We'll have to go south if we are to get out. Take Merrit with us. It will be hard, but I think trying to find our way through the chaos here, and get Breeland out through his own people, will be next to impossible."

Her voice caught for a moment. "Go ... that way?" She looked towards the gunfire. But even as she protested he

147

could see in her face that she understood the reason behind his words. "Will we be able to find Trace?"

He thought for a moment of lying. Was it his responsibility to comfort her, show strength and hope, regardless of the truth? They had never told each other what was comfortable. In fact, they had spent the first year or two of their acquaintance being as abrupt, as brutally honest, as possible. To do less now would be like a denial of what was precious between them, a terrible condescension, as if by marrying him at last she had forfeited his friendship.

"I have no idea," he said with a smile which was a little wild, more than a little crooked.

A flash of humor—and of fear—in her eyes answered him.

He turned, knowing absolutely that she would follow, and bring Merrit with her, dragging her if she must, but surely she would come willingly, towards Breeland?

The battle had become a total flight, with men running and scrambling any way they knew how away from the field and towards the turnpike back to Washington.

"Come!" Hester's voice interrupted him, and he felt her hand on his sleeve and winced.

She glanced at it.

"Nothing," he said quickly. "A scratch."

She shut her eyes tightly for a moment. "William . . . how could they let it come to this? I thought we were the only ones so . . . so arrogantly stupid!"

"Apparently not . . . poor devils," he answered. Now she was no longer pulling at him; it was he who turned to go, taking her hand and half dragging her until she stopped looking and tore her attention away.

Together the three of them went against the tide, towards the still-advancing Confederate troops, always looking for Philo Trace in his pale jacket and trousers against the blues and grays which were now covered in blood and dirt and barely distinguishable in the clouds of dust rising around everyone.

Twice Monk called out the name of Breeland's regiment to fleeing Union troops. The first time he was ignored; the second someone waved a frantic arm, and they turned and went as well as they could judge in the direction indicated.

The ground was littered with bodies, most of them beyond all human help but the decency of burial. Once they heard someone crying out, and Hester stopped, almost pulling Monk off his feet.

A man lay with both legs shattered, unable to move to help himself.

Hester stared at him. Monk knew she was horrified, and at the same time trying to judge what she could do to help him—or if he was dying anyway.

Monk longed to keep on going, to not even look at the pain, the welling blood and the despair in the man's face. And at the same time as all of him shrank from it, he knew he would have lost something irrevocably beautiful if Hester had been willing to leave. He would not have loved her less, but the burning admiration would have dimmed.

The tears were streaming down Merrit's white, exhausted face. She had moved into that realm of nightmare where even movement was hardly real.

Hester bent down to the man and started talking to him, quietly, in a level, cool voice, her fingers trying to move the torn and mangled cloth out of the wounds so she could see what had happened to the bone.

Monk went to find guns fallen when fleeing men had hurled them aside. He got two, broke off the splintered stocks, and returned with the long, metal barrels and gave them to her.

"Well, at last they're good for something," she said bitterly, and with cloth torn from her skirt she padded the wounds and tied the barrels on tightly as splints.

Monk held the man in his arms and gently tilted the one water bottle they had brought to his lips, helping him drink.

"Thank you," the man whispered hoarsely. "Thank you."

"We can't move you," Hester apologized.

"I know, ma'am. . . ."

It was too late to think of such a thing. The Confederate

149

soldiers were on them. Long muskets were pointed, then lowered when it was realized they were unarmed.

The wounded man was lifted up and they did not see what happened to him. He was a prisoner of war, but he was alive.

"And who are you?" a Confederate officer demanded.

Monk told the exact truth, ignoring Merrit. "We have come to arrest a Union officer and take him back to England to stand trial for murder."

Merrit burst into denial, but her words were choked with tears, and there was nowhere for her to run. She could not go back through the confusion of the fleeing Union army. She had no idea what to expect in Washington. No one had. Her only loyalty was to Breeland, and he was somewhere ahead of her, and regardless of his reasons, Monk was doing all he could to find him.

The Confederate officer thought for a moment, turned and asked a man a few yards away, then looked back at Monk, his eyes wide.

"You must surely want him badly to come out here now . . . or didn't you all know about this?"

"We knew," Monk said grimly. "He was a gun buyer for the North, negotiating for six thousand first-class rifles with half a million rounds of ammunition. The dealer and his men were murdered and the shipment stolen for the North, instead of the South. I don't imagine you would be that fond of him either."

The officer stared at him, horror in his tired face, smeared with gun smoke and blood. "Oh, sweet Jesus!" he said almost under his breath, his eyes distant on the carnage of the field. "I hope you find him, and when you do, hang him high. Try that way." He pointed with an arm Monk only now noticed was bandaged and heavily seeping blood. The other arm held his rifle.

They thanked him and moved on as directed, through the dust and smoke, Monk ahead, Hester a yard behind him, holding Merrit by one hand, half pulling her along in case in her stupefied horror she should stop and be lost.

They found Trace first. He was easier to recognize because of his white shirt and pale trousers, unlike any of the uniforms. He carried a pistol, and Monk had also picked one up from one of the dead.

It was quieter here, on the bank on the far side of Bull Run. The dead were everywhere on the ground. It was still hot, the air motionless. Monk could hear the flies buzzing and smell the dust, cordite and blood.

Half an hour later they found Breeland dazed, holding one arm crookedly as if his shoulder were dislocated, still unwilling or unable to believe the battle was over and his men had fled. He was seeking to help the wounded, and bewildered to know how. He was surrounded by Confederate troops but he did not seem to realize it. Most of them simply passed him; perhaps they mistook him for a field surgeon. He no longer carried a gun and offered them no threat.

Trace stood squarely, the pistol in his hand pointing at Breeland's chest.

"Lyman!" Merrit lunged forward. Hester had her by the hand and the impetus of her movement almost overbalanced them both, dragging Merrit to her knees.

"Get up!" Trace said bitterly. "He'll be all right." He gestured to the man on the ground, then jerked his hand at Hester. "She'll stop the bleeding. Then you're coming with us."

"Trace?" Breeland seemed startled to see him. He had not yet looked at Merrit.

Trace's voice was pitched sharp, on the edge of losing control, his face smeared with dust and blood, rivulets of sweat running down his cheeks.

"Did you think I would just let you go?" he demanded. "After all that . . . did you think any of us would let you walk away? Is that your great cause?" He sounded on the edge of hysteria and the gun in his hand was shaking. For a terrible moment Monk was afraid he was going to shoot Breeland right there.

Breeland was nonplussed. He stared at the gun in Trace's hand, then up at his face.

"What are you talking about?" he asked.

151

Merrit swung around to Hester, defiance in every angle of her body, and justification.

Monk kept his gun level, pointing at Breeland. "Get up," he ordered. "Now! Let Hester tend to the soldier. Now!"

Slowly Breeland obeyed, automatically cradling his injured arm. He did not reach for any weapon himself. He still appeared totally confused. Monk was not sure if it was their questions, or more probably that for him the inconceivable had happened: the Union had lost the battle; but worse, far worse, they had panicked and run away. That was not within his belief of the possible. Men of the great cause could not do that.

"We found Daniel Alberton's body, and those of the guards," Monk said between his clenched teeth, remembering what he had seen, even though it was dwarfed by the slaughter around him now. Still there was a moral gulf between war and murder, even if there was no physical one. Different kinds of men committed one from those who were caught up in the other, even if the death was much the same.

Breeland frowned at them, and for the first time he looked at Merrit, and a rush of shame added to the confusion.

"Papa was murdered," she said with difficulty, forcing the words out. She was too drained of emotion to weep. "They think you did it, because they found your watch in the warehouse yard. I told them you didn't, but they don't believe me."

Breeland was incredulous. He looked at each of them in turn as if expecting at least one to deny it. No one spoke; no eye wavered.

"You came for that?" His voice cracked into a squeak. "You came all the way over here . . ." He flung his good arm out. "To this! Because you think I murdered Alberton?"

"What did you expect us to do?" Trace said bitterly. "Just count it as the fortune of war and forget about it?" He rubbed the back of his hand across his face, wiping the sweat out of his eyes. "Three men are dead, not to mention six thousand guns stolen. Your precious Union might justify that for you . . . it doesn't to anyone else."

Breeland shook his head. "I didn't kill Alberton! I bought the guns fairly and paid for them."

Inexplicably, completely unreasonably, it was not the lie that infuriated Monk; it was the fact that Breeland had never once touched Merrit or offered her any compassion. Her father was dead, and he was concerned only that they believed he was guilty of it.

"We're going back to England," he stated. "You are coming with us, to stand trial."

"I can't! I'm needed here!" Breeland was angry, as if they were being stupid.

"You can come back with us to England to trial, or I can execute you here and now," Trace said with a level, almost flat voice. "And we'll take Merrit to stand trial alone. She can tell England what noble men the Union soldiers are . . . they shoot unarmed Englishmen in the back of the head and leave their daughters to take the blame."

"That's a lie!" Breeland moved forward at last, his face filled with anger.

Trace kept the gun aimed at him. "Then come and prove it. I don't mind if you doubt I'll shoot you." He did not need to add the rest; it was wild and glittering in his face, and even Breeland in his indignant dismay could not have misunderstood. He stepped back a little, and turned to face the creek and the way back towards the road to Washington. "You'll not succeed," he said with a very slight smile, gone almost before it was seen.

"Nobody's making it back that way." Trace's contempt was like a lash. "Your good Union citizens crowded out for a Sunday afternoon's entertainment to watch the battle, and they're blocking the roads. We're going south, through the Confederate lines to Richmond, and then Charleston. No one will help you there. In fact, if they learn what you've done, you'll be lucky to make it all the way to the sea. If you really think you can show a British court you are innocent, you'd be very wise to come easily and say nothing to anyone else. Northerners aren't very popular in the Confederacy right now."

Breeland took one last, aching look after the remnant of his men, the clouds of dust showing their retreating route, and his resistance collapsed. He took a deep breath and followed after Monk. Hester and Merrit walked together, a little apart from him, as if to support each other. Trace came behind, still holding the gun.

6

I_T TOOK THEM_ that evening and the next day to reach Richmond. They traveled partly by trains, begging rides where they could, amid the wounded passing back from the battlefront. However, unlike the Union troops, the Southerners were elated with victory, and several spoke of it being the end of the war. Perhaps now the Northerners would leave them alone and allow them to live as they chose as a separate nation. Hester saw in their faces a bewilderment as to why there should have been any fighting anyway. Among some there were jokes, a kind of relief that they had been pushed to the final measure and not been found wanting.

Breeland's bruised and dislocated shoulder had been wrenched back into place and was now in a sling. It must have been painful, but it was not an injury that needed any further treatment. His other cuts were minor. Most of the blood on his clothes was other people's, from when he had been trying to help the wounded. Monk had found him a fresh jacket, not for cleanliness but in order not to give away his Union loyalty. Like all of them, he was exhausted, but perhaps more than they, he was heartsick. He could hardly be otherwise.

Several times Hester glanced sideways at him as they rode south. The sun picked out the tiny lines in his skin, which were dirt ingrained and deepened by weariness. His muscles seemed locked tight, as if, were she to touch him, they would be hard. His hands were clenched on his legs, surprisingly large hands, very strong. She could see anger in him, but not fear. His thoughts were far away. He was struggling with something within himself and they had no part in it.

She watched Merrit, who also was little aware of the lovely country through which they passed with its heavy shade trees and small rural communities. They saw few men working in the fields, and those they did see were white. Merrit could think only of Breeland. She did not interrupt his thoughts, but she watched him with tense anxiety, her face almost bloodless. Hester knew that in spite of her own horror and exhaustion, the girl was trying to imagine herself into his sense of confusion and shame because of the way the battle had turned. His beloved Union not only had lost but had done so with dishonor. He must feel his beliefs threatened. What was there one could say to a man suffering such pain? Wisely, she did not try.

Hester looked also at Philo Trace. She judged him to be almost ten years older than Breeland, and in the harsh sunlight, tired and grimed with dust and gun smoke still, the lines of his face were deeper than Breeland's and there were far more of them from nose to mouth and around the eyes. It was a more mobile face, more marked by character, both laughter and pain. There was not the same smoothness to it, the intense control. It was a private face, but there was no timidity in it.

There was something in Breeland's features that frightened her. It was not a presence so much as an absence, something human and vulnerable she could not see or reach. Was it that which Merrit admired? Or was it simply not there yet because he was younger? Time and experience would write it in the future.

Or did Hester imagine it all because she knew he had killed Daniel Alberton for the guns as coldly as if he were . . . she had been going to think "an animal." But she could not have killed an animal without horror.

They rode in silence except for the necessary words for convenience and understanding. There was nothing else to say; no one seemed to wish to bridge the gulf between them. With Monk there was no need to speak. She knew they felt similarly, and the lack of words between them was companionable.

Nearer Richmond, they passed large plantations, and it was here that they saw black men laboring in the fields, backs bent, working in teams like patient animals. White men kept control, walking up and down, watching. Once she saw an overseer raise a long whip and bring it down across a black man's shoulders with a sharp crack. He staggered, but made no cry.

Hester felt sick. It was a very slight thing—it might happen dozens of times a day somewhere or other—but it was a sign of something deeply alien to all she accepted. Suddenly this was a different land. She was among people who practiced a way of life she could never tolerate, and she found herself staring at Philo Trace with new thoughts. She had liked him. He was gentle; he had humor and kindness, imagination, a love of beauty, and a generosity of spirit. How could he fight so hard to maintain a culture that did this?

She saw the flush on his cheeks under her gaze.

"There are four million slaves in the South," he said quietly. "If they revolt it will become a slaughterhouse."

Breeland turned and stared at him with unutterable contempt. He did not bother to speak. Merrit's expression mirrored his exactly.

The color in Trace's cheeks deepened.

"America is a rich country," he went on steadily, refusing to be silenced. "Towns are springing up all over, especially in the North. There's industry and prosperity—"

"Not if you are a colored person!" Merrit snapped.

Trace did not look at her.

A brief, contemptuous smile curled her lips.

"We export all kinds of things," Trace went on. "Manufactured goods from the North where industrialists grow rich—"

"Not on slave labor!" Breeland spoke at last. "We profit on what we make with our own hands!"

"Out of cotton," Trace said quietly. "More than half our

157

nation's exports are cotton. Did you know that? Cotton grown in the South . . . and that doesn't count sugar, rice and tobacco. Who do you think plants, tends and picks the tobacco for your cigars, Breeland?"

Breeland drew in his breath sharply as if to speak, then let it out again.

Trace turned away and looked across the lovely, gentle countryside. There was grief and guilt in his face, a love for something that was beautiful, and terrible, and that he feared to lose. Perhaps he also expected to lose it, if not for everyone, at least for himself.

They went by train, first from Richmond down through Weldon and Goldsboro to the coastal port of Wilmington in North Carolina. From there they went inland again to Florence and finally to Charleston in South Carolina, where, just over three months before, the first shot of the war had been fired to start the bombardment of Fort Sumter.

Monk and Hester remained with Breeland and Merrit while Trace went to make arrangements for passage to England. The trip south had been tense and exhausting. Breeland had made no attempt to escape, nor had Merrit tried to help him, but Hester and Monk were both aware that only extreme watchfulness could assure that it did not happen. It was necessary for them to take turns in keeping awake, with a loaded pistol always to hand.

Once Breeland glanced at Hester with a look of disdain in his eyes, until he considered her face more carefully, and the contempt was replaced with the knowledge that she had seen more death than he had. He was no longer certain that she would not shoot . . . perhaps not to kill, but certainly to cause extreme and disabling pain. After that he made no attempt to escape from her vigil.

There was much talk in Charleston of the blockade that Mr. Lincoln had declared along the entire coastline of the South, right from Virginia around to Texas. They speculated as to whether it would succeed, and there was talk of gun-running through the Bahamas or other such neutral islands.

But on the second day Trace returned to say he had found passage, and they would leave with the tide the following evening.

The journey back across the Atlantic took only thirteen days, and they seemed to have a fair wind almost all the way. In every physical aspect, it was a pleasure to walk on the deck in the sun with a blue sky around them and a vivid blue sea in every direction, unbroken to the horizon. Merrit was barely recognizable as the girl she had been before the battle and its loss. The determination was still there and the passion, but a joy in her had been destroyed, at least for a time. The heroism of reality had been nothing like that of her dreams. If she had also seen a vulnerability in Breeland, even a flaw, she was too loyal to betray it even in the meeting of a glance.

Emotionally, however, it was quite different.

When Breeland had recovered from his exhaustion of body and the pain in his shoulder was considerably eased, he demanded to speak with Monk. The cabin arrangements had been made so that Trace could keep a reasonable watch upon Breeland. No more was necessary, since escape was obviously impossible. Breeland refused to say anything except if Monk should see him alone.

Monk would have refused him, but his own curiosity was piqued, and he was moved in spite of himself by an urgency in Breeland, as if what he wished to impart was not merely the expected justification of his actions or an offer of some bargain in exchange for his freedom.

They stood on the deck, a little apart from the other passengers, of whom there were far fewer than on the outward voyage. There were no return immigrants, no one coming back from the new world to the old, hoping for better opportunities, greater freedoms. It seemed either no one wished to, or if they did, they were unable to flee the war.

"What is it?" Monk asked a little ungraciously, staring at Breeland as he leaned over the rail watching the blue water churn away to the side and behind them.

159

Breeland did not move or turn to face him. "Mrs. Monk told Merrit that my watch was found in the warehouse yard where Daniel Alberton was killed," he said.

"It was," Monk replied. "I found it myself."

"I gave it to Merrit, for a keepsake." He was still staring at the water.

"How gallant of you," Monk said sarcastically.

"Not particularly." Breeland was dismissive. "It was a good watch, given to me by my grandfather as a gift on my graduation. I intended to marry Merrit . . . I thought then that I would be free to do so."

"I meant how gallant of you to mention the fact, now that it has been found at the scene of her father's murder," Monk corrected him.

Breeland turned slowly, his face cold, contempt in his gray eyes. "You can't possibly imagine she could have murdered her father—shot him, apparently. That is despicable. Even Philo Trace would not stoop to suggesting that."

"No, I don't believe it," Monk agreed. "I think you did, with her there, either helping you or as a hostage." He smiled grimly. "Although I did consider the possibility that you were alone, and you dropped the watch there on purpose, knowing we knew she had it, in order to stop us from following you."

Breeland was startled. "You thought I'd do that! In God's name—" He stopped abruptly, shaking his head, his eyes wide. "You have no idea . . . have you? Your mind, your aspirations are so . . . so low, you think of abominations. You have no concept of the nobility of the struggle for the freedom of others. I pity you."

Monk was surprised he was not angrier, but there was a cold passion in Breeland's face too alien to stir such a familiar emotion in him.

"We have different ideas of nobility," he replied quite calmly. "I saw nothing to admire in the three dead bodies in the warehouse yard, bound hand and foot and shot in the back of the head. Whose freedom were they limiting, apart from yours to steal the guns they weren't willing to sell you?"

Breeland frowned. "I did not kill Alberton. I never saw him again after I left the evening you were there." It seemed to puzzle him. "He sent me a message that night that he had changed his mind and was willing to sell the guns to me after all, at the full price, and he would have his agent, Shearer, deliver them to me at the railway station. I was to tell no one, because he believed Trace would be annoyed when he found out and might even become violent." His lips twisted into a slight sneer. "Tragically, he was right. Only he could not have counted on you being such a fool as to believe Trace . . . except that Trace has been paying much attention to Mrs. Alberton, and she was easily flattered. Or had you not noticed that either? Perhaps like a lot of Englishmen, you have too much of a vested interest in the continuation of slavery to want the Rebels to lose." It was meant as an insult, and said as such.

This time Monk was angry, startlingly so. There was something in the suggestion that Judith Alberton had, at best, turned a blind eye to her husband's murder which filled him with a cold rage. The remark about slavery was perhaps well founded, and mattered not at all. He despised slavery as much as Breeland did. His muscles tensed with the desire to hit Breeland as hard as he could. It took a great effort to use only words as weapons.

"I have no interest in slavery," he said icily. "Perhaps you had not noticed it, but we got rid of it in England a long time ago, generations before you were suddenly moved to take it up. Although we do buy slave-picked cotton . . . from you, actually. Millions of dollars' worth of it. And tobacco too. Perhaps we shouldn't?"

"That's not—" Breeland began, his face a dull red.

"The issue?" Monk cut in, his eyebrows raised. "No, it isn't. The issue is that Alberton refused to sell you the guns you wanted, so you murdered him and stole them. What for, or how noble the cause, is irrelevant." He could not resist sneering. "How brave!"

161

Fury and humiliation flared in Breeland's face. "I did not kill Alberton!" He forced the words between his teeth, standing upright from the rail now and facing Monk, the wind tugging at his hair. "I had no need to—even if you believe I was capable of it. He sold me the guns. Ask Shearer. Why don't you ask him?"

Was it conceivable? For the first time Monk actually considered the possibility that Breeland might not be guilty.

Breeland saw the wavering in his eyes.

"Not much of a policeman, are you?" he said contemptuously.

Monk was stung. He knew he had allowed himself to be read.

"So Merrit gave the watch to Trace, who just happened to go and murder Alberton minutes after someone took the guns from the warehouse yard, and Trace left the watch there?" he said in feigned amazement. "And unfortunately this Shearer, unknown to Alberton or Casbolt, took the guns to you, then took the money you paid him and disappeared?" He shrugged. "Or alternately, Merrit gave the watch to Shearer, perhaps? And he murdered his employer and took the guns to you? His motive would be clear enough, the money. But why did Merrit do that? She did do that, didn't she? You have no idea where she was while you were conducting this elusive business with the vanishing Mr. Shearer."

Breeland drew in his breath sharply, but he had no answers, and the confusion in his face betrayed him. He looked away at the blue water again. "No . . . she was with me at the time. But she'll swear I bought the guns fairly from Shearer, and I never went anywhere near Tooley Street. Ask her!"

Of course Monk did ask her, although he was almost certain what she would say. Nothing that had happened in Washington or on the battlefield, or on the journey through the South to the ship, had altered her devotion to Breeland or the fierce, defensive compassion she had for him in his army's defeat. She watched him in the bitterness of his knowledge and the ache to help was naked in her face. He could never have doubted her.

What Breeland felt for her was far harder to read. He was gentle with her, but the wound to his pride was too raw for anyone to touch, perhaps least of all the woman he loved, and to whom he had spoken so fiercely of the greatness of the cause and the victory they would win. He would not be the first or the last man to boast overmuch of his courage or honor, but he seemed to find it harder than most to accommodate himself to a setback, great or small. There was no flexibility in him, no capacity to mock himself or step, even for an instant, outside his consuming passion.

Monk was uncertain whether he admired Breeland or not. Perhaps it was only such men who achieved the great changes in governments or nations. It might be the price of such mighty gains.

Hester had no doubt about it. She thought him innately selfish, and she said so.

"Perhaps Merrit understands him?" Monk suggested to her as they walked together on the deck as the dying sun splashed across the ruffled water, spilling color like fire over the blue. "Words or gestures are not always necessary."

"Rubbish!" She dismissed the argument, narrowing her eyes against the light and staring seawards. "Of course they aren't. But a look is . . . or a touch, something. She's feeling for both of them now, sharing his pain and loving him desperately. But what about her pain? It's her father who's dead, not his! She's not a soldier, William, any more than you are." Her eyes were very gentle, searching his for the wound she could heal. "Maybe he doesn't have nightmares about the battlefield, about Sudley Church, and the men we couldn't help . . . but she does." Her lips were soft, full of pain. "So do I. Perhaps we should. But we need someone to hold on to."

"Maybe he's already said all he can to her?" he answered, moving closer and putting his arm around her.

Her face in the beautiful light was quite suddenly full of anger, her eyes wide. "She'll die of loneliness . . . when she realizes at last that he isn't going to give her anything of himself. He's always going to love the Union first, because it's easier. It doesn't ask anything back."

"It asks everything back!" he protested. "His time, his career, even his life!"

She looked at him steadily. "But not his laughter, or his patience, or generosity to forget himself for a little while," she explained. "Or think of something that perhaps doesn't interest him especially. It won't ever ask him to listen instead of speaking, to change his mind before he's ready to, to walk a little more slowly or reconsider some of his judgments, let somebody else be the hero, without making a grand gesture of it."

He knew what she meant.

"He'll always do it on his terms," she finished quietly. It was like a damnation.

"Are you sure he killed Alberton?" he asked her.

It was several minutes before she replied. The sky was darkening and the color across the water no longer had the same heat in it. The depth of the sky was indigo shadow, limitless, so beautiful its briefness ached inside her. No matter that there would be dusk tomorrow night, and the night after, and after that; none of them would ever be long enough. And soon she would see them not across the water but over city roofs.

"I don't know," she said at last. "No other answer makes any sense . . . but I'm not certain."

The ship docked at Bristol and Monk disembarked first, leaving the others behind in Trace's care. He went straight to the nearest police station and told them who he was and of his association with Lanyon regarding the murders in Tooley Street, which crimes had been well reported in the newspapers. He told them he had brought Lyman Breeland back, also Merrit Alberton, and proposed to take them to London by train.

The police were duly impressed and offered to send a constable with them for assistance, and to make sure the prisoners did not escape during the journey. Monk noted the use of the plural with a twinge of distress, but not surprise.

"Thank you," he accepted. It was not willingly that he included another person—it robbed him of some of his autonomy—but he would require official help, and it would be idiotic to risk losing all they had gained for a matter of pride and the right to make choices which probably would not make the slightest difference in the end.

As it was, the journey was uneventful. The Bristol police had telegraphed ahead, and Lanyon was at the railway station to meet them. Seeing the crowds, Monk was relieved. It might have proved very difficult to keep Breeland from breaking away without help. Had either he or Trace brandished a pistol they might well have been overpowered by some member of the public brave enough to attempt it and innocent enough to have believed Breeland a victim of kidnap.

Whether the fact that they still held Merrit would have restrained him was not something on which Monk would have wished to rely. Breeland might have justified to himself that the Union cause was of greater importance than the life of one woman, whoever it was. He might even have convinced himself that yielding her up was his sacrifice as much as anyone else's. Or alternatively, he could have chosen to assume she would not be charged with anything, still less found guilty.

Might that be because she was innocent?

Or was it a fair price to pay because she too was guilty?

Now it did not matter, because Lanyon was there with two constables, and Breeland was taken in charge and handcuffed.

"And you, Miss Alberton," Lanyon said grimly, his long face wearing an expression of puzzlement and regret.

The light died out of Merrit's eyes and her shoulders drooped. Monk realized that at least for a while her emotions had been centered on Breeland and she had allowed herself to forget her own jeopardy. Now it was back, and real.

Breeland moved his shoulders, as if, had he been free, he would have touched her, reassured her in some way. But he was already handcuffed.

It was Hester who put her arm around the girl. "We shall do all we can to get you the best help," she said clearly. "We

165

will go first to your mother and tell her you are alive and quite well. At the moment she does not even know that."

Merrit closed her eyes, tears seeping from under the lids. So close to home, courage was harder to find, the pain sharper. Until now her thoughts had all been upon Breeland. Perhaps she had not even considered her mother. But with familiar English voices around her, the sights and smells of home, the adventure was over and the long, quiet payment for it had begun.

She tried to speak, to thank Hester, but she could not do it and still keep control of herself. She chose silence.

Over Lanyon's shoulder Monk could see a knot of people gathering, glancing towards them with curiosity. Their faces were ugly, prying, ready for anger.

Lanyon saw his gaze. He looked apologetic.

"We'd better go," he said hastily. "Before they guess who you are. There's a lot of bad feeling about."

"Feeling?" Hester asked, not immediately grasping what he was afraid of.

Lanyon lowered his voice, his brows drawn down. "In the newspapers, ma'am. There's been a good deal said about Mr. Alberton's death, and foreigners coming over here and seducing young women into murder, and the like. I think we should leave here as quickly as we can." He was very careful not to look behind him as he spoke, but already Monk could see the crowd thickening and faces growing uglier. One or two people were quite openly staring now. They seemed to be moving closer.

"That's appalling!" Hester was angry, a flush spreading up her cheeks. "Nobody's even been charged yet, let alone tried!"

"We can't fight from here," Monk said sharply. He could hear his own voice rising as he thought of how quickly the situation could become violent. He was afraid for Hester. Her indignation could make her careless of her own safety, and a mob would distinguish little between their victim and someone who chose to protect him.

Lanyon said exactly the same. "You come now, quickly,"

he ordered, looking at Breeland. "Don't get any fancy ideas of causing a riot and hoping you'll get away in it. You won't! You'll just get beaten, like as not, and Miss Alberton along with you."

Breeland hesitated a moment, as if he actually weighed such a plan in his mind, then looked at Merrit's white face and the misery in her eyes, and abandoned the idea. As if surrendering, he lowered his head a fraction and walked obediently between Lanyon and the constable.

Merrit followed a few paces behind, with the second constable, leaving Monk, Hester and Philo Trace on the platform.

"We must go to Mrs. Alberton," Trace said anxiously. "She will be distracted with worry. I wish to heaven there were something we could do to clear Merrit of this crime. Surely we can prevent her from being charged?" His words were positive, but his voice belied them. He looked at Monk as if he hoped for help beyond his own power to conceive. "Surely they wouldn't really think . . ." He trailed off. He turned to Hester as if to say more, then saw her face.

They all knew Merrit was in love with Breeland, and loyal. That alone would have forbidden her from abandoning him, whatever the truth of the murder. She would see excusing herself as betrayal, which was to her a sin of even greater evil than the original crime. Perhaps, too late, she would regret it, but in any foreseeable future she would not separate herself from Breeland or her fate from his.

"We'll go straightaway," Monk agreed.

They were tired after the long train journey in the oppressive heat of early August. Hester was acutely aware of being stained with smuts from the engine fires and that at least the lower foot of her traveling dress was grimed with dust, not to mention creased, but she did not demur. It was also nearly seven in the evening, and hardly the hour to make unannounced calls upon anyone. That too was irrelevant. Without further discussion they piled their cases upon the porter's wagon and made for the exit, and the nearest cab to take them to Tavistock Square.

* * *

Judith Alberton received them without even a pretense of formality. Unconsciously, it was Philo Trace to whom she looked first.

"We have Merrit," he responded, his eyes softening as they met hers. "She is very tired, and much distressed by all that has happened, but she is unhurt and quite well."

Her face flooded with relief, but she hesitated.

As if reading her thoughts he answered, "She is not married to Breeland, and she knew nothing of her father's death . . . but then you cannot have imagined that she did."

"No . . . no, of course not." She gazed straight back at him, as if to emphasize her words. She was waiting for something else, something so far unsaid. She recollected herself, and that Monk and Hester were still awaiting her acknowledgment. She flushed slightly, turning to them. "I cannot say how grateful I am to you for your courage and skill in bringing back my daughter. I confess, I thought I was asking the impossible. I—I hope you sustained no injury? I cannot believe there was no hardship. I . . . I wish there were some way I could reward you more than in words, or money, because what you have done is greater than either."

"We succeeded this far," Monk said simply. "That is a very considerable reward in itself. I don't wish to sound graceless, Mrs. Alberton, but would you accept that we did it because we also believed it to be important, and not take upon yourself an additional burden of gratitude."

Hester found herself smiling with a warmth of pride. It was a generous speech, and she knew it was said spontaneously. She reached out her hand and placed it very lightly on his arm, avoiding his gaze, and moved half a step closer to him. She knew he was aware of her by the slightest warmth up his cheek.

Judith Alberton was smiling also, but the fear had not left her eyes. She must have been far more aware than they of what the newspapers had written.

"Thank you. Please come and sit down. Are you hungry? Have you had any rest since you arrived?"

They accepted gratefully, without telling her exactly how

168

arduous the journey had been. They were partway through an excellent dinner when Robert Casbolt arrived, coming straight into the dining room without waiting for the footman to announce him. He glanced at the assembled company around the table, but his eyes rested on Judith.

She looked up at him without surprise, as if he frequently appeared in such a way.

Hester saw the glint of anger in Trace's expression, masked the moment later, but she thought she understood it.

If Casbolt saw it also, he gave no sign.

"She is safe and well," Judith said in answer to his unspoken question.

Something in him darkened, and he could not hide the foreboding in it. "Where is she?"

Judith's mouth tightened. "The police have arrested her, and of course Breeland."

"They have Breeland!" He was startled. For the first time he looked fully at Monk, but still ignored Philo Trace. "You brought him back? I commend you! How did you persuade him?"

"At gunpoint," Monk said dryly.

Casbolt made no attempt to hide his admiration. "That is truly remarkable! I apologize for underestimating you. I admit, I had little hope you could succeed." He seemed overwhelmed. He pulled out one of the empty chairs and sat down. He waved away the footman's offer of food or wine with a smile, not taking his eyes from Monk. "Please tell me what happened. I am most eager to know." He did not ask Judith's permission, but perhaps he already understood that she would care even more than he.

Monk began to recount their adventures, condensing the tale as much as he could, but frequently both Casbolt and Judith interrupted him, asking for more detail and offering praise or expressing alarm at their danger. Judith particularly was distressed at the plight of the American people caught up in a terrible war. It seemed there were vivid, fragmented reports of the battle at Bull Run in the newspaper already. They said the slaughter had been fearful.

Monk said as little as he could about it while still making sense of the account. Judith grew more tense with every few moments. Her face softened once, when Monk very briefly spoke of Merrit's helping to prepare the ambulances for the wounded.

"It must have been . . . terrible beyond words," she said huskily.

"Yes . . ." He did not offer to tell her of it, and watching his face, the brightness of the smooth, burned skin over his cheeks, Hester knew it was his own pain he could not relive, not Judith's he was sparing. She had seen how the horror had overwhelmed him, how the helplessness to do anything in the face of such enormity had robbed him of his belief in himself. She had experienced it herself the first time she had seen battle, and for her it was not so total, because she had at least some medical knowledge, and a function in being there. She could lose herself in the individual she could affect, even if not save. It was not always the success that made it bearable; it was the ability to try.

She had seen it in him, and understood, but it was too raw, too powerful to be touched even by her, or perhaps especially by her. Some wounds have to heal alone, or they do not heal at all.

"Did Breeland not go to the battlefield after all?" Casbolt asked incredulously.

"Yes. It was there we found him."

"And he came with you?" Casbolt frowned in incomprehension. "Why? He did not have to, surely? I cannot believe his own people would give him up to answer English law."

"The Union lost," Monk answered, offering no explanation beyond that simple sentence. He said nothing of the slaughter, the panic, as if the men he had been defending from the shame of it were people he knew. He did not look at either Trace or Hester, or give them time to interrupt. "We went south through the Confederate lines to Richmond, and then Charleston. No one hindered us."

Judith's eyes were wide with fierce admiration. Even in these tragic circumstances, Hester could not help thinking

170

what a beautiful woman she was. She was not surprised that Philo Trace was drawn to Judith. She would have found it harder to understand were he not.

"But the police have arrested Merrit," Judith said to Casbolt. "They found Breeland's watch in the warehouse yard."

"I know," he said quickly. "I was there when Monk picked it up." He seemed puzzled.

Judith lowered her voice. "Breeland gave it to Merrit as a keepsake. I knew that, but I hoped the police would not. However, Dorothea Parfitt told them . . . in all innocence, I imagine. But it cannot be taken back. Merrit showed it to her, boasting a little, as girls will." Her composure cracked and she had to struggle to regain it.

Casbolt put his arm around her shoulders, pulling her a little closer to him. His face was full of pain, and the strength of his emotion was for a moment completely unguarded.

"Breeland is despicable," he said softly. "He must have taken it back from her and dropped it there himself, even accidentally, or with the intention of trying to stop us from pursuing him for the harm it could do her. Either way, Judith, I swear we will fight him. We shall obtain the finest lawyers there are, and a Queen's counsel to defend Merrit, if we cannot prevent it from coming to that." He turned to Monk. "Is it conceivable Breeland will exonerate her? Does he have any love towards her at all, any honor? After all, he is a grown man, she is little more than a child, and she could never in her life have imagined stealing guns for any cause of her own!"

Hester knew what Monk would say before he spoke. She even glanced at Trace and saw the shadow in his face also.

"No," Monk answered bluntly. "He denies he ever killed Mr. Alberton or stole anything." He ignored their disbelief and continued. "He says Mr. Alberton changed his mind about selling him the guns and sent him a message to that effect. He says he bought them quite legally, and paid a man named Shearer for them."

"What?" Casbolt jerked his head up.

Judith stared at Monk incredulously.

171

"And he says he has no idea who murdered the men in the warehouse yard," Monk continued. "But he suggests it might have been Trace, out of revenge for not having been able to purchase the guns."

"Preposterous!" Casbolt could keep silent no longer. "That's totally absurd. No one would believe it." He turned to Judith. "Did you receive any money?"

"No," she said decisively.

"Who is Shearer anyway? Where is he?" Monk asked her.

"I don't know where he is," she admitted. "There has been no money paid for the guns—except, I believe, the money Mr. Trace paid in the beginning."

Casbolt swung around to Philo Trace. "You paid the first half deposit on the whole shipment, did you not?"

"You know I did, sir."

"Did you ever receive any part of it refunded because you were not to make the purchase after all?"

"No, not a cent." Trace's voice was tight and low, as if he was embarrassed for Judith, although it was in no way her fault.

Casbolt looked at Monk. "That should answer your questions, if you still have any. I don't know what he has done to Merrit to persuade her of his innocence, or else to coerce her into swearing a lie to protect him, but she is only sixteen, a child. Certainly far too young to have her word taken seriously regarding a man she is obviously obsessed with." He bit his lip, his expression softening to momentary distress. "Do you think he may have threatened her?"

Again Monk answered honestly. "No. It is my opinion she believes he is innocent. I don't know why. It may be no more than that she cannot bear to think of his guilt. There is little more bitter than disillusion, and we can make ourselves believe what we need to, however preposterous, at least for a while. We call it loyalty, or faith, or whatever virtue counts most highly to us and fits the need."

Casbolt glanced across at Judith, then down at the polished surface of the table with its silver and flowers. "There seems no way in which we can protect her from hurt. The

172

best we can do will be to save her from being implicated in Breeland's guilt in law. The story about our agent Shearer is absurd. Obviously, Breeland organized the stealing of the guns, whether he was there in person or not. We must distance her from that." He looked at Judith, his face softening again, his voice gentle. "Will you call Pilbeam to handle it for you? If you would rather, I can take care of it, make sure the best possible barrister represents Merrit. There is no need for you to do anything."

Her eyes softened. "Thank you, Robert," she said quickly, reaching up and taking his hand. "I don't know how I would have endured these past terrible weeks without your kindness. You have not spared yourself in the slightest, and I know you must be nearly as deeply grieved as I am. Daniel was your friend for even more years than he was my husband. He would be nearly as grateful to you as I am for your tireless care."

Casbolt colored in an oddly self-conscious way, showing a vulnerability that startled Monk.

"I don't believe Merrit will consent to be represented separately from Breeland," Hester said urgently. "And certainly she will not allow him to sacrifice himself for her in any way at all. She is far more disposed to see it as the measure of her love to suffer with him, no matter how innocent she is in fact."

"But that is . . ." Casbolt began, then, seeing her face, fell silent. Perhaps he knew Merrit well enough to realize the truth of Hester's words. He turned to Monk.

But again it was Hester who spoke. "We know Sir Oliver Rathbone quite well. He is the best barrister in London. He can defend her if anyone can."

Judith turned to her quickly, hope flaring in her eyes. "Would he? She may not be willing to be of any help to herself. Will he not refuse . . . in the circumstances?" She bit her lip. "I will pay him whatever his price, if that is the question. Please, Mrs. Monk, if there is anything you can do to prevail upon him. I will sell the house, the jewelry I have, everything, to save my daughter."

"That wouldn't be necessary," Hester said softly. "It will not be money that matters to him, although I will tell him how much you care. It will be a question of finding a way to separate Merrit from Breeland's guilt."

"Try them separately!" Casbolt could not keep from interrupting; his body was locked with tension, his eyes hollow. "It is transparently unjust to charge them as if they were of one mind and one responsibility. Surely a decent barrister could persuade a jury of that?" There was an edge of desperation in his voice, a sharp, high note close to panic.

"Of course!" Monk said quickly, before he could say more, and Judith would know his fear. "We shall tell him all the circumstances, and if he is willing to take the case, he can then come to you and make all the necessary arrangements."

"Thank you!" Judith's face was flooded with relief, and then sudden shame. "You have done so much already. You must be exhausted, and I have sat half the evening pouring out more troubles and expecting your help, when you must be worn to a shadow for lack of sleep, and want more than anything on earth to reach your own home and your own bed. I am sorry."

"There is no need to be." Hester reached across quickly and touched Judith's hand. "We have grown fond of Merrit ourselves, and are almost as angry as you are at the injustice that could be done were Breeland not to pay the price of his crime. Even had you not asked, we should not have wished to leave the task half completed."

Judith said nothing. She was too full of emotion to retain command of herself.

"Thank you." Casbolt spoke for her. "It was a fortunate day for us when you crossed our path. Without you this would have been an unmitigated tragedy." He turned to Trace. "And I have been remiss in acknowledging your part also, sir. Your knowledge and your willingness to take your time and risk your safety in pursuit of justice, and towards Merrit, a very considerable mercy, marks you as a true gentleman. We are in your debt also."

"There is no debt between friends," Trace replied. He

spoke to Casbolt, but Monk was quite certain his words were meant for Judith.

It was not a task to which Monk looked forward. He had half hoped Judith Alberton would have a lawyer in whom she had such explicit trust that she would look no further, but he had always acknowledged the possibility that in the end Rathbone would have to be approached. This was a desperate case.

Still, as he and Hester rode homeward at last, he felt a weight of oppression settle over him at the prospect of having to go to Vere Street the following day and speak to Oliver Rathbone—worse than that, to ask a favor of him.

Their relationship was long, and tense. Rathbone was by birth everything that Monk was not: privileged, financially comfortable, excellently educated, part of the establishment, effortlessly a gentleman. Monk was a fisherman's son from Northumberland, a self-made man, grasping his education where he could, bettering himself by imagination and hard work. He could appear a gentleman to the undiscerning eye. He had every whit as much elegance as Rathbone, but it cost him effort. He had learned how to behave, imitated those he admired, but sometimes made mistakes and remembered them with the fire of embarrassment.

Rathbone never made the point that he was superior; to do so would have been unnecessary. Monk was learning that only now, in his forties.

All of which was only a natural abrasion between two men who had equal intelligence and ambition, quickness of thought and word, passion for justice. The issue that mattered, that was always at the front of both their minds, was that they had loved the same woman. And she had chosen Monk.

Now Monk had to go to him and ask his help, offer him a case which could certainly prove complicated and highly emotive, and very possibly incapable of resulting in a satisfactory conclusion. But it was a kind of compliment that he considered Rathbone the only man who could and would attempt such a task.

Hester insisted on going with him.

They came without an appointment and were told by an apologetic clerk that Sir Oliver was in court. However, if the matter was of the urgency they claimed, considering their long association, a message could be sent to the Old Bailey, and Sir Oliver might meet them there during the luncheon recess.

So it proved. The three of them sat together in a crowded inn, hunched over a small table, talking as softly as possible while still loudly enough to be heard above the babble of voices, which were all attempting to do the same thing.

Rathbone acknowledged Hester, then listened studiously to Monk as he told the story, concentrating on putting the case succinctly. Monk was surprised at how uncomfortable he felt.

"I daresay you will have read of the murders in the warehouse yard in Tooley Street?" he asked.

"Yes," Rathbone said guardedly. "All England has. Extremely ugly. One of the newspapers this morning said that Lyman Breeland had been brought back to London to stand trial, and Alberton's daughter also. It is probably nonsense." He moved the vegetables delicately around his plate. "Someone was seen who resembles them. Why on earth would he leave his cause and his country when they must need him and come back here to face almost certain hanging? I suppose it is conceivable President Lincoln may wish accommodation reached, at a diplomatic level, because of Breeland's importance to the Union cause, but I cannot see any way of making that sit well with public opinion here, not to mention with the law." He frowned. "Why? I assume you have some part in it, or you would not have raised the subject."

"We brought him back," Monk replied, watching Rathbone's long, patrician face with its thin cheeks and sensitive mouth. He saw the start of surprise. "At gunpoint," he added. "But he is not as unwilling as one would suppose."

"Indeed?" Rathbone's eyebrows rose.

"He claims he is innocent, and knew nothing about Alber-

ton's death." He ignored Rathbone's expression. "I don't believe it either, but it is not completely inconceivable. He says
Alberton changed his mind about selling him the guns and
sent him a message to that effect. The hall porter at Breeland's rooms did deliver a message to him that night, on receipt of which Breeland packed his belongings and he and
Merrit Alberton left immediately."

"Could have been anything," Rathbone pointed out. "But
continue."

"He said a man called Shearer, an agent of Alberton's,
brought the entire shipment of guns and ammunition—"

"How much?" Rathbone asked.

"Six thousand rifles and over half a million rounds of ammunition," Monk replied.

Rathbone's eyes widened.

"Quite a weight. Not something you carry around in a
barrow. Do you know how much that is? A wagon load, two,
three?"

"Three at least, large wagons," Monk replied. "He says
Shearer took them to the railway station, where he paid the
full price for them, and Shearer went on his way. Breeland
never saw Alberton at all, and certainly never harmed him."

"And what does Merrit Alberton say?" Rathbone glanced
at Hester.

"The same," she answered. "She says they went by train
to Liverpool, and from there by sea, calling in at Queenstown in Ireland, and then to New York, and further by train
to Washington. We went the same way. She described it
pretty accurately."

Rathbone thanked her. It was impossible to know if he
had read anything of her emotions in her face.

"I had thought the police had traced the guns to a barge
down the river," he said thoughtfully. "Did I misread?"

"No. They did. And I was with them," Monk affirmed.
"We traced the barge all the way to Greenwich, where we
assume it met a seagoing ship and transferred the guns."

"So they are both lying?"

177

"They must be. Unless there is some other explanation we haven't thought of."

"And what is it you want of me?" Although there was a rueful, sad shadow of it already in his eyes, there was a smile on his lips, perhaps in memory of other battles they had fought together, both losses and victories that held their hurt.

Hester drew in her breath sharply and left it to Monk to reply.

"To defend Merrit Alberton," he answered. "She swears she did not murder her father, and I think I believe her."

Hester leaned forward urgently. "Either way, she is only sixteen, and completely under Breeland's influence. She believes passionately in his cause and thinks he is a hero, all the noble and brave ideals that any young woman would have."

Rathbone's dark eyes widened. "The Union of the American states? Why, for heaven's sake? Whatever difference could that possibly make to an English girl?"

"No, not the Union, the fight against slavery!" Her own fierce urgency for it, her utter loathing of all the evils of dominion, cruelty and denial were burning in her face. If Merrit Alberton had felt even part of what she did, it would be painfully easy to believe she would have followed to the ends of the earth a man whose crusade was freedom, and thought little of the cost.

Rathbone sighed. Monk knew in a moment of intense understanding exactly what he thought, and was proved correct when he spoke.

"That may well earn her some sympathy with a British jury, who have no more love for slavery than a Unionist, but it will not excuse anything in the eyes of the law. Is she married to this Breeland?"

"No."

He sighed very slightly. "Well, I suppose that is something. And she is sixteen?"

"Yes. But she won't testify against him anyway."

"I assumed as much. And if she would, that would not help us greatly. Loyalty is a very attractive quality; disloy-

alty is not, even if it is well justified. I swear, Monk, I sometimes think you spend your time trying to find ever more
complicated cases for me, until you have one which will
confound me completely. You have excelled yourself this
time. I barely know where to begin." But the expression on
his face showed that already his mind was racing.

Monk felt the first tiny lift of his spirits. If Rathbone saw
it as a personal challenge, he would take it up. Nothing
would ever allow him to retreat in front of Hester. The flash
of humor, mockery and self-knowledge was there in his
eyes, as if he knew Monk's thoughts as well as he knew his
own, and accepted them. If there was a moment of pain, of
loneliness, it was hidden instantly.

He began to question them both on every detail he could
think of: questions about Casbolt, Judith Alberton, Philo
Trace, and the whole of their journey to America and all they
had done there. Particularly he was interested in Monk's
journey down the Thames with Lanyon.

He looked distressed, and for a moment seriously out of
composure, when Monk told of finding Alberton's body in
the yard, and of almost treading on the watch.

Monk said little of the Battle of Bull Run. The horror of it
was not something for which he had words. The few he
found were difficult and stilted, the emotion too deep to be
shared in this noisy, friendly, peaceful inn. And he was not
ready to look at it again himself. It was too closely bound
with his love for Hester, and with a strange, sharp sense of
his own inability ever to be worthy of that beauty he had
seen in her. And anyway, that was the last thing he could
share with Rathbone. It would be the ultimate cruelty.

He moved on swiftly to the account of finding Breeland,
and how he and Trace had guarded him all the way to Richmond, and then Charleston, and home again.

"I see," Rathbone said when Monk had finished, with
only a few words from Hester. "Then you may tell Mrs. Alberton that I shall call upon her, and she may direct me to
her solicitor for instructions. I have a very considerable battle ahead."

Monk hesitated on the edge of thanking him, then did not. Rathbone had not taken it for him . . . for Hester perhaps . . . for the challenge possibly, for justice, but never for Monk, unless it were to prove himself equal to the challenge.

"Good!" he said instead. "Very good!"

7

RATHBONE RETURNED to the courtroom rather hurriedly. His junior was perfectly capable of conducting the present case. It was a routine one: purely a matter of presenting the evidence, most of which was incontestable. It was as well, because all through the afternoon it was not the subject of *Regina* versus *Wollcroft* which occupied his mind, but how he would handle the case of *Regina* versus *Breeland and Alberton* which he had been rash enough to accept.

He was not only uncomfortable with the case itself but with his own reason for agreeing to take it. He had read something of it in the newspapers, although it did not especially interest him because it seemed so clear-cut, but like most of the editorial writers, he was deeply sorry for Judith Alberton. Compassion was a noble emotion, but it was not a good basis upon which to go to law. Juries might be swayed by sentiment; judges were not. And public opinion was very harshly against Merrit Alberton. It seemed she had conspired with a foreigner to murder her own father. It was an affront to all decencies, to family loyalty, to obedience, to property and to patriotism. If every daughter were free to disobey her father in such a violent and appalling manner, then all society was threatened.

Rathbone found that those assumptions irritated him, and that his respect for the establishment, while deep in the roots of his life—on the surface at least—was becoming a trifle frayed. He despised prejudice, tradition set in rigid minds and no more than habit.

He had also accepted the case in part because he liked the challenge. There was an excitement in stretching himself to the full, and a danger. What if he were not equal to it? What if he failed to secure justice and an innocent man or woman was hanged because he had not been clever enough, brave enough, or imaginative, articulate, persuasive?

Or a guilty man were to be freed? Perhaps to kill again, at the best to profit from his crime and show to others that the law was not capable of protecting his victims?

But even without these he knew he would have accepted it because Hester was involved. She had not said so, but he had seen in her face that she cared for Merrit, might even find something of herself in her, as she might have been at sixteen; wayward, idealistic, too much in love to believe ill of the man in whom she had vested so much, too close to her dream to deny it, whatever the cost.

Was that how she had been? He wished he had known her then. Ridiculous how sharp that ache was, even half a year after she had married Monk. In fact, it was sharper now than it had been when she was still single and Rathbone could have asked her to marry him, if he had only realized how much he had wanted it.

When the case reached its conclusion, satisfactorily and a good hour earlier than he had expected, he accepted his client's thanks and went out into the hot, noisy August street. He hailed the first available hansom that passed him, giving his father's address in Primrose Hill. He settled back for the long ride and deliberately let his mind slip into idleness. He did not wish to think of Monk or of his new case. Especially he did not wish to think of Hester.

After an agreeable supper of fresh bread, Brussels pâté, a very pleasant red wine, and then hot plum pie with flaky pastry and fresh cream, he sat back in his armchair and looked through the open French windows across the lawn to the honeysuckle hedge and the orchard beyond. There was no sound but birds singing, and the faint scratch as Henry Rathbone wiggled a small knife around in the bowl of his pipe, not really achieving anything. He did it out of habit, his mind not on the task, just as he seldom actually smoked the pipe. He filled it, tamped down the tobacco, lit it, and invariably allowed it to go out.

"Well?" he said eventually.

Oliver looked up. "Pardon?"

"Are you going to tell me, or do I have to guess?"

It was both comfortable and disturbing to be understood so well. There was no room for evasions, no escape, and no temptation to try.

"Have you read about the murders in the warehouse yard in Tooley Street?" Oliver asked.

Henry knocked out his pipe on the fire surround. "Yes?" he said, looking anxiously at Oliver. "I thought it was supposed to be an American gun buyer. Isn't it?"

"Almost certainly," Oliver said ruefully. "Monk has just brought him back here to stand trial."

"So what does he want from you? He does want something, doesn't he?"

"Of course." Occasionally he tried hedging with his father. It never worked, because even if he succeeded in misleading him, he felt so guilty he found himself admitting the truth and then feeling ridiculous. Henry Rathbone was transparently honest himself. Sometimes it was a fault—in fact, quite often, when negotiation or management had to be achieved. He would never have made an even moderate barrister. He had not the first idea how to act a part or plead a cause in which he did not believe.

But he had a brilliant grasp of facts and a relentlessly logical mind which was capable of remarkable leaps of imagination.

Now he was waiting for Oliver to explain. Outside the starlings were swirling across the sky, black against the fading gold of the sun. Somewhere close by a lawn recently had been mown, and the smell of the cut grass was heavy.

"He brought the daughter back also," Oliver started to explain. "Extraordinary, but she and Breeland say that they are neither of them guilty of killing Alberton, or of stealing the guns." He saw the look of disbelief in his father's face. "No, I don't think so either," he said quickly. "But he does have a story better than simple denial. He says Alberton changed his mind, but had to do it secretly because of Philo Trace, the buyer from the South to whom he had already given his word and from whom he had accepted a half payment in advance."

Henry's mouth pulled down at the corners in distaste. "And was Alberton the sort of man to do that?"

"Not from what I've read, but I have no personal knowledge," Oliver replied. "Apart from dishonesty, it would ruin his reputation for the future. But more to the point, according to Monk, Trace did not receive his money back." He hesitated. "At least, he says he didn't. And Alberton's estate has no record of having received Breeland's money."

Henry put his pipe in his mouth. He lit a match, and the sharp smell of it filled the air momentarily. He held it to the tobacco and inhaled. It ignited, puffed smoke for an instant, then went out again. He sucked at it anyway.

"The most reasonable explanation seems to be that Breeland is lying," Oliver went on. "Perhaps I need to examine Alberton's business affairs, and what I can of Mr. Trace, to guard myself from unpleasant surprises."

Henry nodded slowly in silent agreement. Oliver was still leaning forward, elbows on his knees. They were facing each other across the space in front of the fireplace, as if the fire were lit, although on this summer evening it was still warm enough for them to be pleased the French doors were open. It was merely a comfortable habit shared over years of discussing all manner of things. Oliver had first done it when he was eleven; then it had been a question of irregular Latin verbs, and trying to find a logic behind their eccentricity. They had reached no conclusion, but the sense of companionship, of having attained some quality of adulthood, was of immeasurable satisfaction.

"The police traced the guns to the river and onto a barge down as far as Bugsby's Marshes," he went on. "Whereas Breeland claims he took delivery of them at the railway station and went by train to Liverpool. Merrit Alberton swears to the same thing."

"That doesn't make a great deal of sense," Henry said thoughtfully. "How competent are the police? I wonder."

"Monk says the man in charge seems excellent. And regardless of that, Monk himself went with him. He says exactly the same. The guns went from the warehouse to the river, and downstream as far as Bugsby's Marshes. From there it would be an easy matter to transfer them to an ocean-going ship, and across the Atlantic. Even Breeland doesn't argue that he took them, and they arrived safely in America. Presumably they were used in the battle at Manassas."

Henry said nothing, absorbed in thought.

"Hester believes the girl is innocent," Oliver said, then instantly wished he had not. He had betrayed too much of himself. Not that Henry was unaware of his feelings. Hester had visited him often enough. She had sat in this room, watched the light fade across the sky and the last sun gilding the tips of the poplars, the evening breeze shimmering through the leaves. She had liked Henry, and she had felt at home here, comforted by more than the beauty of the place, the honeysuckle and the apple trees, also by an inner peace.

"Not that that is a reason, of course!" he added, and as Henry's eyes opened wide, he felt himself blushing. It was exactly a reason. He had only drawn attention to it by denying it.

"There seems to be a great deal that you don't know yet," Henry observed, holding his pipe up and examining it ruefully. "The girl may have been used, and unaware of it."

"That is possible," Oliver agreed. "I need to answer a great many questions if I am to go into court with any chance of competence, let alone success."

Henry looked at Oliver closely. "You have accepted the case, I assume?"

"Well . . . yes."

185

Henry grunted. "A trifle precipitate. But then you are far more impulsive than you like to think." He smiled, robbing his words of offense. There was deep affection in him, and Oliver had never in his life doubted it.

"I shall have to see Mrs. Alberton, of course," he pointed out. "She may not wish to engage me."

Henry did not bother to answer that. He had as high an opinion of his son's professional abilities as had everyone else.

"What does Monk think?" he asked instead.

"I didn't ask him," Oliver replied a trifle tartly.

"Interesting that he did not tell you anyway," Henry said, contemplating his pipe. "He is not usually discreet with his views. He is either being devious or he does not know."

"I shall have more ideas when I have seen Merrit Alberton and heard what she has to say," Oliver went on, perhaps more to himself than to his father. "I shall be able to make some estimate of her character. And naturally, whether I represent him or not, I shall have to speak to Breeland."

"Do you intend to represent him?"

"I would rather not, but if he has any sense he'll do everything in his power to see that they are charged and defended together."

"What if he is prepared to defend her at his own cost?" Henry asked quietly. "If he loves her, he may do that. Will you allow him to?"

Oliver considered for several moments. What would he do if Breeland were willing to take the blame in order to exonerate Merrit, and yet he believed Merrit guilty?

"You had better consider it," Henry warned. "If they are truly in love, they may each try to take the blame for the other, and make your task a great deal more difficult, whomever you represent. You had not thought of that," he observed with surprise.

"No," Oliver admitted. "It was nothing Monk said, rather what he omitted to say, but I had the impression Breeland would not sacrifice himself for anyone else. But I need to know a great deal more than I do, or I am going to run the risk of being caught in this."

186

"Precisely," Henry agreed. "For a start, could the story of Breeland's be true, however unlikely?"

"About the agent, Shearer? I don't know. Certainly I know of no reason that makes it completely impossible—I shall have Monk find out if there is such a person, and if so, what he is like. Could he have murdered Alberton and taken Breeland's money himself?" He went on thinking aloud. "That would be the obvious line of defense, and presumably what Breeland will say. If I use that, either for Breeland or for Merrit alone, then I must be certain it cannot be disproved."

Henry watched him in silence. Oliver realized he would certainly have to work closely with Monk, and he had resisted it until now. He wanted to take the case, but he would rather have been independent, presented Monk and Hester with the defense accomplished, rather than sought their assistance.

"Is it possible Breeland is guilty and the daughter did not know of it?" Henry suggested. "If she knew of it, unless she was taken by force to America, then she is an accomplice at least, and an accessory after the fact."

Oliver said quickly, "I don't know beyond doubt, but from what Monk told me, she cannot be unaware of the truth. She and Breeland were together the whole of the night Alberton was murdered, and she certainly was not in America under duress." He hesitated. "And a watch that Breeland gave her as a keepsake was found in the warehouse yard."

Henry said nothing, but his expression was eloquent.

Outside, the shadows were lengthening on the lawn and the air was definitely cooler. A three-quarter moon was luminous in the fading sky. The sun had gone even from the poplars.

"I am obliged to defend Breeland also." Oliver stated the inevitable. "Unless he insists on his own man, in which case I imagine Merrit Alberton will choose to have the same person, whatever her family wants."

"And will you accept him as a client, believing him guilty?" Henry asked. "Knowing that his condemnation will certainly mean the girl's as well?"

187

It was a moral dilemma Oliver disliked acutely. He found the murders unusually repellent because they were brutal, and as far as he could see, also unnecessary. Breeland, or anyone else, could have stolen the guns without killing Alberton and the guards. They could have been left unconscious and bound, and still been unable to prevent the theft. By the time they were found Breeland had been safely away. The killing accomplished nothing and it was a gratuitous cruelty.

He would far rather have defended Merrit, even if it were no better than pleading her youth and a certain amount of duress or intimidation, and that she had not foreseen the violence. No such argument was feasible for Breeland.

"I don't know," he confessed. "I need to understand a great deal more before I can even formulate what defense to make."

The silence remained unbroken for some time. Henry stood up and closed the French doors, then returned to his seat.

"There is also the matter of the blackmail," Oliver resumed, and to Henry's surprise, told him what Monk had said briefly of Alberton's urgent reason for consulting him. "I suppose that could be involved," he finished dubiously.

"Well, you certainly need to find out who was responsible," Henry agreed. "Perhaps they took revenge for not having been sold their guns."

"But Breeland lied about the guns!" Oliver went back to the one fact that seemed inescapable. "Monk traced them down the river to Bugsby's Marshes, not to the railway station and Liverpool." He stared at the empty fireplace.

"But why murder?" Henry asked. "From what you have said, Breeland did not have to kill Alberton to take the guns. Consider this girl very carefully, Oliver. And consider the widow as well."

Oliver was startled. "A domestic crime?"

"Or a financial one," Henry amended. "Whatever it is, make sense of it in your own mind before you go into court. I am afraid you have no choice but to employ Monk to learn much more before you commit yourself to anything. I think you would be well advised to delay the trial for as long as you are able to, and know far more about the Alberton family before you speak on their behalf, or you will not serve your client well."

Oliver sank further into the chair, content to sit with his thoughts in the quiet room, without any necessity to stand up and light the gas.

Henry sucked thoughtfully on his pipe, but he knew he could allow the subject of the Alberton case to drop for this evening.

Rathbone was startled by Judith Alberton. He had expected the handsome house, suitably draped in black, curtains drawn, wreath on the door, and the straw in the street outside to muffle the sound of the horses' hooves as they passed, the mirrors draped or turned to the wall. Some people even stopped the clocks. All widows wore mourning, the unrelieved black gown, except for perhaps a jet brooch or a locket, the decoration made of hair, which he found repellent.

But Judith Alberton's face was so remarkable in its beauty, and the extraordinary power of emotion in it, that what she wore was irrelevant.

"Thank you for coming so soon, Sir Oliver," she greeted him as he came into the dim withdrawing room. "I am afraid our predicament is very serious, as I expect Mr. Monk has told you. We are desperately in need of the most skilled help we can find. Has he described our situation?"

"An outline of it, Mrs. Alberton," he replied, accepting the seat she indicated. "But there is a great deal more I need to understand if I am to do my best for you." He avoided using the word *success*. He was not sure if there was any possibility of it. What would success be? Merrit acquitted and someone else condemned? Who? Not Breeland; they had been in love then, whether they were now or not. They survived or fell together. He must make her realize that.

"Of course," she agreed. At least outwardly she was perfectly composed. "I will tell you anything I can. I don't know what can help." Her confusion was plain in her eyes.

189

Her hands lay still in her lap on the black fabric, but they were stiff, the knuckles pale.

It was surprisingly difficult to begin. It was always unpleasant intruding on someone's grief, probing into affairs which might show a side of the dead person that others had not known and which would have been so much less painful to have kept secret. But present danger did not allow such luxury. Her dignity in concealing her grief moved him more than weeping would have done.

"Mrs. Alberton, from what I have heard so far, there does not seem any way in which we can defend your daughter separately from Lyman Breeland." He saw her lips tighten, but he could not afford to tell her what she wished to hear, rather than the truth. "They have both stated that they were together the whole of that night," he continued. "Whether she was aware beforehand of what he intended to do, or was in any way a willing partner, can be argued, although we should need better proof than anything we have so far in order to convince a jury of it. Our only hope is to learn exactly what did happen, and then do the best we can to show anything that mitigates the blame. Unless, of course, we can show that there is a highly reasonable possibility that someone else altogether is guilty." He said it with little hope.

"I don't know what the truth is," she said frankly. "I simply cannot believe that Merrit would do such a thing . . . not willingly. I don't care for Mr. Breeland, Sir Oliver. I never did, but my husband had no such qualms. He did not sell him the guns simply because he had already committed himself to sell them to Mr. Trace, and accepted a payment of half the sum."

"You are certain the money had been paid by Trace?"

"Oh, yes."

"What about the money from Breeland?"

Her eyes flew open wide. "From Breeland? There was no money from him. He stole the guns. Surely that was the whole reason for—for murdering my husband and the guards, poor men. I have done what I can for their families, but no recompense makes up for the loss of someone you love."

"One would assume robbery was his reason," he agreed. "And yet surely he could have stolen the guns without killing anyone? A blow to the head would have overpowered them and kept them silent, and they would have been tied adequately to prevent any escape and pursuit."

He saw the shadows in her eyes, the quick shock of pain as the realization came to her that perhaps her husband's death was unnecessary to the theft, that he had been killed in hatred or cruelty, not as a part of war.

"I had not thought of that," she replied very softly, her gaze lowered, as if to defend herself from his understanding.

He was painfully aware of it. He would not have pried were there any alternative, but time and the imperatives of the law allowed no mercy.

"Mrs. Alberton, if I am to defend your daughter, I am forced to defend Breeland as well, unless I can find some way to separate them in the eyes of the public, and therefore of a jury. I must know the truth, whatever that is. Believe me, I cannot afford to be surprised in this courtroom or to face an adversary who knows more of the facts than I do." He shifted fractionally in his seat. "Knowledge is my only weapon, and all the skill in the world cannot defeat a man whose armory is vastly superior. David and Goliath is a fine story, and can be applied as metaphor to certain circumstances, but what is too often overlooked, or even forgotten, is that David did not stand alone. I have not his confidence that God is on my side." He smiled as he said it, but in mockery of himself.

Her chin came up quickly and she met his eyes. "I have total confidence that Merrit did not have any willing hand in the murder of her father," she said without hesitation, her voice strong. "But I do not believe that God intervenes in every miscarriage of justice. In fact, we all know perfectly well that He does not. Tell me what you need from me, Sir Oliver. I will give everything I have to save my daughter."

He did not doubt that she meant it. Even had he not already formed an opinion of her, it was plain in her face, the urgency, the courage and the fear.

"I need all the facts that I can find," he replied. "And I need your agreement that if it is necessary, which it may be, I shall represent Lyman Breeland as well, with whatever consequences may stem from that." He watched her intently as he spoke, seeing the flicker in her gaze, the awareness of how repugnant it would be to ally herself with the man she believed had murdered her husband.

"Please consider it carefully before you reply, Mrs. Alberton," he warned. "I do not know what I shall discover when I begin to look into it with more care, more thoroughness. I cannot promise you that it will be what you wish to know. All I can say is that if you employ me to act for you, I will do everything I can to serve your best interests. I can and will keep every confidence entrusted to me. But I will not lie to you, nor can I protect you from reality."

"I understand." She was very pale indeed, her body stiff, as if, were she to let go of the iron control she willed upon herself, she might collapse completely. "I will face whatever you may find. I believe in the end it will prove my daughter to be innocent of malice, if not of folly. Do whatever is needed, Sir Oliver."

"That will include employing Monk again, to enquire into the case further than he has done so far."

"Anything that you judge appropriate," she agreed. "If you trust him, then I do. And he has already proved himself more than able by bringing Merrit home. How he managed to convince Breeland to come as well I cannot imagine."

"At gunpoint, I understand," he said dryly. "But apparently he claims that was more because Breeland wished to remain with his regiment than because he was afraid to face trial. He claims to have a complete defense, not only to murder but even to robbery."

She said nothing. Emotions chased each other across her face: fear, pain, bewilderment, doubt.

He rose to his feet. "First I shall go and speak with Miss

Alberton. I can proceed little until I have heard what she has to say."

"Will you come back and tell me?" She stood up quickly. She moved with remarkable grace, and he was reminded again what a beautiful woman she was.

"I will keep you informed," he promised. It was not quite the answer she had requested, but it was all he would commit himself to do. He wondered, as the footman showed him out, how deeply he might regret such a promise. He could imagine no outcome of this issue which would not bring with it deep and terrible pain. There seemed no answer which would not add to Judith Alberton's loss.

He had no difficulty in obtaining an interview with Merrit. He stood in the small, bare room in the prison where she was being held prior to trial. It was stone-walled, washed with lime, the floor made of stone blocks. The hinges of the iron door were bedded deep into the jamb on one side, and the lock bit into the other, as if some desperate person might fling himself against it in a blind effort to escape.

There was a table where he could sit and presumably write notes, if he wished, although there was no inkwell. A pencil would have to suffice. There was a second chair for the accused.

When she came in he was again surprised. He had expected someone very girlish, angry, frightened and very possibly disinclined to cooperate with him. Instead he saw a young woman who would never rival her mother in beauty but who nevertheless had some remnant of both charm and dignity, in spite of being very obviously exhausted, her fair hair scraped back and pinned, by the look of it, without benefit of a mirror. Since she had not yet been convicted of any crime, except in public opinion, she still wore her own clothes, a blue muslin dress with a white collar which exaggerated the pallor of her skin. It was clean and fresh. Her mother must have had it sent for her.

"The wardress says you are Sir Oliver Rathbone, and you are to represent me," she said very quietly. "I presume that my mother has engaged you." It was barely a question. They both knew that there was no other explanation.

He began to reply, but she cut across him. "I did not have any part in the murder of my father, Sir Oliver." Her voice trembled only very slightly. "But I will not allow you to use me in order to blame Mr. Breeland." She lifted her chin a fraction as she spoke his name and the corner of her mouth softened.

"Perhaps you had better tell me what you know, Miss Alberton," he replied, indicating the chair opposite for her to be seated.

"Only if it is understood that I will not be manipulated," she answered. She stood quite still, waiting for his word before committing herself even to listen.

He had a sudden sense of how very young she was. Her loyalty was blind, absolute and perhaps the most precious thing to her. He could believe she defined herself by such a value, the ability to love totally, even at such a terrible cost. It was part of being sixteen. He could hardly remember such unequivocal passion. He hoped he had once been so ardent, so careless of hurt to himself, placing love before all.

Time and experience had blunted that . . . too much. Perhaps if he had not been afraid to love like that he would not have lost Hester. But that was a useless thought now, and too brilliantly painful to indulge, even in passing. That was much too real, too wholehearted.

"I have no intention of trying to manipulate you," he said with a fierceness that even surprised him. "I would like to know the truth, or at least as much of it as you can tell me. Please begin with simple facts. We may go on to deduction and opinion later. Perhaps you would begin with the day of your father's death, unless you feel there is something relevant earlier."

She sat down obediently and composed herself, folding her hands.

"Mr. Breeland and Mr. Trace both wished to purchase the guns that my father had for sale. Each, of course, for his own side in the civil war in America. Mr. Trace represented the Confederacy, the slave states; Mr. Breeland is for the Union, and against slavery anywhere." The ring of pride and anger in her voice was unmistakable. Rathbone could not help identifying with her in that much at least.

He did not interrupt.

"My father said that he had already promised to sell the entire shipment of guns, above six thousand of them, to Mr. Trace," she continued. "And he would not change his mind, no matter what Mr. Breeland, or I, for that matter, would say to him. Every argument against slavery was tried, every horror and injustice, every monstrosity of human cruelty detailed, but he would not reconsider." There were tears in her eyes, but she blinked them away furiously, annoyed with herself for betraying such emotion. "I quarreled with him." She sniffed, then shook her head as she realized how inelegant it was.

Rathbone offered her his handkerchief.

She hesitated, then took it, simply so that she might blow her nose, and then continued.

"Thank you. I was very angry indeed. I think the more so because I had always thought well of him before. I had never seen that side of him which . . ." She lowered her eyes, looking away from him. "Which could not admit when he had made a mistake, and yield to a better cause. I said some things to him I wish now I could take back. Not that they are not true, but I could not know they would be the last words he ever heard from me."

Rathbone did not wish to give her time to dwell on the thought.

"You left the room. Where did you go?"

"What? Oh. I went upstairs and packed a small valise with immediate necessities—linens, clean blouses, toiletries, that's all."

"Where was Mr. Breeland during this quarrel?"

"I don't know. At his rooms, I suppose."

"He was not in your parents' house?"

"No. He did not overhear the quarrel, if that is what you are thinking."

195

"It occurred to me. Then where did you go?"

"I left." The color rose up her cheeks delicately. It made him more inclined to believe her awareness of just what a major step she had taken, and that she was as sensible of the risk to her reputation as her mother would have been. She took a deep breath. "I went out of the servants' door, at the side of the house, and walked along the street until I came to the crossroads, where I found a hansom. I took it, directing the driver to Mr. Breeland's rooms."

He did not need to ask the address. Monk had already told him.

"And was Mr. Breeland at home?"

"Yes. He welcomed me, most especially when I told him about the quarrel I had had with my father." She leaned forward across the table. "But you must understand, he in no way encouraged me to defy my parents or behave in any way the least improperly. I require that you should fully believe that!"

Rathbone was not sure what he believed, but it would be foolish to tell her so now. It was not the issue. He could not afford to be concerned with Breeland's morality except as it showed itself in acts that were punishable in law.

"I don't question it, Miss Alberton. I need to know how you spent the rest of that night until you had left London altogether. Very precisely, if you please. Omit nothing."

"You think Lyman murdered my father." Her eyes were direct, her voice perfectly steady. "He did not. What he told Mr. Monk is the exact truth. I know it because I was with him. We spent the evening speaking together and planning what we should do." A first smile touched her lips; it seemed like self-mockery of another more innocent time. "He tried to persuade me to make peace with my parents. He warned me that his country was at war. He explained to me that honor required he join his regiment and fight. But of course I understood that already. I simply wished to be his wife and wait for him, support him and do everything I could myself to help in the fight against slavery. I never imagined I was going to sail off into a new and peaceful life somewhere else."

Rathbone believed her. Her earnestness was transparent and he thought he heard a thread of disappointment she herself was surprised to discover. Something confused her, but as yet he had no idea what it was.

"Please continue," he prompted. "Tell me exactly what occurred. Was Mr. Breeland ever out of your sight?"

"Not for more than a few moments," she replied. "He did not leave his apartment. It was nearly midnight, and we were still talking about what we should do." Pride and tenderness flickered in her for a moment. "He was concerned for my reputation, more than I was myself. If I should have slept the night in his sitting room no one in America would have known it, and that was all my concern. But he cared for me, and it troubled him."

Rathbone was better aware than she how rapidly word traveled, and it flashed through his mind to wonder how much Breeland's concern was for her reputation as it might affect him as her future husband. But it was an uncharitable impulse, and he did not speak it aloud.

She swallowed. In spite of her attempt at calm, and her undoubted courage, the effort was costing her dear.

"A little before midnight a young boy came with a message for Lyman. It was a note. He tore it open and read it immediately. It said that my father had changed his mind about selling the guns, but for obvious reasons he could not say so in front of Mr. Trace. He would return him his money later, and explain that Lyman's arguments regarding slavery had won him over and he could no longer in good conscience sell the guns to the Confederates. Lyman was to go to the railway station at Euston Square and the guns would be delivered to him there. Liverpool was the best port for them to be shipped to America." She was watching him intently, willing him to believe her.

He recognized that she was almost certainly using Breeland's words for the explanation, but he did not interrupt her.

"That was what he did," she continued. "We packed up immediately, taking what was of most importance to him. There was hardly time to do even that. But the guns were the most valuable of all. They were part of the battle for freedom, and a cause that is just must always take precedence over a few material possessions."

"You helped him pack?" he asked.

"Naturally. I had only a few things myself." Again the tiny smile touched her face. She must have been thinking back now on her own hasty departure, in the name of love and principle, with only what she could put into a bag she could carry in her hand. He tried to imagine what precious things gathered in her short lifetime she had had to leave behind. And apparently she had done it without serious regret. He thought how deeply, how unselfishly, she must love Breeland. It hurt him with surprising force that he might be utterly unworthy of it. When he spoke his voice had more anger in it than he had intended.

"And who was this note from? I presume it was signed?"

"Yes, of course," she said indignantly. "He would hardly have acted upon it, leaving everything, had he not known who sent it."

"Who did?"

Color deepened in her face, and there was a moment's confusion as she realized how much depended upon the truth of the issue, and that she thought, after all, not knew it.

"It was signed by Mr. Shearer," she said defiantly. "Of course in light of the . . . murders . . ." She gulped. She seemingly could not bring herself to say her father's name in this connection. Her chin came up. "But when we got to Euston Square the guns were there, already loaded onto a wagon. Lyman never left me for more than a few moments, and that was after the guns were delivered, and he paid Shearer the money. He had written authority to accept on my father's behalf, and it was all perfectly in order. I . . . I was so happy my father had at last seen the justice of what Lyman was fighting for and changed his mind."

"But you did not think to return home and tell him so?"

Misery filled her eyes. "No," she answered very quietly. "I loved Lyman and still wanted to go with him to America. I . . . I was still angry that my father had taken so long to see what had been plain to me from the beginning. Slavery is wicked. Treating a human being like a possession can never be right."

He did not know what to think. The story made no sense, and yet he did not think she was lying to him. She believed what she said. Had Breeland somehow duped her? If he had not murdered Alberton himself, then had he employed someone else to do it? Perhaps this man Shearer? "Tell me about your journey north to Liverpool and what happened there," he instructed.

"How can it matter?" She was puzzled.

"Please do so," he insisted.

"Very well. Lyman showed me to a carriage where I was reasonably comfortable and told me to wait for him while he spoke to the guard. He returned in about ten minutes, and shortly after that the train pulled out."

"Who else was in the carriage?" he interrupted.

"How can it matter? No one I know. I did not speak to them. An old man with a lot of whiskers. A woman with a dreadful hat, quite the ugliest I have ever seen, red and brown. Why would anyone wear red and brown together? I don't know who else. It's all unimportant."

"Where did the train stop?" he pressed.

Obediently she described the journey in its monotonous details.

He wrote down her answers in rapid, almost illegible notes.

"And in Liverpool?"

She told him of Breeland's trouble in having the guns stored temporarily, of finding space on a ship bound first for Queenstown in Ireland, then for New York. With every new fact she spoke of, the pictures became more real, the more he was convinced her story was told from experience rather than imagination.

"Thank you," he said at last. "You have been very patient, Miss Alberton, and you have helped greatly in your defense."

"I will not allow you to defend me at Lyman's expense!" she said quickly, leaning forward across the table, her face flushed. "Please understand that. I shall dismiss you, or whatever it takes, if . . ."

"I understood you when you first told me, Miss Alberton," he said calmly. "I shall not do so; you have my word. I cannot promise what the court will do, and I have never promised to anyone what a jury will do. But for myself, I can answer absolutely."

She sank back. "Thank you, Sir Oliver. Then I shall be very glad if you will act for me and . . . and do what you can."

He rose to his feet, feeling a twist of pity for her, almost like a physical spasm. She was so young, a child, trying to behave like a woman, trying to keep a dignity she was so close to losing. He wished profoundly he could have comforted her, that either her mother or father were here, even that Breeland was . . . damn him. But all he could do to help her was to remain formal, keep the fierce control she depended upon.

"I shall return to tell you how I am progressing," he said carefully. "If you do not see me for a few days, it is because I am working on your behalf. Good day, Miss Alberton." He turned a little quickly, not waiting to look at her as the tears spilled from her brimming eyes.

Rathbone was driven to see Lyman Breeland by curiosity as well as by duty, but it was still not a task he expected to find either easy or pleasant.

He was received in a room markedly similar to the one in the women's section of the prison, with the same bare limewashed walls, simple table and two wooden chairs.

In some ways Breeland was exactly what Rathbone had expected: tall, lean, a hard body used to exercise. One would have judged him a man of action. "Military" was the first thing that came to mind because of his upright bearing and a certain pride in him, even in these crushing circumstances. He was dressed in a plain shirt and trousers an inch or two short for him. Presumably they were borrowed. He would have left the battlefield at Manassas in his dirty, blood-stained uniform.

But Breeland's face surprised Rathbone. Without realizing it he had formed preconceptions in his mind, expected to see a man of readable passions, an arresting face in which one could see zeal and loyalty and a will that overrode all obstacles, all pain or rebuff. Perhaps unconsciously he had envisioned someone like Monk.

Instead he saw a handsome man, but unreachable in an entirely different way. His face was smooth, features perfectly regular, but there was something in it which struck him as remote. Perhaps there were not enough lines yet, as if his emotions were all within, smothered.

"How do you do, Mr. Breeland," he began. "My name is Oliver Rathbone. Mrs. Alberton has engaged me to defend her daughter, and as I daresay you will appreciate, it is necessary that her defense and yours be conducted either by the same person or by two people who are acting as one."

"Of course," Breeland agreed. "Neither of us is guilty, and we were in each other's company the entire time when the crime occurred. Surely you have already been informed of that?"

"I have spoken with Miss Alberton. However, I should like to hear it from you, on your own behalf if you wish me to act for you, and on hers if you prefer to retain someone else."

No smile touched Breeland's face. "I am told you are the best, and it would seem sensible that one person should represent us both. Since apparently you are willing, I accept. I have sufficient funds to meet whatever your charges are."

It was an oddly discourteous way of putting it, as if Rathbone had been touting for business. But he could understand Breeland's feelings. He had been brought back to a foreign country by force to stand trial for a crime for which he would be hanged if he were found guilty. He would be defended by strangers he was obliged to trust without the ability to test them himself. Any man who was not a fool would be defensive, afraid and angry.

201

Rathbone decided not to attempt any kind of rapport, at least not yet. First, quite formally, he would establish the facts.

"Good," he said graciously. "Perhaps if you will sit down we shall be able to begin discussing the details of strategy."

Breeland sat obediently. He moved with ease, even grace, apart from a slight awkwardness in one shoulder.

Rathbone sat opposite him. "Would you begin with your first acquaintance with Daniel Alberton."

"I heard of him through the arms trade," Breeland answered. "His name is well known, and trusted, and he could provide the most excellent guns, and rapidly. I called upon him and attempted to purchase first-class muskets and ammunition for the Union. I told him of the cause for which we were fighting. I did not expect him to understand that the Union itself was of the profoundest value. An Englishman could not be expected to grasp the damage of secession, but I believed any civilized nation would be against the enslavement of one race of people by another." The contempt in his voice was stinging. They had been speaking for only minutes, and surely Breeland must be aware that his own life was in jeopardy, but already he had made an opportunity to express his passion for the Union cause.

Rathbone found it oddly disconcerting, and he was not sure why.

Breeland went on to describe his attempts to deal with Alberton, and his failure. Alberton had given his word to Philo Trace and accepted his money, and he considered himself bound. Breeland allowed a grudging admiration for that, but still believed the justice of the Union cause should have overridden any one man's sense of commitment.

Rathbone's reply was instant, not weighed.

"Can any group claim collective honor without that of the individuals who compose it?"

"Of course," Breeland responded with a direct, almost confrontational stare. "The group is always greater than the one. That is what society is; that is civilization. I am surprised you need to ask. Or are you testing me?"

Rathbone was about to deny it, then realized that in a sense he *was* testing him, but not as Breeland meant.

"What is the difference between that and saying that the end justifies the means?" the barrister asked.

Breeland gazed back at him, his clear gray eyes unwavering. "Our cause is just," he replied with an edge to his voice. "No sane person could doubt it, but I did not kill Daniel Alberton for it, or anyone else, except on the battlefield, face-to-face as a soldier does."

Rathbone did not answer him. "Tell me what happened the night you quarreled with Alberton and later Miss Alberton left her home and came to you."

"You spoke with her. Did she not tell you?"

"I wish to hear your account of it, Mr. Breeland. Please oblige me." Rathbone was angry without knowing why.

"If you wish. She will bear out all I say, because it is the truth." Then Breeland proceeded to describe the evening in essence exactly as Merrit had. Rathbone pressed him for details of the train journey to Liverpool, of the carriage in which they rode and such trivia as the other occupants and what they were wearing.

"I don't see the relevance," Breeland protested, a shadow of anger darkening his face. "How can it have anything whatever to do with Alberton's death what kind of a hat some woman in a railway carriage was wearing hours later?"

"I do not tell you how to purchase guns, Mr. Breeland," Rathbone said tartly. "Please do not advise me how to conduct a case in court, or what information I shall need."

"If you feel you need a description of the woman's hat, Mr. Rathbone, then I shall give it to you," Breeland said coldly. "But Miss Alberton would be in a better position to judge such a thing. It seems to me both trivial and absurd."

"Sir Oliver," Rathbone corrected with a chilly smile.

"What?"

"My name is 'Sir Oliver,' not 'Mr. Rathbone.' And the hat is important. Please describe it."

"It was large and extremely ugly. As far as I can recall,

there was a lot of red in it, and some other, duller shade, brown or something like that—Sir Oliver."

"Thank you. I believe your account of your journey, even though it seems to contradict the facts that the police have." He rose to his feet.

"It is the truth," Breeland said simply, also standing up. "Is that all?"

"For the time being. Is there anything I can do for you? Do you wish any messages sent to your family, or anyone else? Do you have all you require in the way of clothes—toiletries, for example?"

"Sufficient." Breeland gave a slight grimace. "A soldier should think nothing of personal privation. And I have been permitted to write such letters as I wished to, so that my family might know I am in good health. I should prefer they did not learn of this absurd accusation until after it has been proved false."

"Then I shall continue investigating every avenue of proof that someone else is responsible for the deaths of Daniel Alberton and the two guards at the warehouse," Rathbone said, inclining his head in the slightest of gestures and taking his leave.

He was outside in the sun amid the traffic of the street with its noise and haste before he realized why he was so angry. Breeland's account of his actions had tallied so precisely with Merrit's, even to the complete irrelevancies such as the woman's hat, that he did not doubt it was the truth. An invented tale would not run to such trivia. He was quite certain that both Merrit and Breeland had indeed made the journey by train from London to Liverpool, and there seemed no other occasion on which it could have happened. Nevertheless, he would have Monk make absolutely certain, produce witnesses if possible.

What made him clench his hands as he strode along the footpath, holding his shoulders tight, was that not once had Breeland asked if Merrit was all right, if she was frightened, suffering, unwell, or in need of anything that could possibly be done for her. She was little more than a child, in a place that was more terrible than anything her life could have prepared her to meet, and facing the possibility of being hanged for a crime which depended wholly upon his passion for his own political cause, however justified. And yet it had not entered his mind to ask after her, even when he knew Rathbone had only just left her.

Rathbone might admire Breeland's dedication in time, but he could not imagine liking a man who devoted himself to the cause of mankind in general but could not care for the individuals closest to him, and who was blind to their suffering when even a word from him would have helped. The question crossed his mind whether it was people he loved at all, or simply that he needed some great, absorbing crusade to lose himself in as an excuse for evading personal involvement with its sacrifices of vanity, its compromises, its patience and its generosity of spirit. With a great cause one could be a hero. One's own weaknesses did not show; one was not tested by intimacy.

There was a prick of familiarity in that, an understanding of regret. The slow, quiet ache inside when he thought of Hester was also a self-knowledge, now made sharper by coming face-to-face with Lyman Breeland.

It was late afternoon by the time Rathbone went to see Monk. It was not an interview he was looking forward to, but it was unavoidable. Breeland's story must be substantiated by facts and witnesses. Monk was the person to find them, if they existed, and Rathbone was inclined to believe that they did.

He arrived at Fitzroy Street just after six, and found Monk at home. He was glad. He would not have chosen to be alone with Hester. He was surprised by how little he trusted his emotions.

Monk appeared almost to have expected him, and there was a look of satisfaction in his lean face as Rathbone came in.

"Of course," Monk agreed, waving for Rathbone to sit down. Hester was not in the room. Perhaps she was about some domestic duty. He did not ask.

"I've heard her story." Rathbone crossed his legs elegantly and leaned back, exactly as if he were at ease. He was a brilliant barrister, which meant he was articulate, thought rapidly and logically. He was also a very fine actor. He would not have described himself in those terms, however, at least not the last one. "And Breeland's also," he added. "I think it more likely true than not, but naturally we shall require substantiation."

"You believe it," Monk said thoughtfully. It was impossible to tell from his expression what his own ideas were. Rathbone would have liked to know but he would not ask, not yet.

"Merrit gave a very detailed description of the train journey to Liverpool," Rathbone explained, telling Monk about the woman with the hat. "Breeland gave the same description, more or less. It is not proof, but it is highly indicative. You might even be able to find someone else on that train who may have seen them. That would be conclusive."

Monk chewed his lower lip. "It would," he conceded. "Then who killed Alberton? And rather more awkwardly, how did the guns get from the river at Bugsby's Marshes across the city to the Euston Square station?"

Rathbone smiled very slightly. "That is what I shall employ you to discover. There appears to be some major fact which we have not learned. Possibly it has to do with this agent, Shearer. There is also the very unpleasant possibility that Alberton himself was involved in deception of some sort and was double-crossed by Shearer, or even by Breeland."

A flicker of amusement lit Monk's eyes. "I take it that you did not greatly like Mr. Breeland." It was made more in the tone of an observation than a question.

Rathbone raised his eyebrows. "That surprises you?"

"Not in the slightest. There is much in him I admire, but I cannot bring myself to like him," Monk agreed.

"You know, he never once asked me how Merrit was." Rathbone heard the anger and amazement in his own voice. "He can't see anything but his damned cause!"

"Slavery is pretty repugnant."

"A lot of things are, and a great many of them spring from

206

obsession." Rathbone's voice suddenly shook with anger. "And an inability to see any point of view except your own, or to empathize with another person's pain if he is in any way different from yourself."

Monk's eyes widened. "You are absolutely right," he said with sudden, profound seriousness. "Yes . . . Lyman Breeland is a very dangerous man. I wish to hell we did not have to defend him in order to defend Merrit."

"I see no alternative, or believe me, I should have taken it," Rathbone assured him with feeling. "Investigate everything. I don't believe Merrit is guilty of anything beyond falling in love with a cold fanatic of a man. He may be guilty of no more than an ability to love a theory too much and people too little. And that may lead to many sins, but not necessarily the murder of Daniel Alberton. You had better look very carefully at Philo Trace, and at this agent, Shearer, and anything else you find pertinent."

"And as always, you are in a hurry."

"Just so." Rathbone rose to his feet. "Try hard, Monk. For Merrit Alberton's sake, and for her mother's."

"But not Breeland's . . ."

"I don't give a damn about Breeland. Find the truth."

Monk walked towards the door with Rathbone, his face already furrowed in thought. "It has a nice irony to it, doesn't it," he observed. "I hope to hell it isn't Trace. I rather like him."

Rathbone did not reply; they were both too aware of men in the past they had liked, of cases where love and hate had seemed so misplaced. Some tragedies it was too easy to understand, the emotions and judgments not nearly simple enough.

8

$M_{ONK\ WOULD}$ also dearly have liked to find a way to defend Merrit without at the same time defending Breeland, but he was too much of a realist to imagine it could be done. He had watched them together on the long journey home across the Atlantic. He knew Merrit would never allow it. Whatever her belief about Breeland, or her horror at the reality of war, her own nature was based on loyalty. To have saved herself at his expense would be to deny everything she valued. It would be a kind of suicide.

Nor did it surprise him that Breeland was still more concerned with clearing his own name, and thus the cause, than with how Merrit was enduring imprisonment and the fear and suffering that must come with it. He smiled as he thought of Rathbone's distaste, and imagined his regard for Merrit, her youth, her enthusiasm and vulnerability. He wondered also as he strode along Tottenham Court Road, watching for a hansom, what Rathbone had felt for Judith Alberton, and if he had been sensitive to her remarkable beauty.

The August sun was hot, shimmering up from the pavements, winking in hard, glittering light on harnesses, polished carriage doors and, at certain angles, from the windows of busy shops.

A shoeblack boy was accepting a penny from a top-hatted customer. He winked at a girl selling muffins.

Monk hailed a cab and gave the address of the police station, where he hoped, this early in the morning, to find

Lanyon still there. It was the natural place to begin, even though he was now attempting to prove the opposite from that which had seemed to be so obviously the truth at the beginning.

He was fortunate. He met Lanyon just as he was coming down the steps, the sun catching his fair, straight hair. He was surprised to see Monk and stopped, his face full of curiosity.

"Looking for me?" he asked, almost hopefully.

Monk smiled in self-mockery. "I am now retained for the defense," he said frankly. He owed Lanyon the truth, and it was easier than lying or evasion.

Lanyon grunted, but there was no criticism in his eyes. "Money or conviction?" he replied.

"Money," Monk replied.

Lanyon grinned. "I don't believe you."

"You asked!"

Lanyon started to walk, a long, loping step, and Monk kept pace with him. "Sorry for the girl," Lanyon went on. "Wish I could think she was innocent, but she was there in the yard." He looked sideways at Monk, his face shadowed with regret, trying to read Monk's reaction.

Monk kept his own face expressionless. It cost him an effort.

"How do you know?"

"The watch you found . . . it was Breeland's all right, of course, but he had given it to her as a keepsake."

"Did he say so?"

Lanyon's mouth turned down at the corners. "Do you think I would take his word for it? No, he didn't mention it at all, and I didn't bother to ask him. It doesn't really matter what he says. Miss Dorothea Parfitt told us. She's a friend of Miss Alberton's, and apparently Miss Alberton was showing it to her, boasting a little." His expression was rueful, leaving Monk to picture the scene himself and draw his own conclusions.

They passed a strawberry seller's cart.

210

Monk said nothing. His mind was racing, trying to fit into one congruous whole the vision of Merrit bragging about the watch Breeland had given her as a token of his love, Merrit standing in the warehouse yard watching as Breeland forced her father and the two guards into the cramped and humiliating position, then shot them in cold blood, and the Merrit he had seen in Washington and on the ship home, young and loyal, confused by Breeland's coldness towards her, constantly making excuses for him in her own mind, making herself believe the best of him, and now alone and in prison, frightened, facing trial and perhaps death, and yet determined not to betray him, even to save herself.

Perhaps she was one of the world's great lovers, but Breeland was not. He might be one of the world's idealists, or one of its flawed obsessives, not so much a man who supported a cause as a man who needed a cause to support him, to fulfill a nature otherwise empty.

Lanyon was waiting for an answer from him.

"An ugly fact," he granted. "I'm not yet ready to concede its meaning."

Lanyon shrugged.

"What about Shearer?" Monk changed the subject. "What does he say for himself? Have you found the boy who delivered the message to Breeland at his rooms? Who sent it?"

"Don't know yet," Lanyon answered. "Haven't found the boy. Could be any of thousands, and he's not coming forward. Doesn't surprise me. Doesn't want to be connected with a man who committed a triple murder, even supposing he knows we want him. Very likely he can't read. Even if somebody's told him, he'll be keeping his head down."

"Merrit said it was Shearer who sent it."

"Nobody's seen him since the day before Alberton was killed," Lanyon replied again, watching for Monk's response.

They crossed the street just behind an open landau, with laughing ladies holding up pale parasols, their white and blue muslins fluttering in the slight breeze.

A lemonade seller stood on the corner, now and then

shouting out his wares. Lanyon stopped and bought one, looking enquiringly at Monk, who copied him. They both drank the liquid down without interrupting themselves to speak.

"Have you looked for him?" Monk asked as they moved on. Already the air was getting hot, but it was nothing like the stifling closeness of Washington—and London, for all its tens of thousands, its poverty and grime, its magnificence, opulence and hypocrisy, was at peace.

"Yes, of course we have," Lanyon replied. "Not a whisper."

"Don't you think that requires an explanation?"

Lanyon grinned. "Well, the first one that comes to mind is that he was in league with Breeland, but had the good sense to disappear completely, instead of going openly somewhere. But then he didn't have six thousand guns to ship."

"Presumably he just had the money," Monk said dryly.

Lanyon walked in silence for a hundred yards or so.

"You did look into the money?" Monk asked him.

"Of course," Lanyon answered, stepping off onto the cross street, Monk keeping pace with him. "It's clear enough in Casbolt and Alberton's books. He had the half down that Trace paid him. He never received a penny from Breeland."

"Breeland says he paid the full amount to Shearer when the guns were handed over at the Euston Square station."

"Well, he would!" Lanyon skirted around two elderly gentlemen in dark coats and striped trousers, heads bent in earnest conversation. "And if he received the guns in time for the night train to Liverpool, what was it we followed down the river to Bugsby's Marshes?"

Monk thought for several minutes while they walked.

"Perhaps Merrit was his witness," he said at last, the idea forming in his mind as he spoke. "Maybe the guns went from Bugsby's Marshes, and he simply told Merrit they went through Liverpool, but he went that way himself so she would swear to it?"

"On the assumption you would go to America, find him, and bring him back to stand trial . . ." Lanyon finished for him. "You work hard for your money, Monk, I'll give you that! I'd hire you on my case, if I were in trouble."

"Not on the assumption I'd bring him back!" Monk snapped, feeling the color wash up his face. "In order to deceive Merrit, because he didn't want her to know the truth, couldn't afford for her to know. He may well believe that anything he does, including triple murder, is justified by the cause, but he knows damned well that Merrit wouldn't. Especially when one of the victims was her father."

Lanyon's eyes widened, and he slowed his stride considerably. "I suppose that's not impossible. You mean Shearer and Breeland were accomplices, Breeland got the guns, and Shearer got the money? Poor Alberton was killed. Which way did the guns go?"

"Down the river to Bugsby's Marshes, and across the Atlantic from there," Monk answered as they crossed a busy street. "Breeland went to Liverpool and sailed separately, taking Merrit with him. That may have been his original intention, and he might have had to change his mind because of Merrit's obsession with him. Either way, she is innocent of her father's death."

"So Shearer killed Alberton in order to steal the guns and sell them to Breeland?"

"Why not?" Monk's spirits rose. "Doesn't it fit with everything we know?"

"Apart from Breeland's watch at the warehouse yard, yes." Lanyon looked sideways at him, stepping up onto the curb. "How do you explain that?"

"I don't . . . yet. Maybe she dropped it there earlier?"

"Doing what?" Lanyon asked incredulously. "Why would Merrit Alberton be at the warehouse in Tooley Street? Not a usual place for a young lady in the normal course of her summer social round."

Even as he was denying it, Monk realized how desperately he was reaching for an escape for Merrit. "Perhaps she and Breeland went there to make some agreement with Shearer earlier in the evening?"

"Why there?"

"To verify the merchandise. Breeland wouldn't pay for guns unless he knew what he was getting."

Lanyon squinted at him. "Didn't trust him to sell the right guns, even though he was Alberton's agent, but did trust him enough to hand over the whole amount of the money to him and sail off to America in the absolute faith that the guns would be shipped to him, and not either kept or sold to someone else?" He pursed his lips. "What was to stop Shearer from pocketing the money and selling the guns again, or even simply leaving them where they were? Not a lot Breeland could do about it from New York!"

Another idea flashed into Monk's mind. "Maybe that was why he took Merrit with him? Insurance against being cheated."

"By Alberton, maybe . . . but why would Shearer care what happened to Merrit? He killed Alberton anyway."

Monk remembered Breeland's face when he had been told about the murders. "I don't believe Breeland knew about that. He believed Shearer was acting out of principle, that he believed just as passionately as he did himself in the fight against slavery." He saw Lanyon's look of comical incredulity. "Talk to Breeland," he said quickly. "Listen to him. He's a fanatic. In his view, all right-minded people believe as he does."

Lanyon took the point. "I suppose it's possible," he said cautiously. "So Shearer is the villain, Breeland the fanatic, guilty of buying stolen guns and using Merrit's love for him, but not of murder. And Merrit herself is guilty only of being led by her heart and ignoring her head? I suppose at sixteen that's half to be expected." He shrugged. "If a woman wouldn't do all she could to help her betrothed, we'd be just as quick to criticize her."

"Probably," Monk agreed, although privately he wondered just how much blind adoration he could take—perhaps at thirty a lot more than he could now. And would he have used it with the same disregard as Lyman Breeland did? Probably. What was given so freely was often valued too little. But the fact that he himself might have been no better did not soften his dislike for Breeland; if anything it deepened it.

"Are you going to pursue that?" Lanyon asked curiously.

"I'm going to pursue everything," Monk replied. "Unless, of course, I find something so conclusive it isn't necessary." He grinned broadly at Lanyon, but it was ironic, and they both knew it.

Lanyon shrugged. "Good luck." He sounded as if he meant it.

Monk started again at the very beginning, at the warehouse yard, following the trail of the wagons leaving. He remembered vividly going into the closed space in the pale, summer morning and seeing the dead bodies in their grotesque positions. He remembered Casbolt's face in the light, the smell of blood, the wheel tracks over the stones.

He also remembered Manassas and the strange reality of war. The whole of it was like a dream, all smaller than it should have been, the dust and the heat ridiculously commonplace. Gunshots were not like thunder; they were crackling, like dozens of sticks being snapped as a bonfire took hold. Only the cannons roared.

But the blood and the fear had been more real than anyone could imagine, so stark they still came back to him every time he closed his eyes and forgot to guard against them. It was the smell that stayed in his memory.

What were three deaths compared with so many? Some of the soldiers had been shot down without even a fight, just wasted, as thoughtlessly as a man mows down grass.

Was that how Breeland looked at it? Did he see it not as murder but as war? Did he feel a few individual deaths were a small price to pay to secure the end of slavery for a whole race? And perhaps the end of the sin of enslaving for another race, his own? An argument could be made for it. Monk could make one himself.

He knew what Hester would say. At least he thought he did. You did not save a people from sin by committing another sin yourself. But was she a realist? Or did she think of individuals, one man's injuries or pain, one man's grief, because it was what she could help, and refuse to see a wider whole?

Certainly, Lyman Breeland ignored the individual and saw the thousands, the tens of thousands. And Monk found something in Breeland repellent. Did that make Breeland wrong, or only morally braver, more of a visionary and less of an ordinary, limited human being?

Monk stood in the sun in Tooley Street and weighed the possibilities. The wagons had left through the gates and must have turned either left or right. The guns were too heavy to have been transported other than by horse-drawn vehicles or on barges along the river. The river was by far the closer. It was the way Alberton normally moved all heavy goods. It was the way everyone did.

But Breeland was American. Perhaps he did not know that? Could he have gone by road to the Euston Square station? Well over a month had gone by. It would be hard to find witnesses who remembered anything, let alone were willing to testify to it.

Could Breeland's story be true? That was the place to start. The wagons loaded with six thousand guns would be big enough, passing through the streets in the middle of the night.

But time was a whole different question. Breeland had said the note had come to him about midnight. Alberton was still alive then. He was killed around three, according to the medical evidence, and the reasonable deduction as to the loading of the guns. The wagons must have left immediately after. How long would it take them heavily laden, but in the traffic-free still of the night?

He started to walk rapidly, then caught a cab, following the shortest route over the river towards the Euston Square station, thinking furiously all the way. Even at a trot, which wagons could not have done, he could not have made it in less than half- to three-quarters of an hour.

He paid the cabdriver and strode into the station. He

asked to see the stationmaster, quoting Lanyon's name as if he had a right to.

"It is regarding illegal shipment of arms," he said grimly. "And triple murder. My information must be exact. Lives depend upon it, and perhaps Britain's reputation for honor."

The clerk obeyed with alacrity. Let the decision for dealing with this be somebody else's. "I'll fetch Mr. Pickering, sir!"

The stationmaster kept him waiting only fifteen minutes. He was an agreeable man with a thick gray mustache and handsome side-whiskers. He welcomed Monk into his office.

"How can I be of assistance, sir?" he said mildly, but he eyed Monk up and down, weighing his importance and reserving judgment. He had heard wild statements before and was not easily impressed.

Monk would not retreat, but he decided to phrase his request carefully.

"Thank you for your assistance, Mr. Pickering. As you are no doubt aware, there was a triple murder in Tooley Street on June twenty-eighth, and a large shipment of British guns was stolen and exported to America."

"All London is aware of it, sir," Pickering replied. "A very enterprising agent of enquiry tracked down the murderer and brought him back to stand trial for it."

Monk felt a sharp prickle of satisfaction—he did not like to call it pride.

"Indeed. William Monk," he introduced himself, allowing himself a faint smile. "Now I need to be sure that at that trial the man does not escape justice. He is claiming that he bought the guns quite legally, paying full price for them, and that he shipped them out from this station, on the train to Liverpool, the very night that the murders took place. There was a train to Liverpool that night?"

"No trains before six in the morning, sir." Pickering shook his head. "We don't run night trains on this line."

Monk was taken aback. Suddenly the one thing he was sure of had slipped away.

"None at all?" he pressed.

"Well, the occasional special." Pickering swallowed hard, but his eyes did not waver. "Private hire. Don't often refuse one of those."

"Was there one that night? Friday, the twenty-eighth of June? It would really be the early hours of Saturday morning."

"I can look it up," Pickering offered, turning to look at a sheaf of papers on a shelf behind his desk.

Monk waited impatiently. The seconds stretched out into a minute, then two.

"Here we are," Pickering said at last. "Yes, by Jove, there was a special that night, all the way to Liverpool. Goods and a few passengers. Here you are." He held out the sheaf of paper.

Monk snatched it from him. The train had left at five minutes before two o'clock.

"Are you sure it went on time?" he demanded. He heard the edge to his voice, and could not control it.

"Yes, sir," Pickering assured him. "That sheet is written up afterwards. It should have gone five minutes before. That's the time it actually went."

"I see. Thank you."

"Does it help?"

"Yes, it does. The murders could not have happened before about three o'clock."

Pickering looked relieved, and puzzled. "I see," he said, although plainly he did not.

"Do you know if it carried cases of guns?" Monk asked, not expecting an answer of any value.

"Guns? No sir, just machinery, timber and I believe a consignment of bathroom furnishings."

"Why a special train for those?"

"Bathroom furniture's fragile, sir, I suppose."

"Who hired it?"

"On the bottom, there, sir." Pickering pointed at the sheet in Monk's hand. "Messrs. Butterby and Scott, of Camberwell." He regarded Monk curiously. "Did you think the American took the guns on our train to Liverpool? News-

218

papers said he went down the river to Bugsby's Marshes and then across the Atlantic to America. Seems like the sensible thing to do. If I'd just murdered three men and stolen thousands o' guns, I'd get out of the country and away from the law as fast as I could. I wouldn't even hang around on the river; I'd be down there as quick as the tide would carry me, and while it was still as dark as it gets, this time o' the year."

"So would I," Monk agreed. "I'd hope to have weighed anchor and be on the high seas before they'd traced which way I'd gone."

Pickering looked puzzled.

"But if I hadn't stolen them," Monk explained. "If I'd bought them legitimately and didn't know anything about murders, I'd go through Liverpool. It would save considerable time, days, rather than go all around the south coast of England before reaching the Atlantic."

Pickering's bristly eyebrows shot up. "You think he didn't do it? So who did, then?"

"I don't know what I think," Monk admitted. "Except that whoever killed those men in Tooley Street did not travel north on one of your trains."

"I can swear to that," Pickering assured him. "And I will, if I'm called. You get that devil, Mr. Monk. That's no way to treat anybody. Whatever it is you think you're fighting for!"

Monk agreed with him, thanked him and took his leave.

He spent the rest of the day and all the following one retracing his steps down the river from Tooley Street as far as Bugsby's Marshes. Again he spoke to everyone who had seen the barge he and Lanyon had tracked the first time, and a good few others who might have. It was exactly the same as before: a heavily laden barge, piled with crates the size and shape to carry muskets, the barge lying low in the water, moving clumsily to begin with but gathering impetus as it increased speed out in the center of the current. Two men, one tall and lean and with a soft, foreign accent—they thought American. Certainly with its pronounced *r*'s and slightly slurred consonants it was not European of any sort. He had seemed to be in charge and was giving the orders.

It had all been done discreetly, even stealthily, hailing no one else, ignoring the usual comradeship of the river men.

Again he lost them at Bugsby's Marshes. He tried several times to find anyone who had seen them beyond Greenwich, or who had seen an oceangoing ship coming, going or moored, but there was nothing.

A waterman shrugged, leaning on his oars, wrinkling his eyes against the glare of the sun off the incoming tide.

"Not so odd really," he said, chewing on his lip. " 'Idden 'round the bend o' Bugsby's Marshes, 'oo'd be lookin'? Lie there all night and not likely ter be seen, if yer lie close in, like. That's wot I'd do . . . if I 'ad business as was private. Then be off on the first o' the tide. Be out ter sea afore breakfast."

Monk thanked him and was about to turn away and walk back towards the Artichoke Tavern when the man called after him.

"Eh! Yer wanner find out wot 'appened ter it?"

Monk swiveled back. "Do you know?"

"Course I don't, or I'd a' told yer. But yer said yer traced it down this far, an' a blind man can see yer think it 'ad suffink valuable in it, suffink stolen."

Monk was impatient.

"Well, 'aven't yer asked them wot 'as the barge?" the waterman said, shaking his head.

"Asked . . ." Then it struck Monk almost like a physical blow. He had followed the trail of the barge as far as Bugsby's Marshes, but his mind had been fixed on Breeland and the guns. He had not thought of the barge's returning upstream to wherever it was now! That might provide proof of Shearer's complicity, and if not where he was now, then at least where he had gone after the murders. Monk could have kicked himself for not having done that straightaway. It seemed Lanyon had not thought of it either. They had both been so convinced that catching Breeland was everything, it had not seemed to matter. Presumably, Breeland's undenied possession of the guns, plus his watch at the scene, had been proof enough without finding out where he had hired the barge, and from whom. That in itself was not incriminating. Breeland would claim he had done so in the hope of being able to purchase the guns in the usual way.

But now it mattered.

"Yes," he said grudgingly. It pricked him to be taught the obvious by a river man whose job it was to row boats and understand tides. "Yes, I'll trace the barge back up. Thank you."

The river man grinned and pushed his cap back farther on his head before picking up his oars again and pulling away.

But even though he spent that evening until dusk, and all the day after, Monk found no trace of the barge's return journey, nor did the river police know anything about a barge stolen or missing.

" 'Appens," a gap-toothed sergeant told him, standing on the dockside in the sun, the tide lapping high at the pier stakes below them. "Mebbe it was stole from someone as stole it 'emselves, so they couldn't say much. Or could be it were put back afore it were missed?"

"Or maybe it belonged to whoever used it," Monk added. "They might have been well paid to keep silent."

"Could be," the sergeant agreed glumly. "Daresay yer'll never know. Sorry I can't 'elp yer. I can't even tell yer w'ere ter begin. There's 'undreds o' wharfs an' docks along the river, an' scores of 'em 'd do yer a favor, if yer paid 'em right, an' keep their mouths shut."

Monk stared across the busy river, light reflecting off the gray water between strings of barges going upstream with the incoming tide. They carried goods from all over the world, everything from timber, coal and machinery, to silks, spices and exotic furs, perhaps cotton from the Confederate states to feed the mills of Manchester and the north, and tobacco for the gentlemen's cigars in Mayfair and Whitehall.

A pleasure boat passed, decks lined with people, their straw hats on against the sun, scarves and handkerchiefs bright. Somewhere a hurdy-gurdy was playing. The air smelled of salt and fish and a whiff of tar.

"Do you know an agent named Shearer?" Monk asked.

The sergeant thought for a few moments. "Tall feller, thin, long nose an' a lot o' teeth?" he asked. "Crooked at the front, like?"

"Actually, I don't know. I've not met him." And he had not seen Judith Alberton to ask her for a physical description. "He worked for Daniel Alberton, in Tooley Street."

"That's the one. Sharp feller. Very quick ter see the advantage in anything."

"Do you know him, professionally, I mean?"

"Criminally, like? No. Too fly for that, an' no need, as I can see. Jus' 'eard of him up an' down the river."

"Do you know anything else about him?" Monk pressed him. "Do you know where he came from? Has he any political beliefs?"

"Political beliefs?" The sergeant looked startled. "Like wot? Anarchist, or the like? Never 'eard 'e were dangerous, 'ceptin' if yer crossed 'im over money. Could be nasty then, but so can a lot o' folk."

"I was thinking of sympathies with either side in the American civil war." Monk knew it sounded ridiculous as he said it, standing side by side with this river sergeant watching the barges nudging each other upstream towards the docks, the commerce of the world coming and going. This was trade, cargo, profit. It was tides, weather, tonnages, who bought and who sold and at what price. Washington and Bull Run were another life.

"Shouldn't think so." The sergeant shrugged. "Shouldn't think 'e even knew there was a war, 'less they bought summink for someone an' wanted it shipped. S'pose that's the guns, eh? Wouldn't think a man like Shearer'd give a toss where they went, long as they were paid for."

That fit in with Monk's theory that Breeland could have paid Shearer with the price of the guns, and Shearer could have been the one who murdered Alberton and took the guns down the river while Breeland himself and Merrit went to Liverpool by train. The only question then was why had Breeland been rash enough to trust Shearer? And obviously he had been right to do so, because the guns had arrived in Washington.

But Monk could not believe it, not without some compelling reason why Breeland would trust Shearer. Yet it seemed there must have been such a fact.

Was there another person involved? Not likely, unless it had in some way been Alberton himself, and he had then been betrayed by Shearer. Breeland had said the note sent to him had been from Shearer, but he would not know that. Anyone could sign Shearer's name.

One thing was absolutely certain: Monk was still a considerable distance from the truth.

He made his way back to Tooley Street and the warehouse. It was busy now. Storage and shipment, buying and selling continued in spite of Alberton's death. Perhaps it was not as thriving as it had been, but his reputation had been excellent, and Casbolt was still alive, although his part in the business had apparently been more to do with purchase.

Monk went in through the open gates with an icy shiver of memory. There was a wagon in the center of the yard, horses shifting restlessly on the cobbles, flies buzzing around, a smell of manure, wood shavings, oil, sweat and tar heavy in the air. Two men were working together lowering a wooden crate from the winch into the back of the wagon, and they finished as he approached them. One lashed the crate firmly so it would not shift; the other went to close the warehouse doors.

"Yeah?" The one at the wagon turned to Monk civilly enough. He was a square, heavy-shouldered man with a mild, blunt face. " 'Elp yer, sir?"

"I hope so. I'm looking for Mr. Shearer. I believe he used to work with Mr. Alberton," Monk replied.

"Yeah, 'e did an' all," the man responded, pushing his hand through what was left of his hair. "Poor Mr. Alberton's dead, murdered. 'Spect you know that, all Lunnon does. But

I ain't seen Shearer for weeks. In fact, not since poor Mr. Alberton were done in, an' that's a fact." He turned to the man coming back from closing the warehouse doors. "Eh, Sandy, feller 'ere's lookin' fer Shearer. Yer see 'im lately? 'Cos I ain't."

Sandy shook his head. "Ain't seen 'im since . . . I dunno. Reckon not in weeks. Mebbe day afore poor Mr. Alberton got done in." His face reflected sadness and an undisguised anger. Monk was surprised how much it pleased him. He had liked Alberton. He had not allowed himself to think about that lately, suppressing it in his concentration on solving the question of who was responsible for Alberton's death and proving exactly how it had been accomplished.

"What was he like?" he asked aloud. Then he realized he had not introduced himself. "My name is Monk. Mrs. Alberton has employed me to help her with regard to Mr. Alberton's death. She believes there is much more to learn about it than we know at present, and there may be other people involved." That was true literally, if not in its implication. He did not wish to tell them it was to clear Merrit of the charge of murder. They might well believe her guilty. If the newspapers were accurate, which was highly debatable, the general public had little doubt as to her involvement.

"Eh! Bert! Over 'ere!" Sandy called to a third man, who had appeared at the warehouse doors. "Come an' 'elp this gent 'ere. 'E's workin' fer Mrs. Alberton."

That was sufficient to make Bert move with alacrity. Whether they knew Judith personally or not, mention of her name ensured complete cooperation.

"Wot yer reckon ter Shearer, then?" Sandy prompted. " 'Ow would yer describe 'im fer someone as 'ad never met 'im an' knew nuffink?"

Bert considered carefully before he answered. "Clever," he said at last. "Clever as a rat."

"Eye ter the best chance," the first man added, nodding sagely.

"Ambitious?" Monk asked.

They all three nodded.

"Greedy?" Monk ventured.

"Gonna get 'is share," Bert agreed. "Never knowed 'im ter cheat, though, ter be fair."

"Don't do ter cheat, not if yer get caught at it," Sandy added. "This sort o' business yer'll be lucky ter land in the clink. More like facedown in the river. But I never knowed 'im ter cheat, neither. Can't say as I ever 'eard 'e did."

"Had ambitions, but not dishonest as far as you know," Monk summed up.

"S'right, guv. There's another five 'undred guns was 'ere, an' they're gorn too. But we reckoned as 'ooever was 'ere took 'em all. You think as Shearer 'ad summink to do wif doin' in the gaffer?" the first man asked, squinting a little at Monk. "Papers says as it were that Yankee."

"I'm not sure," Monk said honestly. "Breeland got the guns, no doubt about that, but I'm not sure he actually killed Mr. Alberton."

"Then 'ow'd 'e get 'em?" Sandy said reasonably. "An' if it weren't for them guns, why'd anyone do 'im like that? That ain't even a decent way ter kill anyone. That's . . ." He searched in vain for a word.

"Barbaric," Monk supplied.

"Yeah . . . that an' all."

Bert nodded vigorously.

"Yer reckon as Shearer 'ad summink ter do wif it?" Sandy persisted. "An' then he scarpered, like? 'Cos nobody 'round 'ere's seen 'im since then."

"Does it fit in with what you know of him?" Monk asked.

They looked at each other, then back again. "Yeah, near enough," Sandy agreed. "Don' it?"

"Yeah. If the money were right," Bert added. " 'Ave ter be. 'E wouldn't do it fer nuffink. Sort o' liked the gaffer, in 'is own way. 'Ave ter be a lot." He bit his lip. "Still an' all, the way it were done. I don't see Shearer doin' it like that. That 'ad ter be the Yankee."

"What about for the price of six thousand first-class rifled muskets?" Monk persisted.

"Well—s'pose so. That's a lot o' money in any man's reckonin'," Sandy acknowledged.

"Could he have sympathized with the Union cause?" Monk tried a last question on the subject.

They all looked mystified.

"Against slaving," Monk explained. "To keep all the states of America as one country."

"We don't 'ave no slaving in England," Sandy pointed out. "Least not black slaving," he added wryly. "There's some as thinks they got it 'ard. An' as for the states o' America, why should we care? Let 'em do whatever they likes, I says."

Bert shook his head. "I'd be agin slavery. In't right."

"Me too," the first man added. "Can't say as Shearer gave a toss, though, not so as ter kill anyone over it, like."

"Do you know where Shearer lives?" Monk asked them.

"New Church Street, just off Bermondsey Low Road," Bert replied. "Dunno the number, but ends in a three, as I recall. About 'alfway along."

"Was he married?"

"Shearer? Not likely!"

Monk thanked them and left the yard to try New Church Street.

It took him nearly half an hour to find where Shearer had lived, and an irate landlady who had waited three weeks with an empty property.

"Bin 'ere near on nine year, 'e 'ad!" she said belligerently. "Then ups and goes Gawd knows where, an' without a by-your-leave! Says nothing to nobody, an' left all 'is rubbish 'ere fer me ter clear out. Lorst three weeks o' rent money, I did." Her eyes glared stonily at Monk. "You a friend o' 'is, then?"

"No," Monk lied quickly. "He owes me money too."

She laughed abruptly. "Well, yer got no chance 'ere, 'cos I got nuffink an' I ain't partin' wif the li'l I got from sellin' 'is clothes ter the rag an' bone, an' I tell yer that fer nothin'."

"Do you think something could have happened to him?"

Her thin eyebrows shot up.

"That one? Not likely! Too fly by 'alf, 'im. Got a better offer an' took it, I s'pec. Or the rozzers is after 'im." She looked Monk up and down. "That wot you are, a rozzer?"

"I told you, he owes me money."

"Yeah? Well, I never knew a rozzer wot was close kin ter the truth. But if 'e owes yer money, I reckon as 'e's in for trouble if yer finds 'im, like. Yer look like trouble ter me."

Monk had an instant of recollection, as if someone else had said exactly the same to him, but it was gone before he could place it. Such jolts of memory from before the accident were becoming fewer, and he no longer actively searched for them or tried to hold them with him. What she had said was probably true. He did not forgive easily, and if someone had cheated him, he would have pursued the culprit to the last hiding place and exacted what was due. But that was a long time ago. Then his carriage had overturned, robbing him of all his past, in the summer of 1856. In the five years since he had built a new life, a new set of memories and characteristics.

He thanked her and left. There was nothing more to be learned here. Shearer had disappeared. What mattered was where he had gone, and why. Tomorrow he would speak with dockers and bargees who would have known him. He might even find where the barge had come from that had taken the guns down the river. Then he would go on to the shipping offices Shearer would have dealt with to export Alberton's guns, or machinery and whatever else he traded in.

That evening he told Hester a little of what he had learned.

"Do you think it was Shearer who actually killed Mr. Alberton?" she asked with a lift of hope in her voice.

They were sitting at the table over a meal of cold chicken pie and fresh vegetables. He noticed that she looked a little tired.

"Where have you been all day?" he asked.

"Do you?" she insisted.

"What?"

"Do you think Shearer killed Daniel Alberton?"

227

"Possibly. Where have you been?"

"At the Small Pox Hospital at Highgate. We're still trying to improve the quality of staff caring for the patients there, but it's difficult. I've been writing letters most of the time."

It was on the edge of his tongue to make some remark about Florence Nightingale, who was inexhaustible in her letter writing in her efforts to bring about hospital reform, but he forbore. It explained Hester's tiredness. He had promised months ago to employ a woman to keep house, and forgotten about it.

"It would mean Merrit was not guilty," she said, watching him keenly. "It would explain how Breeland did it without her knowledge."

He smiled. "You'd like that, wouldn't you." It was a statement.

She hesitated only a moment. "Yes," she admitted. "I can't see any way he is innocent, but I really want to believe she is."

He relaxed a little. "You should start looking for someone to come in every day, even if it's only for a few hours."

She thought about it for several minutes, watching his face, trying to judge if he was being overgenerous.

He could read her thoughts as if they were written in front of him.

"Look for someone," he repeated. "Maybe three days a week, long enough to clean and do some cooking."

"Yes," she accepted. "Yes, I will." She looked at him very levelly, a smile beginning in her eyes.

He felt remarkably pleased, as if he had given her the best gift imaginable, and perhaps it was, because his real gift was time to devote to what she was good at, time to use the skills she possessed in abundance, instead of laboring to develop those she would never find natural. He smiled back, more and more broadly.

She knew his thoughts too. She bit her lip. "I can cook!" she said quickly. "Moderately."

He did not argue; he just grinned.

* * *

In the morning he began on the river, speaking to dockers and bargees yet again, this time not about the movement of the guns but about Shearer. It took him till early afternoon to find anyone who knew Shearer and was willing to talk about him, but all he could say reinforced what Monk had already heard from the men at the warehouse. Shearer was hard, ambitious, competent, but to all outward appearances loyal to Daniel Alberton. He was not spoken of with liking, but there was a definite respect in the men's faces and in the tone of their voices.

It left Monk further confused. The picture of Shearer that emerged did not sit easily with the facts. He walked along the street almost unconscious of the passing traffic, the heavily laden wagons, the men shouting to one another, the cranes rising and lowering, the jostling crowds of masts as the tide jiggled the boats, the occasional gull wheeling overhead.

Shearer had disappeared, that seemed unarguable. The guns had gone to America, as had Breeland and Merrit. Alberton and the two guards were dead, murdered.

The barge with the guns had gone down the river towards Bugsby's Marshes, and was untraceable after that. Breeland and Merrit seemed to have traveled by train to Liverpool, but the only train in which they could have gone had left before the murders, and thus before the guns had left the warehouse.

It seemed Shearer's involvement was the only fact which could link all three things together and make any kind of sense of them.

Someone must know more of Shearer, and might even know of the ship which had come up the Thames as far as Bugsby's Marshes and loaded the guns and then weighed anchor and gone out to sea again. Was it a British ship or an American one?

Perhaps what he had already learned would be enough to raise reasonable doubt as to Merrit's guilt, if there were no prejudice and jurors were able to disregard their emotions. But it would certainly not be sufficient to clear her name. There would always be those who would believe her guilty, simply that it had not been proved. She had got away with it. That was only a little better than hanging, a kind of life in limbo. Although if she returned to America with Breeland, perhaps England's opinion of her would matter less.

But was it also enough to save Breeland from the rope, against the hatred there was for him, the conviction in the public's mind that he was guilty? And would he inevitably drag her down with him?

Not that it made any difference to what Monk had to do. Probabilities of a verdict one way or the other were Rathbone's business, although he was certain Rathbone would want to know the truth as much as he did. Someone had bound up three men and shot them through the head. He needed to know who that someone was, beyond any doubt at all, reasonable or not.

He went into the nearest shipping office and asked to speak to the clerks.

"Shearer?" A young man in a tight jacket repeated the name. "Oh, yes, very good fellow. Agent for Mr. Alberton." He sucked in his breath. "Terrible business, that. Awful. Thank goodness they got the man who did it. Kidnapped the daughter too, by all accounts." He made a clicking sound with his tongue.

"When did you last see Shearer?" Monk asked.

The clerk thought for a few minutes. "Doesn't deal with us a lot," he replied. "Certainly I haven't seen him for a couple of months or more. I expect he's very busy, what with poor Mr. Alberton gone. Don't know what's going to happen to the business. Good reputation, but won't be the same without Mr. Alberton himself. Very reliable, he was. Knew a lot about shipping, and trade too. Knew who had what, and always paid a fair price, but nobody's fool. Can't replace that, even though Mr. Casbolt is brilliant at the buying, so I hear. Terrible shame."

"I can't find anybody who has seen Shearer since Mr. Alberton's death," Monk told him.

The clerk looked surprised. "Well, I never. Knew he thought the world of Mr. Alberton, but didn't think he'd go off like that. Thought he'd stay around to look after the business best he could, for the widow's sake, poor woman. Goes to show, you never know, do you?"

"No. Who did Shearer deal with mostly, if not you?"

"Pocock and Aldridge, up on the West India Dock Road. Big place. Ask anyone."

Monk thanked him and left. It was some distance to the West India docks, so he took the first hansom he saw and arrived twenty-five minutes later. He paid the driver and alighted, then turned towards the building, and suddenly he knew exactly what it would be like inside, as if he had visited it frequently and this were only one more routine call.

It was unnerving. He had no idea why he would have come here, or when. It was no time he could recall since the accident. He strode across the pavement, almost bumping into a thin man in gray, and without apologizing, he went up the few steps and pulled the door open.

Inside was completely strange to him, not as he had seen it in his mind's eye at all. The proportions were more or less the same, but there was a desk where he had not seen it, the walls were the wrong color, and the floor, which had been the most individual feature, tiled in gray-and-white marble, was now wooden.

He stopped abruptly, confused.

"Mornin', sir. Can I 'elp yer?" the man behind the desk asked.

Monk collected himself with difficulty. He found he was fumbling for words, trying to bring himself back to the present.

"Yes . . . I need to speak to . . ." The name Taunton came into his mind, but he had no idea from where.

"Yes, sir? 'Oo was it yer wanted?" the man asked helpfully.

"Do you have a Mr. Taunton here?"

"Yes, sir. Would that be the elder Mr. Taunton or the younger?"

Monk had no idea. But he must answer. He went with instinct rather than sense.

"The elder."

"Yes, sir. What name shall I say?"

"Monk. William Monk."

"Right, sir. If yer'd care ter wait, sir, I'll tell 'im."

The message came back within minutes, and Monk was directed up a stair that curved graciously onto a landing. He could not remember what the man in the hall had said, but he had no hesitation in turning left and walking to the end of the corridor. This was familiar, a little smaller than he recalled, but he even knew the feel of the handle when he touched it, recalled the catch as the door stuck before it swung wide.

The man inside the comfortable room was standing. There was surprise in his face, and unease in the angles of his body. He was a little older than Monk, perhaps fifty. His hair was receding, auburn in color, his cheeks ruddy. Monk knew that Mr. Taunton the younger was his half brother, not his son, a taller, darker man with a sallow complexion.

"Well, well," Taunton said nervously. "After all these years! What brings you here, Monk? Thought I'd seen the last of you." He looked puzzled, as if Monk's appearance confused him. He could not help staring, first at Monk's face, then at his clothes, even his boots.

Monk realized that Taunton was older than he had expected. He could not recall him with a full head of hair, but the gray in it was new, the lines in his face, a certain coarsening of features. He had no idea how long it had been since they had last met, or what the circumstances were. Was it to do with police work, or even before that? That would make it twenty years or more, well into the past that Monk had lost completely, not even patched together from fragments learned here and there, people he had come across in investigations since the accident.

He could not afford to trust that Taunton was a friend; he could not assume that of anyone. The little he knew of his life showed he had earned more fear than love. There might be all manner of old debts left unpaid, his and others'. This was a time when he wished fiercely that he knew himself better, knew who were his enemies, and why, knew their weaknesses. He was without armor, without weapons.

He searched Taunton's face, and saw no warmth in it. The expression was guarded, careful, but already there was a beginning of pleasure, as if he had seen a vulnerability in Monk, and it pleased him.

Monk racked his mind for something to say that would not betray his ignorance.

"The place has changed." He played for time, hoping Taunton would let slip some information, so at least he would know how long ago they had last met, perhaps even the mood, whether their enmity was open or concealed. Because with every passing second he was more and more certain that it was enmity.

"Twenty-one years, I make it," Taunton said with a faint curl of his lip. "We're doing well. Did you think we couldn't have the odd renovation here and there?"

Monk looked around the office. It was well appointed, but not luxurious. He allowed his observation of it to reflect in his expression—unimpressed.

The color deepened in Taunton's cheeks.

"You've changed too," he said with a faint sneer. "No more fancy shirts and boots. Thought you'd have had everything made 'specially for you by now. Fall on hard times, did you?" There was a keen undertone of pleasure in his voice, almost relish. "Dundas take you down with him, did he?"

Dundas. With blinding clarity Monk saw the gentle face, the intelligent, clear blue eyes with laughter deep in the lines around them. Then as quickly it was overtaken by grief and a raging helplessness. He knew Dundas was dead. He had been fifty, perhaps fifty-five. Monk himself had been in his twenties, aspiring to be a merchant banker. Arrol Dundas was his mentor, ruined in some financial crash, blamed for it, wrongly. He had died in prison.

Monk wanted to smash the sneering face in front of him. He felt the rage burn up inside him, knotting his body, making it difficult even to swallow, his throat was so tight. He must control it, hide it from Taunton. Hide everything until he knew enough to act and foresee the results.

How much did Taunton know of Monk since then? Did he know he had joined the police? Monk could not be sure. His reputation had spread widely. He had been one of the best and most ruthless detectives they had had, but he might never have had occasion to work here in the West India docks.

"A little change of direction," he answered the question obliquely. "I had certain debts to collect." He allowed himself a smile, wolfish, as he intended it to be.

Taunton swallowed. His eyes flicked up and down Monk's very ordinary clothes, the ones he had chosen in order to be inconspicuous on the river and in the docks.

"Doesn't look like they amounted to much," he observed.

"I haven't collected them all yet," Monk answered, the words out before he gave them thought.

Taunton was rigid, his hands moving restlessly by his sides, his eyes never leaving Monk's face.

"I don't owe you anything, Monk! And after twenty-one years, I don't know who does." He let out a little snort. "We always did very well by you. Everybody made their profit. No one got caught, far as I know."

Caught! The word struck Monk like a physical blow. Caught by whom? Over what? He did not dare ask. What had Dundas been accused of in the end, what was it that had ruined him? Monk could remember only the fury he had felt, and the absolute conviction that Dundas was innocent, blamed wrongly, and he, Monk, should have known some way to prove it.

But was it something to do with Taunton? Or did Taunton know about it because everyone did?

Monk hungered to have the truth, all of it, more than almost anything else he could think of. It had haunted him ever since the first shafts of memory had struck him, fragments, emotions, small moments of recollection gone before he could perceive anything more than an impression, a feeling, a look on someone's face, the inflection of a voice,

234

and always the sense of loss, a guilt that he should have been able to prevent it.

"Worried?" he asked, staring back at Taunton.

"Not in the least," Taunton replied, and they both knew it was a lie. It hung in the air between them.

For once Monk was pleased that he inspired fear. Too often his ability to intimidate had disturbed him, made him feel guilty for that part of him which must have liked it in the past.

"Know a man named Shearer?" He changed the subject abruptly, not to discomfort Taunton but because he did not know what else to say to him about the past. Above all Taunton must not guess that Monk himself did not know.

"Shearer?" Taunton was startled. "Walter Shearer?"

"That's right. You do know him." That was a statement.

"Of course I do. But you wouldn't have come here if you didn't know that already," Taunton answered. He frowned. "He's an agent for shipping machinery and heavy goods, marble, timber, guns mostly . . . for Daniel Alberton—or he was, until Alberton was murdered." His voice dropped. "What's that to do with you? Are you in guns now?" He shifted his weight slightly.

Monk could smell fear, sudden and sharp, physical rather than the slow anxiety there had been before. Taunton's imagination had taken a leap forward. When he spoke again his voice was a pitch higher, as if his throat had tightened till he could scarcely breathe.

"Is it something to do with you, Monk? Because if it is, I want no part of it!" He was shaking his head, stepping backwards. "Working for men who make their money slaving is one thing, but murder is something else. You can swing for that. Alberton was well liked. Every man's hand'll be against you. I don't know where Shearer is, and I don't want to. He's a hard man, gives no quarter and asks none, but he's no killer."

Monk felt as if he had been hit so hard his lungs were paralyzed, starved for air.

Taunton's voice rose even higher. "Look, Monk, what

happened to Dundas was nothing to do with me. We made our deal, and we both kept our sides of it. I don't owe you anything, and you don't owe me. If you cheated Dundas, that's between you and . . . and the grave, now. Don't come after me!" He held up his hands as if to ward off a blow. "And I want nothing to do with those guns! There's a rope waiting at the end of those. I'm not shipping them for you, I swear on my life!"

Monk found his voice at last.

"I haven't got the guns, you fool! I'm looking for the man who killed Alberton. I know where the guns are. They're in America. I followed them there."

Taunton was stunned—nonplussed.

"Then what do you want? Why are you here?"

"I want to know who killed Alberton."

Taunton shook his head. "Why?"

For a moment Monk could not answer. Was that really what he had been like, a man who did not care that three men had been murdered, or who had done it? Did his need to know require explaining?

Taunton was still staring at him, waiting for the answer.

"It doesn't matter to you." Monk jerked himself out of his thoughts. "Where is Shearer?"

"I don't know! I haven't seen him for close on two months. I'd tell you if I knew, just to get rid of you. Believe me!"

Monk did believe him; the fear in his eyes was real, the smell of it in the room. Taunton would have given up anyone, friend or foe, to save himself.

How had Monk ever been willing to trade with such a man? And worse than that, larger and far uglier, to make profit by trading with a man whose money came from slaving! Had Dundas known that? Or had Monk misled him, as Taunton implied?

Either thought made him sick.

He needed the truth, and he was afraid of it. There was no point in seeking an answer from Taunton; he did not know. What he believed of Monk was indictment enough.

Monk shrugged and turned on his heel, going out without

236

speaking again. But as he walked past the man at the desk in the hall, his thoughts were not on Taunton, or Shearer, but on Hester and her face in his mind's eye as she had spoken of slavery. To her it was unforgivable. What would she feel if she knew what he now knew of himself?

Already the thought of it bowed him down, crushed him inside. He walked out into the sun, and was cold.

9

FOR THE FIRST TIME since he had been married, Monk was reluctant to go home, and because he dreaded it, he did it immediately. He did not want time to think any more than he had to. There was no possibility of avoiding seeing Hester, meeting her eyes and having to build the first lie between them. Earlier in their knowledge of each other they had fought bitterly. He had thought her opinionated, quick-tongued and cold-natured, a woman whose passion was all bent towards the improvement of others, whether they wished it or not.

And she had thought him selfish, arrogant and essentially cruel. This morning he would have smiled at how happy they both were. Now it twisted inside him like a torn muscle, a pain reaching into everything, blinding all other pleasures.

He opened the door and closed it behind him.

She was there, straightaway, giving him no time to recompose his thoughts. All his earlier words fled.

She misunderstood, thinking it to do with his search along the river.

"You found something ugly," she said quickly. "What is it? To do with Breeland? Even if he's guilty, that doesn't mean Merrit is." There was so much conviction in her voice he knew she was frightened that somehow she was mistaken, and Merrit had played a willing part.

It was the perfect chance to tell her what he had really found, uglier than she could imagine, but about himself, not

Breeland. He could not do it. There was a beauty in her he could not bear to lose. He remembered her in Manassas, bending over the soldier, half covered in blood, tending to his wounds, willing him to live, sharing his pain and giving him her strength.

What would she think of a man who had made money out of dealing with the profits of slaving? He had never been more ashamed of anything in his life, anything he knew about. Or more afraid of what it would now cost him . . . and he realized that was the most precious thing he would ever have.

"William! What is it?" There was an edge of fear in her voice and in her eyes. "What did you find?"

She was concerned for Merrit, and perhaps for Judith Alberton. She could not guess that it was her own life that was threatened, her happiness, not theirs.

The truth stuck in his throat.

"Nothing conclusive." He swallowed. "I didn't find any trace of the barge coming back up the river. I've no idea whose it was. Probably someone who lent it willingly, or it was stolen from someone who daren't report it. Or maybe they stole it themselves." He wanted to touch her, as he usually did, feel the warmth of her body, the eagerness of her response, but self-disgust held him back, closing him in like a vise.

She moved back again, a flicker of hurt in her face.

It was the first taste of the overwhelming loneliness to come, like the fading of the sun before nightfall.

"Hester!"

She looked up.

He had no idea what to say. He could not face the truth. He had had no time yet to work out what words to use.

"I think Shearer may be the one who killed Alberton." It was a lame thing to fill the place of what was in his mind. It was hardly a revelation.

She looked a little puzzled. "Well, it would explain the odd time with the train, I suppose," she conceded. "A conspiracy between Shearer and Breeland which Merrit did not know about? Perhaps she and Breeland were at the yard earlier, and that was when she dropped the watch?" Then her face clouded. "But why would they go there? It doesn't make sense. Why was Daniel Alberton there anyway, at that time of night?" She frowned. "Was it something to do with Merrit running away, do you suppose? And he was still there when Shearer came to steal the guns?" She shook her head. "It doesn't sound likely, does it?"

It did not. There was still some major fact they were missing. He had to concentrate hard to make himself feel that it mattered.

"Are you hungry?" she asked, her eyes bright again.

"Yes," he lied. He guessed she had gone to some trouble. Now that he thought about it, there was a warm, savory odor coming from the kitchen.

She smiled. "Fresh game pie and vegetables." She looked pleased with herself. "I found a woman today. She's Scottish. Her name is Mrs. Patrick. She's a bit fierce, but she's a terrific cook, and she's prepared to come every weekday afternoon for three hours, which is good, because most people like to do all day or not at all. Some even expect to live in." She searched his face. "She's half a crown a week. Do you think that will be all right?"

He did not even think to add it up. "Excellent! Yes. If you like her, then make it permanent."

"Thank you." Her voice lifted. "I do appreciate it." She touched him lightly, but there was intimacy in it, a sweetness that sent his pulse racing, and a pain through him at his deception. He had no idea how he was going to live with it. An hour at a time, then a day at a time. Maybe he would learn to forget it for whole periods. He would probably never know exactly what he had done with Taunton, if he had betrayed Arrol Dundas or not, or what had driven him to it. It might have been as simple as greed, the desire for the power of success. Or possibly there was some mitigating circumstance—if only he knew it!

He followed her into the kitchen, pleasantly cool with the

back windows open and full of the delicious aromas of expertly seasoned food. In other circumstances it would have been a perfect meal. It took all the skill he possessed, all the self-mastery, to pretend it was.

Hester was unaware of the turmoil within Monk. She believed it was no more than the frustration of a case he could not understand which made him shrink away, and she resolved to play her own part in the detecting as soon as possible.

By the time he left the following morning, still in search of more knowledge of Shearer, she had determined what to do. Dressed in her best morning gown of pale blue-gray muslin, she set out to visit Robert Casbolt. She had no doubt he would see her, because of the depth of his regard for Judith Alberton, and for Merrit. He could not fail to know how desperate the situation was, and regardless of his other commitments, he would make time to help.

She knew where he lived because he had mentioned it that first evening at dinner. She arrived shortly after nine o'clock in the morning and gave her card to the butler, with a respectful note written across the back saying simply that she felt it most urgent to speak with him at his earliest convenience, in Merrit Alberton's interest.

She was kept waiting only fifteen minutes, then shown into a beautiful sitting room full of warm colors. The walls were paneled with mellow oak, and a red Persian rug covered the floor in front of the huge, stone-manteled fireplace, which at this time of the year was half hidden by a tapestry screen. The sofa and chairs were all odd, some covered in velvet, some in brocade and one in honey-colored leather, but the whole effect was one of the greatest comfort. There were two tall lamps, of different sizes, but both with brass columns and large hexagonal shades fringed in deep gold.

Casbolt himself was dressed casually, but obviously with care. His linen was immaculate, his soft indoor boots polished and shining.

"How good of you to come, Mrs. Monk," he said earnestly. "After you have already done so much. Judith told me that your husband is still working almost night and day to find some way of proving Merrit's innocence. What can I do to help? If I knew of anything at all, believe me, I would have done it."

She had already planned carefully what she intended to say.

"I have been giving a great deal of thought to the matter for which Mrs. Alberton first engaged my husband's services," she said, accepting the seat he offered her but declining any refreshment. She did not need the excuse of a social amenity to keep his interest. No pretense was necessary between them.

He looked startled, almost as if he were not sure of her meaning. He sat down opposite her, on the edge of the chair rather than leaning back. There was no relaxing in him at all.

"Whoever was willing to resort to blackmail to obtain the guns may have taken it a step further, do you not think?" she explained.

His face cleared, then he frowned again. "Has Mr. Monk found some evidence which suggests Breeland is not guilty after all? Surely the fact that he has the guns precludes that possibility?"

"Of course he is involved," she agreed. "And perhaps we are seeing something more than is there because we all so badly wish Merrit to be innocent. We are trying to think of any solution that excludes her. . . ."

"Of course!" he agreed. His face had a crumpled, hurt look, as if the optimism in his voice were at odds with his belief. Hester wondered if he knew a side to Merrit they did not, and it was that which now caused him to hesitate. Then he smiled. "I think Merrit may have been completely duped by Breeland. She is young, and in love. One does not always see clearly. And all the experience she has had is with honorable people." He looked down at the rich carpet on the floor, then up again quickly. "I know she quarreled very badly with her father, but believe me, Mrs. Monk, Daniel Alberton was a totally honorable man, a man whose word anyone could trust absolutely and who would never stoop to a cruel or greedy act. She was angry with him, but she spoke in haste

243

and the heat of emotion. In her heart she knows, just as I do, that he was as good a man as walks the earth."

She met his gaze very frankly. "What are you telling me, Mr. Casbolt? That she could not imagine duplicity, therefore Breeland could easily have misled her; or that she loved her father too much to have been party to hurting him, regardless of her anger that evening?"

"I suppose I'm telling you both, Mrs. Monk." A sad, self-mocking expression filled his face. "Or that I care very much for the outcome of this tragedy, and I would do anything to spare the family further pain."

There was no way she could be unaware of the power of his feelings. The air between them was charged with the knowledge of fear, horror, the grief of loneliness. In that moment Hester glimpsed the reality of Casbolt's involvement with the Albertons, and the depth of his lifelong love and devotion to his cousin.

But she was not here to offer sympathy or encouragement.

"Could Breeland have been part of the attempt at blackmail?" she asked. "He seemed willing to do anything at all to get the guns. He is a man whose belief in his cause seems to him to justify anything. He would see it as helping to preserve the Union and freeing slaves."

Casbolt's eyes widened very slightly. "I had not thought of it, but it is possible. Except how could he know of Gilmer, and Daniel's kindness to him?"

"Any number of ways," she responded. "Someone obviously knew."

"But he had only been in England a few weeks at that time."

"How do you know that?"

He drew in his breath slowly. "I don't!"

"And he could have had allies. Whatever the truth of it," she pointed out, "it seems Breeland was on a special night train to Liverpool and could not actually have killed Mr. Alberton himself. And Merrit was with him, so that excludes her also, thank heaven."

He leaned forward. "Are you sure? Mrs. Monk, please,

please don't raise Judith's hopes unless there is no doubt whatever . . . you understand it would be unbearably cruel."

"Of course. I understand. This is why I came to you, not to her," she said quickly. "And because I can speak to you more frankly about Mrs. Alberton. But do you think it is possible that the whole blackmail attempt is connected with the final theft of the guns—whether it was an unsuccessful attempt by Breeland, or even by Mr. Trace?"

His eyes widened.

"Trace? Yes . . . it could be. He is . . . devious enough . . . for that." Then he frowned. "But even if it were so, how would that help Merrit? And to be honest, Mrs. Monk, that is really all I care about. I am not concerned with justice. I hope I don't shock you in saying that. I am sorry if I do. Daniel was my friend, and I need to see his murderers brought to justice, but not at the cost of further loss to his widow and daughter. He was my best friend from youth, and I knew him well. I believe their welfare is what would have concerned him far above any revenge for his death. And that is all it would be now." He looked at her earnestly, searching her eyes for understanding.

She tried to think how she would feel in Judith's place. Would she care above all things that Monk be avenged, or would their child's safety and happiness come first? If she were killed, would she want Monk to pursue vengeance for her?

The answer to that came immediately. No. She would want the living protected. Let time take care of justice.

"I see you understand," he said softly. "I thought you would." There was gentleness in his voice, and relief. He could not hide it, and perhaps he did not want to.

But she could not let go of the truth, the need to worry at the problem until she had unraveled it. She would decide afterwards who to tell and what decisions to make.

"I wonder why they asked for the guns to be delivered to Baskin and Company, instead of direct to them. Do you suppose they believed Mr. Alberton had some reason not to sell to one side or the other in the American war?"

He understood exactly what she meant. "I know of none. But it would suggest someone who was unfamiliar with his family history. Anyone who knew him would never imagine he would do business that would profit pirates, however indirectly. So you are right in that it may be an American rather than someone British." He shook his head a little. "But I don't see how that helps Merrit. In fact, I don't even see how it brings us any closer to the truth. What we need is something that shows Merrit had no knowledge of Breeland's intention to harm Daniel. Either that, or that she knew but was unable to help. She was under threat herself, or imprisoned in some way."

"We couldn't prove that because it is quite obviously untrue," she pointed out. "She went with him willingly, and is still prepared to defend him. She believes he is innocent."

"She believes it because she has to." He shook his head and smiled very slightly. "I've known Merrit since she was born. She is the closest I have to a child of my own. I know she is passionate and willful, and when she gives herself to something, or someone, it is wholeheartedly, and not always wisely. I have watched her through a love of horses, the determination to be a nun and then a missionary in Africa, and a deep infatuation with the local doctor, a very nice young man who was quite unaware of her regard." Amusement and affection lit his face. "Mercifully, it passed without incident, or embarrassment." He shrugged. "I think it is all part of growing up. I seem to remember a few turbulent emotions myself which I blush to recall now, and certainly will not speak of."

Hester could do the same, including the vicar she had mentioned to Monk. She had also had periods of being quite convinced nobody loved her or understood her feelings, least of all her parents.

"Nevertheless," she persisted, "the blackmail attempt was quite real. If it was not either Breeland or Trace, then it was someone else. Could it have been Mr. Shearer, the agent?"

He was startled. "Shearer? Why . . ." He stared at her intently. "Yes, it could, Mrs. Monk. It is a very disagreeable thought, but it is not at all impossible. Shearer acting as intermediary for pirates, and when that did not work, then for Breeland!" His voice rose. "And if Breeland himself cannot have killed poor Daniel, then perhaps Shearer did? Certainly he seems to have left London since Daniel's death. I have not seen him since a day or two before. That would explain a great deal . . . and best of all, it would account for Merrit's belief that Breeland is innocent."

The quiet room seemed to glow around them. A bowl of golden midseason roses shone amber and apricot, reflected in the polished surface of the table beneath. The grace of a Targ horse filled an alcove.

"Poor Daniel," he said quietly. "He trusted Shearer. He was ambitious, always looking for the advantage, driving the hardest bargain for shipping of any man on the river, and believe me, that is saying a great deal. But Daniel thought he was loyal, and I confess, so did I." His lips twisted in a bitter grimace. "But then I suppose the greatest betrayals are from where they are least expected."

Another thought occurred to Hester, one she would far rather not have entertained, but it would not be dismissed.

"Do you have any control over who buys the guns, Mr. Casbolt?"

"Not legally, but I suppose effectively I do. If Daniel had done something I found intolerable I could have overridden it. Why do you ask? He never did, or anything even questionable."

"Would you have sold them to the pirates?"

"No." Again he was meeting her eyes with candor and a fierce intensity. "And if you are thinking that Daniel would, then you are mistaken. Judith would never have borne it, after what happened to her brother. Nor would I. And Daniel would not have done it even if she had never known. Believe me, he hated the pirates as much as we did." He looked down for a moment. "I'm sorry if I sound harsh, Mrs. Monk, but you did not know Daniel or you would not have asked. What they did to her brother was monstrous. Daniel would not give them air to breathe, let alone guns to continue their crimes. Nor would I have allowed it, whatever the threat or the price."

Hester believed him, but she could not help wondering if perhaps Daniel Alberton had needed the sale sufficiently to connive at it, and hope Judith would never know. With the American war, guns appeared to be scarce, and at a premium. She did not wish to believe it. She had liked Alberton. But she knew people would do desperate things if faced with ruin, not even so much for the loss of material goods as for the shame of failure.

"Thank you, Mr. Casbolt, you have been very kind in giving me so much of your time."

"Mrs. Monk, please do not pursue this idea any further. I knew Daniel Alberton better than any man, in some ways even better than his wife did. Nothing in the world would have persuaded him to sell guns to any pirate on earth, and least of all to those in the Mediterranean. You have met Judith. You must have some sense of what a remarkable woman she is, how . . . how . . ." It was obvious in his face that he could find no words adequate to name the qualities he saw in her. "Daniel adored her!" he said fiercely, his voice thick with emotion. "He would have lived out his days in debtors' prison rather than break her trust by doing such a thing. He was a most honorable man, and . . . and she loved him for it. He . . . this is difficult for me to say, Mrs. Monk." He shook his head very slightly, as if to dismiss some cloud around him. "He did not have great passion or wit, great imagination . . . but he was a man you could trust with anything and everything you possessed. Could you not sense that for yourself, even in the brief time you knew him?" His smile was twisted with pain. The agony in him seemed to fill the room. "Or am I thinking you could see in a few hours what I saw in half a lifetime?"

She was embarrassed for her thoughts, and ashamed of having allowed him to see them.

"I imagine it will prove as absurd as you say." She made it half an apology, in tone if not in words. "Perhaps if we could find Mr. Shearer it would give us the solution."

A strange bitterness filled his face for a moment, then vanished.

"I have no doubt that that is true. Who knows what hungers drive a man to the betrayal of those who trust him? Please just do what you can to save Merrit, Mrs. Monk, for Judith's sake. It is something I cannot do." He swallowed. "I don't have the skill. I can care for her in many other ways, ways of business affairs and seeing that she is provided for and that she always has the respect of society. But . . ."

"Of course," she promised quickly, rising to her feet. "I shall do it for Merrit's sake also. We worked side by side for a little while on the battlefield. I know her courage. And I like her."

He relaxed a little. "Thank you," he said quietly, standing also. "Please God that Monk will find Shearer, or at least proof of his part in this."

When she spoke of her thoughts to Monk he found the idea of Alberton's having connived to sell guns to the pirates repellent, but he was obliged to consider the possibility. She saw the wince of pain in his face as they sat over Mrs. Patrick's excellent supper, which included a rhubarb pie whose pastry melted in the mouth.

She saw the darkness in his face. It had been there the previous evening also, and she wondered if the same fear had occurred to him then, and he had been unwilling to say so. He had liked Alberton instinctively, more than most clients, and his death had left a sense of loss as well as anger. But there was no way to blunt the thought. Only the truth could banish it . . . perhaps.

"What did Casbolt say?" he asked her.

"He denied that it was possible. He said Alberton adored Judith and would rather have gone to debtors' prison than deal with pirates." She hesitated.

"But . . ." he prompted.

"But he was Alberton's closest friend and he could not bear to think he would betray Judith like that. Or that he was . . . so much less than they all believed him. He's very loyal. And . . ." She smiled very faintly at the memory of Casbolt's face in the beautiful, glowing room, the intensity of the emotion filling his body as he sat on the edge of his seat. "And he is pretty devoted to Judith himself. He would do anything to protect her from further hurt."

"Including lying to hide Alberton's guilt?" he pressed.

"I should think so," she answered frankly, weighing her words and aware that she believed them true. "It would also be a matter of protecting the reputation of a dead friend, for Judith's sake too. I can understand that, even if I don't know whether I would do it myself or not."

His eyes widened. "At the expense of the truth? You!"

She looked back at him, trying to read his expression, but not with any intent to moderate how she answered.

"I don't know. Not all truths need to be told. Some shouldn't. I just don't know which they are."

"Yes, you do." There was a black shadow in his face. "They are those which cause the innocent to suffer, and create a divide between people because of lies . . . even lies of silence."

She did not understand the depth of feeling behind his words. It was as if he were angry with her, as he had been when they had first known each other and he had thought her hypocritical, even cold. Perhaps then there had been parts of her that were locked away, too quick to condemn what she did not understand and was afraid of, but not now!

She did not know how to break through the barrier. She could not find it, touch it, but she knew absolutely that it was there. What had she said that had created it? Why did he not know her better than to misunderstand? Or love her enough to break it himself?

"I don't know what the truth is," she said quietly, looking down at the table. "I think it more likely it had to do with

250

Shearer, whether he meant to sell the guns to the pirates, or Trace, or Breeland, or just anyone who wanted them."

"I can't find Shearer." His voice was flat. "No one has seen him since before the murders."

"Doesn't that say a great deal in itself?" she asked. "If he were not involved somehow, wouldn't he still be here? Wouldn't he be doing all he could to help, and perhaps improve his own position in the business? He might even hope to be some sort of manager."

He pushed his chair away from the table and stood up, moving about the small room restlessly.

"It isn't enough," he said grimly. "You can see it, and I can, but we can't rely on a jury. Breeland had the guns. He was involved. He might have persuaded Shearer actually to commit the murders, probably for the price of the guns, which could be enough to corrupt many men. I admit, I don't care if Breeland hangs for it. To corrupt another man to betrayal and murder is an even deeper sin than doing it yourself. But it won't help Merrit because it doesn't prove she had no knowledge of it."

"But . . ." She started to protest, then realized with a crushing weight that he was right. Not only would the jury be less likely to believe it because of her closeness to Breeland, and the fact that she had gone willingly with him, dropping her watch in the warehouse yard, but she herself, in her misguided loyalty to him, would not deny it.

"There are dark places in everybody," he said in the silence. "People you believe you know have violence and ugliness it is hard to accept, and impossible to understand." There was anger in his voice and a pain she heard only too clearly. She wished to ask what he had discovered that he had not told her, but she knew from the angle of his body, the part of his face she could see, half turned away from her as it was, that he would not tell her.

She stood up to clear away the dishes and carry them through to the kitchen. She would not mention it again, at least not tonight.

251

Monk went to bed early. He was tired, but far more than that he wished to avoid speaking with Hester. He had shut himself out, and he did not know how to deal with it.

In the morning he woke early and left Hester still asleep. At least he thought she was. He was not certain. He wrote a hasty note telling her he had gone to the river again to pursue the matter of the guns, the money, and anything he could learn about the company who dealt with the pirates, then he left. He would find something to eat, if he felt like it, somewhere on the road. There were plenty of peddlers around with sandwiches and pies. The general mass of working people had no facilities to cook, and ate in the street. He did not want to risk Hester's waking and finding him in the kitchen, because he would have to give some explanation, or openly avoid it, and he was not ready to face so much inward pain.

From the very moment he awoke in the hospital his past had been an unknown land which carried too many areas of darkness, too many ugly surprises. He should have had the sense, the self-restraint, to have guarded his feelings more. He had known then that marriage was not for him. Love and its vulnerabilities were for those with uncomplicated lives, who knew themselves and whose darkest recesses of the soul were only the ordinary envies and petty acts of retreat that affected everyone.

He had not been prepared for someone like Hester, who forced from him emotions he could not stifle or control, and in the end could not even deny.

He should have found the strength to! Or at least the sense of self-preservation.

Too late now. The wound was there, wide open.

He went out of the house, closing the front door softly, and walked as quickly as he could along Fitzroy Street and into Tottenham Court Road. He had no choice but to examine the blackmail issue more closely. His revulsion against the idea was no excuse; in fact, it impelled him to do all he could to test it against the facts, and if possible disprove it.

It was too early to obtain permission to examine Alberton's finances. Rathbone would not be at his offices in Vere Street at this hour. However, Monk could write a note asking for the necessary authority, and leave it for him.

Then he would pursue Baskin and Company, who had been named as the intermediary for the pirates' guns.

The river was busy in the early morning. Tides waited on no man's convenience, and already dockers, ferrymen, bargees and stokers were busy. He saw coal backers, bent double under their heavy sacks, keeping a precarious balance as they climbed out of the deep holds. Men shouted to one another, and the cries of gulls circling low in hope of fish, the clatter of chains and metal on metal, were loud in the air above the ever-present surge and slap of water.

"Never 'eard of it, guv," the first man answered cheerfully when Monk asked for the company. "In't now'ere 'round 'ere. Eh! Jim! Yer ever 'eard o' Baskin and Company?"

"Not 'round 'ere," Jim replied. "Sorry, mate!"

And so it continued down as far as Limehouse and around the curve of the Isle of Dogs, and again across the river at Rotherhithe. He had been certain the ferrymen would know if anyone did, but even the three he asked had never heard either name.

By midafternoon he gave up and went back to Vere Street to see if Rathbone had obtained the necessary permission to go through Daniel Alberton's accounts.

"There's no difficulty," Rathbone said with a frown. He received Monk in his office, looking cool and immaculate as always. Monk, who had been traipsing up and down the dockside all day, was aware of the contrast between them. Rathbone had no shadows in his past that mattered. His smooth, almost arrogant manner came from the fact that he knew himself, better than most men. He was so supremely confident in who he was he felt no need to impress others. It was a quality Monk admired and envied. He had come to understand himself well enough to know that his own moments of cruelty came from self-doubt, his need to show others his importance.

He recalled himself to the present. "Good!"

"What do you expect to find?" Rathbone was looking curious and a trifle anxious.

"Nothing," Monk replied. "But I need to be certain."

Rathbone leaned back in his chair. "Why didn't you ask me to look?"

Monk smiled thinly. "Because you may not want to know the answer."

Humor flashed for an instant in Rathbone's eyes. "Oh! Then you had better go alone. Just don't leave me walking into an ambush in court."

"I won't," Monk promised. "I still think Shearer is the one who actually committed the murders."

Rathbone's eyebrows rose. "Alone?"

"No. I think it would have taken more than one, even holding a gun. They were tied up before they were shot. But he could have hired help anywhere. He certainly lived and worked where he would be able to find plenty of men willing to kill a man, for a reasonable price. The price of those guns would be enough to buy nine decent-sized houses. A small percent of the profit would give him sufficient to obtain all kinds of assistance."

Rathbone's fastidious face expressed his distaste.

"And I suppose we have no idea where Shearer is now?"

"None at all. Could be anywhere, here or in Europe. Or America, for that matter, except it's not the best place to be, unless he has designs on making more money in the armaments business." He debated with himself whether to mention the whole blackmail affair, and his failure to find any trace of Baskin and Company, and decided against it for the moment. It might be easier for Rathbone if he did not know.

"He could well do that," Rathbone said thoughtfully, leaning back and placing his fingertips together, elbows on the arms of his chair. "He might have bought more guns somewhere with the money from Breeland, if what Breeland says is true. There's a very murky area in arms dealing, and he would be in a position to know more about it than most."

It was a thought which had not occurred to Monk; he was annoyed with himself for it. His preoccupation with the past, and its destruction into the present, was costing him the sharp edge of his skill. But it was second nature to conceal it from Rathbone.

"That's another reason I need to see Alberton's books," he said.

Rathbone frowned. "I don't like this, Monk. I think perhaps I had better know what you find. I can't afford to be taken by surprise, however much I may dislike what it shows. No one has accused Alberton of anything yet, but I know the prosecution is going to use Horatio Deverill. He's an ambitious bounder, and they didn't nickname him 'Devil' for nothing. He's unpredictable, no loyalties, few prejudices."

"Doesn't his ambition curb his indiscretion?" Monk asked skeptically.

Rathbone's mouth turned down at the corners. "No. He's got no chance of a seat in the Lords, and he knows it. His hunger is for fame, to shock, to be noticed. He's good-looking, and a certain kind of woman finds him attractive." A quiver of humor touched his lips. "The sort whose lives are comfortable and a trifle boring," he continued. "And who think danger would give them the excitement their rank and money shield them from. I imagine you are familiar with the type?"

"Do you?" Then, like a wave of heat inside him, Monk knew why Rathbone had smiled. Monk himself carried that sort of danger, and he knew it and had used it often enough. It was a hint of the reckless, the unknown, even a suggestion of pain, another reality they wanted to touch but not be trapped in. Boredom held its own kind of destruction.

He stood up. "Then we had better know everything we can, good or bad," he said tersely. "If I see anything I don't understand, I'll send you a message, and you can find me an accounts clerk."

"Monk . . ."

"Only if I need one," Monk said from the door. He did not intend to tell Rathbone about his merchant banking days, and that he knew very well how to read a balance sheet, and what

255

to look for if he suspected embezzlement or any other kind of dishonesty. He wanted to block the whole of the past, most especially to do with Arrol Dundas, from his mind.

Monk examined the books of Alberton's business far into the night. Alberton and Casbolt had dealt in a number of commodities, mostly to considerable profit. Casbolt had been extremely knowledgeable as to where to obtain goods at the best price, and Alberton had known where to sell them to the best advantage. They had left a good deal of the shipping to Shearer, and had paid him well for his services. Read in detail, the movement of money showed a trust among the three men stretching back nearly twenty years.

Even with the skills he half remembered and which came back with startling clarity as he read, added, subtracted, Monk found nothing that was less than completely honest.

But he also had no doubt whatever, when he finally closed the last ledger at twenty-five minutes to one, that the guns the pirates' agents had demanded through blackmail would be worth roughly £1,875. The guns unaccounted for from the warehouse after Alberton's death and the robbery had not been paid for through the books. There had been no money in Alberton's possession at the time of his death, and nothing concealed in the warehouse. If money had changed hands at all, it had gone with whoever had left Tooley Street that night, or else Breeland had passed it to Shearer at the Euston Square station, as he had said.

Tomorrow he would go back and speak to Breeland.

When Hester awoke she found Monk's note. It left her with an increasing sense of loss. She was almost grateful that the trial of Merrit and Breeland loomed so close; it left her less time to torture herself with questions and fears as to what had changed between them.

Thoughts had flickered darkly across her mind that perhaps he regretted the commitment of marriage, that he felt trapped, closed in by the expectations, the constant companionship, the limits to his personal freedom.

256

But the change in him had been so sudden it made little sense. There had been no hint of it before; indeed, the opposite was true. Finding Mrs. Patrick had been a stroke of good fortune. It freed Hester to pursue her interest in medical reform without neglecting domestic duties. And Mrs. Patrick was undeniably a better cook.

She forced it from her mind and dressed in soft gray, one of her favorite colors, then set out to call upon Judith Alberton. She was not exactly sure what she wished to ask her, or even what she hoped to learn, but Judith was the only person who knew what had happened to her brother and his family, and Hester still had the feeling that the blackmail attempt was at the heart of the murders, whether it had been brought about by Shearer, or by Breeland, or even possibly by Trace, although that was a thought she hoped profoundly was not true. She had liked Philo Trace. The fact that he was from the South, and his people countenanced the keeping of slaves, was an accident of birth and culture. It had nothing to do with the charm of the man or the pleasure she felt in his company. The conflict of morality was something she sensed he was already facing within himself. Perhaps that was because she wished to believe it, but until forced to do otherwise by evidence, she would suppose it to be so.

It might be coincidence that the murders and the theft had followed so soon after the blackmail, for which the price of silence had been guns, but she did not think so. There was a connection, if she could find it.

Judith seemed pleased to see her. Naturally she was not receiving social calls and was wearing full mourning for her husband, but she was perfectly composed and whatever grief she felt was masked by a dignity and warmth which immediately drew Hester's admiration—and made her task more difficult and seem more intrusive.

Nevertheless, only the truth would serve, and Merrit's situation was desperate. The trial was due to start at the beginning of the following week.

"How nice of you to call, Mrs. Monk," Judith welcomed her. "Please tell me what news you have. . . "

Hester hated lies, but she knew from many years of nursing that sometimes half-truths were necessary, for a period at least. Some truths were better unknown altogether. The ability to fight the battle was what was needed, and without the death of hope.

"I have never believed Merrit was involved," she answered, following Judith into a small room which opened onto the garden and was decorated in greens and white, and at the present moment was filled with the morning sun. "But I am afraid it seems unavoidable that Mr. Breeland was, even if not directly."

Judith stared at her, no anxiety in her eyes, only confusion.

"If not Mr. Breeland, then who?"

"It seems most likely it was Shearer. I'm sorry." She did not know why she apologized, only that she regretted that Alberton should have been betrayed by someone he had trusted so long, and so closely. It added to the pain.

"Shearer?" Judith questioned. "Are you sure? He's a hard man, but Daniel always said he was completely loyal."

"Have you seen him since Mr. Alberton's death?"

"No. But then I have only met him once or twice anyway. He hardly ever came to the house." She did not need to add that they were not social acquaintances.

"No one else has seen him since then either," Hester told her. "Surely if he were innocent he would be here to help, to continue to work in the business and to offer all the support he could? Would he not be as anxious as we are to catch whoever is responsible?"

"Yes," Judith said quietly. "I suppose the answer had to be terrible, whatever it was. It was foolish to have hoped it would be . . . something . . . bearable . . . someone easy to hate, and dismiss."

There was nothing Hester could say to mitigate that. She turned to the other matter she needed to probe. "Mrs. Alberton, your husband and Mr. Casbolt received a very ugly letter requesting that they sell guns to a company which is known to be an intermediary who would sell them on to most undesirable quarters."

258

Judith's face registered no comprehension of why Hester should ask.

"They refused, but they asked my husband's assistance in finding out who was making the request. The letter was anonymous, and threatening—"

"Threatening?" Judith said quickly. "Have you informed the police? Surely they must be responsible, then. . . ."

"Mr. Breeland has the guns that were stolen."

"Oh . . . yes, of course. I'm sorry. Then why are you asking about these people?"

Again Hester told less than the truth.

"I am not quite certain. I just feel that the coincidence of time, and the fact that it was guns, may mean that they are connected somehow. We need all the knowledge we can possibly obtain."

"Yes, I see. Of course. What can I tell you?" Judith made no demur at all. She leaned forward, her face watchful and intelligent.

Hester hated opening the subject, but it was a past loss, raised perhaps to avoid a present one.

"I believe you lost your brother in dreadful circumstances. . . ." She saw Judith wince and the color pale in her cheeks. Hester did not retreat. "Please tell me at least the main story. I don't ask lightly."

Judith looked down. "I am half Italian. I daresay you knew I was not entirely English. My father came from the south, about fifty miles from Naples. I had only one brother, Cesare. He was married and had three children. He and his wife, Maria, used to love sailing."

Her voice was tight and low. "Seven years ago their boat was boarded by pirates off the coast of Sicily. The whole family was killed." She swallowed convulsively. "Their bodies were found . . . later. I . . ." She shook her head minutely, little more than a shiver. "Daniel went out. I didn't. He . . . he wouldn't tell me the details. I asked . . . I was glad he refused. I saw in his face that it was terrible. Sometimes he dreamed . . . I heard him cry out in the night, and wake up,

259

his body rigid. But he would never say what had happened to them."

Hester tried to imagine the crushing weight of horror that had remained with Alberton so vividly, and the love for his wife which had taken him to Sicily, and then kept him silent all the years between. And yet he still dealt in guns! Did he feel they were also used for good, to fight just causes, defend the weak, even keep a balance of power between otherwise violent forces?

Or was it simply the only business he understood, or the most profitable? They would probably never know. She wished to think it was one of the former.

"How long was he away?" she asked aloud.

"I don't know. Almost three weeks," Judith answered. "It seemed an age at the time. I missed him dreadfully, and of course I feared for him also. But he was determined to do everything he could to have the pirates found and punished. He pursued word of them from one place to another, but always they eluded him. And most of the forces of law were those who had no interest in catching them." A fleeting love and sorrow filled her eyes. "Italy is a culture, a language, a great art, a way of life, but it is not a nation. One day it may be, if God is willing, but that day is not yet."

"I see."

Judith smiled. "No, you don't. You are English, forgive me, but you have no idea at all. Neither had Daniel. He did all he could, and when he realized that they could simply disappear anywhere in hundreds of miles of coastline, thousands of islands anywhere between Constantinople and Tangiers, he came home again, angry, defeated, but prepared to care for me and for Merrit, and let justice be God's, in whatever manner it may."

There was nothing for Hester to add. Of course it was possible Alberton had made contact with gun buyers in the Mediterranean, pirates or otherwise, fighters for or against Italian unification. But there was no way she could find out. Probably Judith did not know; certainly she would not say.

260

"How did you know of the blackmail?" Judith asked, interrupting her thoughts.

"Mr. Casbolt told me." Hester realized that needed some explanation. "I was seeking his help regarding his knowledge of Mr. Breeland, and of the munitions business in general. He told me of the pressure to sell to the pirates, and why Mr. Alberton never would, whatever the threat or the price."

Judith's face relaxed into a smile. "He always understood. He knew Daniel before I did, you know? They were friends at school here in England, and one year he brought Daniel with him to Italy. That was where we fell in love." She looked down for a moment. "Without Robert's help I don't know if I would be able to commit to Sir Oliver's fee for representing Merrit, and that would be more than I could bear." She raised her head quickly, her eyes wide, fear naked in them. "Mrs. Monk, do you think Sir Oliver is going to be able to save her? The newspapers are so certain she is guilty. I had no idea written words could hurt so much . . . that people who don't even know you could be so passionately certain of what you are like, what is in your heart. I don't go out, not at the moment, but I don't know how I will be able to when the time comes. How will I face people when everyone I pass in the street may believe my daughter is guilty of . . ."

"Ignore them," Hester replied. "Think only of Merrit. Those with any honesty will be ashamed of themselves when they discover their error. The others are not worth battling with, and there is nothing you can do about them anyway."

Judith sat quite still. "Will you be there?"

"Yes." There had been no decision to make.

"Thank you."

Hester stayed another half hour, but as a matter of companionship. They talked of nothing important, carefully avoiding speaking of the case, or of love and loss. Judith showed her around the garden, vivid with color as the roses began their second flush. It was warm even in the shade, the heavy perfume of flowers dreamlike. It made Monday's opening of the trial harsher by contrast, as if this were so soon to end. For a long time neither of them spoke. Platitudes would insult the reality.

Monk went to see Breeland on Saturday. He had not found enough to help Rathbone beyond hope, doubt, issues to raise. He would continue seeking during the trial, but he was beginning to fear that there was no proof to find that Merrit was innocent. It might end in being no more than a matter of judgment.

There was one question to ask Breeland, the answer to which would do him no injury, so Monk had no hesitation in asking it.

Breeland was brought into a small square cell. He looked pale and thinner than when Monk had last seen him. His face had hollows around the eyes and a certain leanness to the cheeks where the muscles showed tight-clenched. He stood stiffly, looking at Monk with resentment.

"I have already told you everything I have to say," he began before Monk had spoken at all. "You brought me back to stand trial and to prove my innocence. I assume your friend Rathbone will do his duty, although I have little confidence in his belief in my innocence. I trusted you, Monk, but I now fear my trust may have been misplaced. I think you would be pleased enough to see me hang, as long as Miss Alberton is acquitted and you are paid your fee for rescuing her. I apologize if I accuse you unjustly. I hope I do."

Monk searched the smooth, chiseled face and saw no surface emotion, no fear, no weakness, no doubt in his own courage to face the ordeal now only two days away. He should have admired it. Instead it filled him with a strange fear of his own. He was not certain whether Breeland's demeanor was more than human, or less. He could see none of his own vulnerabilities reflected there.

"I accept your apology," he said coolly. "Certainly I would like Miss Alberton acquitted, and I admit I don't give a damn whether you hang or not ... provided you are guilty ...

whether you actually fired the gun doesn't matter. If you corrupted Shearer, or anybody else, into doing it for you, that's all the same to me. If you didn't, and it had nothing to do with you, then I'll fight as hard to clear you as I would any man."

There was no flash of humor in Breeland's face, not even the ghost of recognition of irony. Monk had a sudden thought that Breeland did not perceive himself except as a hero, or a martyr. Human foibles and absurdities eluded his grasp. Monk saw a vision of an endless desert of existence, always on the grand scale, stripped of the laughter and trivia that bring proportion to life and are the measure of sanity.

Poor Merrit.

He pushed his hands into his pockets. "How many guns did you buy?" he asked casually. "Exactly."

"Exactly?" Breeland repeated, his eyebrows lifted. "To the gun? I didn't count them. There was hardly time. I assumed every crate was full. Alberton was a stubborn man, with limited views and no moral or political understanding, but I never doubted his financial integrity."

"How many guns did you pay for?"

"Six thousand. And I paid him the agreed amount per gun."

"You paid Shearer?"

"I already told you that." Breeland frowned. "For that amount of money you could build several streets' worth of four-bedroom houses in any part of London. It seems obvious to me that Shearer double-crossed Alberton, shot him and the guards in a manner to make it look as if it were Union soldiers who did it, sold the guns to me, and escaped with the money. I am innocent, and Rathbone will be able to demonstrate that."

Monk made no reply. Breeland was perfectly correct. Monk did not care whether he hanged or not . . . not at this moment.

10

On the following Monday the trial began of Lyman Breeland and Merrit Alberton, jointly accused of the Tooley Street murders. Oliver Rathbone was as well prepared as he was able to be, given the information he possessed. From what Monk had told him, he believed Breeland had not committed the crimes himself, but assuring the jury that he had not instigated them, and profited from them knowing what had occurred, was quite another matter. And Rathbone was aware of having a client who would not naturally elicit the sympathy of the jury.

He had spoken to both Merrit and Breeland on the Friday before. He had weighed whether to suggest to Breeland a softer manner, more expression of humility, even of regret for the tragedy of Alberton's death, but he formed the belief that it would be a wasted attempt, perhaps even produce a pattern of behavior that was obviously false.

Now as the court was called to order and the proceedings began, Rathbone looked up at Breeland's face in the dock, expressionless, staring straight ahead as if he had no interest in the people assembled there, no regard or respect for them, and Rathbone wished he had made some effort to warn him how dearly that could cost.

Merrit, on the other hand, looked young and frightened, and very vulnerable indeed. Her skin was pale, blue-shadowed around her eyes, and her hands were clenched on the rail so hard it would be easy to think she was holding on to it to save

265

herself from falling. As Rathbone watched her, she squared her shoulders and lifted her chin a little, and looked up at Breeland. Very tentatively she reached out her hand and touched his arm.

The shadow of a smile moved his lips, but he did not speak to her. Perhaps he did not wish the court to witness any emotion in him. Perhaps he felt that love was a private thing, and he would not share it with those who had come to stare, and to judge.

Rathbone was acutely conscious of Judith Alberton, as were most of the people in the court. There was a beauty in her carriage, and in what could be glimpsed of her features. He saw people nudge each other as she came in, and several men were unable to keep the admiration, or the interest, from their expressions.

Rathbone wondered if she was accustomed to being stared at, or if it made her uncomfortable. She looked at Merrit, who was still turned towards Breeland, then across at Rathbone. It was only a glance before she sat down, and he could not see her eyes through the veil. He only imagined the desperation she must be feeling. All the help anyone could give her could not cross the barrier of loneliness she must face, the fear of what these days would bring.

Hester was beside her, dressed in dark and pale grays, the light catching her fair skin and a little white lace at her throat. He would have recognized the curve of her cheek anywhere, and the individual way she carried her head. The greatest beauty in the world did not catch his breath that way with the ache of familiarity, the memory of so many shared struggles for victory over ignorance and wrong. Winning had mattered, of course it had, the causes had always been worth the fight, but he realized how good the battles themselves had been. This was another one, but they were not together in it as they had been in the past. Monk was between them in a new way.

He saw Breeland stiffen and a look of extraordinary dislike fill his face. Rathbone followed his glance. A slender, dark-haired man had entered the courtroom and was making his way towards a vacant seat on the edge of the aisle in the public gallery. He moved with an unusual grace and made no sound at all, taking a place where it was unnecessary to excuse himself to anyone. His remarkable eyes studied Judith Alberton, even though she was in front of him and he could not have seen her face.

Rathbone wondered if this was Philo Trace. He knew it was not Casbolt, since they had already met.

Opposite him, across the aisle, Horatio Deverill was rising to open his case. He was a tall man, slender in his youth but now thickening around the middle. His once-handsome features were slightly coarsened but still full of power and character. But it was his voice which commanded attention and forced one to listen. It was rich, idiosyncratic, with perfect enunciation. Many a jury had been mesmerized by it. When he spoke, no one's attention wandered.

"Gentlemen," he began, smiling at the jurors, sitting upright and self-conscious in their high, carved seats. "I shall tell you about a heinous and terrible crime. I shall show you how an honorable man, much like yourselves, was conspired against to be robbed, and then murdered, in order to gain guns for the tragic conflict which is even now being fought out in America, brother against brother."

There was a murmur of horror and sympathy around the room.

Rathbone was not surprised. He had expected Deverill to play for any emotional reaction he could draw. He was perfectly capable of doing the same, were he to suppose it would win him a case. He did not care about individual points, only the verdict.

"And I shall show you," Deverill continued, "that this terrible deed was not only an offense against the law of this land, and the laws of God, but against the very laws of nature itself, acknowledged by every race and nation in mankind. It was carried out at the behest and to serve the purposes of the accused, Lyman Breeland. But, gentlemen,

267

it was aided and connived at by the victim's own daughter, Merrit Alberton."

He received the desired gasp of horror, shimmering around the room like a hot wind before a storm.

"She was infatuated with Breeland," he continued. "And what he did to induce this obsession in her I cannot prove, so I shall not attempt even to tell you, but suffice it to say, after the terrible deed was done, she fled to America with him, that very night." He shook his head. "And it was only by the good offices of a private agent of enquiry, employed by her own mother, the widow of the murdered man, that she and Breeland were brought back to this country, at gunpoint, to face you, and your decision as to how justice may be served.

"To this end, my lord . . ." He turned at last to face the judge, a lean man with powerful features and clear, silver-gray eyes. "To this end, I call my first witness, Robert Casbolt."

There was intense interest as Casbolt came into the court and crossed the open space of the floor in front of the judge and jury and climbed up the short, curving steps to the witness stand. He was immaculately dressed in dark gray, and looked pale but composed. There was not even the shadow of the smile he so often wore, and which had etched the lines around his mouth.

He swore as to his name and residence, and awaited Deverill's first questions calmly. Once he glanced down at Judith and his expression softened, but it was only for an instant. He looked like a man at a funeral. He did not look towards the dock.

"Mr. Casbolt . . ." Deverill began, smiling apologetically and walking up and down the open floor like an actor facing an audience to deliver a great soliloquy. Although it was the jury to whom he was playing, he never once looked in their direction. "I realize this is acutely painful for you, sir. Nevertheless it is necessary, and I hope you will bear with me while I take the court through the events which led to this tragedy. You were aware of almost all of them, even

268

though you can have had no idea to what terrible end they were destined."

Rathbone looked at the jury. They ranged from about forty to sixty in age, and seemed decent and prosperous, like most jurors. There were qualifications of property required which ruled out many younger men, or those of a different social class. They sat serious, unhappy, and concentrating fiercely upon every word that was said.

"Mr. Casbolt, would you tell the court how and when you first encountered Lyman Breeland?"

"Of course," Casbolt said quietly, but his voice fell with perfect clarity in the faint rustling around the room. "I do not recall the exact date, but it was early in May of this year. He presented himself at the business premises of Daniel Alberton and myself." He lifted one shoulder very slightly. "He was interested in the armaments aspect of our business."

"And what did Mr. Breeland say to you?" Deverill asked innocently.

"That he was authorized to purchase guns for the Union cause in the American conflict," Casbolt answered. "He said he was entrusted by his superior with a very large sum of money, approximately twenty-three thousand pounds, which he had deposited at the Bank of England."

There was a gasp of amazement around the room. It was a fortune beyond most men's imagination. Several people looked up at Breeland in the dock, but he studiously ignored them all, keeping his eyes on Deverill.

"Did you see this money?" Deverill asked, his voice hushed with awe.

"No, sir. One would not have expected him to bring it with him," Casbolt answered. "It is a . . . a fortune!"

"It is indeed. But he told you, and Mr. Alberton, that the government of the Northern states of America had sent him with this money in order to purchase guns, is that so?"

"Guns and ammunition for them, yes, sir."

"And you believed him?"

"We had no cause to doubt him. I still have not," Casbolt

replied. "He presented credentials, including a letter from Abraham Lincoln bearing the seal of the President of the United States. Both Daniel Alberton and I were well informed as to the escalating hostilities across the Atlantic, and naturally we were also aware of the fact that representatives from both the Union and the Confederate states had been purchasing guns wherever they were available all over Europe."

"Just so," Deverill agreed. He pushed his thumbs into the armholes of his waistcoat, stared at the polished toes of his boots, then looked up at Casbolt. "And had you, or Daniel Alberton, sold guns before to either party in this war?"

"We had not."

"And you are sure that Daniel Alberton had not, for example, made a private agreement with Lyman Breeland, unknown to you or Mr. Trace?" Deverill prompted.

Casbolt's face filled with a curious mixture of emotions which were only too apparently painful. His eyes flickered towards Judith, sitting in the front seat of the gallery.

Everyone in the room must have been aware of the tension and the personal grief.

Rathbone looked up at Breeland. He was watching intently, but if he felt any sorrow or fear it was too tightly under control to betray itself. His pride could serve him ill. It looked too much like indifference. The next time he had the opportunity to speak to his client, Rathbone would tell him so, for any good it would do.

"Are you sure?" Deverill prompted.

Casbolt drew his attention back. His expression cleared.

"The other reason was that Daniel Alberton was my friend, and one of the most honorable men I have ever known. In twenty-five years I never knew him to break his word to anyone." His voice caught. "One could not ask more of a business associate than that, coupled with skill and knowledge of his field."

"Indeed one could not," Deverill agreed softly, looking again at the jury.

Rathbone swore under his breath. He had never imagined defeating Deverill would be easy, but the reality of his task was becoming sharper by the minute. Brilliant as Rathbone was, and ruthless, he could not alter the truth, nor would he try.

"What, precisely, was the agreement made with Mr. Trace?" Deverill asked ingenuously.

"Daniel had given his word to sell six thousand P1853 Enfield rifled muskets," Casbolt replied clearly.

Deverill was supremely satisfied. It glowed in his face. Rathbone knew the jurors saw it, and had judged its importance accordingly. They believed he had scored a major point, even if they did not know what it was. One of them, a man with magnificent side-whiskers, shot a malevolent glance up at Breeland.

Merrit looked as if she had been struck. She moved a fraction closer to Breeland in the dock. The movement was not lost on the jury.

Rathbone knew how to manipulate emotion also, although at times he found it repugnant. He would have used the slave issue, one most Englishmen deplored, even though many of them favored the South. But he was conscious of Hester sitting beside Judith Alberton, and how she would despise him for the moral dishonesty of it. He was angry with himself that he allowed it to hurt.

"Why was he prepared to sell guns to Mr. Trace, sir?" Deverill enquired innocently. "Was he a sympathizer with the Confederate cause?"

"No," Casbolt answered. "I am not aware that he had a loyalty to either side. The only opinion I heard him express was one of sadness that the issue had come to war at all. In the several months previously he had hoped it would be resolved by negotiation. It was simply that Mr. Trace presented himself and was desperate to purchase. He did not argue his cause greatly. He said the South wanted to be free to decide its own destiny and choose its form of government, but little more than that. It was Mr. Breeland who tried to persuade him that his cause justified the sale of arms to the Union rather than anyone else."

271

"So Mr. Trace obtained the sale simply because he was first?" Deverill deduced.

"Yes. He paid half the sum as an evidence of good faith. The second half was to follow upon delivery of the guns and ammunition."

"And Breeland wished Mr. Alberton to renege on that agreement and sell the guns to him instead?"

"Yes. He was most insistent . . . to the point of unpleasantness." Casbolt's face was twisted with regret, even a degree of self-blame, as if he should have foreseen the tragedy.

Deverill was quick to seize on it. "What sort of unpleasantness? Did he threaten anyone?"

"No . . . not so far as I am aware." Casbolt's voice was soft, his mind very much in the past tragedy. "He accused Daniel of being in favor of slavery, which of course he was not. Breeland was passionate about his cause, both to abolish slavery in America and to keep all the states in the Union, whether they wished it or not. He frequently argued his opinion—his obsession—that the South should not be allowed independence . . . only he called it secession. I admit, I don't understand the difference." This time the faintest smile touched his face.

Deverill opened his eyes very wide. "Nor I, to be frank." He gestured very slightly towards the dock, but did not look up at it. "But fortunately it is not our concern." He dismissed it. "In his attempts to change Mr. Alberton's mind about the guns, did he call upon him at his place of business, or at his home, do you know?"

"Both, he told me, but I know for myself that he called often at his home, because I was there on half a dozen occasions. He was offered hospitality and accepted it."

Again several jurors shot Breeland a look of loathing.

"There is something peculiarly repellent in the ultimate betrayal of eating at a man's table and then rising up and murdering him. Every society abhors it," Deverill said quietly, his voice very low, and yet carrying to every corner of the room.

The judge glanced at Rathbone. He would have objected to the irrelevance of the comment, but it was not irrelevant except legally, and every man and woman in the room knew it. It would only betray his own desperation. He shook his head minutely.

Deverill continued. "During these visits, Mr. Casbolt, did you observe any relationship growing between Breeland and Merrit Alberton?"

Casbolt winced and shivered a little. "Not as much as I should have done." His voice was tight in his throat, strained with regret. Even sitting several yards away, and looking upwards at him on the stand, Rathbone was moved by the emotion in him. It was too genuine for anyone to doubt it, or be unaffected.

There was a ripple of compassion around the room. A woman sniffed. One of the jurors shook his head slowly and glanced up at Merrit in the dock.

Rathbone turned to Judith, but her expression was hidden by her veil. He saw Philo Trace look towards her, and his emotion also was laid bare to see. Rathbone realized in that moment that Trace loved Judith, silently, without expectation of return. He knew it with a depth of understanding because that was how he loved Hester. The time for her responding to him was gone. Perhaps it was only an illusion that it had ever been.

Deverill had milked the silence for all he could get from it. He resumed his questioning.

"And did you see Miss Alberton return his attentions?" he asked.

"Indeed." Casbolt cleared his throat. "She is only sixteen. I believed it was an infatuation which would pass as soon as Breeland left to go back to America."

Instinctively, Rathbone looked up at Merrit and saw the pain and defiance in her face. She leaned a little forward, longing to tell them the truth, how much she truly loved Breeland, but she was not permitted to speak.

Casbolt went on. "He was an officer in an army." Suddenly anger burst through, raw and hard in his voice. "About to engage in civil war five thousand miles away from England. He was in no position to make an offer to a woman, let alone a child of Merrit's age! It never occurred to me that he would! I don't believe it entered her father's mind either. And if Breeland had had the ill judgment, the effrontery, to do so, Daniel would naturally have refused."

In the dock Breeland stirred, but he also could not defend himself yet.

"If Breeland loved her," Casbolt went on, "and were an honorable man, he would have waited until the war was over, and then returned with a proper offer, when he could support her and care for her as a man should. Provide a home for her . . . not leave her with strangers in a besieged city while he went off to a battle from which he might never return . . . or return crippled and unable to care for her." He was shaking as he stood gripping the rails, his face white.

He had not given a single fact tying Breeland to the murder of Daniel Alberton, but he had damned him in the eyes of every person in the room, and Deverill knew it. It was there in the confident stance of the barrister's body, the smooth velvet of his voice.

"Just so, Mr. Casbolt. I am sure we all feel as you do, and might well have had no more foresight as to the tragedy to come. We hold no condemnation, sir, no wisdom after the event. Could you now tell us what you observed the night of Daniel Alberton's death . . . ?"

Casbolt closed his eyes, his hands still gripping the rail.

"Are you all right, Mr. Casbolt?" Deverill said anxiously. He stepped forward, as if afraid that Casbolt might actually collapse.

"Yes," Casbolt said between his teeth. He took a deep breath and lifted his head, staring with fixed eyes at the paneled wall above the gallery. "I know only from learning what happened earlier that evening. I assume you will call Monk, who was present, to tell you what he saw and heard. I had been dining late with friends and had not yet retired. It was about half-past three when a messenger brought me a note from Mrs. Alberton."

"Exhibit number one, my lord," Deverill said to the judge.

The judge nodded and the usher handed a piece of paper to Casbolt.

"Is this the note you received?" Deverill asked.

Casbolt's hand trembled as he took it. He had difficulty finding his voice. "It is."

"Will you read it for us?" Deverill requested.

Casbolt cleared his throat.

" 'My dear Robert: Forgive me for disturbing you at this hour, but I am deeply afraid something serious may have happened. Daniel and Merrit had a terrible quarrel this evening. Mr. Breeland was here, and Mr. Monk. Mr. Breeland swore that he would not be defeated in his cause, regardless of what it cost him. Merrit has left home. I discovered an hour ago that she has packed a bag and gone, I fear to Breeland. Daniel left shortly after the quarrel. He must have gone after her, but he has not returned. Please find him and help. He will be so distressed.' "

He looked up, his voice thick as if he fought tears. "It is signed 'Judith.' Of course I did not hesitate more than a moment to wonder what was the best course of action. I realized it would be to enlist Monk's help, in case of unpleasantness, and then go straight to Breeland's rooms. If necessary we could bring Merrit back by force . . . before her reputation was ruined." A bitter humor flashed across his face and disappeared, replaced by misery.

Deverill nodded his head slowly.

The jury looked suitably grieved.

The judge glanced at Rathbone to see if he had any response, but there was none to make.

"Please continue," Deverill requested. "I assume you went to find Mr. Monk?"

"Yes," Casbolt agreed. "I awoke him and told him briefly what had happened. He came with me, first to Breeland's rooms, which were empty. We were let in by the night porter, who told us Breeland and a young lady had left. . . ."

Again the judge glanced at Rathbone.

"I have no objection, my lord," Rathbone said clearly. "I intend to call the night porter myself. He has information which supports Mr. Breeland's version of events."

The judge nodded, and turned to Casbolt. "Please restrict yourself to what you know, not what others have told you."

Casbolt bowed acknowledgment and continued with his story. "Because of what the night porter told us, we went with all possible haste back to my carriage, which was waiting outside, and drove to the warehouse in Tooley Street." He stopped for a moment to regain his composure. It was obviously a struggle for him. Anyone in the room could see that the events of that night were so overpowering that he was transported back to the yard in the early-morning light, and the horror he had seen there. He spoke in a harsh, almost toneless voice, as if he could not bear to remember with the reality of feeling.

Rathbone listened, finding the story more devastating than when Monk had told him. There was something in Casbolt's reliving of it which carried an even greater power. If he had asked the jury for a verdict now, they would have hanged Breeland and Merrit today, and pulled the lever for the trapdoor themselves.

Casbolt had described finding the bodies in their grotesque positions with only the briefest of words, almost too spare to re-create the picture. His horror filled the room. No man could have acted such searing emotion.

He did not mention finding the watch. Deverill had to remind him of it.

Casbolt looked startled. "Oh. Yes. Monk found it. He picked it up. It had Breeland's name engraved on it, and a date. I don't recall what it was."

"But Lyman Breeland's name was on it, you are certain of that?"

"Of course."

"Thank you. Just one thing more, Mr. Casbolt."

"Yes?" He looked puzzled.

"Forgive me for such an enquiry, sir," Deverill apologized. "But just in case anyone might wonder, or my learned friend raises the issue, allow me to spare him the trouble. Exactly where were you that evening, before you received Mrs. Alberton's desperate note? You said you dined with friends?"

"Yes, Lord Harland's house, in Eaton Square. I am afraid the party went on rather longer than expected. I did not arrive home until a little after three. I was still up when the messenger arrived."

"I see. Thank you." Deverill turned with a flourish towards Rathbone, waving a hand in invitation.

Casbolt had said nothing Rathbone disputed, nothing he wished to clarify. He would have liked to stretch out the proceedings in the hope Monk might yet discover something more, but if he did so now Deverill at least would know it, possibly the jury would also.

He half rose from his seat. "I have no questions for the witness, my lord."

"Good. Then we may adjourn for luncheon," the judge said bleakly.

Rathbone was barely outside the courtroom when he saw Hester and Judith Alberton coming towards him. Philo Trace was a few yards away, but he did not approach them. It flashed through Rathbone's mind to wonder again exactly what Trace's part was in the purchase of guns. Could he have been the one who tried to blackmail Alberton, and was that why Alberton had absolutely refused to deal with Breeland . . . because he dared not? Had Monk been the catalyst which made him change his mind? It was only the thread of an idea, but it persisted.

"Sir Oliver?" Judith was in front of him. He could hear the fear in her voice.

"Please don't worry, Mrs. Alberton," he said with more confidence than he felt. It was a part of his profession he had been obliged to practice so often: the comforting of people

277

in desperate situations, the giving of courage and hope he had no knowledge he could justify. "We have our turn after Mr. Deverill has done all he can. I don't feel any certainty that I can prove Breeland innocent, but with Merrit it will be far easier. Don't lose heart."

"The watch," she said simply. "If Merrit was not there, how did it come to be in the warehouse yard? She was so proud of it, I cannot imagine her willingly letting it out of her possession."

"Can you imagine her lying to protect Breeland?" he asked gently. He could not help looking for a moment at Hester and saw in her eyes the fierce need to help, and confusion because she did not know how to.

"Yes," Judith said quietly. "Sir Oliver . . . I am terribly afraid I should not have sent Mr. Monk to bring her back. Have I condemned her to death—" Her voice broke.

Hester tightened her grip on Judith's arm, willing her to have strength. But she could not argue, could not think of any words that would comfort.

"No," Rathbone lied with authority. He heard the ring of conviction in his own voice, and was stabbed with fear that he would be proved wrong. But he was used to risk, to defying the rules and trusting to fortune, because it was all he had. He was acutely conscious that he did not deserve to succeed as often as he had. "No, Mrs. Alberton. I do not believe that Merrit is guilty of more than foolishness. I am very sorry that I may have to demonstrate that the man she loves is in no way worthy of her, and she will find that very hard. There is little in life as bitter as disillusion. And when it happens she will need your comfort. You must remain strong for that time. It will not be long."

Judith's expression could not be seen, but the emotion, the effort at self-mastery and the fear were all in her voice.

"Of course. Thank you, Sir Oliver." It was painfully apparent that she wanted to say more, and also that she would be asking for something he could not give her. She waited only a moment longer, then slowly turned away. After she had moved a step or two she was facing Philo Trace. She must have seen his expression, his remarkable eyes. Perhaps she was the fortunate one, to be able to hide behind a veil, to have no one know how much she had seen of his emotions, or to pretend she had not read them.

Then the moment was gone, and with Hester beside her she walked away. Rathbone went to find himself some luncheon, although he had little appetite for it.

The afternoon resumed late with Lanyon giving evidence for the police. In the rather stiff language of officialdom he corroborated all that Casbolt had said, at Deverill's insistence, also confirming that Casbolt had indeed dined with friends and remained in their company until after the time Alberton and the guards were believed to have been killed.

It was unnecessary. Rathbone had never considered Casbolt a possible suspect, nor did he believe anyone else had.

Deverill thanked Lanyon effusively, as if he had made an important point.

Rathbone was pleased to see several jurors looking mystified.

"And did you find anything remarkable at the scene of the murders which led you to the identity of any of the persons present, apart from the victims?" Deverill asked.

"Yes," Lanyon said unhappily. "A gentleman's gold watch."

"Where did you find it?"

The jury were only mildly interested. They already knew, and their distaste was apparent. A couple of them looked up at Breeland.

He ignored them almost as if he were unaware. Rathbone had seen innocent men with that sublime detachment, knowing the crime spoken of had nothing to do with them. He had also seen guilty men with a coldness that appeared just the same, because they had no understanding that what they had done was repellent. They felt no pain except their own.

Merrit was utterly different. She was pale, shivering, and it cost her a very obvious effort to muster even a semblance of composure. She had been stunned by Casbolt's account of finding the bodies. Lanyon's less emotional telling of essentially the same facts had been even harder for her. His tightly controlled voice made it more real. Yet in his own way he was also shocked. It was in the keenness of his speech, the way he kept his eyes down and did not once look at Judith in the front row of the gallery, nor up at Merrit herself.

Deverill took Lanyon through the exact circumstances of finding the watch, and of the name engraved on the back. Then he moved on to Lanyon's following of the trail of wagons from the yard to Hayes Dock and the beginning of their journey down the river by barge.

At four o'clock the judge adjourned the court for the day.

In the morning, Deverill resumed exactly where he had left the story. It took him the rest of the morning to proceed detail by detail until Lanyon admitted to losing the trail at Bugsby's Marshes. Deverill very graciously offered to call every bargee, docker and waterman who had given Lanyon evidence.

Wearily, the judge asked Rathbone if he contested the issue, and immensely to the court's relief Rathbone said that he did not. He was happy to concede that everything Lanyon had said was true.

Deverill looked startled, and pleased, as if his adversary had unexpectedly surrendered.

"Are you well, Sir Oliver?" he enquired solicitously.

There was a faint titter around the gallery, instantly hushed at a glare from the judge.

"In excellent health, thank you," Rathbone replied. "Quite well enough for a trip down the river to Bugsby's Marshes, if I felt like it. I don't. But please don't let me stop you, if you feel it will serve your cause."

"It will certainly not serve yours, sir!" Deverill returned.

"Nor harm it either." Rathbone smiled. "It is irrelevant, a diversion. Please continue. . . ."

The judge had a very dry smile and directed them to proceed.

"Your witness," Deverill invited.

Rathbone stood up and walked across the floor to stand in the middle of the open space. This time every eye was on him, waiting for him to begin the fight. So far he had not even parried a blow, much less struck one. He knew he must make a mark immediately or forfeit their attention.

"Sergeant Lanyon, you very diligently followed the trail of this barge all the way from Tooley Street, near Hayes Dock, down the Thames as far as Bugsby's Marshes. It carried a cargo of something heavy, and we have assumed it was the guns from Mr. Alberton's warehouse. Do you know the identity of the men who were seen by these various witnesses to whom you spoke? I mean know it, Sergeant, rather than deduce it from a dropped watch or a chance to purchase armaments for a cause."

"No, sir. I only know they knew where the guns were and they wanted them enough to commit murder to take them," Lanyon answered with only a flicker of expression in his mild, thin face.

"Just so," Rathbone agreed. "But who were they?"

Lanyon's jaw set hard. "I don't know. But someone dropped that watch, and recently. Gold watches don't lie around warehouse yards long before someone notices them."

"Not in daylight, anyway." Rathbone smiled very slightly. "Thank you, Sergeant Lanyon. You seem to have fulfilled your duty excellently. I have nothing more to ask of you . . . except . . . did you find out what happened to the guns after Bugsby's Marshes? Or what happened to the barge afterwards?"

"No, sir."

"I see. Don't you find that curious?"

Deverill stood up.

Rathbone held out his hand. "I rephrase that, Sergeant Lanyon. In your experience as a police officer, is that a usual occurrence?"

"No, sir. I've looked hard for anything further, but I can't find any trace of where the guns went after that, or the barge."

"I shall enlighten you," Rathbone promised. "About the guns, at least. The barge mystifies me as much as it does you. Thank you. I have nothing further to ask."

After the luncheon adjournment Deverill called the medical officer, who described the exact manner of the killings. It was gruesome and distressing evidence, and the court heard it in near silence. Deverill seemed to begin with the intention of drawing from him every agonizing detail, then just in time realized that the jury were acutely aware of the pain it had to cause the widow, and this not only produced in them a very natural rage against the perpetrators but also against himself, for subjecting her to hearing, perhaps for the first time, a clinical description of horror she had been protected from before.

Rathbone looked up at Merrit in the dock and saw the agony in her eyes, her ashen skin now so bleached of color as to seem bruised, and the achingly rigid muscles of her arms and body as silent weeping racked through her. It would be a hard man indeed who could look at her and not believe that if she had had even the slightest knowledge of this before, let alone complicity, she was tortured with remorse now.

He also wondered what went through her mind regarding Breeland, sitting bolt upright as if on some military duty, his features composed, almost without expression.

In Rathbone's mind the thing that burned up inside him with a rage he could not control was that Breeland never once extended his hand towards Merrit or made any gesture of pity for her. If he were distressed within himself, it was inside a loneliness nothing could break. Whatever he felt for her, he cared more for his cause, and the dignity and stoic innocence he presented to the world. If he had any human vulnerability, no one must see it. If he had weighed the cost to Merrit at all, it had not been heavy enough on the scales to show.

A military expert was called who testified that this peculiar method of binding the arms and legs over a pole was known to be practiced by the army of the Union to punish those of its members who had been found guilty of various crimes, the *T* indicating "thief." It was not an execution, but usually lasted for six to twelve hours, by which time the man concerned was barely able to stand, even after release. He had no opinion as to the shooting, but his anger was palpable that an accepted form of discipline should have been so misused. It was an insult to the honorable man who had designed it.

Whether the court agreed with him it was impossible to say; they were overwhelmed with the savagery of the only case they had witnessed, and they were not at war. The necessities of the Union army, of any army, were unknown to them. The fact that the practice was specific to the army for which Breeland fought was an added condemnation. The hatred for him could be felt in the air like a hot, stinging smell.

Rathbone's mind raced as to how he could undo the emotional damage. Mere facts would be drowned in the revulsion of feeling.

The last witness of the day was Dorothea Parfitt, the seventeen-year-old friend to whom Merrit had shown the watch and bragged a little of her love affair. Dorothea walked across the open space of the floor and tripped on the very first step up to the box. She had hold of the railing, so it was only barely noticeable, but she let out a little gasp and straightened herself, blushing.

Deverill was extremely gentle with her, doing all he could to ease her obvious consciousness that her words could condemn her friend, perhaps to the rope. What motive she had had in first saying this to the police no one else could know. It might have been envy, because Merrit had won the love of a most glamorous man who was older, braver, more mysterious and exciting than the youths she knew. It is very natural to want to prick vanity, especially if it is exercised at your expense. She could not then have foreseen the terrible consequences. She would not even have been able to imagine standing here now, about to repeat her words, because she could not take them back, and give Deverill the power to place a rope around Merrit's neck.

She faced Deverill like a rabbit in front of a snake. Never once did she allow her eyes to stray towards Merrit in the dock.

The watch was passed up to her but she refused to touch it.

"Have you seen it before, Miss Parfitt?" Deverill asked gently.

At first her throat was so tight, her lips so dry, that her voice would not come.

Deverill waited.

"Yes," she said at last.

"Can you tell us where, and in what circumstances?"

She swallowed convulsively.

"We all realize that you would immeasurably rather not," Deverill said with a charming smile. "But loyalty to the truth must outweigh the desire not to cause trouble for a friend. Just tell me exactly what happened, what you saw and heard. You are not accountable for the actions of others, and only an unjust or guilty person would hold you to be. Where did you see this watch, Miss Parfitt, and in whose possession?"

"Merrit's," she answered, her voice little above a whisper.

"Did she show it to you?"

"Yes."

"Why? Did she say?"

Dorothea nodded. Deverill held her gaze as if she were mesmerized.

"Lyman Breeland had given it to her as a token of his love." Her eyes brimmed with tears. "She really thought he loved her. She had no idea he was wicked . . . honestly! She must have found out, and given it back to him, because she would

284

never have had anything to do with killing her father . . . not ever! I know she argued with him because she thought he was terribly wrong to sell the guns to that man from the South, because the South keeps slaves. But you don't kill people over things like that!"

"I am afraid they do in America, Miss Parfitt," Deverill said with wry regret. "It is a subject about which some people feel so violently that their behavior is beyond the bounds of ordinary law and society. One of the most tragic of all kinds of war is beginning, even as we stand here in this peaceful courtroom and argue our differences. And we none of us know where it will end. Please God, we will not, with our own prejudices and greeds, make it any worse."

It was a sentiment Rathbone felt profoundly, and yet Deverill's giving voice to it irritated him like a scraped elbow. Whether Deverill meant it or not, Rathbone had no doubt he expressed it to manipulate the emotions of the court.

Dorothea had no idea what to make of it. She stared at him with open confusion.

"Mr. Deverill," the judge admonished, leaning forward, "are you chastising the witness for her lack of knowledge as to the outcome of the present tragedy across the Atlantic?"

"No, my lord, certainly not. I am simply trying to point out that some people feel passionately enough about the issues of slaving to kill those who differ from them."

"It is unnecessary, Mr. Deverill. We are aware of it," the judge said dryly. "Have you anything further to ask Miss Parfitt?"

"No, my lord, thank you." Deverill turned to Rathbone. His foretaste of victory was plain in his face, in the confidence of the way he stood, balancing with his back a trifle arched and his shoulders squared. "Sir Oliver?"

Rathbone rose to his feet. The watch was the most powerful piece of evidence against Merrit, the one thing he could not explain away. Deverill knew it as well. What mattered was what the jury saw.

"Miss Parfitt," he said, matching Deverill smile for smile, gentleness for gentleness. "Of course you have no choice but to tell us that Merrit Alberton showed you the watch that Breeland gave to her as a token of his feelings for her. You said it first with no knowledge of its meaning, and now cannot withdraw it. We all understand that. But Mr. Deverill omitted to ask you exactly when this incident occurred. Was it the day of Daniel Alberton's death?"

She looked suddenly relieved, seeing escape. "No! No, it was several days before that. At least two, and maybe three. I don't recall exactly now. I could get my diary?"

"I don't think that will be necessary," he declined. "Not for me, anyway. Could she have given it back to him for any reason? A quarrel, possibly? Or to have the catch altered, or put on a chain, or something else engraved?"

"Yes!" she said eagerly, her eyes widened. She seemed to hesitate for a moment.

"Thank you," he said quickly, afraid she would embellish it and be caught in an invention. "That is all we need to know, Miss Parfitt. Please do not strive to help. Only what you know is evidence, not what you may wish, or even believe."

"Yes . . ." she said awkwardly. "I . . . I see."

The judge looked at Deverill.

Deverill shook his head with a slight smile. He knew he did not need to make more of it.

The court adjourned for the day, and Rathbone went straight to see Merrit. He found her alone in the cell used for such meetings. The wardress was stationed outside the door, a big woman with her hair scraped back severely and a pink, scrubbed face. She shook her head slightly as Rathbone went past her and the key clanked in the lock.

"It's not going well, is it?" Merrit said as soon as they were alone. "The jury think Lyman did it. I can see it in their faces."

Did she instinctively think of Breeland before herself, or had she not yet grasped that she also was charged equally with him? No one believed she had fired the shots

286

herself, but an accomplice in such a crime would be held just as responsible and punished with the same finality. He could not afford to be gentle with her. She must face the truth of the situation before it was too late even to try to save it.

"Yes, they do," he agreed candidly. He saw the pain in her eyes, the trace of unreasonable hope that she was wrong die away. "I am sorry, but it is inescapable, and I would not be helping your cause if I were to pretend otherwise."

She bit her lip. "I know." Her voice was hoarse. "They are so mistaken in him. He would never do anything so vile . . . but even if they could not understand that, surely they can be made to see that there was no cause to? He received a note that my father had changed his mind and would sell the guns to him after all. He had found a way of escaping his commitment to Mr. Trace and was free to offer them to the more honorable cause. They were there at Euston Square Station. There was even a special train just to transport them."

"I believe I can prove that he could not have fired the shots himself," he agreed, allowing no lift of hope into his voice. He must not mislead her, even by implication. "What I cannot prove is that whoever did it was not paid to by Mr. Breeland. And that is just as serious a crime. Since you and he left England with the guns, you are accomplices in robbery and murder. . . ." He held up his hand as she began to protest. "I can make a good argument that you were unaware of what had happened, and therefore innocent—"

"But Lyman is innocent too!" she cut in, leaning forward urgently, her eyes bright. "He had no idea anyone had killed to get the guns!"

"How do you know that?" he asked very gently. It was not a challenge. There was no confrontation.

"I . . ." she started to answer. Then she blinked, her face puckering with dismay. "You mean how can I prove it to them? Surely . . ." Again she stopped.

"Yes, you do have to," he answered the question he thought had been in her mind. "In law one is presumed innocent unless you can be proved to be guilty beyond a reasonable doubt. Consider the word *reasonable*. Do you believe, after listening to the evidence so far, that the men in the jury box will have the same idea of what is true as you will have? We lose reason in emotion. When you think of issues like war, injustice, slavery, the love of your family or your country, your way of life, are any of us guided purely by reason?"

She shook her head minutely. "No," she whispered. "I suppose not." She took a deep breath. "But I know Lyman! He would not stoop to anything dishonorable. Honor, what is right, is dearer to him than anything. That is part of the reason I love him so much. Can't you make them see that?"

"And are you absolutely certain that what is right would not include sacrificing three men to the cause of obtaining guns for the Union?" he asked.

She was very pale. "Not by murder!" But her voice shook. Her eyes filled with tears. "I know he was not in the warehouse yard that evening, Sir Oliver, because I was with him all the time, and I was not there. I swear that!"

He believed her. "And how did the watch come to be there? How do I explain that to the jury?"

Fear rippled through her. He could not mistake it.

"I don't know! It doesn't make any sense. I can't explain it."

"When did you last see the watch?"

"I've been trying to think, but my mind is in such turmoil the harder I try the less clear it becomes. I remember showing it to Mrs. Monk, and I had it the day after that, because that was when Dorothea admired it, so of course I told her about it." She flushed very faintly, hardly more than a suspicion of color in her pale face. "After that . . . I'm not certain. Times get muddled in my memory. So much happened, and I was furious with my father. . . ." The tears spilled over her eyes and she fought for self-control.

Rathbone did not interrupt her or try to offer words they both knew he could not mean.

"Could you have lost it, or left it on a garment you were not wearing?" he asked at length.

"I suppose so." She seized the explanation. "I must have. But Lyman would never have left it in the yard, and who else could?"

"I don't know," he admitted. "But I shall have Monk investigate it. It may now be possible your father took it with him."

"Oh, yes! That could be, couldn't it?" At last there was a lift of hope in her voice. "Sir Oliver, who was it that killed him? Was it Mr. Shearer? That is very dreadful. I know my father trusted him. They had worked together for years. I only met him once. He was rather grim, sort of . . . I'm not sure . . . angry. At least I thought he was." She searched his face to see if he understood what she found so difficult to say. "Was it for money?"

"It seems as if it was."

"How could my father have been so wrong about him?"

"I don't know. Perhaps because we tend to judge others by our own standards."

She did not answer. And within a few moments he took his leave, trying to encourage her to keep heart.

He did not especially wish to see Breeland, but it was a duty he must not shirk. He found him standing by the chair and small table in the room assigned for him. His face was stiff, his shoulders locked so tight they strained the fabric of his jacket. He looked accusingly at Rathbone, and Rathbone could not blame him for it. He disliked the man, and Breeland must know it, and also that Rathbone's first loyalty was to Merrit Alberton. It was Judith, after all, who was paying him. It was Merrit's desire, not Breeland's, that they be charged as one, and she would not claim any special innocence. She was determined to stand with him, although Rathbone wondered if it was now love for Breeland or love of loyalty which kept her.

Without warning he felt a keen pity for Breeland, thousands of miles from home and overwhelmingly among strangers who hated him for what they believed him to be.

Perhaps had Rathbone been in similar circumstances he would have wrapped himself in the same icy dignity. It was the last protection Breeland had left, to seem not to care. And why should anyone parade his vulnerability for his enemies to stare at?

Could Shearer have murdered Alberton without Breeland's knowledge, and certainly without his complicity? And should Breeland, owing all his allegiance to his own people, locked in a terrible war, not have taken the guns so fortuitously offered him—simply because he suspected they had been obtained by deceit? It was war, not trade. For him they were the survival of a cause, not a matter of profit.

Breeland stared at him. "I assume that at some point in this farce you will attempt to defend at least Miss Alberton, if not me?" he said coldly. "Although I would remind you she came willingly with me to America, and Monk will testify to that."

"I am more concerned to hear him testify as to the exact times of the events on the night of the murders, and your train to Liverpool," Rathbone replied levelly. "It will be a simpler matter to convince them of the fact that Shearer may well have planned and committed the murders and the theft of the guns, with the intention of selling them to you, and you buying them in good faith, than it will be to make them feel well disposed towards you."

"What does that matter?" Breeland said bitterly. "I am a foreigner. They don't understand my cause, or sympathize with it. They don't know what America stands for. They have not caught our dream. I can't help that. Surely they at least understand justice?" It was said with an air of challenge, and not a little of insult.

Rathbone reminded himself of the man's isolation, of how much he had already sacrificed for a cause that was both noble and unselfish. Would he himself have done any better, any more wisely? Would such threat, and such lack of understanding and respect all around him, not have made him lash out also?

"Juries are people, Mr. Breeland, and subject to emotional impulses like the rest of us," he said as mildly as he could, keeping the edge out of his voice. "They will not remember everything that is said to them. In fact, they will probably not even hear it all, or perceive it in the way we wish them to. Very often people hear what they think they will hear. Make them feel some respect for you, some liking, and they will see the best, and recall it when it matters. This is not peculiar to English juries; it is part of the nature of all people, and we choose to be tried before a jury precisely because they are ordinary. They work on instinctive judgment and common sense as well as the evidence presented to them. Your own common law is based upon this."

"Yes, I know." Breeland's lips were tight. Rathbone felt there was fear as well as anger and idealism behind the mask of his face. He did well that it was not the overriding thing. "I cannot make people like me. And I will not grovel. My cause speaks well enough for me. I would abolish slavery from the earth." Now his voice rang with passion, his eyes alight. "I would give every man the chance to be his own master, to believe what he chooses and speak his mind without fear."

"It sounds marvelous," Rathbone said wearily, but with total sincerity. "I am not sure if it can exist. Liberty is always a matter of balancing one thing against another, gains and losses. But that is not the issue. You can fight for whatever you wish once you are free to leave the dock. First accomplish that, and to do it you will need to behave with a little more humanity. Believe me, Mr. Breeland, I am very good at my profession . . . easily as good as you are at yours. Take my advice."

Breeland stared at him, his eyes steady and fixed, fear far down in their depths bright and hard.

"Do you . . . do you think you can prove me innocent?" he said softly.

"I do. Now make the jury pleased to see me do it!"

Breeland said nothing, but some of the ice in him melted.

291

* * *

In the morning Monk was called to the witness stand to corroborate first Casbolt's evidence of their visit to Breeland's rooms, and then their terrible discovery in the warehouse yard in Tooley Street.

Deverill treated him with civility, but he could draw him to say little beyond a simple "Yes" or "No." He knew perfectly well, as was his skill to know, that Monk worked with Rathbone and his interest was in the defense. He had no intention of allowing Monk to cloud the issue or raise questions.

Monk wished there were some he could raise. So far he could think of nothing to add, even had Deverill allowed him to.

He substantiated all that Lanyon had already told them about their pursuit of the barge down the river as far as Greenwich and Bugsby's Marshes beyond.

"Now tell me, Mr. Monk, when you reported your findings to Mrs. Alberton, did she then request you to undertake any further activities on her behalf?" Deverill asked with wide eyes and acute interest in every line of his body.

It angered Monk to have to play out Deverill's charade, but he had no choice. Deverill asked his questions far too cleverly to give him room to say anything else without lying, and being caught at it.

"She asked me to go to America and bring her daughter back," he replied.

"Alone?" Deverill was incredulous. "A superhuman task, surely—and one not designed to enhance Miss Alberton's honor or reputation."

"Not alone," Monk said tartly. "She suggested I take my wife with me. And Mr. Philo Trace also expressed a desire to go, which I was glad to accept, since he knew the country and I did not."

"Most practical, at least as far as it extends," Deverill damned it with faint praise. "Mrs. Alberton can hardly have foreseen this situation today." He turned on the spot, his

292

coat swinging. "Or perhaps she did. Perhaps she loved her husband and wished his murder avenged. Even at this cost!"

Rathbone started to rise.

"Not very logical," Monk criticized with a cold smile. "If all she wanted was justice, she would have employed someone to go to America and kill Breeland—and Miss Alberton also, had she thought her guilty." He ignored the gasps around the room. "That would have been easier to accomplish, and less expensive. Only one man necessary, and no return fare for Breeland or Miss Alberton, and no chance of their escape."

"That is an appalling suggestion, sir!" Deverill said in well-displayed horror. "Barbaric!"

"No more so than yours," Monk retorted. "And no sillier."

There was a faint titter of laughter around the gallery, more a release of tension than amusement.

The judge half hid a smile.

Deverill was annoyed, but as he framed his next question his wording was a great deal more carefully considered.

"Did Breeland return with you of his own free will?"

"I gave him no choice," Monk replied with slight surprise. "But actually he did express a willingness to answer the charge. He said he—"

"Thank you!" Deverill cut him off, raising his hand, holding the palm forward for silence. "That is sufficient. Whatever Breeland wishes to say, he will no doubt be given the opportunity in due course. Now—"

"And of course you will believe him," Monk said sarcastically.

Rathbone smiled.

"What I believe is irrelevant," Deverill snapped. "It is the members of the jury who matter here, Mr. Monk. But while we are considering beliefs, did you believe Breeland's eagerness to prove his innocence, or did you feel it advisable to bring him back under some restraint?"

"I have learned that my beliefs may be mistaken," Monk

answered. "I kept him under restraint. However, I did not think the same necessary for Miss Alberton. I used no restraint whatever upon her."

Deverill's face tightened with irritation. He should have foreseen that Monk might say that.

"Thank you. I know of nothing further you could usefully add to our deliberations. Unless my learned friend has something to ask you, you are excused."

Rathbone rose to his feet slowly, not until the very last minute certain of what he was going to say. How wise was it to pursue the matter? How far could he predict what Monk would say? Should he allow Deverill the opportunity to reexamine? Everything Monk would corroborate in Breeland's story would be better told by Breeland himself.

"Thank you." He inclined his head very slightly. "I agree with Mr. Deverill."

The judge looked slightly surprised, but Monk was allowed to return to the body of the court, where he sat beside Hester and Judith Alberton, only once glancing at the brooding figure of Philo Trace.

Deverill's last witness was a banker who testified that no money whatsoever had reached Daniel Alberton's account since the payment made by Philo Trace as a deposit in good faith.

Deverill offered to have both Casbolt and Trace testify to this, but the court was willing to accept the banker's word and his documents.

"The prosecution rests," Deverill said, facing the jury with a smile. "The guns were stolen. No payment was made to Alberton and Casbolt. Mr. Alberton was murdered in the warehouse yard in Tooley Street and the guns taken and shipped to America, quite openly by Lyman Breeland, in the willing company of Merrit Alberton, whose watch was found at the scene of the murders. None of these things has the defense even attempted to deny. They cannot! Gentlemen, Breeland is manifestly guilty, albeit because he believes in his cause at any cost. And Miss Alberton is swept off her feet in her consuming obsession for him, which even

294

now she does not abandon. But murder is a deed he cannot walk away from with impunity. We shall show him so!" And he turned to Rathbone with an inviting gesture of his hand. "But please give us your best efforts to try . . . when the court reconvenes tomorrow."

11

Monk was angry on the witness stand, but once the court had adjourned for the day and the heat of antagonism had died down, his feelings were different. Hester had gone with Judith Alberton. Casbolt had been there also, but perhaps a sense of decorum had prevented him from remaining too close to her.

The other, far uglier thought came unbidden—that perhaps he was beginning to suspect that Alberton himself had been involved in the sale of the extra five hundred guns to the pirates, and had been betrayed by them, and he could not bear Judith to know it. He did not want to face having to lie, nor did he know enough to tell her beyond doubt. Perhaps Alberton had intended that she should never know.

How much does one protect the people one loves? What is protection, and what is stifling, denial of their right to be themselves, to make their own choices? He would bitterly have resented such protection himself. He would have felt it belittled him and made him less than equal.

The sun was fading a little in the street, but the air was still hot from the day. The slanted light was hazy and the dust rose in clouds from the dry cobbles.

Monk had looked at Breeland from the witness-box and wondered what he felt, what emotions there were under his cold exterior. He had never been able to read him except perhaps on the battlefield at Manassas. There his passion, his dedication and his disillusion had all been naked. But he was an acutely private man. He seemed driven to speak of his ideals to rid America of slavery, but whatever more personal, human emotions he felt he could not show. It was almost as if his fire were all in the mind, nothing in the heart or the blood.

Was it actually an evasion of real feeling, a way of making sure the object of his passion never asked of him anything he could not govern, direct, guard from hurting him?

Love was not like that. No choice could be made between the giving and the taking. He saw that in Philo Trace's eyes as he looked at Judith Alberton. Trace held no hope of receiving anything from her more than friendship, and perhaps he would not have withdrawn his help from her if she had refused even that. Whether he could have escaped from it was irrelevant. He had not tried to. There was no meanness of spirit in him, no self-regarding, at least where she was concerned.

But was Monk thinking of Philo Trace or what he himself had learned of love?

He crossed the street and continued walking. He passed a muffin seller, barely aware of her.

He had never intended to love Hester. He had realized very early in their acquaintance that she had the power to hurt him, to demand of him a depth of commitment he had no intention of giving. All the life he could remember he had avoided such a loss of his freedom.

And he had lost it anyway. She had effectively taken it from him, whether he wished it or not.

That was not true. He had chosen to embrace the fullness of living, instead of playing on the edge and lying to himself that he was retaining control, when all he was doing was abstaining from experience, running away from himself.

He despised cowardice as much as he did self-deception.

He hailed the next hansom and gave the driver his address in Fitzroy Street. He could not go back on his decision, whatever it cost.

He had been home for nearly an hour when Hester came in. She looked tired and frightened. She hesitated even before she took off her jacket. It was linen, of the dusty blue-gray she liked so well. Her eyes searched his anxiously.

He knew what disturbed her, more even than her fear for Judith or Merrit Alberton. It was his evasion over the last few days, the distance he had opened between them. He must bridge it now, whatever the result.

"How is she?" he asked. The words were trivial. He could have asked her anything. What mattered was that he met her eyes.

She saw the difference. It was almost as if he had touched her with the old intimacy. Something inside her warmed like a flower opening.

"She is frightened for Merrit," she answered. "I hope Oliver can make as powerful an argument as Deverill did. I wish Breeland would reach out to Merrit. She looks so alone there." Again it was not the words that mattered, but the softness in her mouth, the fact that her eyes did not even flicker away from his.

"He believes in his cause," he said, wishing beyond almost anything else that he could avoid this moment, that somehow it would go away. "He can see a million slaves and the moral wrong of their state, the mass injustice and cruelty—but he doesn't dare to look at the loneliness or the need of one human who needs him. It is too . . . personal, too intimate, too close under his own skin."

She unfastened the pin that secured her hat and took off the hat itself, all the time watching him. She knew he had not yet reached the point of what he was saying.

"Does he love Merrit?" she asked.

"Is that what matters?"

She stood quite still. She did not know why, her puzzlement was in her eyes, but she sensed he was asking for reasons deeper than the mere words he used, or the personal question.

"It's part of it," she said carefully. "The issues he fights for matter as well."

"And Philo Trace?" he went on. "He loves Judith. I suppose you've seen that?"

A smile touched her mouth, then vanished. "Of course I've seen it. It's so plain even she has seen it. Why?"

"And does she care that he's a Southerner, fighting for the slave states?"

Her eyes widened a little. "I have no idea. Why do you ask? You like him? So do I."

"But you abhor slaving. . . ."

The shadow was at the back of her eyes. She knew he still had not said what he needed to, although she could not guess what it would be. Would the warmth go from her then? Would these be the last few seconds he would ever look at her and see that undisguised tenderness in her face, and the honesty? Could he stretch the minutes out, make them last so he would never forget?

"Yes," she agreed.

"I learned something about myself when I went down to the river looking for Shearer." Now there was no going back.

She understood. She saw the fear in him. She knew the darkness already. She could not have forgotten that first, terrible, drowning fear in Mecklenburg Square, the horror which had nearly destroyed him. It was her courage which had made him fight.

Now she came forward, standing just in front of him, so closely he could smell the perfume of her hair and skin.

"What did you find out?" she asked, only the slightest tremor in her voice.

"One of the shipping companies knew me. The man expected me to be wealthy. . . ." This was every bit as difficult as he had expected. Her clear eyes allowed no evasions or euphemisms. If he lied now he would never be able to regain what he lost.

"As a policeman?" Her face was white, her voice catching in her throat. He knew she envisioned corruption. She was shaking her head a little, denying the possibility.

"No!" he said quickly. "Before that. As a banker."

She did not understand. It was time to put it into unmistakable words, words that could not be misunderstood or evaded anymore.

300

"Doing business with men who had made their money out of slaving . . . and it seems I knew it." He must say it all. Easier now than raising the subject again later. "I was bargaining for Arrol Dundas, my mentor. I don't know whether I told him that that was where the money came from . . . or not. Perhaps I misled him."

For a moment she was silent. Time ballooned out to seem like eternity.

"I see," she said at last. "Is that why you've been . . . away . . . these last few days?"

"Yes . . ." He wanted her to know how ashamed he was, he needed her to know it, but the words were too trite. None of them meant enough for the bitter weight of regret now that he should have allowed himself to be without honor. He had degraded his own worth.

She smiled, but her eyes were filled with sadness. She reached out her hand and touched his cheek. It was a soft gesture. It did not dismiss what he had done, or excuse it, but it set it in the past.

"You've looked back enough," she said quietly. "If you profited from it, it's gone now."

He wanted to kiss her, to be as close as people can be, to hold her tightly and feel her answering strength, but he had created the gulf and it must be she who crossed it, otherwise he would never be sure she had wished to, that he had not precipitated it.

She looked at him a moment longer, weighing what he thought, what he felt, then she was satisfied. Her eyes filled with warmth and, smiling, she put her arms around him and kissed his lips.

Relief washed over him in a warm, sweet tide. He had never been more grateful for anything in his life. He responded to her with a whole heart.

Rathbone began his defense when the trial resumed in the morning. He wore an air of confidence he was far from feeling. There was still no trace of Shearer and no sign of where

301

he had gone. Of course, with his shipping connections that could be anywhere in Europe—or the world, for that matter.

But juries liked a person they could see and whose guilt had been shown them, not a reasonable alternative who was nothing more than a name.

He must repair the damage Deverill had done, the emotional impression he had created in the jurors' minds. He began by calling Merrit to the stand. He watched her walk across the floor of the court. Everyone in the room must have been aware of how nervous she was. It was there in the pallor of her face, in the slight misstep as she climbed up to the witness-box, and in the quaver of her voice as she took the oath.

Again Hester sat beside Judith. Monk had given his evidence and was free to return to searching for more information about Shearer, anything at all, however tiny, that would give proof of the theory that it was he alone who had planned the robbery and the murder, knowing he would sell the guns to Breeland, but without Breeland's foreknowledge.

Rathbone began very gently leading Merrit through her story, starting as late in events as the day of the murders itself. He did not wish to open the subject of their early acquaintance, in case Deverill should pry out of it the appearance that Breeland had courted her not for herself but purely as a means to corrupt her into helping him obtain the guns. It might not be difficult to do, given her loyalty to him, her passion against slavery and how much she had already committed herself to the cause, and could not now retreat.

Beside Hester, Judith sat a little forward, her black, lace-gloved hands knotted together in her lap. She was listening to every word, watching every gesture, each expression of the face. Hester knew she was seeking meanings, hope, wrestling with fear, trying to outguess the future. She had been there too many times herself.

On Judith's other side, Robert Casbolt, his evidence also given, was offering silent support. He was too wise to mouth comforting words that could have no meaning. Everything lay in the balance. It all depended on Rathbone, and Merrit.

"You quarreled with your father that evening," Rathbone was saying, looking up at Merrit on the stand. "What about . . . precisely?"

She cleared her throat. "His selling guns to the Confederates instead of to the Union," she answered. "I believed he should have found a way to get out of his bond to sell them to Mr. Trace, even though he had promised to. He should have given back the money Mr. Trace had paid in advance."

"Did he still have that money?" Rathbone asked curiously.

"I . . ." It was very obvious she had never considered that possibility. "I . . . don't know. I assumed . . ."

"That he had not paid for the guns with it?" he asked. "But he did not manufacture the guns, did he?"

"No . . ."

"Then it may not have been possible."

"Well . . . I suppose . . . I thought he bought them first." Involuntarily she glanced at Casbolt as she spoke, then back to Rathbone. "But if he still owed anything, I am sure he would have made some way . . . I mean, when Lyman . . . Mr. Breeland, paid for them in full, as he could, then anything my father owed could have been paid—couldn't it." She spoke with confidence, sure she had the solution.

"If indeed Breeland did have the money," Rathbone agreed.

Hester knew what he was doing—demonstrating for the jury Merrit's trust, her naïveté, and her transparent belief that the dealings were legitimate. She did not yet see how he was going to extricate Breeland from the suspicion of deceit.

"But he did!" Merrit said urgently. "He actually paid it to Mr. Shearer, at Euston, when we took the guns."

"Did you see that?" Rathbone enquired.

"Well . . . no. I was in the carriage. But Mr. Shearer would not have handed over the guns without the money, would he!" That was a challenge, not a question.

"I think it excessively unlikely," Rathbone agreed with a smile. "But may we return to your parting from your father? You accused him of being in favor of slavery, is that right?"

She looked abashed. "Yes. I wish now that I hadn't said those things, but I believed them then. I was terribly angry."

"And you believed that Lyman Breeland wanted to purchase the guns for a highly honorable cause, far more honorable than that of Mr. Trace?"

Her chin lifted sharply. "I knew it. I was in America. I witnessed the most terrible battle. I saw . . ." She gulped. "I saw so many men killed. I had never realized it would be so dreadful. Until you have seen a battle, heard it, smelled it . . . you can have no idea of what it is really like. We don't begin to know what our soldiers endure for us."

There was a murmur of appreciation around the room, even of awe.

Rathbone allowed the jury to see her remorse just long enough that he did not seem to be doing it deliberately, then he continued.

"After your quarrel, where did you go, Miss Alberton?"

"I went upstairs to my bedroom, packed a few personal belongings—toiletries, a change of costume—and I left the house," she replied.

"A change of costume?" He smiled. "You were wearing an evening gown?"

"A dinner dress," she corrected him. "But not suitable for travel, of course."

Deverill looked exaggeratedly weary. "My lord . . ."

"Oh, yes, it does matter," Rathbone said with a smile. He turned back to Merrit. "And then you left for Mr. Breeland's rooms?"

She flushed very slightly. "Yes."

"That must have been a very emotional time for you, and required courage and decision."

"My lord!" Deverill protested again. "We do not doubt that Miss Alberton has extraordinary courage. An attempt to arouse our sympathy—"

"It has nothing whatever to do with courage, or sympathy, my lord," Rathbone interrupted. "It is purely practical."

"I am glad to hear it," the judge said dryly. "Proceed."

"Thank you. Miss Alberton, what did you do just when you arrived at Mr. Breeland's rooms?"

She looked confused.

"Did you talk together? Eat something, perhaps? Change your clothes to the ones you had brought?"

"Oh . . . we spoke for a little, of course, then he stepped out for a few moments while I changed my clothes."

Deverill murmured under his breath.

"And the watch?" Rathbone asked.

Suddenly there was utter silence in the room.

"I . . ." Her face was white.

Deverill was on the point of interrupting again.

Rathbone wondered if he should remind Merrit that she had sworn to tell the truth, but he was afraid that she would consider the truth a small price to pay not to betray Breeland.

"Miss Alberton?" the judge prompted.

"I don't remember," she said, looking at Rathbone.

He knew she was lying. In that moment she had recalled very clearly, but she would not say so. He changed the subject.

"Was Mr. Breeland expecting you, Miss Alberton?"

"No. No . . . he was very surprised to see me." The color washed up her face. She was acutely conscious of the fact that she had gone uninvited. It seemed to Hester, seeing her discomfort, that Breeland had not welcomed her as a lover might, but rather as a young man would who had been taken very much by surprise and been obliged extremely hastily to rearrange his plans. She hoped that was not lost upon the jury.

Rathbone was standing elegantly in the open space of the court, his head a little bent, the light shining on his fair hair.

Hester glanced up at Breeland. He also looked self-conscious and uncomfortable, although it was not so easy to know for what cause.

"I see. And after you had greeted each other, you had explained your presence, and he had permitted you to change your clothes, what did you do then?" Rathbone asked.

"We discussed what we should do," she replied. "Do I have to tell you what we said? I am not sure I can remember."

"It is not necessary. Were you together all the time?"

"Yes. It was not so very long. At a little before midnight a messenger arrived with a note saying that my father had changed his mind and would sell Lyman the guns after all, and we should go straight to the Euston Square station with the money."

"Who wrote this note?"

"Mr. Shearer, my father's agent."

"Surely it surprised you? After all, your father had been adamant, only a few hours before, that it was completely impossible for him to change his mind. It was a matter of honor," Rathbone pointed out.

"Yes, of course I was surprised," she agreed. "But I was too happy to question it. It meant he had seen the justice of the Union cause after all; he was on the right side. I thought perhaps . . . perhaps my argument meant something to him. . . ."

Rathbone smiled ruefully. "And so you went to the station with Mr. Breeland?"

"Yes."

"Would you describe that journey for us, Miss Alberton?"

Step by step, in tedious detail, she obliged. They adjourned for lunch, and then resumed. By midafternoon, when she had completed her account, anyone still listening might well have felt as if they themselves had made the train journey to Liverpool, stayed in a boardinghouse and embarked upon the steamer to cross the Atlantic.

"Thank you, Miss Alberton. And just to make sure we have not misunderstood you, was Mr. Breeland out of your company at any time during the night of your father's death?"

"No, absolutely not."

"And did you see your father after you left home, or go anywhere near the warehouse in Tooley Street?"

"No!"

"Oh . . . one thing more, Miss Alberton . . ."

"Yes?"

"Did you actually see Shearer at the Euston Square station? I assume you do know him by sight?"

"Yes, I do. I saw him very briefly, talking to one of the guards."

"I see. Thank you." He turned to Deverill, inviting him to take his turn.

Deverill considered carefully, perhaps more to test Rathbone than in actual indecision. Merrit had already made it plain she would defend Breeland to the last degree, and the more she did so the more the jury respected her, whether they believed her or not. They did not think she was lying, except perhaps about leaving the watch in Breeland's rooms, but they may well have thought her duped and used by a man unworthy of her. He would alienate them if he made that any more publicly apparent than it already was.

It was a difficult night. The tension made sleep difficult, in spite of exhaustion. Monk had been up and down the river all day, and intended to resume the day after as well, determined to find something. Hester did not ask him for an account of progress; she needed to keep hope alive, for Judith's sake.

On Friday Rathbone called Lyman Breeland to the stand. This was the most dangerous gamble of the whole defense, but he had no choice. Not to have called Breeland would have demonstrated his fears, not only to Deverill but more important, to the jury. Deverill would have made the most of it in his summing up.

Above all Rathbone would have liked to separate Merrit from Breeland in the jurors' minds, even in the legal charge, but that was morally impossible. He had already done too much with the watch. He had undertaken to defend Breeland, and he must do so to the very best of his ability.

Standing in the witness-box with shoulders squared and chin high, Breeland swore that he would tell the truth, and gave his name and his rank in the Union army.

Rathbone drew from him the bare facts of his journey to England and the reason for it. He did not ask him why he was prepared to go to such lengths in his cause; he knew Breeland would tell them anyway, spontaneously and with a passion that would ring through whether they wanted to believe him or not.

"And you presented yourself to Daniel Alberton in the hope of purchasing the guns you needed?" Rathbone asked, meeting Breeland's eyes and willing him to keep his answers brief. That they might also be respectful was beyond his hope, in spite of his efforts to convince Breeland that antagonizing everyone now might cost him his life, the balance was so fine. Breeland had replied simply that he was innocent and that should be enough.

Rathbone had dealt with martyrs before. They were exhausting, and seldom open to reason. They had a single view of the world and did not listen to what they did not wish to hear. In some ways their dedication was admirable. Perhaps it was the only way to accomplish certain goals, noble ones, but it left a trail of wreckage behind. Rathbone had no intention that Merrit Alberton should be part of Breeland's destruction.

Breeland agreed with unexpected brevity that he had indeed gone to see Alberton in hope of purchasing guns, and when he had met with resistance and learned that the reason for it was a commitment to Philo Trace, he had done all in his power to change Alberton's mind by convincing him of the Union's morally superior cause.

"And during this time you made the acquaintance of Miss Merrit Alberton?"

"Yes," Breeland agreed, a flicker of warmth at last lighting his face. "She is a person of the deepest compassion and honor. She understood the Union cause and espoused it herself immediately."

Rathbone would have wished he had phrased it in more romantic terms, but it was better than he had foreseen. He must be careful not to lead Breeland so his emotions seemed coached.

"You found you had in common the most important values and beliefs?"

"Yes. My admiration for her was greater than I had expected to feel for any woman so young and so unacquainted with the actuality of slavery and its evils. She has an ex-

308

traordinary gift for compassion." His face softened as he said it and for the first time there was something like a smile on his lips.

Rathbone breathed a sigh of relief. The jurors' expressions relaxed. At last they saw the human man, the man in love, with whom they could identify, not the fanatic.

He did not look at Merrit, but he could imagine her eyes, her face.

"But in spite of all both you and Miss Alberton could do to change his mind," he continued, "Mr. Alberton did not agree to go back on his word to Mr. Trace, and sell you the guns instead. Why did you not simply go to another supplier?"

"Because he had the finest modern guns available immediately, and in quantity. I could not afford to wait."

"I see. And what plans did you make as a result of this, Mr. Breeland?"

Breeland sounded slightly surprised.

"None. I confess, I was very angry with his blindness. He seemed incapable of seeing that there was a far greater issue at stake than one man's business reputation." The hard edge had returned to his voice and he directed his attention entirely towards Rathbone. Merrit seemed to have gone from his mind. He leaned a little forward over the rail of the witness-box. "He could see nothing but the narrow view, his own word and what Philo Trace thought of him. He was a man without vision. No matter what I told him of the evils of slavery." He waved his hand in a small dismissive gesture. "And all your gentlemen here have no idea what a cancer of the human soul it is when you have seen human beings treated with less dignity than a good man treats his cattle." His voice rang with the fire of his anger; his face burned with it. Rathbone could easily see why Merrit had fallen in love with him. What was less easy to see was what tenderness or patience he could give her in return, what laughter or tolerance or simple joy in daily life, what gratitude for little things—above all, perhaps, what forgiveness for failing and understanding of its needs. He had no compassion for weakness.

But Rathbone was in his middle forties; Merrit was sixteen. Perhaps she had years ahead before she would come to realize the value of such things. Now Breeland was a hero, and heroes were what she wanted. She knew his vulnerabilities and loved him the more for them. She did not see his limitations.

"We have heard that you quarreled with Mr. Alberton on the night of his death, and on leaving his house you told him that you would win in the end, regardless of what he might do. What did you mean, Mr. Breeland?"

"Why, that the Union cause was just and in the end would prevail against any ignorance or self-interest," Breeland replied clearly, as if the answer should have been obvious. "It was not a threat, simply a statement of the truth. I did not harm Mr. Alberton, as God is my judge!"

Rathbone kept his voice calm, almost matter-of-fact, as if he had barely heard Breeland's denial or the passion in him.

"Where did you go after you left Mr. Alberton's house?"

"Back to my rooms."

"Alone?"

"Of course."

"Did you make any agreement with Miss Alberton that she would follow you?"

Breeland opened his mouth to respond instinctively, then changed his mind. Perhaps Breeland remembered Rathbone's warnings about the sympathies of the jury. "No," he said gravely. "I had no wish to come between Miss Alberton and her family. My intentions towards her were always honorable."

Rathbone knew that he was on dangerous ground, full of pitfalls. He wished he could have avoided asking at all, but the omission would be so glaring it would have done more harm.

"You went to your rooms. Mr. Breeland, had you, for any reason, taken back from Miss Alberton the watch you gave her as a keepsake?"

Breeland did not hesitate. "No." His gaze was unflinching.

Rathbone had not meant to look at the jury, but in spite of

310

himself he did. He saw the coldness in their faces. They believed Breeland, but they did not like him for it. In some
subtle way he had enlarged a gulf between himself and Merrit. Her loyalty was to him; his was to his cause. It was not
what he had said which jarred; it was the manner in which
he said it, and perhaps it was also what he did not say.

"Have you any idea how the watch came to be in Tooley
Street?" Rathbone asked.

"None at all," Breeland responded. "Except that it was not
dropped by either Miss Alberton or myself. She arrived at my
apartments at about half-past nine, and remained there with
me until we both left a little before midnight, when the note
came from Shearer that Mr. Alberton had changed his mind
and was willing to sell the guns to the Union after all. Then
we left together and went to the Euston Square station, and
from there to Liverpool." He summed up the entire story in a
few sentences, leaving Rathbone less to draw from him than
he had intended, but it was spontaneous and spoken with
such force that perhaps it was better than a carefully guided
response would have been.

"Were you surprised by the note from Shearer?" Rathbone began, then was aware of Deverill rising to his feet. "I
apologize, my lord," he said quickly. "The note that pur-
ported to come from Shearer?"

"I was amazed," Breeland conceded.

"But you did not doubt it?"

"No. I knew the justice of my cause. I believed that Alberton had at last realized it himself, and that the issue of
freedom from slavery was far greater than the business dealings, or the reputation for honor, of any one man. I admired
him for it."

There was total silence in the room. Rathbone felt as if a
kind of darkness had descended over him. He drew in his
breath with difficulty. Breeland had in a few moments laid
bare his philosophy and shown them an indifference to the
individual which was like a breath of ice, a road whose end
could not be known.

Rathbone looked at the jury and saw that they did not yet

311

perceive the fullness of what Breeland had said, but Deverill did. Victory was in his eyes.

Rathbone heard his voice in the high-ceilinged room as if it were someone else's, echoing strangely. He must continue, play it out to the very last word.

"Did you show the note to Miss Alberton?"

"No. I had no reason to. It was important to pack up my few belongings and leave as quickly as possible. He had allowed us very little time to get to the Euston Square station." Breeland was quite unaware of there having been any change. Nothing was altered in him, not the set of his shoulders, his hands gripping the rail, the confidence in his voice. "I told her what it said, and she was overjoyed . . . naturally."

"Yes . . . naturally," Rathbone repeated. Detail by detail he took Breeland through the ride to the station, a description of the place, of the guards, of Shearer himself, of the train and all the passengers in the carriage they shared. It coincided with Merrit's description so honestly he began for a moment to feel hope again. All the events and people were recognizable as the same she had seen, and yet with a sufficiently different perception, a different use of words, that it was clear they were not copied from each other, or rehearsed.

He even noticed a couple of jurors nodding, candor in their expressions, acceptance. Perhaps they too had made the journey from Euston to Liverpool and knew the truth of what Breeland was saying.

In the afternoon he took him more briefly through the voyage across the Atlantic and his short stay in America.

Deverill interrupted to ask if any of this was relevant.

"I do not doubt, my lord, that Mr. Breeland bought the guns for the Union army, or that he believes unequivocally in its cause. It is not difficult to see why any man might wish to abolish slavery in his own land, or any other. Nor do we doubt that he fought at Manassas, probably bravely, as did many others." He lowered his voice. "That he would pay any price whatever for Union victory is only too tragically clear. That he should sacrifice others to it is the substance of our charge."

312

"It is not my aim to prove that," Rathbone argued, knowing he was telling less than the truth, and that Deverill knew it also. "I wished to show that his treatment of Miss Alberton was always honorable and quite open, even when Monk and Trace were in Washington, because he knew he was innocent of any crime and had no cause to fear them."

Deverill smiled. "I apologize. You were so far from it I had not realized that was your aim. Please continue."

Rathbone was foundering, and they both knew it. But he could not now retreat. He took Breeland through his confrontation on the battlefield with Monk and Trace, and his acceptance of returning to England.

"You offered no resistance?"

"No. Many men can fight the physical battle in America," Breeland answered. "Only I can answer here for my actions, and fight the moral cause by persuading you here in England that our cause is just and our behavior honorable. I bought guns openly and paid a fair price for them. The only person I deceived was Philo Trace, and that is the fortune of war. He would expect it of me, as I would of him. We are enemies, even if we treat each other politely if we chance to meet in London. We are not barbarians."

He cleared his throat. "I am not afraid to answer for my acts before a court of law, and I wish you to think of my people as the just and brave men they are." He lifted his chin slightly, staring straight ahead of him. "The time will come when you will have to choose between the Union and the Confederacy. This war will not cease until one side has destroyed the other. I will give everything I have, my life, my freedom if necessary, to ensure that it is the Union that wins."

Rathbone looked up at Merrit and saw the flash of pride in her face, and that it cost her an effort. He thought he also saw a deepening shadow of loneliness.

There was a very slight murmur of applause from somewhere in the back of the court, instantly hushed.

Deverill's smile widened, but there was also a flicker of

313

uncertainty in it. He wanted the jury to think he was confident, perhaps that he perceived something they did not. It was a game of bluff and double bluff.

Rathbone could play it too. At the moment it was all he had.

"I cannot imagine that there is any man here who does not share your sentiments," he said very clearly. "It is not our war, and we grieve for your country, and we hope profoundly that some better solution may be found than the slaughter of armies and the ruin of the land. We have no desire to take the freedom of an innocent man who is serving his people in such a cause." He bowed very slightly, as if the battle against slavery were the question at issue.

His achievement was short-lived. Deverill rose to cross-examine Breeland, swaggering very slightly into the center of the floor. He began with a broad, dramatic gesture.

"Mr. Breeland, you speak with great passion about the Union cause. No one here could mistake your dedication to it. Would it be true to say you hold it dearer to you than anything else?"

Breeland faced him squarely, with pride. "Yes, it would."

Deverill considered for a moment. "I believe you, sir. I am not sure I could be so wholehearted myself. . . ."

Rathbone knew what was coming next. He even considered interrupting, diverting the jury for a few moments by pointing out that what Deverill had said was hardly a question, and not relevant to the case. But it would be delaying the inevitable. It would emphasize the fact that he had not wished Breeland to answer. He remained in his seat.

"I think . . ." Deverill resumed, turning sideways to look up at Merrit. "I think that rather than declare the justice of my cause, and my own innocence, I should have been tempted to protest my love for a young woman who had given up everything—home, family, safety, even her own country—to follow me into a foreign land, at war with itself . . . and to expend my energy in doing all I could to see that she did not hang for my crimes, at the age of sixteen . . . barely yet a woman, on the verge of her life. . . ."

The effect was devastating. Breeland blushed crimson. One could only guess what anger and shame consumed him.

Merrit was white with misery. Perhaps never in her life again would she face such a terrible understanding, or humiliation.

Judith bent her head slowly, as if a weight had become too much to endure.

Philo Trace's lips were twisted with a pity he could not reach across and express.

Casbolt also stared at Judith.

The jurors were torn as to whether they would look at Merrit or not. Some wished to grant her privacy by averting their gaze, as if they had unintentionally intruded upon someone caught naked in an intimate act. Others glared at Breeland in undisguised contempt. Two looked up at Merrit with profound compassion. Perhaps they had daughters her age themselves. There was no condemnation in their faces.

Rathbone forced himself to remember that he was charged equally to defend Breeland and Merrit. He could not take advantage of this, and let Breeland hang to accomplish Merrit's acquittal, but at that moment he wished he could.

Deverill did not need to add more. Whatever the facts, and those he could not shake, he had stifled any possible act of mercy. The jury would want to convict Breeland, not for the murders, but because he did not love.

While Rathbone was struggling in the courtroom, Monk was trying to trace Shearer's actions on the night of Alberton's death and for the few days before. The only way to clear Breeland of the charge would be to prove that he had not conspired with Shearer. The times of the quarrel at Alberton's home, the delivery of the note to Breeland's rooms, and his arrival at the Euston Square station all made it impossible for him to have been at Tooley Street, but they did not prove that he had not either deliberately corrupted Shearer into committing the murders or at the least conspired with him and taken advantage of it.

He began at Tooley Street again, with the surviving warehousemen. It was a dusty, warm day with scurries of wind making little eddies over the cobbles.

"When did you last see Shearer?" Monk asked the man with the sandy hair to whom he had spoken before.

The man's face creased in concentration. "Not rightly sure. 'E was 'ere two days afore that. Tryin' ter 'member if 'e was 'ere that day. Don't think so. In fact I'm certain, 'cos we 'ad a nice load o' teak in, an' it weren't anything as 'e 'ad ter be 'ere for. Dunno w'ere 'e was, but Joe might know. I'll ask 'im." And he left Monk standing in the sun while he did so.

"At Seven Sisters, 'e was," he said on his return. "Went up ter see a feller abaht oak. Can't see as it's got anything ter do wi' guns."

Neither could Monk, but he intended to follow every movement of Shearer regardless. "Do you know the name of the company in Seven Sisters?"

"Bratby an' summink, I think," Bert replied. "Big firm, 'e said. On the 'Igh Street, or just off it. What does it 'ave ter do with poor Mr. Alberton's death? Bratby's deals in oak an' marble an' the like, not guns."

"I'd like to know where Shearer was from then onward," Monk said frankly. There was no point being evasive. "He was at the Euston Square station to pass over the guns to Breeland at just after half-past midnight, and no one has seen him since, for certain."

"So where is 'e?"

"I should dearly like to know. What does he look like?"

"Shearer? Ordinary sort o' bloke, really. 'Bout your 'eight, or a bit less, I s'pose. Lean. Not much 'air, but darkish. Got green eyes, that's different, an' a spot on 'is cheek, 'bout 'ere." He demonstrated, touching his cheekbone with his finger. "An' lots o' teef."

Monk thanked him, and after a few more questions which elicited nothing of worth, he took his leave and spent the next hour and a half taking a hansom to Seven Sisters. He found the firm of Bratby & Allan just off the main street.

"Mr. Shearer?" the clerk asked, pushing his hand through his hair. "Yes, we know 'im, right enough. What would that be about, sir, if I may ask?"

Monk had already considered his reply. "I'm afraid he has not been seen for several weeks, and we are concerned that some harm has come to him," he said gravely.

The clerk did not look much concerned. "Pity," he said laconically. "S'pose people 'oo work on the river 'ave haccidents, like. Not certain wot day it was, but I can look at me books an' see, if you want?"

"Yes, please."

The clerk put his pencil behind his ear and went to oblige. He returned several moments later carrying a ledger. " 'Ere," he said, putting it down on the table. He pointed with a smudged finger and Monk read. It was quite clear that Shearer had been at Bratby & Allan on the day before Alberton's death, until late in the afternoon, negotiating the terms of sale of timber and the possibility of transporting it south to the city of Bath.

"What time did he leave here?" Monk asked.

The clerk thought for a moment. " 'Alf after five, as I recollect. I s'pect you'll be wantin' ter know w'ere 'e went next?"

"If you know?"

"I don't, but then I could give yer a guess, like."

"I would be grateful."

"Well 'e'd go ter a cartin' company what 'as yards close by. Stands ter reason, don't it?" The clerk was pleased with his status as an expert. It pleased his self-respect quite visibly.

Monk gritted his teeth. "Indeed."

"And there's not many as goes as far as Bath," the clerk went on. "So if I was you, I'd try Cummins Brothers, down the road from 'ere a bit." He pointed to his left. "Or there's B. & J. Horner's the other way. An' o' course the biggest is Patterson's, but that's not ter say they're the best, an' Mr. Shearer likes the best. Don't stand no nonsense, 'e don't. 'Ard man, but fair . . . more or less."

"So who is the best?" Monk said patiently.

"Cummins Brothers," the clerk replied without hesitation.

"Costly, but reliable. Yer should ask ter see Mr. George, 'e's the boss, an' Mr. Shearer'd go to the top. Like I said, an 'ard man, but good at 'is business."

Monk thanked him and asked for precise directions to the premises of Cummins Brothers. Once there he requested Mr. George Cummins and was obliged to wait nearly half an hour before being shown into a small room very comfortably appointed. George Cummins sat behind his desk, the light shining through his thin white hair, his face pleasantly furrowed.

Monk introduced himself without evasion and told him honestly what he had come for.

"Shearer," Cummins said with surprise. "Disappeared, you said? Can't say I expected that. He seemed in good spirits when I last saw him. Expecting a nice profit on a big deal. Something to do with America, I think."

Monk felt a quickening of interest. He controlled it to protect himself from hope, or forcing circumstances to fit his wishes.

"Did he elaborate on that at all?"

Cummins's eyes narrowed. "Why? Just what is your business, Mr. Monk? And why do you want to know where Shearer is? I consider him a friend, have done for years. I'm not speaking about him to just anyone until I know why."

Monk could not tell him the truth, or it might prejudice any evidence Cummins could give. He must be honest, and yet evasive, something he had learned to do well.

"The deal with the American went badly wrong, as you may be aware," he replied gravely. "No one appears to have seen Shearer since then. I am a private enquiry agent acting on behalf of Mrs. Alberton, who is concerned that some harm may also have come to Mr. Shearer. He was a loyal employee of her late husband for many years. She feels some responsibility to ascertain that he is alive and well, and not in need of assistance. And of course, he is sadly missed, especially now."

"I see." Cummins nodded. "Yes, of course." He frowned. "Frankly, I can't understand him not being there. I confess,

318

Mr. Monk, you have me worried now. When I didn't see or hear from him, I took it he was away on a trading matter. He does go to the Continent now and then."

"When did you last see him?" Monk pressed. "Exactly."

Cummins thought for a moment. "The night before Alberton was killed. But I suppose you know that, and that's why you're here. We talked about moving some timber to Bath. As I said, he was in good spirits. We had dinner together, at the Hanley Arms, next to the omnibus station on Hornsey Road."

"What time did you leave?"

Cummins looked anxious. "What is it you're thinking, Mr. Monk?"

"I don't know. What time?"

"Late. About eleven. We . . . we dined rather well. He said he was going back to the city."

"How? Cab?"

"Train, from Seven Sisters Road Station. It's just down the bottom of the street from the Hanley Arms, then along a bit."

"How long would the journey take?"

"That time of night? Not many stops: Holloway Station, through Copenhagen Tunnel, then into King's Cross. Best part of an hour. Why? I wish you'd tell me what it is you're thinking!"

"Anyone see you together, swear to what time he left?"

"If you want. Ask the landlord of the Hanley Arms. Why?" Cummins's voice was sharp with alarm.

"Because I believe he was at the Euston Square station at half-past one," Monk answered, rising to his feet.

"What does that mean?" Cummins demanded, standing also.

"It means he couldn't have been at Tooley Street," Monk replied.

Cummins was startled. "Did you think he was? Good God! You . . . you didn't think he did that? Not Walter Shearer. He was a hard man, wanted the best, but he was loyal. Oh, no . . ." He stopped. He knew from Monk's face

319

there was no need to say more. "It was the American!" he finished.

"No, it wasn't," Monk replied. "I don't know who the hell it was. Will you swear to this?"

"Of course I will! It's the truth."

Monk checked with the landlord of the Hanley Arms, but he received the answer he expected, and corroboration from the landlord's wife. He retraced Shearer's steps to the Euston Square station, and found thirty-two minutes unaccounted for. No one could have gone south to Tooley Street, murdered three men and loaded six thousand guns in that time. But he could have stopped at King's Cross and walked from there to the Euston Square station to claim a wagon load of guns already stored there and waiting.

He recounted all these things to Rathbone that evening.

In the morning Rathbone asked for the court to be delayed for sufficient time for the landlord of the Hanley Arms to be called, and it was granted him.

By early afternoon all evidence had been given and both Deverill and Rathbone had made their summations. No one knew who had murdered Daniel Alberton or the two guards in Tooley Street, but it was quite clear it could not have been either Breeland or Shearer—acting for Breeland, or with his knowledge. Rathbone could not say how Breeland's watch had come to be in the yard, or account for the movement of the guns from Tooley Street or to Euston Square, but a mystified and unhappy jury returned a verdict of not guilty.

Judith was weak with relief. For her the immediate fact that Merrit was free from the threat of death was sufficient. She allowed herself to have a few moments' respite from grief.

Hester stood in the crowded hallway outside the courtroom watching as Merrit came towards her mother, hesitantly at first. Philo Trace was standing a dozen yards to the left of them. He did not wish to be included in the circle, but it was nakedly apparent in his face how much it mattered to him that Judith should be happy. His eyes were soft as he looked at her, oblivious to everyone else coming and going.

Robert Casbolt was closer, pale-faced, exhausted by the emotional turmoil of the trial, but now also, if not relaxed, at least no longer struggling to rescue Merrit.

Lyman Breeland stood back. It was impossible to tell from the stunned pallor of his face what he felt. He was free, but neither his character nor his cause had been understood as he would have liked. He was at least sensitive enough to the pain that had been experienced not to come forward now. Of this immediate reunion he was not a part. They were left with the grief, and the anger, all the things that had had to be unsaid, even unthought, until the battle was over.

Merrit's eyes filled with tears. Perhaps it was the sight of her mother in black, the color and vitality in her stifled, drained away by loss and then by fear.

Judith held her arms out.

Silently, Merrit stepped forward and they clasped each other, Merrit sobbing, letting go of all the terror and pain that she had held so desperately in control over the last month since Hester had first told her of her father's death.

Philo Trace blinked hard several times, then turned and walked away.

Robert Casbolt remained.

Rathbone came out of the courtroom door, smiling. Horatio Deverill was a couple of steps behind him, still looking surprised but not exhibiting any ill will. They passed Breeland without apparently noticing him.

"Did you do that on purpose?" Deverill asked, shaking his head. "I really thought I had you, on intent if not facts. I'm still not sure I wasn't caught by sleight of hand somehow."

Rathbone merely smiled.

Merrit and Judith parted and Judith thanked Rathbone formally, and moved a little apart with him. Merrit turned towards Hester.

"Thank you," she said very quietly. "You and Mr. Monk have done far more for me than I can ever express to you in words." There was still confusion and unhappiness in her face.

Hester knew what it was. The victory of acquittal was deeply shadowed by the disillusion of Breeland's isolation from her. Now that the immediate danger was over she had to face a decision. They were not forced together by common circumstances any longer. Suddenly it was a matter of choice. That she had to make it at all was painful enough, and her misery was clear.

"It was a very mixed blessing, wasn't it?" Hester replied equally quietly. She did not wish anyone else to hear their exchange, and with as many conversations as there were going on, it was not difficult to submerge themselves in the sea of voices.

Merrit did not answer. She still did not wish to commit herself to saying aloud that the certainty was gone. The crusade was glorious, but it was not really love, not enough for a marriage.

"I'm sorry," Hester said, and she meant it profoundly. She had mourned dreams herself, and knew the pain of it.

Merrit lowered her eyes. "I don't understand him," she said under her breath. "He didn't ever really love me, did he? Not as I loved him."

"He probably loves you as much as he is able to." Hester searched her mind to find the truth.

Merrit looked up. "What shall I do? He's an honorable man. I always knew he wasn't guilty! Not just of actively being there, but of persuading Shearer to do it either."

"Are you sure he wouldn't have taken the guns even if he had known that they were tainted by murder?" Hester asked.

Merrit gulped. "No . . ." she whispered. "He believes the cause is great enough to justify any means of serving it. I . . . I don't think I can share that belief. I know I can't feel it. Maybe my idealism isn't strong enough. I don't see the great vision. Perhaps I'm not as good as he is. . . ." That was almost a question; the pleading for an answer was in her eyes. Even now she was half convinced the fault was hers, that it was she who lacked a certain nobility that would have enabled her to see things as he did.

"No," Hester said decisively. "To see the mass and lose

322

the individual is not nobility. You are confusing emotional cowardice with honor." She was even more certain as she found the words. "To do what you believe is right, even when it hurts, to follow your duty when the cost in friendship is high, or even the cost in love, is a greater vision, of course. But to retreat from personal involvement, from gentleness and the giving of yourself, and choose instead the heroics of a general cause, no matter how fine, is a kind of cowardice."

Merrit still looked doubtful. Part of her understood, but she had not found words to explain it to herself. She frowned, struggling to make final the realization she had been trying not to see for days.

"I couldn't love anyone who would put me before what he believed was right. I mean . . . I could love him, but not with a whole heart, not the same way."

"Neither could I," Hester agreed, seeing the momentary relief in Merrit's eyes, then the confusion return. "I would want him to do what was right, no matter how it would hurt. That's the difference. I would want the cost to me to tear him apart . . . not to add to his sense of glory."

Merrit trembled on the edge of tears. "I . . . I really believed . . . you can't leave it behind so easily, can you?"

"No." Hester touched her arm very gently. "Of course not. But I think going with him, pretending all the time, watching the reality grow sharper, would be even more difficult."

Breeland was coming towards them. He looked a trifle awkward, uncertain what to say now that the tension had passed. He had the guns; he was proved innocent and acquitted. Perhaps he did not even understand the chill in the air.

Judith turned to watch, but she remained where she was.

"Thank you for your efforts on our behalf, Mrs. Monk," Breeland said stiffly. "I am sure you did it because you believed it to be right; nevertheless we are grateful."

"You are mistaken," Hester said, meeting his eyes. "I had no idea whether it was right or not. I did it because I care for Merrit. I hoped she was innocent, and I believed it as long as I could, because I wanted to. Fortunately, I still can."

"That is the sort of reasoning a woman is free to have, I suppose," he said with faint disapproval. "But it is too emotional." A very small smile touched his lips. "I do not wish to be ungracious." He turned to Merrit. "Perhaps you would prefer to remain some time with your mother before we return to Washington. I understand that. I can wait at least a week, then I should rejoin my regiment. I have very little reliable news of what is happening at home. At least now my honor is vindicated and England will know that the officers of the Union are upright in their dealings. I may well be sent back to purchase more arms."

There was a moment of silence before Merrit replied with her voice level, but it was apparent it cost her all the strength of will she possessed.

"I am sure your honor is vindicated, Lyman, and that for you that is the most important thing that could have happened. I am happy it is. I am equally certain that you deserve it. However, I do not wish to return to Washington with you. I thank you for the offer. I am sure you do me great honor, but I do not believe we should make each other happy, therefore I cannot accept."

He looked as if he had not grasped what he had heard. It was incomprehensible to him that she could have changed from the girl who had adored him so completely to the young woman who now made such a considered judgment that, incredibly, amounted to a rejection.

"You would make me very happy," he said with a frown. "You have all the qualities any man could wish for, and what is more, you have shown them under the greatest pressure. I cannot imagine I could find any woman I should admire more than I do you."

Merrit drew in a deep, shuddering breath. Hester saw the resolve flicker in her face.

"Love is more than admiration, Lyman," Merrit said with tremendous difficulty, gasping to control her breath. "Love is caring for someone when they are wrong, as well as when they are right, protecting their weakness, guarding them un-

324

til they find strength again. Love is sharing the little things, as well as the big ones."

He looked stunned, as if she had struck him, and he had no idea why.

Then quite slowly he bowed and turned and walked away.

She gave a little gulp, drew in her breath to call him back, and remained silent.

Judith came and put her arms around her, allowing her to weep with deep, wrenching sobs that were the end of a dream, and already just a thread of relief.

12

MONK AND HESTER dined out on the most excellent poached fish, fresh vegetables and plum pie with cream. They walked home arm in arm along the quiet, lamp-lit streets. There was an arch of light across the sky between the rooftops, and a few windows glowed yellow.

"We still don't know who killed Daniel Alberton," Hester said at last. They had both refrained from saying it all evening, but it could no longer remain a ghost between them.

"No," he agreed somberly, tightening his arm around her. "Except that it wasn't Breeland, even indirectly, and it couldn't have been Shearer. Who does that leave?"

"I don't know," she admitted. "What happened to the other five hundred guns?"

He did not reply for several minutes, walking in silence with his head down.

"Do you think Breeland took them too, and he lied?" she asked.

"Why should he?"

"The money? Perhaps what he paid wasn't enough?"

"Since there's no trace of any money at all, there doesn't seem to be any reason," he pointed out.

There was no response to make. Again they walked a short distance without speaking. They passed another couple and nodded politely. The woman was young and pretty, the man openly admiring of her. It made Hester feel comfortable and very safe, not from pain or loss, but at least from the agony of disillusion. She gripped Monk's arm a little more tightly.

"What is it?" he asked.

"Nothing," she said with a smile. "Nothing to do with Daniel Alberton, poor man. I really want to know what happened . . . and to prove it."

He gave a little laugh, but he held her equally close.

"I can't forget the blackmail," she went on. "I don't believe its happening at the same time was just coincidence. That's why he called you in. The blackmailer has never been back! Pirates don't give up, do they?"

"Alberton's dead!"

"I know that! But Casbolt isn't! Why didn't they pursue it with him? He also gave money and help to Gilmer."

They crossed the road and reached the pavement on the far side. They were still half a mile from home.

"The ugliest answer to that is that they didn't give up," he replied. "We still don't know what happened to the barge that went down the river, who took it, or what was on it. Certainly something went from Tooley Street; there are five hundred guns not accounted for . . . the exact amount demanded by the pirates."

"You think Alberton sold them after all?" she asked very quietly. It was the thought she had been trying to avoid for several days. The tension of the trial had allowed her to; now it could no longer be held away. "Why would he do that? Judith would loathe it."

"Presumably he never intended her to know . . . or Casbolt either."

"But why?" she insisted. "Five hundred guns . . . what would they be worth?"

"About one thousand eight hundred and seventy-five pounds," he answered. He had no need to add that that was a small fortune.

"You looked at his company books," she reminded him. "Could he possibly have needed that much?"

"No. He was doing well. Up and down, of course, but overall it was very profitable."

"Down? You mean times when no one wanted to buy guns?" she said skeptically.

"They dealt in other things as well, timbers and machinery particularly. But I wasn't thinking of that. Guns were the main profit makers, but also the only bad loss." They reached the curb. He hesitated, looked, then crossed. They were close to Fitzroy Street now. "Do you remember the Third China War you said Judith told you about the first night at the Albertons' home?"

"Over the ship and the French missionary?"

"Not that one, the one after . . . only last year."

"What about it?" she asked.

"It seems they sold some guns to the Chinese just before that, and because of the hostilities they were never paid. It wasn't a large amount, and they made it up within a few months. But that was the only bad deal. He didn't need to sell to pirates. Trace had paid him thirteen thousand pounds on account for the guns Breeland took, which, of course, will need to be paid back. Breeland says he paid the full price, around twenty-two thousand five hundred pounds. And there's the ammunition as well, which would be over one thousand four hundred pounds. The profit on all that would be a fortune." He shook his head a little. "I can't see why he should feel compelled to sell another one thousand eight hundred and seventy-five pounds' worth of guns to pirates."

"Nor can I," she agreed. "So where are they? And who killed Alberton, and who went down the river? And for that matter, where is Walter Shearer?"

"I don't know," Monk admitted. "But I intend to find out."

"Good," she said softly, turning the corner into Fitzroy Street. "We have to know."

In the morning Monk woke early and left without disturbing Hester. The sooner he started the sooner he might find some thread that would lead to the truth. As he walked towards Tottenham Court Road past the fruit and vegetable wagons heading for the market, he wondered if perhaps he already had that thread but had failed to recognize it. He rehearsed all he knew, going over it again in his mind, detail by detail, as he rode in a hansom across the river, ready to begin again the journey down to Bugsby's Marshes.

This time he did the trip hastily, concentrating more on the description of the barge, any distinguishing marks or characteristics it might have had. If it had returned even part of the way, surely someone must have seen it?

It took him all morning to get as far as Greenwich, but he learned a little about the barge. It was large and yet still so heavily laden it rode almost dangerously low in the water. One or two men who were used to working on the river had noticed it for precisely that reason. They described the dimensions very roughly, but in the dark, even had there been any other distinguishing marks, no one saw them.

From Morden Wharf, beyond Greenwich, he went by boat back across the river and up a little to Cubitt Tower Pier and then by road again past the Blackwall entrance to West India South Dock, still asking about the barge. He stopped for a tankard of cider at the Artichoke Tavern, but no one remembered the night of the Tooley Street murders anymore. It was too long ago now.

He went increasingly despondently to the Blackwall Stairs, where he had a long conversation with a waterman who was busy splicing a rope, working with gnarled fingers and a skill at weaving and pulling with the iron spike which in its way was as beautiful as a woman making lace. It pleased Monk to watch, bringing back some faint memory of a long-distant past, an age of childhood by northern beaches, the smell of salt and the music of Northumbrian voices, a time he could not fully recall anymore, except like bright patches of sunlight on a dark landscape.

"A big barge," the waterman said thoughtfully. "Yeah, I 'member the Tooley Street murders. Bad thing, that. Pity they in't got 'oo done it. But then I don't like guns neither. Guns are fer soldiers an' armies an' the like. Only bring trouble anywhere else."

"The ones for the Union army seem to have gone by train

to Liverpool," Monk replied. Not that it mattered now, and certainly not to the waterman.

"Yeah." The man wove the unraveled end of the rope into the main length and took out his knife to tidy off the last threads. "Mebbe."

"They did," Monk assured him.

"You see 'em?" The waterman raised his eyebrows.

"No . . . but they got there . . . to Washington, I mean."

The waterman made no comment.

"But there were others," Monk went on, narrowing his eyes against the sunlight off the river. They were directly across from the gray-brown stretch of Bugsby's Marshes and the curve of Blackwall Point, beyond which he could not see. "Something came down on that barge. What I don't know is where those boxes went, and where the barge went to after it was unloaded."

"There's plenty of illegal stuff goes back and forward around 'ere," the waterman ventured. "Small stuff, mostly, and farther down towards the Estuary, 'specially beyond the Woolwich Arsenal an' the docks on this side. Down Gallion's Reach, or Barking Way and on."

"It couldn't have got that far in the time," Monk replied.

"Mebbe it waited somewhere?" The waterman finished his work and surveyed it carefully. He was apparently satisfied, because he set it down and put away his knife and hook. "Margaret Ness, or Cross Ness, p'raps?"

"Any way I could find out?"

"Not as I can think of. You could try askin', if there's anybody 'round. Wanter go?"

Monk had nothing else left to try. He accepted, climbing into the boat with practiced balance and sitting easily in the stern.

Out on the water the air was cooler and the faint breeze on the moving tide carried the smell of salt and fish and mud banks.

"Go down towards the Blackwall Point," Monk directed. "Do you think there's enough cover there to conceal a seagoing ship, one big enough to cross the Atlantic?"

"Well now, that's a good question," the waterman said thoughtfully. "Depends where, like."

"Why? What difference does it make?" Monk asked.

"Well, some places a ship'd stand out like a sore thumb. See it a mile off, masts'd be plain as day. Other places there's the odd wreck, for example, an' 'oo'd notice an extra spar or two? For a while, leastways."

Monk sat forward eagerly. "Then go past all the places. Let's see what the draft is and where a ship could lie up," he urged.

The waterman obeyed, leaning his weight against the oars and digging them deep. "Not that it'll prove anything, mind," he warned. " 'Less, o' course, yer find someone 'as seen it. It's going back, now. Must be two months or more."

"I'll try," Monk insisted.

"Right." The waterman heaved hard and they picked up speed, even against the tide.

They moved around the wide curve of the Blackwall Reach as far as the Point, Monk staring at the muddy shore with its low reeds, and here and there the occasional driftwood floating, old mooring posts sticking above the tide like rotted teeth. Mudflats shone in the low sun, patches of green weed, and now and then part of a wreck settling lower and lower into the mire.

Beyond the Blackwall Point were the remains of two or three ancient barges. It was difficult to tell what they had been originally; too little was visible now. It might have been one barge, broken by tides and currents, or it might have been two. Other odd planks and boards had drifted up and stuck at angles in the mud. It was a dismal sight, the falling and decaying of what had once been gracious and useful.

The waterman rested on his oars, his face creased in a frown.

"What is it?" Monk asked. "Isn't this too shallow a lane for an oceangoing ship? It would have to stand far out, or risk going aground. It can't have been here. What about farther down?"

The waterman did not answer, seemingly lost in contemplation of the shore.

Monk grew impatient. "What about farther down?" he repeated. "It's too shallow here."

"Yeah," the waterman agreed. "Just tryin' ter 'member summink. There's summink I seen 'ere, 'round about that time. Can't think on what."

"A ship?" Monk said doubtfully. It was more of a denial than a question.

A yard-long board drifted past them towards the shore, submerged an inch or two below the surface of the water, one end jagged.

"What kind of a thing?" Monk said impatiently.

Another piece of flotsam bumped against the boat.

"More wrecks than that," the waterman answered, gesturing towards the shore. "Looks different. But why would anyone go an' move a wreck from 'ere? Ain't worth nothin' now. Wood's too rotten even ter burn. Ain't good for nothin' 'cept gettin' in the way."

"Another . . ." Monk started, then as his eye caught the jetsam drifting away, an extraordinary thought occurred to him—daring, outrageous, almost unprovable, but which would explain everything.

"Is there anybody else who would know?" His voice was surprisingly hoarse when he spoke, urgency making it raw.

The waterman looked at him with amazement, catching the sharp edge of emotion without understanding it.

"I could ask. Ol' Jeremiah Spatts might a' seen summink. Not much as gets by 'im. 'E lives over t'other side, but 'e's always up an' down. Mind yer'll 'ave ter be careful 'ow yer asks. 'E's no time fer the law."

"You ask him." Monk fished in his pocket and pulled out two half crowns and held them in his open palm. "Get me a careful, honest answer."

"I'll do that," the waterman agreed. "Don' need yer money, jus' wanner know what yer guessed. Tell me the story."

Monk told him, and gave him the half crowns anyway.

* * *

That evening Monk called upon Philo Trace, and fortunately found him in his lodgings. He did not ask him why he was still in London, whether it was in the hope of purchasing guns for the Confederacy or only because he was loath to leave because of his feelings for Judith Alberton. The trial was over; he had no legal or moral duty to remain.

He recalled Trace's having mentioned diving in the Confederate navy, and he needed to speak to him about it now, urgently.

"Diving!" Trace said in disbelief. "Where? What for?"

Explaining his reasons, and briefly what he had seen, Monk told him why.

"You can't go alone," Trace agreed the moment Monk was finished. "It's dangerous. I'll come with you. We'll have to get suits. Have you ever dived before?"

"No, but I'll have to learn as I do it," Monk answered, realizing how brash it sounded even as he spoke. But he had no alternative. He could not send anyone else, and the look in Trace's eyes betrayed that he knew that. He did not argue.

"Then I'd better explain some of the dangers and sensations you may feel, for your own safety," he warned. "There must be divers somewhere along the river, for salvage at least, and to mend wharfs and so on."

"There are," Monk agreed. "The waterman told me. I've already made enquiries. We can hire equipment and men to assist us from Messrs. Heinke. They are submarine engineers in Great Portland Street."

"Good." Trace nodded. "Then I'm ready when you wish."

"Tomorrow?"

"Certainly."

Monk had told Hester of the idea that had come to him on the river, and of his plan to take Philo Trace and dive beneath the Thames at Blackwall Point. Of course she had asked him about it in minute detail, and he answered only with assurances of his safety, and generalities as to how that was going to be assured, and what he expected to find.

The next afternoon just before two o'clock he left, saying he would meet with Philo Trace and the men from Messrs. Heinke at the river, and would return either when he had discovered something or when the rising tide made further work impossible. She was obliged to be content with that. There was no possibility whatever of her accompanying him. She knew from the look on his face that pressing the issue would gain her nothing at all.

Monk found the entire experience of diving extraordinary—and terrifying. He met Trace at the wharf where they were to be fitted out with all they would need for the proposed venture. Until this point Monk had been concentrating on what he expected to find on the bottom of the river, and what he would learn from it, if they were successful. Now, suddenly, the reality of what he was going to do overwhelmed him.

"Are you all right?" Trace asked, his face shadowed with anxiety.

They were side by side on the vast wooden timbers of the wharf, the gray-brown water opaque, twenty feet below them, sucking and sliding gently, smelling of salt, mud and that peculiar sour odor of receding tide which left behind it the refuse of the teeming life on either side of it. It was so turgid with scraped-up silt it could have been a foot deep, or a mile. Anything more than a foot beneath the surface was already invisible. It was just before ebb tide turned to flood, the best time for diving, when the currents are least powerful and the visibility of the incoming salt water offered almost a foot of sight.

Monk found himself shivering.

"Right, sir!" a thin man with grizzled hair said cheerfully. "Let's be 'avin' yer." He eyed Monk up and down with moderate approval. "Not too fat, anyway. Like 'em leaner, but you'll do."

Monk stared at him uncomprehendingly.

"Fat divers in't no good," the man said, whistling between his teeth. "Can't take the pressure down deep. Their 'ealth goes an' they're finished. Off with yer clothes, then. No time ter stand abaht!"

"What?"

"Off with yer clothes," the man repeated patiently. "Yer don't think yer was goin' down dressed up like that, did yer? 'Oo'd yer think yer'll see down there, then? The flippin' Queen?"

Another man had arrived ready to assist, and Monk looked across and saw that Trace was also being undressed and redressed by a cheerful man who was wearing a thick sweater in spite of the warm August morning.

Obediently he stripped off his outer clothes, leaving only his underwear. He was handed two pairs of long, white woolen stockings, then a thick shirt of the same material, then flannel knee breeches which had the effect of keeping the other garments together. They were suffocatingly hot. He had little time to imagine the ludicrous figure he must cut, but seeing Trace he knew he would appear much the same.

His dresser produced a cap of red wool and placed it on his head, adjusting it as carefully as if it had been an object of high fashion.

A string of barges moved past them, men staring interestedly, wondering what was happening, what they would be looking for, or if it was only a matter of shoring up a falling wall or broken pier stake.

"Watch yerself!" Monk's dresser warned. "Keep that straight, just like I put it! Get yer air 'ose blocked up an' we'll be pulling yer up dead, an' all! Now yer'd best be gettin' down them steps onter the barge. No need ter put the rest o' yer suit on yet. It's mortal 'eavy, specially w'en yer in't used ter it. Watch yerself!" This last was directed to Monk when he took a step in his stockinged feet perilously close to an upstanding nail.

Trace followed after him down the long ladder to the low boat which was bumping up against the wharf. It was already occupied by a wonderful array of pumps, wheels, coils of rubber hose and ropes.

Normally, Monk would have kept his balance easily in the faintly rocking boat, but he was tense and uncharacteristically awkward. It flashed into his mind to wonder what they would think of him if they found nothing. And who would pay him for this expedition?

Trace was looking grim, but his fine features were composed. At least outwardly he felt no misgivings. Had he believed Monk's extraordinary story?

The three men who had dressed them and helped so far put their backs against the oars and pulled away from the wharf, then began to swing wide and go downstream with the outgoing tide, towards Bugsby's Marshes and beyond. No one spoke. There was no sound but the creak of the oars in the oarlocks and the splash and dip of the water.

The sky was half overcast from the smoke of thousands of chimneys in the dock areas on the north side. Masts and cranes showed black against the haze. Ahead of them lay the ugly flats of the marshes. He had already told them as nearly as he could where they wished to begin the search. It was only approximate, and he became increasingly aware of just how huge the area was as they approached the Point, and the wreck he had seen on his earlier trip.

The men rested on their oars. It was just about slack tide.

"Right, sir," one of them said. "Where'd yer be wantin' ter begin, then?"

It was time to seek the counsel of experts.

"If a man wanted to sink a barge with the least chance of its being found, where would he choose?" he asked. It sounded ridiculous even as he listened to himself.

Overhead, gulls wheeled and cried. The wind was rising and the water slurped against the sides of the boat, rocking it very gently.

It was the man who had begun helping Monk dress who answered.

"In the lee o' one o' the sandbanks," he answered without hesitation. "Water's deep enough ter 'ide a barge even at the lowest tide."

"What would sink a barge?" Monk asked him.

The man screwed up his face. "Not much, actual. Mostly age, overloading, which some fools do."

"But if you wanted to sink one?" Monk pressed.

337

The man's eyes widened. "Bash an 'ole in it, I reckon. Below the waterline, o' course. Not the bottom. That's made of elm. Too 'ard. Sides is oak."

"I see. Thank you." He had all he needed. Now there was no avoiding putting on the rest of the suit and going over the side and into the murky water.

A few more pulls on the oars, five minutes perhaps, and he was climbing into the diving suit with the help of two of the men. It looked rather like a very baggy, all-in-one jacket and trousers made of two layers of waterproof cloth with india rubber between. It felt as though he were pulling on a heavy sack, but with arms and legs in it.

He had had no idea how difficult it would be to force his hands through the tight india rubber cuffs. He was obliged to grease his hands with soft soap and then narrow his palms as much as possible while an attendant opened the cuff and he pushed his hand into it so violently he was afraid he was going to tear his flesh.

The dresser nodded with approval. If he noticed the cold sweat on Monk's face he made no comment on it.

"Sit down!" he ordered, pointing to the thwart behind Monk. "Gotta get yer boots on, an' yer 'elmet. Gotta make sure everything's right." He bent down and began the process with the enormous weighted boots. "If they in't right, you'll lose them in the mud. Sucks summink awful down there. An' 'old still while I put on yer breastplate. That comes loose an' yer a gonner."

Monk felt his stomach clench as his imagination visualized the darkness and the bottomless, greedy mud. It cost him all his self-control to sit obediently motionless while the helmet was placed over his head and screwed, metal rubbing against metal, until it was tight. The front glass was left off for now. Monk was surprised by the almost crushing weight of the helmet. The air hose was passed under his right arm and the end attached to the inlet valve, then the breast line was brought up under his left arm and secured. Next came the belt and the heavy, razor-sharp knife in its leather sheath. The man looped a rope around Monk's waist.

" 'Ere now, 'old this in yer 'and, and if yer get in trouble pull on it six or seven times an' we'll get yer up. That's w'y we call it the lifeline." He grinned. "This 'ere other rope we've tied to yer, we're gonna tie the other end ter the ladder—we don't wanter lose yer—least not until we're paid." He laughed heartily.

"All right, lad?" the man asked.

Monk nodded, his mouth dry.

He looked at the brown water around their vessel, still drifting idly on the slack tide, and felt as if he were about to be buried alive. The three men were busy at their tasks, careful, professional.

Trace sat on the other thwart, dressed exactly the same. He smiled, and Monk smiled back, wishing he felt as confident as the gesture implied.

One of the men straightened up. "All right, boys, let's get the pump going!" There was a loud *click-clack,* and in a moment Monk felt the air rush into his helmet. The man smiled. "Aye, it's working all right. Now, don't you worry, lad. Just 'member ter stick close ter the other feller an' 'ow ter inflate yer suit wi' that valve, an' yer'll be fine." He did not sound quite as confident now, as if at this final moment he had realized just what a novice Monk was, and the risks he was taking.

The front glass of his helmet was screwed into place and for a moment Monk was overcome with panic. He gasped for air and drew it into his lungs. Gradually his wild heartbeat subsided.

"Right," the man said with a slightly forced smile. "Time ter go!"

Monk lumbered towards the ladder, thinking with each step that the weight of the helmet would buckle him at the knees. He climbed down awkwardly, and when the water was to his waist two fifty-pound leads were fastened to his chest and back. He gasped at the sudden increase in weight.

He was handed a waterproof lantern with a candle in it.

His suit began to inflate slightly as the air expanded it. Now he appreciated why it needed to be so large on him.

339

Trace was already below him in the water, almost submerged.

The river closed over his head and in moments he was blinded by gloom. The only contact with Trace and the surface was by rope, and he tried to unscramble what the men had told him: Stay calm. Don't panic. Remember, you are not on your own. Pull on the rope if you're in trouble. We'll get you up.

The pressure built up in his eardrums. He swallowed to clear it.

Gradually his sight cleared a little as his eyes became accustomed to the gloom. He could make out the form of Trace, coming towards him, taking Monk by the hand.

With leaden feet just touching the muddy bottom, Monk followed after him.

He lost all sense of time. He was amazed how difficult it was to keep his balance. The tide was far more powerful than he had foreseen, pulling one way and another at him as current eddied and swirled, sometimes going one way at chest height, the opposite way at his thighs and knees. More than once he found himself falling and regained his footing with difficulty. And all the time he was acutely aware that only one thin hose of pumped air supported his life, one thin set of ropes could pull him back to the surface.

The ground sloped up beneath his giant boots. They were on the mud bank. It was hard work trying to climb up it. He was sweating as he went, but his hands and feet were cold. The murky water swirled around his head, a brown, blinding mass.

The dim figure of Trace was still just ahead of him, close enough to hold his hand, but was no more than a deepening of the gloom.

Time seemed endless. He longed for light. This was all an idiotic idea. What had made him think the barge had been sunk, simply because he could find no trace of its going back upstream again? And if it were down here, what did that prove? Only that fraud had been the intention all along. Would it prove by whom? Or who had murdered Alberton?

It was impenetrably dark ahead. How long had they been down here?

Trace was still guiding him along, turning slowly in the water, raising his other arm.

Monk lost his balance again. He should have left this to professionals. Except he could not; he must find this himself, hold the proof in his own hands, see everything there was, miss nothing, destroy nothing.

Still holding Monk's hand, Trace swung his arm around and pointed. Ahead of them was a deeper murk, blocking off even the swirling brown of the water.

Trace started to move again and Monk followed, agonizingly slowly.

Then suddenly his feet were swept from under him and he felt a hard yank on the ropes. Awkwardly he tried to look down at what had caught him. It was the boards of a sunken wreck.

Trace was climbing up onto an angle of the boat.

Monk went after him. The effort to move made his muscles ache. They seemed to be on a deck, slipping slightly as the bow settled deeper into the mud. Moving hand over hand they found the cabin.

It took a long, slow examination, a foot at a time, holding on to each other, to discover what was inside.

It was Trace who found the crates. It was impossible to tell how many there were of them, but moving with infinite slowness they found at least fifty. Far more than Monk had expected. More like the original shipment to Breeland.

But why here at the bottom of the river and not on their way over to America, or to the Mediterranean?

Monk felt Trace's hand on his shoulder. He could see almost nothing. There was barely sufficient light to tell which way the surface lay.

He reached out for Trace, then drew back his hand, now numb with cold. This was no time to be foolish.

A hand came after him. Then he felt the rest of the body, a shoulder, perhaps a head. It bumped into his helmet and something covered the glass in front of his eyes.

Hair! Loose human hair in the water! Trace was drowning!

Monk reached up and clasped the arm, trying to pull desperately on the rope at the same time. He must get help! What had happened?

There was no resistance on the arm, no weight! God Almighty! It was loose . . . just an arm, bloated and almost naked! He could dimly make out where his fingers had sunk into the flesh, like squeezing soft fat.

He felt himself gag, and only just controlled himself from retching. The rest of the body was there, almost whole, huge, disintegrating at the touch.

He saw Trace's light in the gloom, waving around. Another body floated across his vision and disappeared.

It made no sense. Who were they? Why were they dead? He forced himself to govern his revulsion and move slowly after one of them. Deliberately he felt around until he found the head. He shone his light on it, close up, trying not to look at the unrecognizable features. The bullet hole was still there, not easy to see in the white, half-eaten flesh of the forehead, but plain enough in the splintered skull.

It seemed to take endless time swishing around almost helplessly in the current inside the cramped cabin, bumping into each other, into the trapped and hideous corpses, before they ascertained beyond doubt that there were three men, all of whom had been shot dead.

Trace came right up to him, holding Monk by one arm and touching his helmet to Monk's. When he spoke, incredibly, Monk could hear him almost as normal.

"Shearer!" Trace said distinctly, waving his other arm, with the lantern, in the direction of one of the corpses.

Shearer. Of course! This abomination was why no one had seen Walter Shearer since the night of Alberton's death. He had been loyal to Alberton after all. He had followed the barge down here, and been shot with these other two. Were they the ones who had actually committed the murders? Why? On whose orders?

He made a sign of acknowledgment, then turned and

blundered out of the fearful cabin and stopped abruptly as his air hose tightened and almost broke. Terror stifled his breath. He was covered in cold sweat. Trace! Of course! He would die down here in this filthy water, alone with his murderer. He would never see light again, breathe air, hold Hester in his arms or look at her eyes.

When Monk left home that afternoon, Hester had tried, at first, to busy herself with domestic tasks. Mrs. Patrick arrived at exactly two o'clock, the agreed time. She was a small, thin woman with crisp white hair full of natural curl, and very blue eyes. Hester judged her to be about fifty years old. She had a strong face, albeit a little gaunt, and a brisk manner. She spoke with a slight Scottish burr. Hester could not place it, but she knew it was not Edinburgh. She had too many memories of that city to mistake its tones.

Mrs. Patrick, neat in a white, starched apron, began to clear up the kitchen and consider what other tasks needed doing: clean and black the small stove, put on the laundry, scrub the kitchen floor, clean out the larder and make a note of what needed restocking, take out the rugs, sweep the floors, beat the rugs and return them, hang the laundry out, and do the ironing from the previous day. And of course prepare the dinner.

"What time will Mr. Monk be home?" she enquired while Hester was sitting in the office out of the way, stitching on a shirt button.

"I don't know," Hester replied honestly. "He's gone diving."

Mrs. Patrick's eyebrows shot up. "I beg your pardon?"

"He's gone diving," Hester explained. "In the river. I'm not sure what he expects to find."

"Water and mud," Mrs. Patrick said tartly. "For heaven's sake, why would he be doing such a thing?" She looked at Hester narrowly, as if she suspected she had been lied to regarding the nature of Monk's employment.

Hester was very keen to keep Mrs. Patrick's services. Life had been altogether much easier since her advent. "He is still trying to find out who killed Mr. Alberton in the Tooley Street murder," she said tentatively.

Mrs. Patrick's eyebrows were still raised and a trifle crooked, her mouth twisted into profound skepticism.

"There are other guns," Hester went on, not sure if she was making matters better or worse. "Something went down the river on the barge from Hayes Dock. It might have been to pay the blackmailers."

Mrs. Patrick had not intended to admit that she had been following the case. She disapproved of reading about such things, but the words were out of her mouth before she realized their implication. "That was why they asked for Mr. Monk in the first place, wasn't it?"

"Yes, it was," Hester admitted.

"If you ask me, they don't exist." Mrs. Patrick smoothed her apron over her narrow hips. "I reckon as Mr. Alberton did that himself . . . probably sold the guns to the pirates anyway!"

"That wouldn't make any sense," Hester argued. "If there were no blackmailer then he could sell them anywhere he wanted."

"Highest bidder," Mrs. Patrick said darkly. "Money, mark my words, that's what'll be at the bottom of it . . . the love of money is at the root of all evil." And with that she turned and went back to the kitchen and her duties.

Hester sat for another fifteen minutes turning it over in her mind, then she went through to the kitchen herself and informed Mrs. Patrick that she was going out and had very little idea when she would be back.

"You're not going along the river?" Mrs. Patrick asked in some alarm.

"No, I'm not," Hester assured her. "I'm going to consider the question of blackmail again, more carefully."

Mrs. Patrick grunted and returned her attention to the sink, but her square, stiff shoulders were eloquent of her mixed satisfaction and disapproval. She was obviously not at all certain that the position she had accepted was a wise

344

one, but it was undoubtedly interesting, and she would not leave just yet, unless it seriously threatened either her personal safety or her reputation.

Hester went again to see Robert Casbolt. She hoped to find him at home. If not she would have to seek an appointment with him in his offices, or wait there for him to return from whatever business had taken him away.

Fortunately he was at home, apparently reading. An ancient manservant informed her Mr. Casbolt would be happy to see her, and led her, not into the golden room in which they had talked before, but to an upstairs room which was, if anything, even more beautiful. French doors opened onto a balcony which overlooked the garden, at the moment full of flowers and quiet in the sun. The room was done entirely in soft earth colors and creams, extraordinarily restful, and Hester felt immediately comfortable in it.

Casbolt welcomed her, inviting her to be seated in one of the chairs facing the garden, a little to the left of a magnificent Italian bronze lion.

"It's beautiful!" she said, moved by something more than mere admiration. There was a tenderness in the room, as if it were a place apart from ordinary life.

He was pleased. "You like it?"

"More than that," she said honestly. "It's . . . unique."

"Yes, it is," he agreed simply. "I spend time here alone. When I am out it is locked. I am glad you see its quality."

Hester hoped even more profoundly that it was not as Mrs. Patrick suggested, but she must face the truth. If Alberton had intended to deal with the pirates in any manner at all, or had given them to believe he would, then perhaps his death had nothing to do with the American civil war but was a matter of money, or perhaps after all those years, an old vengeance for Judith's brother's death. Since Casbolt was her cousin, and obviously cared for her deeply, perhaps he even knew that, or had guessed it since. If it were either of these two answers, she longed for it to be the latter. A vengeance would be understandable. Any man might well have hungered to exact some kind of justice in the circumstances, and reached where the law could not.

"What can I do for you, Mrs. Monk?" Casbolt asked graciously. "I feel we owe you so much, believe me, you would have only to name your favor."

"We still do not know who was responsible for the crimes." She chose evasive words and she spoke softly. Somehow in this lovely room it would seem coarse to use words like *murder* when euphemisms would be understood.

He looked down at his hands for a moment. He had fine hands, strong and smooth. Then he raised his eyes.

"No, and I fear we may not," he answered. "I had believed it was Breeland himself, or Shearer at his instigation. I am delighted that Rathbone proved it was not Merrit, and not learning who it was is a small price to pay for that."

"It is not necessarily a trade, Mr. Casbolt," she argued. "Merrit is perfectly safe now. I have considered the matter quite carefully, and I have wondered if it does not stem back to the original letter of blackmail over which you first consulted my husband. After all, they asked for guns as a payment for their silence. And they have been silent."

He frowned, uncertainty in his face. He hesitated for several moments before replying.

"I'm not sure what it is you believe, Mrs. Monk. Do you think they killed Daniel and stole the guns, because he would not yield to their demands? Was Breeland simply caught up in it by an unfortunate accident of timing? Is that what you are suggesting?"

It was not as simple as that, but she was reluctant to tell him what she feared. Daniel Alberton had been his closest friend, and any slur against him would reflect on Judith, and on Merrit. Did the truth matter now, the detailed truth as to why, as long as they knew who?

"Is it possible?" Hester said evasively.

Again Casbolt sat silently for several moments, his brows drawn down in thought.

As she waited, she realized how unlikely it would be. If

guns could be so simply stolen, why would they have bothered with the sophistication of blackmail in the first place?

He was watching her.

"You don't believe that, do you?" he said softly. "You are afraid Daniel yielded to them, aren't you? You know he was in the yard that night . . . it must have been to meet someone."

"Yes," she said unhappily. She loathed having to do this, but the truth lay between them, huge and inevitable. There was no possibility of avoiding it now.

"Daniel would not sell guns to pirates," Casbolt said, shaking his head, denying it to himself.

"The guns missing from Breeland's shipment were exactly the amount asked for in the blackmail letter," she pointed out.

"He still wouldn't do that. Not to pirates!" But his voice was losing its conviction. He was talking to persuade himself, and the unhappiness in his eyes betrayed his knowledge that she could see it.

"Perhaps he had little choice," she said.

"The blackmail? We would have fought it through! I believe your husband might well have discovered who it was. It had to be someone in London. How could a Mediterranean pirate know about Gilmer?"

"How would anyone?" she said so quietly he leaned forward to hear her. She could feel the heat in her face and yet her hands were cold.

He stared at her. "Are you . . . are you saying what I think . . ." He stumbled over the words. "No! He would not do that!"

Just as Breeland could not be guilty because of the times of events, Casbolt could not either. She hated hurting him, but he was the one person she could trust, and who would be in a position to find the truth, and maybe to keep it silent.

"Perhaps he needed the money?"

His eyes widened. "The money? I don't understand. I am quite familiar with the company books, Mrs. Monk. The finances are more than adequate."

At last Hester spoke aloud the ugly thought that she had been trying to suppress or deny all day. "What if he invested privately as well, and lost money?"

He looked startled, as if the thought rattled him. It took him a moment to regain his composure.

"In stocks, you mean?" he asked. "Or something of that sort? I don't think it is likely. He was not a gambler in even the mildest way. And believe me, I have known him long enough that I would be aware of it." He spoke very gravely, still leaning forward, his hands locked together, knuckles white.

Hester had to pursue it, explain to him what she meant. "Not stocks or shares, and I had never thought of gambling, Mr. Casbolt. I was thinking of something which seemed at the time a certain business deal, with no risk attached."

He gazed at her, his eyes clouded, waiting for her to continue.

"Like selling guns to the Chinese," she answered.

His face was unreadable, his emotions too profound to measure.

It was at that moment that she believed he knew. He had concealed it to protect Alberton, and possibly even more to protect Judith. She realized with a jolt how much this whole room spoke of his love for her, and why it was special. Perhaps there would be no need to tell anyone. They did not have to know any more than they did now. Mystery, unanswered questions, would be better than the truth.

"The Third Chinese War," she finished the thought. "If he invested in guns to sell to the Chinese, shipped them out, and then they refused to pay because a war had broken out between us and them that was completely unforeseeable by anyone, then he would have sustained a heavy loss . . . wouldn't he?"

His lips tightened, but his eyes did not waver from hers. "Yes . . ."

"Is that not possible?"

"Of course it is possible. But what are you suggesting

348

happened the night he was killed? I still don't understand how a loss to the Chinese would bring that about."

"Yes, you do," she said softly. "What if Breeland were telling not only what he thought was the truth, but what actually was the truth? Alberton could have taken Philo Trace's money, given in good faith, then sold the guns to Breeland, using Shearer to deliver them to the Euston Square station. He would then have had two separate amounts of money which would come to an excellent profit . . . more than sufficient to make up for the Chinese losses."

He did not argue. His face had a bruised, almost beaten look. "Then who killed him? And why?"

"Whoever represented the pirates," she answered.

"I . . . suppose so."

"Or else there was a confrontation," she added, her voice lifting with hope in spite of herself. "Perhaps he knew who they were, and he may have said he would deal with them because he planned to exact some kind of justice for Judith's family." She chose the word *justice* deliberately, instead of *revenge*.

He considered it. It was apparent in his face that he was weighing all the possibilities. He seemed to make a decision at last.

"If your suggestion about Daniel having lost private money on the Chinese war is correct, and that he did indeed sell the guns to Breeland just as Breeland said, and kept Philo Trace's money . . . then when Trace discovered that, would he not be the one to exact revenge—or, from his point of view, justice? And the method of . . . murder . . . was a peculiarly American one, remember. Do you not think it more likely that Trace went to Tooley Street to face Daniel about it, and there was a furious quarrel, and Trace killed them? Whether he went there alone or not we may never know. Perhaps he had help. He will have had allies here ready to move the guns when he bought them, just as Breeland had. Possibly one man could have made the guards tie each other, at gunpoint, and he could have tied the last himself . . . I imagine."

He looked pale, very strained. "Trace seems a gentle man, full of charm, but he is a gun buyer for the Confederate army, fighting to preserve the way of life of the South, and the right to keep slaves. Underneath the easy manner there is a very desperate and determined man whose people are at war for their own survival."

He hesitated, biting his lip for a moment. "And there is another thing, Mrs. Monk . . . the watch. Merrit said in court that she didn't know where she left it, but she was lying. We all know that. She took it off in Breeland's rooms when she changed her clothes, and forgot it. Someone went up there before we did. The porter said so." He was looking at her very shakily. "If that were Trace, then he could have taken it and dropped it in the yard to incriminate Breeland. What would be more natural?"

Hester felt her heart lurch and her skin break out in a hot, prickly sweat of horror. Monk was alone with Trace at the bottom of the Thames, trusting him, his life dependent upon Trace's skill and his honor.

She shot to her feet, her breath rasping. "William is diving." She almost choked on the words. "He has only Trace with him! They're looking for the barge that took the guns down." She turned and stumbled towards the door. "I've got to get there! I've got to warn him . . . help . . . him."

Casbolt was beside her instantly. "I'll go," he said. "I'll get to them as fast as I can. I can get out on the river. You stay here, safely. You couldn't help even if you were there. I'll tell the river police." And he moved past her, touching her gently on the arms, as if to hold her there.

"Remain here," he repeated. "You'll be safe. I'll take the police and confront Trace. Monk will be all right." And before she could argue he went out of the door, closing it behind him, and she heard his footsteps fade away.

She moved back to the center of the room. It really was beautiful. There was a miniature portrait at one end of the pale marble mantel. At first she had not realized who it was. Now she could see it was Judith as a young woman, perhaps

350

twenty or so. That would be when she had first met Daniel Alberton.

There was another picture, no more than a sketch, three young people climbing over the rocks on a beach, Judith laughing, close to Casbolt, Alberton a little distance away, looking towards them. It was obvious that Judith and Casbolt were the couple, Alberton the newcomer.

Trace, who was so much in love with Judith, was a newcomer too. Had his love for Judith had anything to do with the reason he had killed Alberton, instead of merely rendering him unconscious? Was it Judith herself, as much as the guns?

Monk was alone with him, possibly this moment under the water, dependent on him for skill, for life!

But Casbolt had gone to fetch Lanyon and rescue him. He would be there far before . . . There! Where?

Suddenly she froze like ice, her limbs shaking. Casbolt had not asked her where Monk was diving for the barge! He knew!

Everything that was true about Alberton and the private investment in the Chinese war was equally true about Casbolt himself. He could have lost money, and all the glamour and generosity that money allowed. This beautiful house and everything in it, the admiration and respect that go with success. And Casbolt was used to success. Everything around him showed he had had it all his life . . . except with Judith. She had given him no more than the love of a cousin and friend, never passion. He was too close.

She went over to the door and turned the handle. But it was locked. Damnation! That old manservant must have seen Casbolt leave and locked it up behind him.

She rattled the handle and called out.

Silence.

She tried shouting.

Either he was deaf or he did not care. Perhaps Casbolt had even told him to keep her there?

The watch! Casbolt would have seen it when he and Monk had gone to Breeland's rooms looking for Merrit. He

351

could easily have taken it then, concealed it from Monk, and then dropped it himself when they were in the Tooley Street yard. No wonder he had been so startled when he discovered Breeland had given it to Merrit.

She shook the door as violently as she could, shouting for help. It had no effect whatever.

She swung around and went to the French doors and opened them. The balcony had wisteria climbing up it. Was it enough for a toehold? It would have to be! Monk's life depended on it. Gingerly, disregarding the ruin of her skirts, she clambered over the edge, refusing to look down, and began to slip and clutch and slip again until she could jump the last few feet to the grass, landing in a heap.

She stood up, brushed herself down and set off at a run to reach the street.

It had all been about money, not guns, and because of Judith. The American war had nothing to do with it at all. The guns had been sold twice, and paid for at least once and a half. Casbolt had employed Shearer, and someone else who had committed the actual murders, carefully making sure he was accounted for that night. Then, as Monk had guessed, the following night they had all met up down the river at Bugsby's Marshes to pay and be paid.

She ran out into the middle of the road, waving her arms and shouting out, her voice high and shrill, verging on hysteria.

A carriage slowed to a stop to avoid striking her. A hansom pulled up with a screech and a curse.

She called up to the driver. "I need to get to the Bermondsey police station. My husband's life depends on it . . . please!"

There was an elderly man already inside. He looked momentarily alarmed, then seeing the anguish in her face and every aspect of her body, he acquiesced with startling generosity, offering his hand to help her.

"Come in, my dear. Driver, as the lady wishes, with all possible speed!"

The coachman hesitated only long enough to make certain Hester was safely inside, then he swung the whip wide and high, and urged the horses forward.

Monk gasped, then the hose fell loose. Air surged back around his face. There was a touch on his shoulder and he tried to swing around, but he was too slow, achingly clumsy.

Trace was beside him, shaking his head, holding the air hose, smiling.

Monk was ashamed of his thoughts, of his panic, but above all weak with relief. He was grinning idiotically at Trace through the filthy water and the thick glass.

He raised his hand in thanks.

Trace waved back, still shaking his head, then pointing to the nearest of the piled crates.

Monk took out his knife and together they prized the lid off. There were guns there. He could feel their outlines.

Trace held up his lamp, close, only inches above them. Now it was possible to see that they were old models, flintlocks mostly, many of them useless, without firing pins, a far cry from the latest Enfields Breeland had purchased. They were little more than sham.

Laboriously they unpacked the top layer. Underneath was only bricks and ballast.

They tried a second case, and a third. They were all the same; a few guns on top, then just weight.

Now at last Monk understood almost all of it. The real guns had never been at Tooley Street. They had been stored somewhere else, and taken to Euston and loaded onto the freight wagons on the train before Shearer even got there the night of the murders. He had merely accepted Breeland's money. Where he had been the rest of that night, they would probably never know.

These cast-off guns laid over bricks and ballast had been stolen by the wretched men whose bodies floated in this ghastly cabin below the Thames. They had hidden the barge, disguised among the wrecks on the shore of Bugsby's Marshes, until the following night, then floated it again to

353

keep a rendezvous they thought was to deliver their goods and receive payment for murder. Instead, along with Shearer, they had met their own deaths. If he looked again he would find all the times fitted.

He put his hand on Trace's arm to signal they should leave. They had seen all there was. They moved slowly away. And was it all simply greed, a matter of selling the guns twice and thus having more money? Admittedly, a vast amount more.

He lurched through the gloom, fumbling his way, awash in clouds of mud, pulled by tides as the flow increased, and they were trying to fight against it. It seemed an endless journey. His legs ached from the weight of his boots. He was imprisoned behind the glass plate, breathing pumped air. He struggled to remember what they had told him to do. Use the outlet valve. Get more buoyancy. That was better. Life and sunlight were only a few fathoms away, but like another world.

Trace was beside him, moving more rapidly, surer-footed. He was waving his light, guiding and urging Monk forward. Then suddenly Trace dropped his light. Monk saw his hands scrabble at where his throat would be beneath the helmet; his face appeared contorted behind the glass, as though he were gasping, choking for air.

Then his ropes tightened, and he was dragged backwards and up, disappearing into the murk, leaving Monk completely alone.

Where was the boat? He strained upwards, looking for its shadow through the cloud of sand that swirled around him, and did not see it.

Then at last the steps were there. He grasped them, hauling himself up, desperate to reach the top, the light, to get out of the cold, clammy, imprisoning suit. It seemed to take forever. He was leaden-weighted. There was no help from the ropes. They had stopped pulling him. He had to climb on his own. The effort was overwhelming.

At last his head broke the surface and instinctively he gasped, drawing in only more pumped air. Hands reached out to help him aboard, and as the water drained off him and the attendant removed the front glass from his helmet, he recognized Robert Casbolt. Then a shot rang out, and another, and another. The attendant crumpled forward, his chest scarlet, and slid into the water.

The other two men lay sprawled beside the pumping equipment, one partly on his back next to Trace, staring sightlessly upward, a dark hole in his head, the third doubled over the after thwart, blood on his hair. Philo Trace was slumped in the bottom of the boat, eyes closed, barely conscious, his helmet beside him.

Casbolt was holding a gun, its muzzle pointed towards Monk.

"You found something down there that showed you it was Trace," he said with a sad little shake of his head. "But you weren't quick enough for him. He shot you. He nearly got away with it, too. If your wife hadn't come to me with the truth, and I raced here to try to rescue you, then he would have succeeded! Tragically, I was just too late. . . ." He swallowed hard. "I really am sorry. All I wanted was Judith . . . back again, as it used to be. And enough money to look after her. That was all I ever wanted." He raised the gun a little higher.

A shot rang out, then another. Casbolt teetered for a moment and then overbalanced, falling into the brown, swelling tide.

Across the water another boat was coming towards them, Lanyon in the bow, a pistol in his hand. Beside him, Hester was ashen-faced, the wind whipping her hair and blowing her torn and wet skirts.

The boat reached the barge and Lanyon jumped over. A look of horror filled his eyes as he saw the bodies. It was a moment before he collected himself and came over to Monk. Trace coughed and sat up a little straighter, one of the other boat's crew helping him.

Hester scrambled from one boat to the other and ran forward, falling on her knees beside Monk, saying his name over and over, searching his face, desperate to know he was

355

all right. Her voice caught in her throat; her breathing was wild and jerky.

He grinned at her, and saw the tears of relief run down her cheeks. He could understand so very easily that you could love one woman so much that no one else filled your heart or mind. For a moment he could almost have been sorry for Casbolt. He had wanted Judith all his life. Love could hurt. It would ask for sacrifices greater than the imagination could foresee, and it was not always returned, or even understood. But it did not excuse what he had done. The end does not justify the means.

Lanyon unfastened Monk's helmet and lifted it off.

Hester put her arms around Monk's neck and buried her head on his shoulder, clinging to him with all the strength she possessed, until it hurt them both, but she could not let go.

A FUNERAL IN BLUE

by Anne Perry

❧

Elissa Beck, the wife of Dr. Kristian Beck, a prominent London surgeon, is found strangled along with another woman in the studio of a well-known London artist. Hester Monk presses her husband, Inspector William Monk, to search for evidence that will save her former colleague from the hangman's noose as well as solve the riddle of Elissa Beck's secret life and murder.

Published by Ballantine Books.
Available at bookstores everywhere.

THE TWISTED ROOT

by
Anne Perry

As private investigator William Monk listens to the young Lucius Stourbridge plead for help in tracking down his runaway fiancée, he feels a sense of heavy foreboding. Miriam Gardiner disappeared suddenly from a croquet party at the luxurious Bayswater mansion of her in-laws-to-be and has not been seen since. But on Hampstead Heath, Monk finds the coach in which Miriam had fled and, nearby, the murdered body of the coachman. There is no trace of Miriam.

What strange compulsion could have driven the beautiful widow to abandon the prospect of a loving marriage and financial abundance? Monk's attempt to answer that question proves a challenge, as Miriam Gardiner's fateful flight ends in a packed London courtroom and a charge of murder. And in a race with the hangman, Monk and clever nurse Hester Latterly—themselves now newlyweds—desperately pursue the elusive truth. . .and an unknown killer whose malign brilliance they have scarcely begun to fathom.

Published by Ballantine Books.
Available at bookstores everywhere.

Immerse yourself in the mysterious world of
Anne Perry's Victorian London. Look for this
thrilling William Monk novel,
available in paperback!

A BREACH OF PROMISE
A William Monk Novel

by Anne Perry

Stripping away the pretty masks that conceal society's darkest transgressions, Anne
Perry unflinchingly exposes the human
heart's deepest hiding places—and creates
the most mesmerizing courtroom drama of
her distinguished career.

Published by Ballantine Books.
Available at bookstores everywhere.

THE SILENT CRY

by Anne Perry

The reign of Queen Victoria brought Londoners fabulous wealth; however, not all citizens of the British capital enjoyed these amenities. For deep in the filthy and dangerous slums of London one could transact secret and shameful business—even the privileged like Leighton Duff who pays for this privilege with his life.

Rhys Duff, the son of Leighton Duff, is found barely alive next to his father's body. Inspector William Monk is called to investigate the brutal assaults of the Duffs as well as a series of rapes and beatings of local prostitutes. Could there be a connection? Monk soon uncovers shocking evidence that points to the young Rhys Duff and the possibility that he murdered his own father. . .

Published by Ballantine Books.
Available at bookstores everywhere.